Kulubi

By the Same Author

THE PASSION PLAYERS

KULUBI

EDMUND P. MURRAY

CROWN PUBLISHERS, INC.
NEW YORK

Inquiries should be addressed to Crown Publishers, Inc.,
419 Park Avenue South, New York, N.Y. 10016.
Library of Congress Catalog Card Number: 72-96658
ISBN: 0-517-504235
Printed in the United States of America
Published simultaneously in Canada by General Publishing Company Limited

Designed by Ruth Smerechniak

DEDICATED

. . . to all the Ethiopian authors who might have written it if such books could be published in their beautiful, sad country

CONTENTS

AUTHOR'S NOTE

Kulubi IS A NOVEL. IT IS SET IN A COUNTRY CALLED "ETHIOPIA," but it is an Ethiopia of the mind. All of the characters and events are fictional, and none is intended to represent actual persons, living or dead. Even the very real figure of His Imperial Majesty Haile Selassie I here is rendered not as a known historical personage but as an imagined character in fiction. Some of the events alluded to, the various intrigues, the student riot, and so on, also have some basis in recent history but are telescoped in time and otherwise distorted to serve the fictive design of a novel. Similar freedoms are taken with historical background and contemporary detail. It is hoped, therefore, that no one will read what follows as anything but a novel and certainly not as a factual book about Ethiopia, Ethiopians, or foreigners who may have lived there.

A list of major and secondary characters follows. There is a glossary of frequently used Ethiopian words and place names at the back of the book.

E.P.M.

MAJOR CHARACTERS

TESFAYE TESSEMA	*an Ethiopian journalist*
HARRY COMFORT	*an American gathering material for a book on Ethiopia*
JULIE COMFORT	*his wife*
JONATHAN COMFORT	*an infant*
BARIA MEDHANE ALEM	*a painter*
HAILE SELASSIE I	*born Teferi Makonnen, Emperor of Ethiopia*
DEJAZMATCH TESSEMA BEKELE	*the Emperor's old friend and adversary, father of Tesfaye*
NEGASH MENGISTU	*an official close to the Emperor*
WANDIMU GETAHUN	*a peasant*

SECONDARY CHARACTERS
(In Order of Appearance)

CHRISTINA ANTONAKOS	*a hotel keeper at Awash Station*
MAJOR TSGAYE	*a police officer at Awash*
ELENI (HELEN)	*an official of the Organization of African Unity*
ZENEBETCH DESTA	*glamorous radio and television personality*
HAGOS	*a young university lecturer*

MAKONNEN SEYOUM	*a young bureaucrat*
CLAUDE JACKSON	*a black American photographer*
FIKR	*a bus driver*
A YOUNG MATRON	*who won't reveal her name*
COLONEL WILSON	*a British eccentric*
TIRUWORK	*a young matron*
ALGANESH	*her friend*
ZEWDITU	*an Ethiopian Airlines hostess*
ONE THOUSAND EIGHTY	*a famous madame*
FAT MARGARET	*her friend*
GENERAL TADESSE ADERA	*known as "The Hyena," an admirer of One Thousand Eighty*
HILARY BLANKENSHIP	*an aging American pilot with EAL*
NEGUSSIE	*a younger EAL pilot*
SHALEKA SHIFERAW ASFAW	*a government official, husband of Tiruwork*
SENATOR GETACHEW TESSEMA	*son of Dejazmatch Tessema and elder half-brother to Tesfaye*
THE CROWN PRINCE	*sole surviving son of Haile Selassie*
BALCHA AMARL	*a popular writer*
FREHIWOT	*a singer*
MAJOR ABEBE	*in charge of police at Kulubi*
RUFAEL	*a friend of Baria Medhane Alem*
WOLDE MEDHANE ALEM	*Baria's brother*
A MAD STUDENT	*who declaims at a funeral*

and

SAINT GABRIEL	*the archangel, patron saint of the church at Kulubi*

PART ONE

THE ROAD TO KULUBI

THE SUN CAME ON LIKE A SPOTLIGHT. TESFAYE SAW IT CATCH BARIA'S station wagon on the road that twisted through morning fog into the rocks above them.

"There they go," said Harry.

Tesfaye glanced at him, but Harry was absorbed in his driving. There they go. Tesfaye let the words echo in his mind, like a shout bouncing off the brown and dun rocks around them. He knew that for Harry the words would have no echo. They were only words, something said to fill a hole in the early morning silence. It was Tesfaye who read meaning into them, surprised that Harry had even noticed the station wagon for he missed so much of what happened around him.

Beyond the tightly shut windows, the morning mist stretched, yawned. Only that single, still gauzed shaft of the sun's light had broken through, pointing dimly at the mud-spattered station wagon. There they go. Baria and Harry's wife. Not, there they are, but, there they go, Harry had said. He was right. The mist rolled over. The sun faded out.

Tesfaye heard a whimper from the back seat of the Volkswagen. He prayed. He knew that infant's capacity for crying. He'd been there, just outside the delivery room door, the night the loud child had screamed itself into existence. No. Not night. It had been morning by then. A wet dawn three months ago. Another chapter in Harry's obsession with Kulubi. Tesfaye blamed himself for that obsession, for last year making the pilgrimage to Kulubi had been his idea. Now, Harry was hooked, convinced that he'd been at the center of a miracle. Tesfaye was skeptical, faithful no longer to the religion of his people, but to his foreign training as a newspaperman. He could record the events, the same events Harry had witnessed, but he could not make Harry's leap into belief.

It had begun the year before. Tesfaye remembered the night they had wandered among the tens of thousands of pilgrims on the eve of the feast of St. Gabriel. As they tried to make their way into the church, he had teased Harry about making a *silet* to Gabriel.

"It's like a vow," Tesfaye had explained. "And if Gabriel grants the favor you ask, you have to come back on his feast day next year and bring him a gift."

It was Harry who'd been skeptical then. Not until the night the infant in the car bed behind them had been born did Harry confess that he had made a *silet* to Gabriel in the church at Kulubi. The whimpers from the back seat seemed to have stopped. Tesfaye sighed with relief.

"He'll sleep a good while now," said Harry.

"God bless."

"And don't start in on why isn't he with his mother."

"I hadn't mentioned it."

"Julie will be stuck with him the whole time we're at Kulubi and you and I are out wandering around."

Tesfaye looked over his shoulder at the bundle in the back seat. No sound. No movement. The baby, untimely ripped from his crib two hours before dawn, had howled in protest for the first hour of their trip. Then, as dawn had begun to filter through the mist, he'd at last cried himself to sleep.

"Have to admit he doesn't give up easy," said Harry. "He's a fighter. Like his daddy. Remember the night he was born?"

"All too well."

The mist had again closed in around them. The windshield wiper thumped dully, uselessly against it. Harry inched forward in second gear. Remembering was no problem. Tesfaye didn't even have to close his eyes. He could remember, but what puzzled him still was why he let himself become so often involved in Harry's continuing comedy of errors. And in Harry's sadness.

Yet, Harry wanted so eagerly to see and understand that Tesfaye, functioning as his translator and guide, had become far more aware of his own country than he'd ever been before. Trying to make Harry see Ethiopia clear had forced Tesfaye to look at it with fresh eyes. He was grateful for that, but he wondered if he would ever be able to do as much for Harry.

They'd first met at a cocktail party soon after Harry had arrived in Addis Ababa. Prepared only by some courses he'd taken at a university in California, Harry had come to Ethiopia to write a book about a country he'd never before seen. Tesfaye had been amazed.

Harry told him he had taken a doctorate in African studies under Horst Eisler, the famous Semitic language scholar who had lived many years in Ethiopia. Tesfaye knew Eisler well and could understand the sway the old man might have had over Harry. But Eisler's mastery of Amharic and several other Ethiopian languages clearly hadn't rubbed off on Harry. After well over a year in the country, Harry and Amharic were still strangers.

Though Tesfaye still found Harry puzzling, he no longer considered him either as bold or as foolish as he had at first. Harry, whatever his shortcomings, was passionately involved in what he was trying to do. Watching Harry, Tesfaye had begun to realize how he himself, in his work as a journalist, tended to stand apart, detached, observant, but never deeply involved. It was an attitude he'd admired in other newspapermen he'd met—the older American and British professionals he wanted to be like. He prized objectivity, but he had lately begun to wonder what his objectivity had cost him. He suspected that in trying to adopt the foreign ideal of what a journalist should be, he had become detached from his country, even from himself. He knew it wasn't a question of wanting to be like Harry, but of recognizing in Harry something he had lost in himself.

He stood a bit in awe of Harry's relentless need to know, to understand, to be able to explain. Particularly since Kulubi had become the focus of the book he wanted to write, Harry drove himself like a man possessed. His hunger for information was so intense that at times Tesfaye feared Harry would swallow the country whole. Like the father of a child with a new toy, Harry jabbed endlessly at the buttons of his tape recorder, feeding fanciful data into it, hoping reality would play back. But for all his effort, Ethiopia remained as much of a mystery to Harry as Harry himself was to Tesfaye.

Tesfaye wondered if he would ever be able to fathom the silent enigma who rode beside him now. Like the country that had nurtured him, Harry was so full of contradictions and so deeply buried within himself. Tesfaye was convinced that somewhere under all those layers of soft American flesh there was a hard core of trapped humanity. He wondered if it could ever be unlocked.

It had been the night the child was born that Tesfaye had caught his closest glimpse of the depths within Harry. Harry had called him well after midnight. Julie had begun labor. Harry was aware that reluctant night watchmen often refused to unlock hospital gates for emergency patients late at night. He was afraid that with his poor Amharic he would never be able to talk his way in.

Tesfaye said he would meet them at the hospital gates. But Harry had another problem. He couldn't find his car keys. Tesfaye sped to his house and drove Harry and Julie to Empress Zewditu Hospital. The night *zabagna*, even denser than most, was deaf to Tesfaye's urging. It had only been when Harry bellowed in an explosive mixture of garbled English and Amharic that the *zabagna* relented. It took another, briefer argument to get Julie into the delivery room and examined.

Harry and Tesfaye then settled down to wait Julie's long ordeal. They sat together on a backless bench, leaning against a whitewashed corridor wall. Staring at a delivery room door that was flanked by a panel painting of the legend of Solomon and Sheba. It was Tesfaye who had called Harry's attention to it. He regretted it later.

"Appropriate, isn't it?" he had said. "Another legend of birth on a delivery room wall. Solomon seduces Sheba. Menelik, our first emperor, is born."

"Menelik," said Harry. "Maybe if it's a son . . . you know, I never told this to anyone before. Not even Julie. But I did make a vow, a *silet* to Gabriel that night when we were at Kulubi."

"You did?"

As they sat on the hospital bench, Harry explained the strange evolution of a vow he had made half in jest, skeptically. Wanting a son and wanting to write a book about Ethiopia were both part of it. But what Harry was really after, Tesfaye realized, was some sense of himself.

"There are so many things," Harry had said, "so much on my mind. I never–it's hard to know what to do–or think. Or even say. You know what I mean?"

"I do," Tesfaye had said. He knew Harry didn't want an answer, only a chance to talk.

"That's why, another reason I want to write this book. About Ethiopia. It's a mystery, isn't it? Ethiopia. Hard for foreigners to understand."

"Very hard," said Tesfaye.

"If I can organize, you know, get together, what I think. If I can. If I can do that, get together about Ethiopia. I don't know. Maybe it will help me get myself . . . organized. Anyway, maybe a little bit better.

"Maybe that's why, that night you were kidding me about making a vow to Gabriel, maybe that's why, just as a joke, I said I wanted a son. It would mean a lot to me, having a son. It's another way of seeing yourself, you know, outside yourself. Watching him grow, becoming a man, can help you understand, maybe, you know, the man you've become."

They'd sat, listening to Julie's moans and, later, her screams through the delivery room door, behind the painting of Solomon and Sheba. "If it is a son," said Tesfaye, "what did you pledge to Gabriel?"

"To write that article. The one your ministry made a pamphlet of. About Kulubi. And walk with it from Dire Dawa, like people do, you know, and bring a copy to the priests at the church."

Tesfaye had been impressed. "You're original," he said. "It isn't everyone who can fulfill a *silet* to Gabriel by writing a pamphlet about his church. And you've already done it. Without even knowing if Gabriel will give you what you asked for."

"You have to at least pretend . . . pretend to have faith."

"Congratulations," said the American missionary doctor when he finally emerged from the delivery room. "It's a boy." Tesfaye and Harry looked at each other. Then shyly looked away. They had another long wait before Harry was allowed to see his wife and the child.

"This business of Kulubi," said Harry. He was staring at the painting by the delivery room door. "You don't . . . you don't believe in miracles, do you?"

"I might," said Tesfaye. "If I saw one."

"You don't think this . . ."

Tesfaye shrugged.

"I don't know why I think this has to be a miracle." He stood and crossed to study the painting that spelled out in forty-four cartoonlike panels the legend of Solomon and Sheba. "Tesfaye, what would you think if . . . our son. Our first . . . born in Ethiopia. Do you think . . . what if we named him Menelik? Like the son Solomon and Sheba had. What would you think?"

Tesfaye looked at him. He could see that Harry was in earnest. "Well, it would be, if Madam agrees, I suppose a very nice thing to do."

"People wouldn't mind? I mean we're foreigners. Taking something Ethiopian."

"No one would mind."

"I want . . . to understand. To write. Kulubi. Ethiopia. I guess . . ."

"Yourself?"

"Yes."

Tesfaye looked away. Without knowing quite why, he grieved for his friend. He wanted so much. A son. A miracle. Ethiopia. Harry wanted to understand, but Tesfaye wondered how he could tell him that some people might mind very much indeed if a foreigner named his son Menelik. Born in this country, the child technically could be an Ethiopian citizen. But for three thousand years after Menelik's legendary rule, no emperor even had dared to take the name. And the king who did finally call himself Menelik the Second dared much and proved himself the finest ruler the country had known. Harry might well wonder, What is Ethiopia? Who is this child? A miracle? My own? Tesfaye shook his head. The child might be Ethiopian. But he was not Menelik.

"It must be awful," said Harry when he came back into the corridor after visiting Julie and seeing the newborn child. "Awful what a woman has to go through."

"It's hard on fathers, too," said Tesfaye. "And especially on their friends."

"Don't make fun," said Harry. "She was very brave."

"Come on. You need a drink—and some sleep."

"But it's dawn," said Harry.

"As far as I'm concerned it's late last night. Come on. I'll drive you home and pour us each some of that Scotch you Americans always have so much of."

He took Harry by the hand, something he'd never before done with a foreigner, and walked with him to the car. Now, sitting beside him as they drove through the low hills over the Wonji plain, he wondered why Harry had given up so easily on his idea of naming the baby Menelik. The baptism had been at the Holy Saviour Catholic Church in Addis, a concession to Harry, but the name had been Jonathan, at the insistence of Julie. Tesfaye later learned that it had been her father's name. Americans were strange, but he thought that even among Americans a man would have the right to name his own son. But Harry as usual had given in to his wife. It had been the same with their trip to Kulubi. Harry had wanted to leave a day early to allow for a leisurely journey. Julie had insisted on accepting an invitation for Christmas dinner with some properly academic Americans attached to the university in Addis. Now they would have to shotgun through to Dire Dawa in a single day.

Poor Harry, thought Tesfaye. His wife seems to have colonized him the way the foreigners colonized Africa. She ruled by keeping Harry in the dark, unsure of himself, frightened of giving offense. He had noticed how much calmer, more competent Harry could be when his wife wasn't on the scene. But such women didn't seem to want their men at their strongest, their best. They preferred them weak, dependent. He wondered if Harry ever thought of himself as a colony. Surely not. Harry had no doubt been persuaded his marriage was a partnership. Tesfaye thought of the term the French had used in gulling their colonies—a special relationship. You provide the resources and the labor; we'll tell you what to do.

But women like Julie, Tesfaye suspected, were even more clever than the colonialists. The foreigners had made real contributions to Africa's development and even to the enlightenment of some Africans. He wondered if Julie would ever enlighten Harry. Or contribute to his development. He doubted. But what can an outsider, a bachelor know? Not much, he realized, but perhaps enough to keep him a bachelor.

Ethiopia, except for the brief time of the Italians, had been spared the colonial experience. There were times when he envied other, more advanced African countries that had benefited from foreign development. But he did not envy Harry.

He watched the care with which Harry edged his small car into the last sweeping curve that would ease them down from the hills. Below the fog had already lifted from the plains. He could see the green carpet the Dutch had woven along the irrigation canals of the sugar plantation they had created in the arid scrubland. Baria's station wagon was already streaking along the open highway. Harry, intent on his own driving, didn't notice.

"The fog is lifting," he said.

Tesfaye wondered. True to his culture and language, he did

not just listen to Harry's words. He interpreted them, read double, multiple meanings into them. And wondered if for Harry the fog would ever lift.

They sped through the still sleeping town of Nazaret and were soon in open country. They left the tarmac behind but still made good time on the well-graded dirt highway. The landscape was a bleak chaparral of acacia and thornbush. There seemed no color in it anywhere. Withered leaves dull as the bark of knotted trees. Tree bark dun as the parched earth.

Tesfaye remembered other trips just after the rains when the unpromising scrub of this region had been green and jeweled with the sudden growth of scentless desert flowers whose names he would never know. In the highlands where he'd been born it was different. There he knew the cycles of the year and what each meant, not just to the land, but to the people as well.

There were times when he wondered if the rains of the highlands, coupled with the rich soil and easy climate, were not more God's curse than his blessing. God and other foreigners brought grace to Ethiopia. And, whatever he might tell Harry, Tesfaye had misgivings about the bounty of both.

He thought of the rains as a kind of unearned foreign investment. They came with their benefits and demanded from Ethiopians nothing more than ritual prayer. The rains made life, not a rich life, but an easy life possible almost without effort.

He was convinced that the rains, the warm sunshine, and fresh breezes of the highlands were as dangerous as the easy handouts of a foreign government. Even coffee, which brought the country most of its foreign exchange, grew wild in such quality and profusion that no one had ever bothered to cultivate the crop.

The coffee grew wild by the grace of God, and the Americans had come and built the highways to haul the coffee more easily to market.

In the highlands the rains came and Ethiopians alternated days of hard work with primitive tools and days wasted at prayers, at endless court cases, at festivals and drinking. In the lowlands where planning and hard work were needed for a life of more than nomadic emptiness, it was the foreigners who came and planned and worked and plundered the profits. Exploiting manual workers from other areas, never the restless nomads or indolent Christians.

He remembered the Wonji plains, vibrating like a sudden splash of green on a dark canvas, as though a single rain cloud spilled itself on an isolated patch of scrub and left the rest of the world barren. But it wasn't the rains that had come to Wonji.

It was Dutchmen driven out of Indonesia by Sukarno. They came with their solemn puritan work habits and their knowledge of irrigation and their skills at exploiting rich soil and cheap labor. And they brought with them their colonialist ways.

A mixed blessing, thought Tesfaye. But still a blessing for the dead land they developed and the dying people they employed. For a man who had nothing before, a dollar a day was a fortune. The field hands at Wonji, Kambettas imported from their homeland hundreds of kilometers to the south, lived in hovels, but the hovels were better than the grass or mud huts they'd lived in before. The Dutch built for themselves a Holland-like paradise complete with pines and tulips and swimming pools but with irrigation ditches in place of dikes.

They even allowed a few educated Ethiopians who held staff jobs to live in paradise—not with them—but near them. The Dutch took perhaps ten dollars a day in profit from the labor of a man they paid a dollar. And yet, God save the Dutch, thought Tesfaye. The dollar was better than nothing.

The Americans had come like a thunderstorm with their roads and airplanes and their experts and their military equipment and their military bases and their Peace Corps teachers who were better, thought Tesfaye, than the Indians who were the only teachers we could afford before.

He remembered the jokes they used to invent about their Indian teachers when they'd been students.

The English language, they joked, had been born in Great Britain, fell ill in America, died in India, and was being buried in Ethiopia. Which made life difficult for the editor of an English-language newspaper. Tesfaye even had to put up with Indian teachers who moonlighted as proofreaders.

And yet, he could be grateful even for the Indians. Terrible teachers of history and English, they were good at science and mathematics. And they'd come at a time when any teacher was better than none.

And now, he thought, we have Americans teaching us and helping us fight malaria and rinderpest and showing us how to breed superior cattle and we have Germans who cure our lepers and teach them to be productive farmers and Russians to build us an oil refinery and a technical school and to pass out subversive pamphlets and scholarships to indoctrinate our students in Moscow. We have Swedes who build schools in the countryside and teach countryside people to grow two bushels of *teff* or maize or wheat where a cupful had grown before and the British who came with their cotton plantations and the French who had come long before and built a railroad.

All the foreigners came and brought with them their loud, arrogant wives whom they leave in their villas surrounded by servants while the men develop our cottage industry brothels into major factories till the number of prostitutes begins to rival the number of priests and bureaucrats.

The foreigners had come in a deluge like the life-giving rains. But the rains also brought erosion and murderous floods and foreigners brought their expensive liquors and cars and all the costly and complex gadgets we all long for now and still only a handful can buy. A generation ago none of us could buy and a handful is better than none. Except what are we buying? With their radios and their high-powered stereo the foreigners gave us their cheap music and taught us their vulgar dances. They had come, thought Tesfaye, and we learned to want the worst they had brought but we hadn't learned to achieve the best they could do.

The centuries of easy life, of gifts of the rains and the soil, had taught us that work was only for servants and outcasts. A good man owned land that someone else worked or he was a soldier or at worst a priest. Even our radical students and educated elite act out the belief that work ends when a degree has been earned. A degree, especially a foreign degree, was a passport to the civil service and its bureaucracy and the endless drinking of coffee and the useless shuffling of papers.

The government, omnipresent as God, had replaced God in the cities as the giver of all things. In the countryside it was still God who was the giver—of rain and its blessings. Everywhere the Emperor is our father and still to many in the countryside the Emperor is god and our father is the giver of all things. From the giver, many took. Few worked. Someday, Tesfaye was convinced, we will have to work.

Ethiopians had learned to fly airplanes and drink whisky and perform operations and dance the jerk as skillfully as Americans could fly and operate and jerk, but they had not learned to work and sacrifice and postpone pleasure in order to build the airplanes and hospitals and earn the leisure to drink and do the jerk.

Tesfaye was willing to accept miniskirts and pollution, loud and overcrowded cities and even the slow corruption of girls who in towns were still beautiful but no longer innocent or shy.

The clichés he typed for the paper proclaimed that Ethiopia would take the best of foreign civilization and preserve the best of its own culture. It was one of the mildest of lies the papers told.

He had seen too much of the world and too much of what was actually happening in Ethiopia not to know that the worst would come with the best. He told Harry that he was prepared to accept the worst. But in his own mind he wasn't sure how much of what he told Harry he really believed himself. He secretly feared that Ethopia would swallow the worst of what the rest of the world was made of, spit out the best, and in the process lose its appetite for all that was gracious and sacred in its own traditions.

They drove in silence through a region littered with giant volcanic boulders. It was an area where Tesfaye always felt oppressed by a history older than history. Traces of fog sat like lingering ghosts on the gray lava. He began to look forward to their arrival at Awash Station where they had agreed to stop for breakfast at the Café de la Gare. But he knew that Awash was well over an hour away. He had to fight sleep and hoped that the effort of driving would keep Harry awake.

He poured them each a plastic cup of black coffee from a thermos he held on his lap. The baby slept. There was no sign of the station wagon, not even a cloud of dust on the horizon ahead. They were soon into the grassland marked out as an animal preserve, and Tesfaye began to look for game. He spotted ostrich, Grant's gazelle, a fleeting glimpse of zebra, countless tiny dik-diks, and a family of hartebeest. He avoided calling Harry's attention to what he saw. They had driven together often enough that he knew distracting Harry could be dangerous. But when he saw the dead kudu by the side of the road, there was nothing he could do.

"Harry, stop."

"What? Huh?" Harry, as though startled from a dream, looked frantically from right to left. "Where?"

"Just slowly, Harry. Slowly."

Harry braked too sharply. The car skidded to a stop just short of the edge of a ditch. The baby woke, screaming.

"What happened?"

"I saw something back there," said Tesfaye. "Look after the baby. I'll be right back."

He popped his door open and swung his long legs out of the cramped car. He ran the fifty meters back to where he'd seen the kudu stretched out in a pool of blood. He was breathless when he stopped and looked down at a barrel-chested bull that would have stood four feet at the shoulder. Its widespread corkscrew horns were nearly as tall. Its throat had been slit from shoulder to shoulder.

The blood was still fresh; the body, warm to the touch of Tesfaye's hand. The wide, sensitive ears, the lean intelligent face with the handsome white markings across the bridge of the nose and above the eyes still seemed to quiver with life. But flies already festered in the dust-darkened blood that framed shoulders and head.

The numerous dik-diks he had been seeing as they drove through the game preserve were the tiniest of antelopes; the kudu was king. And, for Tesfaye, who had once kept a kudu in his compound in Addis, he was also the most beautiful of all animals.

In death, the white mane on the underside of the slaughtered bull quivered in the light breeze. The coloring of the brown mane on the ridge of the back and even of the white stripes across the deep, powerful chest were muted in the mist of the clouded-over dawn.

But Tesfaye knew how magnificent this six hundred pound stag would have looked alive, standing at his full height in the sunlit plain. The kudu he'd kept in Addis, sent to him from his father's land in Mota, had never grown to the size of the mature bull whose corpse he stood over that morning.

His city-bound kudu had died, not from the savage blade of a tribesman, but from the ills of civilization. The vet who failed to save him called it bronchial pneumonia. Tesfaye called it the foul air of Addis.

He had named the beast Toto. Like his own tawny dik-diks, the blue guinea fowl, the fawn bushbuck, and even the spotted cheetah cubs, Toto and all the other animals the bachelor Tesfaye kept in his compound had eaten from his hand. Toto's favored food had been saltine crackers though Tesfaye imposed a balanced diet of cabbages and grasses and lettuce. Of all the animals he'd kept, only Toto had captured his heart.

That morning, seeing the murdered kudu in the game park, he had mourned again, not only for this bull and for Toto, but for all of his vanishing past.

Born in the countryside of the Chercher Mountains, Tesfaye had come to the city to continue his education only in adolescence. Now, each year, even in the provinces, he saw more of the best of his past disappearing as swiftly as the dik-diks who had vanished from the roadside. The best was disappearing while the worst, the poverty and ignorance, remained.

He might joke about Ethiopia with others. His jokes often confused some listeners, usually earnest foreigners like Harry, and enraged others, especially Ethiopians like Baria who played allegiance to cultural preservation. But inside himself he could not joke. And this morning, over the body of the kudu, the death of his past descended on him, taking vengeance for his jokes and the times he managed to ignore what was happening to his country.

Harry hadn't seen the kudu lying on its side as they sped past on the relatively good stretch of road through the game park. Now, Harry lumbered up beside him.

"What is it?" panted Harry. "What is it?"

"A kudu."

"A what? But it's dead."

"Yes," said Tesfaye.

"Oh God." They could hear the baby's cries. Harry dragged himself back to the car to fuss over it while Tesfaye squatted by the dead kudu.

Later he wondered why his first thought had been that the kudu had been murdered by foreign hunters. He knew better. Foreigners killed with guns and were scrupulous about not hunting in the game preserve.

But to the impoverished Kirayu Gallas who lived in the area the huge kudu meant a hide and horns that could be sold and meat that could be eaten.

He looked off into the sparse bush on either side of the road. The land was all but barren. There was no one in sight and few hiding places in view. Yet he knew there were many living things in that seemingly naked landscape, including the eyes of the men who had killed the kudu.

They would wait till he and Harry drove off, check the road to make sure no pillaring dust heralded the approach of another car, then hurry from their thin sanctuary and drag the heavy carcass deeper into the bush. There it would be skinned and dehorned and as much of the flesh as the hunters could haul off to eat that day and dry for the future would be hacked loose. The rest would be left to the jackals and hyenas and vultures to fight for.

He studied the kudu. Except the slashed throat, there was no other wound or sign of blood he could see. It was unlikely that a healthy kudu could have been surprised by even the stealthiest of hunters. Probably the animal was already ill or injured when its killers managed to get a knife around its throat.

If sick, its flesh might well poison all who would eat it. But sick or lame, even after its throat had been slit, the kudu with its dying power had managed to escape its attackers as far as this shallow ditch. A trail of blood leading from the bush confirmed his guess that the wound had been inflicted elsewhere. But it was here, beside the civilized, man-made road, despite the civilized protection of the man-designated game preserve, that the kudu had finally died. Tesfaye knew no white hunter had killed the kudu. And yet . . .

He looked up the road to where Harry's head bobbed in and out of the car. The baby's crying was a distant wail. The scrub, still cool under the clouds and mist, was strangely silent. There was only the buzzing and occasional stinging of the blood-drunk flies that swarmed around the carcass.

Innocent Harry, thought Tesfaye.

Squatting low on his heels, he looked back at the kudu, so much like his Toto, even bigger, more magnificent, but now just as dead. He thought of tying it to the back of the Volkswagen and towing it a hundred kilometers to deny its bounty to the poachers who'd killed it. But he knew he couldn't drag that beautiful corpse through the dirt. And, like policemen everywhere, a team of the game park's few and ineffective rangers would doubtless appear when most unneeded to accuse them of killing the kudu. Better to let his real assassins enjoy the fruits of their labor. They had earned it.

Unlike Europeans and Europeanized Ethiopians, the tribesmen didn't kill for sport. Their killing was wasteful, illegal, and most of the dead flesh would feed not them but hyenas and vultures. As he thought of it, Tesfaye hoped the flesh wasn't poisoned with disease. He hated to see beauty killed, but to Tesfaye this killing did not cry out for vengeance.

He touched the still-warm coat of the kudu for the last time. Be glad, he thought. At least it was an Ethiopian who killed you.

He stood up. He knew Ethiopians had been killing their big

game long before the great influx of foreigners had come. He knew it was only the relatively early arrival of the British in Kenya that had preserved the wildlife there for herds of modern tourists to flock to. For in Kenya, too, hungry Africans killed the game to keep themselves alive. And white men and whitewashed Kenyans preserved the game to keep the tourists coming in. Even this meagre and poorly protected game park he stood in was a white man's concept indifferently applied in a black man's country.

Whatever he told Harry half or wholly in jest, and whatever proud Ethiopians tried to tell themselves, Tesfaye knew that he and all Ethiopians were black. Not a well-baked brown halfway between burnt African and underdone white. Tesfaye knew he was black. Ethiopia was Africa and black Africa's problems were Ethiopia's problems, too. For all their British superiority, Kenyans were his brothers. For all their French haughtiness, Senegalese were his cousins. For all their arguments about borders, Somalis and Sudanese were his neighbors, his friends.

For all the distance between them, Nigerians, Congolese, the Zulus of South Africa, the Ashantis of Ghana, were all his kin. He looked down on the kudu and he told himself again he was an African. I'm African and Africans are murdering our own past. Because we want to. Because our past is misery and hunger and slavery and ignorance. And yet, how beautiful the dumb, dead beast was.

He turned and walked back to the car. Harry was waiting for him, a soiled white diaper lying in the road at his feet, drawing flies. Tesfaye asked himself how he could blame the Harrys of this world for destroying Ethiopia's past. How could he blame them? He could think of no answer. But he did blame them.

As they drove on through the game preserve. Tesfaye couldn't shake the thought from his mind. There were times when he could understand the young radicals and the old reactionaries among his people who agreed on one idea: drive the foreigners out. Not just the exploiters. Even the harmless foreigners like Harry. Harry, who would bury his eyes in wildlife books by the hour but couldn't bear to look at a dead kudu. Harry, who had come to Ethiopia with a fixed, scholastic idea of the Ethiopian personality and set about with an open mind but closed eyes to find material to illustrate a theory concocted in California.

Harry, his vision fixed rigidly on the road, oblivious to the land he drove through, would write a book that would help blur and obscure and thereby destroy the Ethiopia that Tesfaye knew and loved. The Ethiopia he knew and loved and—in the most progressive chambers of his mind—the Ethiopia he wanted to destroy.

"Harry," he said, "do you know who killed that kudu?"

"Huh. That which?"

"Don't turn around, Harry. Keep your eye on the road. That kudu we saw with its throat slit back there."

"Oh. Was that a kudu?"

"Yes. It was a kudu."

"Oh." His arms were locked to the wheel. A minute or more went by before he asked, "Who killed it?"

"I don't know," said Tesfaye. "Some Gallas, probably." But to himself he chanted, You and I, Harry. You and I. You and I are the killers of the kudu.

There was another long silence before Harry nodded and said, "Oh. Uh-huh. Some Gallas. I guess they live in the game park. Gosh. They shouldn't let people live there. It's bad for the animals."

"We'll drive them away," said Tesfaye. "And let them live in the city."

"I'm not so sure about that," said Harry. "I'm not so sure that's a good idea."

But that's what you're doing, thought Tesfaye. You kudu killer. You're murdering my country, my past. And I'm helping you.

"They could starve in the city," said Harry. "They don't have any skills."

"We'll teach them," said Tesfaye.

"Maybe you're right," said Harry. "Education's the answer."

As they drove on the motion of the car lulled the baby back to sleep. Tesfaye, to avoid distracting Harry, lapsed into the quiet that was his usual mode except when he was forced to explain Ethiopia and its people to his hard-to-convince friend. Harry was anxious to learn but difficult to inform.

Soon after he arrived in Addis, Harry had told Tesfaye that the people of Ethiopia were orally oriented. In his own books, Horst Eisler had demonstrated that this was the key to understanding the country.

"Orally oriented?" Tesfaye had asked. "Does that mean we talk too much?"

"Well, something like that."

Beneath the disposable diapers in the flight bag on the floor of the car, Harry had packed travel books and animal guides, bird books and relief maps. He had told Tesfaye he had been determined to make the trip at a more leisurely pace than they had the year before. He wanted to check what he saw against his reference material and to query Tesfaye and Baria about the countryside and the people along the road to Kulubi, so that the trip itself could become part of the book he would write. But staying in Addis Ababa to celebrate Christmas by the Western calendar had spoiled his plan. Now he tried to concentrate only on his driving. He knew they had to hurry. As they sped through the countryside, birds and wildlife, the exotic tribesmen marching along the side of the road, unfamiliar trees and shrubs and strange outcroppings of rocks and volcanic slag failed to distract him.

Harry was writing his book because of a theory of the Ethiopian personality he had developed under Eisler's guidance. He had told Tesfaye that he knew people would read the book not for his ideas but for the information it would include about a strange and exotic land. But Tesfaye feared that in his hasty pursuit of facts and his straining for a theory to explain them, Harry was running blind. The facts were elusive and the country too complex and changing too rapidly to pose for a theory. Harry's book would be full of mistakes and opinions that would be far off target.

But at least he would get the book written, as foreigners always do. Ethiopians would attack it, as Ethiopians always attack books by foreigners. But no Ethiopian would take the trouble to write such a book himself. A nation of critics, thought Tesfaye. A nation of talkers and gossips and backbiters. Harry's right. Orally oriented. But we never do anything. Unhappy the nation that needs heroes—and foreigners. But heaven help us, thought Tesfaye, how we do need them.

The relative quiet while the baby slept created a vacuum that Harry's nervous mind filled. His thoughts skipped like jumping beans. He thought of the festival they were driving to. Then Kulubi as it had been the year before. Then he remembered he hadn't completed the forms requesting an extension of his foundation grant. And a letter to Eisler. He owed Eisler a letter.

He wondered if Julie had answered that last letter from his mother. She must have. What would he do without Julie? Soon he'd be able to show her Kulubi. And the magic of it. His *silet;* his vow. Could it only be coincidence? And wanting to name the baby Menelik. He didn't want to think about that. When he told Julie about it she'd only laughed. The article he'd written. This year with Tesfaye for reluctant company he would walk among the pilgrims from Dire Dawa to Kubuli.

Kulubi. He was glad Baria was with them. Someone to keep Julie company while he and Tesfaye were walking. While he was busy with his research. Kulubi. Microcosm of Ethiopia. Kulubi: Key to Ethiopia. Not a bad title perhaps for his book.

He'd been bogged down on the book. So many other things. Julie. The baby. Being a father. Get the grant extended. Then it would be possible to finish. If not all the writing—no—he couldn't finish all the writing but surely the research. Kulubi: Microcosm of Ethiopia. Everyone from the Emperor himself to the lowliest peasant. All the tribes. Christians and pagans and Muslims. Hundreds of foreigners. Ethiopia, the macrocosm, converging in the needle's eye of Kulubi. A theory to explain Ethiopia based on the power of Kulubi to draw Ethiopia together. Harry believed in theories. It was more than an academic habit. Theories were a way of ordering the chaos. Even when facts contradicted a theory, he preferred to cling as long as he could. Not just the chaotic, contradictory facts about Ethiopia, but of his own life as well. Like the miracle that teased him to explain the birth of a child. He'd wanted a child from the first and had worn down Julie's early reluctance. But, as the childless years went by, he'd wondered if she still wore that reluctance coiled inside her. She would swear it had been removed, even challenging him to feel if the string were still there. He never had. And then as if by magic the seed had borne fruit. If the miracle theory was true, it had begun at Kulubi.

He remembered the night of the eve of Gabriel's Day a year ago when he and Tesfaye had wandered among the tens of thousands who dotted the hillside above the tiny village and filled the bowl where the gold-domed new church now stood on a hillock. His first glimpse of the church and the gathering crowds had made Harry wish he'd brought Julie.

Though she teased him, sometimes cruelly, about the lingering shreds of his Catholicism, he knew she could be moved by a spectacle like this. He felt himself drawn by the faith of the pilgrims. Julie would be impressed by the Byzantine richness and African rhythms of the services and the swirling masses of the people in costumes as varied as the dozens of languages they spoke.

Harry had but slowly discovered Julie's taste for the exotic. Two lonely Americans, they had met and married in bourgeois Geneva. In the first years of their marriage he'd dragged her to Fatima and Lourdes. She'd labeled them frauds. Crass, commercial middle-class fakes. Preying on the sick, the hysterical.

Her own world she'd found as they traveled. The crowded markets of Algiers. The jasmine-scented streets of Alexandria. The remoter villages of northern Iran where fabulous rugs were woven by wizened peasants. The rivers of people, viewed from a distance, flowing into the sacred waters of the Ganges. The saffron-robed monks of Vientiane and the temples of Angkor Wat. The shops and restaurants on junks in the harbor of Hong Kong.

They had finally made their eastering way back to the States, and Harry drifted again into the academic world he had tried to escape.

For Harry it was a full circle. He'd left the sanctuary of Southern California with a vague hope of work more meaningful than either his father's shirt factory or the scholastic plants at Stanford and UCLA. He drifted from Chicago to Washington to New York but found he could adjust to neither the pace, the climate, nor the people. Europe beckoned. Harry went. Found Julie. And came back to California.

Stanford, where he'd earned his master's degree, was only a few miles from his parents' indulgent home. The pull was hard to resist. Then, at a cocktail party given by friends on the campus, Harry met Horst Eisler. The aging Semitic scholar was then busy drumming Amharic into the ears of Peace Corps trainees destined for Ethiopia.

The chance encounter focused Harry's blurred attention on a new realm of possibility. He'd taken his master's in sociology. Switching to African studies would make returning to school more like a new adventure than surrender to a well-worn routine. Julie was intrigued. Eisler encouraged him. His parents approved and were soon subsidizing his doctorate as well as his marriage. The prodigal remittance man had returned to the fold.

"One thing you can't deny." It was his mother's favorite joke. "Your parents are a comfort."

He'd always hated the family name. It had been abstracted from an unpronounceable Ukrainian patronymic when Harry's grandfather had migrated to America. His parents compounded the crime by naming their only child Harriston. His mother thought it sounded English.

"Dr. Harriston Comfort," she said when he told her of his study plans. "Won't it sound nice?"

Harry was soon plodding his way through to the doctorate he would earn with a never-to-be-published thesis, "Cross-Cultural Bias as Reflected in the Writings of Foreign Commentators on Ethiopia." Horst Eisler alone among the countless foreign commentators on Ethiopia was revealed to have no biases, cross-cultural or otherwise.

Though grieved by Harry's inability to grasp even the rudiments of the Amharic language he loved so well, the old Semiticist was impressed by the younger man's earnest footnoting of the history of Ethiopia's historians. Harry seemed reasonably fluent in French, one of the few languages Eisler himself did not know well. He considered Harry a disciple and was confident he would master the complex language of the Amharas if he had the chance to live in Ethiopia.

He backed Harry for the foundation grant which guaranteed two years (extendable) to research and write what Eisler was confident would be the definitive study of Ethiopian culture.

With the help of Baria and Tesfaye, Harry had begun to learn something about the country. With Baria he'd traveled to the farthest reaches of Galla country in the west, to Wollega and to the rain forests beyond where outcast Negroid tribes lived a life of their own. It was Baria who had taken both Harry and Julie to the Muslim festival at Shek Hussein in the mountains of Bale. To Falasha villages in Begemdir where Ethiopia's black Jews read the Pentateuch in Ge'ez, the ancient church language of the country. To Lalibela where Christian descendants of Moses had ruled and to Axum with its ancient pagan monuments built by an unknown people. To Asmara and Keren and Massawa where Eritreans waged a sporadic revolt against the government in distant Addis Ababa.

"If you're really going to write a book about Ethiopia," Baria had warned him, "I can't leave you just in Tesfaye's hands. You have to remember we aren't all Amharas. We aren't all Christians. Most of us are Gallas. Many are pagans or Muslims. A few are Jews."

Harry wasn't convinced.

"But the heart of it all," he began. "It's the highlands. The

Christians. The Amharas. Even you have a Christian, an Amhara name."

"A slave name," said Baria. "Gebre Medhin is an Amhara name. Servant of the Saviour. It was the name of the family that made slaves of my grandparents. And you know what Baria means."

"Yes. You told me. It means slave."

"So it does. Like Shankila, Baria is the name of a tribe from which many slaves have been taken. Our people weren't Barias. They were Gallas. But when they were taken as slaves, their masters made Christians of them. Taught them to speak Amharic and gave them that name. Many people tell me I should change it. But I don't want to deny. Or forget."

It was seldom Baria spoke of himself. Talking was not his style. He seemed to prefer pointing things out, forcing Harry to see for himself. Perhaps, Harry reasoned, it was because Baria saw with a painter's eye. It was Tesfaye, the journalist, who was the great explainer. He had learned far more about Ethiopia from Tesfaye, yet, there was so much that he admired, even envied in Baria. To be a bachelor again. Unchained. He thought of living an artist's, a writer's life. If his book on Ethiopia was successful. And he were still a bachelor like Baria. No responsibilities. No obligations to anyone. But he remembered how empty his life had been as a bachelor. And, whenever he had found a girl, how anxious he'd been for involvement, commitment. He wondered if Baria wasn't the same. He remembered that Baria had told him that for all his drinking in the brothels and chasing he would never play with married women. That's where trouble lies, he had said. And nothing real can come of it.

Harry was impressed by the quiet strength, the competence Baria showed in everything he did. Especially his work. His paintings were disciplined abstractions which captured the anguish and beauty of his country in a way that Tesfaye's words never could.

Harry recognized that Baria was acutely sensitive, yet, like his paintings, tightly controlled. He affected a cynicism about men and a contempt for women that Harry saw as a mask to hide his real feelings. Harry suspected that Baria's mottled skin was only one of the problems. He knew how grimly self-conscious his friend was about the vitiligo that spotted his skin. Many Ethiopians thought it was leprosy and shunned him because of it.

In recent months he and Julie had seen relatively little of Baria. Harry thought he knew why. Though Baria made much of the joys of his bachelor life, Harry was sure he was lonely.

"I don't know what's wrong with him lately," said Julie one evening as they were returning from a party they'd risked during the last week of her pregnancy. Baria had been there but had hardly spoken to them. "He's gotten so nasty. And cold."

"He's sensitive," said Harry.

"Like an iceberg, he's sensitive."

"Only a third of an iceberg shows," said Harry.

"And the rest is just as cold."

"He's afraid of being hurt. I understand Baria."

"Better than I do I'm sure."

Though he admired Baria, Harry admitted to himself that he felt more comfortable with Tesfaye. Tesfaye was far more open and had opened more of Ethiopia's closed doors to Harry. Through Tesfaye he had met several important figures in government. He had been introduced into the homes of many old aristocratic families usually wary of foreigners.

He had met Tesfaye's father, who knew more of the history of his country than perhaps any living man. And it was Tesfaye who had been his patient guide through the labyrinthine ways of the church, the life of the peasants, the ritual of the seasons, the devious ways in which power was won and used, and even, in theory at least, the workings of the language.

With Tesfaye he had been to the old capitals of Ankober and Gondar, to the tiny Shangri-la of a village, Ejersa Goro, where the Emperor had been born. They had been to the monasteries of Debra Birhan, Quosquam, and Gishen Mariam, and, most important of all, to Kulubi.

It had been his discovery of Kulubi that had given a sudden focus to Harry's study of Ethiopia. Tesfaye had suggested the trip, and it had been Tesfaye who had pointed Harry's persistent nose to the follow-up research that had resulted in his one solid piece of work since coming to the country.

His article on Kulubi had been published in the latest issue of *The Journal of Ethiopian Studies*. It had not only pleased old Eisler, but had won approval in official Ethiopian circles.

Tesfaye had suggested the title, "The Church of Unity: Kulubi Gabriel." Now shorn of Harry's carefully compiled one hundred and forty-seven footnotes, the article was being reissued by the government as a handsomely illustrated pamphlet in both Amharic and English.

Harry's instinctive mastery of the bland style of Ethiopia's apologists had won him an audience with the Emperor. The government was even planning an Arabic edition to demonstrate the religious unity that prevailed in a country where Christians and Muslims had been slaughtering each other for centuries. It had been Harry's happy discovery that Gabriel, a saint of the Koran as well as of the Bible, was, at Kulubi, worshipped jointly by members of the two warring faiths.

He was proud of the pamphlet he'd done and aware that Kulubi had given him a focus for his efforts to understand the country. Since that visit he had thrown himself into his research with all the energy that had seemed blocked, frustrated in everything else he'd ever tried. Each day his tape recorder and notebooks swallowed great hunks of information which he realized he was still a long way from understanding, digesting, synthesizing. But he drove himself with a furious energy, confident that it would all fall into place in time. Perhaps now, with the birth of a son. Perhaps with another visit to Kulubi the genesis would be complete.

He had read of saints and mystics who had known the presence of God. And of people who had witnessed or experienced miracles. It had never happened to him. He had become a Catholic for the most secular of reasons. Before he met Julie, he'd fallen in love with a Catholic girl. She'd left him. But the faith he'd adopted lingered. He wanted to believe. He envied the mystics, the witnesses of miracles. He envied the pilgrims he'd seen at Kulubi.

Even when they were sure Julie was pregnant, he tried not to think of the *silet* that he'd made as more than a joke. A joke he'd been goaded into by Tesfaye.

During the two days they spent at Kulubi, Harry had first learned about the concept of the *silet*. About the people who made them. And what happened. In his article on Kulubi he had written:

> Though the miracles attributed to St. Gabriel of Kulubi are many and varied, the largest percentage relates in one way or another to children. The most frequent of all is an appeal to the saint, usually by barren women, for a child. Many families long childless report that their prayers for a child were answered after a visit to Kulubi on St. Gabriel's Day.
>
> The story of one Indian couple echoes the Biblical story

> of Gabriel's appearance to Zacharias and the subsequent birth of a child to his long-barren wife. The couple, who are Hindus, had been childless for twenty years. Inspired by the stories they had heard of St. Gabriel of Kulubi, they went to the church and followed the custom of making a *silet* or pledge to return in a year with a gift for the saint if a child should be born to them. The next year they returned, not only to bring an offering to Gabriel, but also to have their child blessed by the priests of the church. The couple have since continued to make annual pilgrimages of thanks to the saint.
>
> Skeptics are fond of explaining away miracles in psychological terms such as wish fulfillment, hallucination, psychosomatic influences, etc., or simply as coincidence. . . .

Harry, however, was no longer disposed to explain away his miracle. He had tried not to think of it as a miracle. But the theory fit.

Midway through Julie's pregnancy, Harry had again begun going to Mass. He went each Sunday by himself. He hadn't taken communion or been able to bring himself to confession. But he did want to pray and he wanted a church to pray in.

He wondered if he had faith. He wondered if this birth really was a miracle.

At Kulubi he'd been separated from Tesfaye by the crowds in the church. He had been pressed close to a high, canopied pulpit. A deacon halfway up the steps was passing out what Harry later learned were packets of dirt from the ground around the church.

As he watched the massed arms of the pilgrims reaching toward the pulpit, he made his *silet*. Silently, skeptically, his joke with Gabriel. He told no one. And, somehow, he had gone on to promise what he would do to fulfill his *silet* if his plea was granted . . .

> Even a few minutes spent talking to the pilgrims reveals something of the variety of the people and prayers in evidence at Kulubi. A man from Asmara carrying a girl of ten on his head reveals that the child had been speechless for years but that after he took her on a pilgrimage to Kulubi she regained her speech. A heavyset woman from Addis Ababa crawled on the ground before the church till her knees and palms were sore. Like many pilgrims she was shy about revealing the nature of her vow and would say it was in thanks for "the miraculous performance of Kulubi Gabriel."

> Though most of the supplicants who ask for a child are women, many fathers who have had only daughters will pray for a son. One man, already in difficulties because of the large size of his family, said he asked Gabriel to spare him further children for a while. One year recently a woman from Gambella brought a lion cub as a gift for Gabriel. The woman said she had asked Gabriel to cure her of a uterus problem, according to Aleka Tiume Lisan, religious educator of the church. "Blood became flesh and the woman returned to the church after a year with her newly born son," said the religious leader.

That night, bleary-eyed from lack of sleep yet keenly alert, Harry had pressed Tesfaye into service interviewing pilgrims who were willing to tell their stories. There was enough of the academic in Harry that he also sought responses to twenty-five Thematic Apperception Test cards he had specially prepared for Ethiopia.

The TAT cards, in which he held a mystical faith, drew a blank from most of the pilgrims. They couldn't figure out what this crazy white man wanted them to say about his little drawings. Not knowing what answers were expected of them, they cautiously kept silent.

"We shouldn't have rushed them," Harry said later. "You can't rush TAT interviews with primitive people. It takes time to build confidence."

Tesfaye agreed.

They had wandered among groups dancing and singing in the level area beneath the church. They explored the improvised nightclubs in roughly put together grass and wood frame shelters. They talked to people in the campsite where the well-to-do pitched elaborate tents and on the hillsides where the poor huddled in blankets around smoky eucalyptus fires.

As he drove, his mind clung to that previous December. *Tahsas*. On the Ethiopian calendar Gabriel's day was *Tahsas* 19. For us, December 28, just three days after our Christmas. At first Julie had wanted to make the trip. Tesfaye thought it might be too rough for her.

"Good God," she protested to Harry. "After driving across half of Europe and the Middle East . . ." She turned to Tesfaye. "Did he tell you we drove all the way from Geneva to Afghanistan in a 1950 *Ford*, for God's sake."

Did we really do it for God's sake? Harry wondered now as he remembered her words. The meaning of meaningless curses had begun to trouble him. He used them himself. And that troubled him even more.

But Julie also wanted to be in Addis, she admitted, for the opening of an exhibition of paintings by Baria. Baria had asked Harry to write a review of the show. Harry compromised by doing an advance article which Tesfaye had run in his paper the Sunday before the opening. Julie had agreed that at least one of them should be there for the exhibition and let herself be talked out of the trip.

But Harry wished she had been with him that night at Kulubi. For that was the night, he now believed, the miracle had begun. This year, perhaps, they would be there together. He wanted to share the trip with her exactly as he'd known it. Except that now, after years of barren marriage, they would have a child and that child would be with them. In his article he had reported:

> Women with babes in arms make their way to the holy water spring. Water piped from an adjoining hill to a tank in the church compound and in the old church below is blessed by priests who work in shifts baptizing children and adult pilgrims alike. Over a thousand infants, all born to women who had made their plea to Gabriel the previous year, are baptized.

He remembered how he had wanted to have the child baptized Menelik. They had talked about the possibility of an Ethiopian name for the child when Julie was pregnant. Julie had said she'd be willing if it were a girl. But a boy she wanted to name Jonathan. It had been her father's name.

To Harry it sounded too much like Harriston. One of those names parents inflict on defenseless children. Who would then go through life insisting their name was Harry or John. It hadn't occurred to him that Menelik would be at least as much of a burden as Harriston. He saw only the romance, the legend.

Chapter One, thought Harry. The Birth of Menelik. He thought of the quote from Gibbon that everyone who wrote a book about Ethiopia felt compelled to use. "Surrounded by the enemies of her religion, Ethiopia slept a thousand years, forgetful of the world by whom she was forgot."

So much of history was a long sleep. Filled in by legends. Waiting for something to happen. Like waiting for a child to be born. Like waiting for a miracle.

The word tripped another memory. It was a memory he didn't want, but he had begun to wonder again about faith and its miracles. That miracles could come despite, or perhaps because of, a belief that was weak.

He didn't want to think about the faith he had found on the heels of love. Or about the faithless girl, faith's tool, who had brought him to it. He didn't want to remember—Marie des Anges. Her name. A name like a nun's.

He didn't want to think about Marie. But now she was there.

A plain provincial girl but with something that seemed both pure and stable about her when Harry had met her in Paris. Before he knew Julie.

In those days he had convinced himself he was no longer an American. Not even an exile. But a European. An umbilical two hundred dollars a month from his parents still tied him to home. But he managed not to think about that.

He worked half days trying to sell a Swiss-based mutual fund to expatriate Americans living in Paris. He wasn't good at it, but his draw helped stretch the remittance from home. Marie des Anges was one of the house's bilingual typists, one of the few not monotonously pursued by other salesmen.

She wore no makeup on her pinched features. Her lips and nose were thin; her eyes, narrow. She had no breasts but a peasant's strong legs and hips. Her loneliness wore a mask of innocence, and Harry, at that dissolute, mildly alcoholic phase of his life, was ready to be attracted by purity.

He wasn't quite ready for the passion he discovered when she accompanied him to his flat the second evening he'd taken her to dinner. Even thinking about it now, he felt himself grow tense. He soon found she was as passionate about her religion as she was about sex.

The combination of apparent purity, underlying passion, and a deep faith seemed specially designed to fill those vacuums by which Harry was beginning to define himself. Mixed up as so often. Faith and desire. And the dreams we're raised on. Women with pneumatic, center-fold breasts. True love, first love with a girl who had kept herself pure for you. But he had never known a virgin. Nor slept with a woman whose breasts were dirty words like knockers or boobs or literary metaphors like melons or clusters of grapes.

As a young man he had first taken sex from a skinny prostitute bought on the streets of Los Angeles. Then at college with casual girls who had known other lovers.

He wondered why he should envy mystics and people who had known miracles and men who had slept with virgins. And why mystics and miracles and virgins and women with breasts like metaphors should all be so mixed up in his mind. Mixed up as so often. A passion for the virginal Marie des Anges who wasn't a virgin leading him to church. And not just because he had wanted to marry her. But to believe. Or try. He didn't want to think about Marie. But she was there.

It had been a Saturday evening that they first slept together. The next morning he'd accompanied her to Mass. When marriage was discussed, it had been his idea, not hers, that he should convert. He was sure it would be necessary to win her parents' approval. She'd shrugged, agreed.

He'd taken his instructions with a Sorbonne-educated priest, a disciple of Maritain, chosen by his superiors for such tasks because of his ability to handle Americans in search of both faith and culture.

Harry proceeded rapidly through the sacraments. Baptism, first confession, communion, confirmation followed each other within a month during that magical Parisian spring. But he never quite made it to Catholic matrimony.

Marie disappeared. She left a note at his apartment saying she must go to prepare her parents for meeting him. Weeks passed. He wrote to the address she'd left. Then he received a postal from a city in the south telling him not to come—maintenant.

A few weeks later another salesman from the securities house told Harry he'd met her in the metro with a bearded, bohemian type. She didn't come to the apartment. She didn't call work. She avoided their old haunts.

Harry began prowling the fourteenth arrondissement. He never saw her again. By then, however, he'd been hooked on his new faith. For a time, matrimony denied, he even thought of holy orders. His astute young confessor suggested a year's consideration.

The last he'd heard of Marie was from a mutual friend, an American journalist to whom she'd sold a brick of hashish in Tangier. She'd been with a silent, bearded young man. Harry was left with a hollow echo in his heart and a dry faith he couldn't call his own.

He deserted Paris for the less troubling atmosphere of Geneva.

He worked, full-time now, as a statistician in the main office of the same giant mutual fund. It was here that he met Julie, herself a refugee from a shattered romance at home.

Like Marie, she was a typist for the securities firm. Though no more attractive, she wore an aura of availability that made her desirable and heavily pursued. A full, pouting lower lip was the one sensuous feature in a face otherwise plain. Her hair was long, lank. She was small breasted, but a narrow waist and full hips made her look good in a bikini. She was often invited on Riviera weekends. Men enjoyed showing her off. And quickly forgetting her. She and Harry met like two strays, coupled, felt need, married civilly, and steadily clawed their way toward a punishing love.

When she decided to marry Harry, Julie feared she was pregnant. She believed the father to be an elderly German stock analyst with a tenacious wife and five grown children. She was terrified equally of abortion and of raising a child by herself. When the alarm proved false, she secretly blamed Harry for the deception under which he married her. He'd suffered for his ignorant sin.

He hadn't noticed the village they were approaching.

"Slow down," said Tesfaye. "This is Awash we're coming to."

"Gosh, that was quick," said Harry. "What time is it?"

Tesfaye looked at his watch. He kept it set for Western time but automatically translated it into the Ethiopian system.

"Two thirty," he said.

"Uh-huh." Harry's mind struggled. Add six. To get Western time from Ethiopian you add six. Two thirty. Eight thirty. "Not bad. We're making good time."

"Not bad," said Tesfaye.

At a service station at the edge of town they saw Baria's station wagon parked off to the side. Harry pulled up beside it, but there was no sign of Baria and Julie. No attendants appeared. The station seemed deserted.

"Where is everybody?" said Tesfaye.

"Never mind everybody," said Harry. "Where's Julie and Baria?"

"Maybe they're closed," Julie had said. There was no sign of life at the service station.

"They can't be closed." Baria leaned on his horn again. And

again. No response. He saw a Kirayu tribesman coming up the road from the center of the village. Baria climbed from the station wagon and hailed the man in Galligna. They exchanged greetings and Baria asked, "Where are the people from this place?"

"Ah, they're all down there." He nodded back toward the village. "Some madwoman has chained herself to a pole. Everyone's gone there to play with her." He swung his walking stick over his shoulder, draped his arms over it and went on his way. "Everyone in this place is mad."

Baria told Julie what the man had said. "Come on," he urged. "Let's lock this thing up and leave it here. We can walk down and see the circus. It should be amusing."

"No thank you," said Julie. "I don't want to go wandering around to see a madwoman. This place scares me anyway. They're liable to put me in chains, too."

"Shall you wait for me here then?"

She looked around the deserted station. Vultures perched on the unattended gas pumps. Fog rising from the nearby river swirled damp and chill around them.

"Are those my choices?"

He nodded.

"Can't we drive down?"

"We should leave the car where it can be seen from the highway. So your husband and Tesfaye will know we're here."

"Knowing Harry, he'll drive right by without seeing it."

"Tesfaye won't. Come on."

She followed him along the edge of the highway and around the crumbling, tin-roofed Orthodox church. They followed the badly rutted road down toward the railroad tracks. They saw the crowd standing in a strangely silent circle around what looked like a flagpole. They couldn't see the woman. As they drew near the edge of the circle, the crowd, seeing Julie's white face, politely made way for her.

"Good," said Baria. "We'll get a front seat." He took her elbow and steered her through the crowd. Julie saw the woman and recognized her at once.

"I know her. She runs the hotel here."

"You're right," said Baria. "She's part of that Antonakos clan. They run these hotels all along the railway."

A major and a dozen rifle-bearing policemen held back the

crowd around the concrete-based remnant of the flagpole to which the woman was chained.

"She really is strung up," said Baria. "See? There are bolts through the rings of the chains."

"But why?" said Julie.

The woman's arms were stretched above her head. She was slumped back against the base of the shaft. Her bare feet were on the ground. Her black dress, bleached with dust, clung to a full, stocky figure. She looked to be forty, haggard and worn, yet still strangely attractive. The sight of another woman in chains was too much for Julie.

"We've got to get her down," she said, more loudly than she'd intended.

The police major turned toward them. He and Baria recognized each other. The major approached them.

"*Gashe* Baria."

Gashe Tsgaye. *Tadess?* You've arranged quite a spectacle for us."

"Arranged? Not at all. This crazy Greek did all the arranging herself."

"Really? She must be quite gifted. To slip those bolts up there through the chains herself."

"Yes, that," said the major. He was a dark-complexioned Amhara, still young but already paunchy. "Her son did that. The son does what she tells him. And the damned Greek bitch is crazy."

"What do you mean, Greek?" snapped the woman in flawless Amharic. "I'm as Ethiopian as you are."

Suppressed laughter snickered through the crowd.

"She thinks just because she was born here that makes her an Ethiopian," said the major.

"It does," said Baria. "It makes her a citizen."

"A citizen third class," said the major.

"A citizen," said the woman. "And who is your father, son of a dog?"

This time the crowd's laughter broke into a roar.

"Quiet, you fools," yelled the major. The policemen behind him raised their rifles. "And you, hold your tongue, crazy Greek bitch."

"Ethiopian," screamed the woman. Her black eyes flashed. "I'm an Ethiopian the same as you. Hah. I have a right to be in chains if I want."

"That's supposed to be comic," said the major to Baria. "She thinks she's a comic, too. But she's only crazy. She's been mocking us all morning."

"Will someone please explain it to me?" said Julie.

"I beg your pardon," said the major in English. "She's crazy and making a spectacle of herself, isn't it?"

"But you can't just leave her like that."

"We won't be leaving her like that. She had herself chained up there. But when we try to take her down she spits and kicks like a mule. We got her shoes off but that's all. I don't want to use real force, but I will if I have to."

"My name is Mrs. Comfort," said Julie. "My husband is Dr. Harriston Comfort. We're all driving to Kulubi together, and my husband will be here in a few minutes with a friend of his, a very important Ethiopian journalist."

"You know Tesfaye," said Baria. "Tesfaye Tessema."

"Of course," said the major.

"I think you better have these chains removed," said Julie, "before my husband and Ato Tesfaye arrive. They'll be shocked."

"With all due respect," said the major, "to your husband and Ato Tesfaye, I have an even bigger problem. His Majesty the Emperor will be coming through here soon. He's going by train to Dire Dawa for this Kulubi business. I can assure you she'll be down before His Imperial Majesty arrives." He turned to Baria and added in Amharic, "She'll be down if I have to cut her arms off to do it."

"I'm sure," Baria answered, still in Amharic. "What is this thing she's chained to anyway?"

"That? It's something the Italians put up. During the occupation. It was their flagpole. The chains came down and made a big web around it to keep Ethiopians from getting too close. Then, when the Emperor came back and liberated the country, the Italians here ran off and the people broke the chains and tore down their damn flag."

"Very nice," said Baria. "All the millions they spent in Addis to build war monuments. Here it's better. A flagpole. Broken chains. Liberation. Very nice."

The major glanced back at the flagpole. "It doesn't look like much of a liberation monument right now," he said.

"With a *faranj* chained to it?" said Baria. "It's even better."

"I'm no *faranj*, you damn leper. An Ethiopian. But to hell with your liberation. This is my revenge."

"It's some kind of crazy vow she made to Kulubi Gabriel," said the major.

"To hell with your vows. It's my revenge."

"You see?" said the major. "She is crazy."

"It's Kulubi fever," said Baria. "Very contagious this time of year. Even foreigners get it. This lady's husband is another victim."

"How long has she been this way?" Julie asked the major.

"She's always been crazy."

"I mean in chains."

"That," said the major, lapsing forgetfully into Amharic, "that she did last night."

"I did it at sunrise, you bastard. Give me some water."

"I'll give you my piss, Greek bitch."

"ETHIOPIAN . . ."

The woman's howls were operatic, but Julie felt there was real emotion behind the half-mad performance.

"Will you let me talk to her?" she said to the major. "Perhaps a woman could help."

"Dear lady, if you can talk her into coming down off that damn thing without violence, I will be grateful to you. But I'm afraid she doesn't speak English."

"She speaks French," said Julie. "I've talked to her before. My husband and I stayed at her hotel."

"She speaks French," said the major. "But not so much." He shrugged. "Try if you want, but watch her. Don't stand too close. She's dangerous. When we tried to get her down, she kicked two policemen so bad they had to be put in the clinic. That's where we put her son too, when he tried to fight us. Talk her down if you can. But one way or another she comes down and out of sight before that train comes in."

Julie took a step closer to the woman. She greeted her in French and asked, "Do you remember me? My husband and I stayed at your hotel. We hired your son to guide us down to the Palm Springs."

"I don't know you," said the woman. "I don't know your husband. I only know Gabriel let my husband die."

The major evidently had understood. "That's what the vow

was about," he said to Julie in English. "He wasn't a bad sort. The husband. But this one has always been crazy. They ran the hotel here. She's part of that family of Greeks that run the railway hotels all the way from Djibouti to Addis. They tried to get this one to move to Addis when the husband died and let some other cousin run this place. But she insists on staying here. That's part of the crazy vow, too."

"He knows nothing. Send him away." The woman looked at Julie, studying her more closely. "Yes, I know you. Your husband is a little fat man. With glasses."

"That's Harry."

"Get me some water."

"No," said the major. "No water. She wants to make a scandal, but in comfort. She knows the Emperor's train is coming, and she wants to make a scandal."

"Never mind," said Julie. "Can you get these people out of here? Let me talk to her alone. I'll do what I can."

The major glanced at Baria.

"Let her try."

The major spoke to his men. They raised their rifles and one fired a shot in the air. The crowd began to back away, prodded by the rifles of the police. One Somali, muttering over his shoulder as he slowly moved off, was struck on the back of his head with such force that blood flowed from the wound. The police let him lie and moved the rest of the crowd off. The major and Baria followed them.

The two women were left in the chill mist at the base of the flagpole. Julie knew a hundred pairs of eyes were still on them, yet she felt isolated, alone.

The blood had drained from the Greek woman's upraised arms. They were deadly white except at the wrists where the chains had bitten into the flesh.

"Tell me," said Julie. "You said it isn't a vow. You said it's revenge."

"They let my husband die," said the woman. "I'll have my revenge."

"How did he die?"

The woman stared up into the swirling mist. She shook her head violently. Her tangled, shoulder-length hair fell about her face. Sounds of weeping came from her mouth, but there were no tears.

"He died in my arms." She shook the heavy chains. "These arms."

Julie could see there were work-hardened muscles under the white flesh.

"Tell me."

"In Greece," sobbed the woman.

"Not here?"

"In Greece. It was his brain."

Julie went closer and brushed the woman's hair back from her face. With her fingertips she dried the drops of moisture that dribbled from the woman's heavy, sensual mouth.

"Ai, he was a man, by God. A beautiful man. Tall and strong as an ox. Hair like a raven, and gentle with my heart, gentle as the lamb. Ai . . ." She laughed deep in her throat. "Don't talk to me of men. There was only one."

"I understand," said Julie. "My father was like that. I've never known a man like him."

"Huh. But you didn't go to bed with your father. You didn't know him like I knew my man."

Julie looked down at her shoes. She felt terribly conspicuous in the naked square, pleading with a mad woman.

"You must have . . ." She paused, knowing how trite her words would sound. But she could think of no others. "You must have loved him very much."

"Love? There's no love in me now. I'm withered like a raisin. Love I don't know it. I spit the filth of this village from my mouth, and my mouth is still dry.

"I have three days to stay here. Three days to spit on Gabriel. He let my man die. Like the rest." She looked down at Julie. "Have you ever . . . have you ever known a man like . . ."

"No," said Julie. "I never have."

"Huh. I suppose you'll tell me you're some innocent virgin."

"No. Not that either."

"What are you then?"

"A woman. Like you. Only not as lucky as you. At least you've known a real man."

"Oh, God, I knew him."

"Won't you tell me what happened?"

"His brain. It was his brain. And they let it rot."

She fell silent, staring over the tin roofs of the railroad sheds that stood between them and her hotel.

"What's your name?"

"Me? Huh. Christina. A good Christian name. Christians. Greeks. Ethiopians. Priests. They're all useless. The doctors in Addis Ababa, at that hospital named for our dwarf of a king, the doctors were Germans. Useless. They could do nothing. I took him to Greece. They said they could save him. Cut out the front of his brain that was rotting. Some kind of tumor, they said. Cut out half his brain and he'd live. Like a vegetable, he'd live. They wanted to make him as useless as they were, and they said that would be living. He'd have to be fed. He'd have to be carried. He wouldn't know it when he shit or he pissed. Useless to a woman. Useless to himself. And they said that would be living. I prayed. I prayed to them all. Gabriel. Mary. Giorgis. The lot. I watched him dying and I prayed. I begged the doctors. I prayed to the saints. And I watched my man die . . .

"Oh, God. My arms are like lead."

"Let me take you down. Please."

"Huh. Let Gabriel take me down. With his miracles. I prayed to Gabriel above all. Let my man live like a man. That was my *silet*. I vowed that every year my man went on living like a man I would walk from this hole of a village to Kulubi with a stone on my head. Not even a year did he live. Oh, God, I would have walked. Do you think I'm weak? Do you think a weak woman could hold a man like mine?"

"I know you're strong. But you must be strong now."

"I am strong. My arms feel like lead, but I'll hang here three days. I'll hang here and spit dust in the face of your Gabriel."

"If he loved you, and I know he loved you, he wouldn't want to see you in chains."

"Huh. What would he want then? To see me running loose?"

"He'd want to see you strong. Happy. Not hanging there like a vegetable. He'd rather see you dead than that."

The woman stared at her. A hard, masculine beauty haunted her face, as though the man she'd loved still lived somewhere behind her coal black eyes.

"Dead," she said. "Like him. Then let them kill me."

"They won't kill you."

"Then I'll hang here."

"Vegetable," said Julie sharply. "Hang there like a vegetable. Is that what you want? Is that what you wanted for him?"

"Oh, God. What did I want for him?"

"Life," said Julie. "Not death. Not this."

"Not death. I wanted life."

"Chained to a pole?"

"No. Not chains. I didn't want chains."

"Christina, come with us. Please."

"Ai. You sound like my family." Tears brimmed in her eyes. "Come to Addis, says this one. Come to Dire Dawa, says that one. Come to Djibouti. Come, and we'll find you a new husband. Come. Huh. Where will they find a man like mine? There's none."

She gave up trying to hold back her tears. The mannish hardness of her face softened as she wept.

"Take me down," she said. "It's no good."

Julie turned and motioned to the major and Baria. They covered the short distance quickly.

"Help me take these bolts out," said Julie. Shiny nuts held the threaded bolts in place on the rusty chains. They spun off easily. Baria pulled out first one bolt, then the other. Julie caught the woman's arms as they fell.

The major stood behind them.

"Where can we take her?" asked Julie.

"To her hotel if she'll go," said the major. "I have no objection."

"Christina, can we go to your hotel?"

"No, not yet. I don't want to face them there now."

"Then to my office," said the major. "Follow after me." He turned smartly on his heel. Baria walked with him.

Julie supported Christina, and the two women walked behind Baria and the major. The crowd began to close. Julie felt a sudden terror constricting in her throat. She became aware of Christina's weight sagging against her. Harry, she thought. Where is he? Whenever I want him.

She could see his car on the far side of the river as they began their own descent to the bridge. Now, with the muddy Awash between them, she wished the bridge would collapse, leaving Harry to pursue his hegira to Kulubi alone with Tesfaye.

He had found them in the police compound just after Christina had decided she would, after all, return to her hotel.

"We've always run this place," she had said. "We'll go on."

They watched her cross the open, rough ground back toward her hotel. A stocky, shabby figure in black. Walking alone.

"You were very brave," said Harry.

"She's the brave one," said Julie.

"She's always been a little crazy," said the major.

"Don't you think she should be in custody?" said Tesfaye.

"Don't you worry. I'll send a guard to her hotel. To make sure she stays put till after the Emperor's train passes through."

"That isn't what I meant," said Tesfaye. "The woman needs help."

"That one? She's tough as nails."

The major had invited them to a *wat* and *injera* breakfast at his home, a modest, mud-walled house within the police compound. Julie sat with the baby on her lap, listening to the men joke about Christina. She barely touched the highly spiced food.

"Fantastic she should carry on like that about the poor man now that he's dead," said the major. "When he was alive she treated him like a servant."

Julie looked up. "She loved him very much."

"Perhaps in her way. But she never let him forget it was her family he married into that owned the hotel, her family he owed his livelihood to. Today she put herself in chains. When the husband, poor Dimitri, was alive, she kept him in chains. Now, she talks about him as though he were some kind of god. But I tell you she gave him a hell of a time."

"He must have been very attractive," said Julie.

"Dimitri? Not so much attractive. But a very decent sort. Very quiet. She was always the tough one in the family. Always a little crazy, but tough as anything, that one."

"I remember the husband," said Baria. "Always so much polite. Walked a little stooped."

"That was him," said the major. "Poor Dimitri."

She wanted to blot out their words. To think of the man as Christina had described him.

"Anyway," said Harry, "you did a very brave, wonderful thing. Going out there like that."

She wouldn't look up. She stared down at her child. Now, she could see Harry's car, watching her from across the river. She thought of the night her child had been born. While Harry and Tesfaye sat in the corridor outside. Her arms strapped to a table. Her feet raised, tied into braces. And her screams. She looked away. She didn't want to think about that night. She didn't want to think about Harry.

Baria guided the station wagon down the twisty, rock-strewn dirt road toward the rotting wood planks of the bridge over the Awash. Downriver towered the remaining stone pylons of the bridge built by the Italians three decades before. Beyond it Julie could barely make out the steel trestle of the railway shrouded in the mist that still clung to the river.

Harry's car again caught her eye, an accusing blur slowly making its way up along the sheer slate wall of the opposite bank. There were times when Harry frightened her. She had begun to recognize the terrible, frustrated intensity that jangled just beneath the surface. A poorly wrapped bundle of nerves, she once had called him. She knew the remark hurt, but there were times she feared she had made a mistake in choosing soft, awkward Harry. She had seen the passion he brought to his work. She wondered what he would be like if he were ever successful, if he ever finished his book. If he ever began to believe in himself. As she watched Harry's car, she still felt trapped by his presence. He rode with Tesfaye so the young journalist could continue to educate him into the languages and legends, the flora and fauna, the people and problems of Ethiopia. As she thought of Harry in his beetle of a car, she tried to mimic his weakness for alliteration: the past and the present, the priest and the peasant, the fishes and fowls, the leeches and the lechers. It didn't help. She still felt trapped. The soft folds of his body, the endless circles of his talk overflowed his distant, ascending car. Her awareness of Harry slithered down the canyon wall, spilling over the river and the bridge.

The station wagon, loaded down with their camping gear, took the rough descent to the bridge smoothly. Trying to drive Harry from her mind, Julie turned to watch Baria. He eased from one low gear to another, lightly tapping the brakes. Harry rode with Tesfaye and her child. She rode with Baria. She was content not to talk. She tried to concentrate on Baria. His face, his hands on the wheel. She knew so little of Baria. She knew his face; the slow, almost bored rhythms of his body. The diseased patches of his flesh.

She had studied his paintings. She had listened to him reading poems he had written. The poems were in a language she didn't understand. The language of his paintings was recognizable enough. Strange perhaps to an Ethiopian but not to anyone who had dutifully trudged through the galleries of New York and Europe.

His paintings meant no more to her than his poems. But what did they mean to him? Ask and he would only make jokes. What did she mean to him? More jokes. What did anything mean? The biggest joke of all.

Harry, the theologian of the family, no doubt could explain it. Endlessly. But she knew enough of herself to recognize what she sought in Baria. Sin and its punishment. All wrapped up in one. Illicit desires; casual abuse.

She was afraid to ask what it was that diseased his skin. She knew it wasn't leprosy. Another of his jokes. But there were moments when she wished it were contagious. The thought of his flesh made her own flesh tingle. She needed its danger, its threat. She wondered what he would be like without those discolored patches.

Someday she would have to tell Harry. So he could explain.

She cursed.

God damn him. Why do I have to think about Harry? I want to think about Baria.

God damn him.

And then she remembered. What Harry had told her about swearing. It was a way of calling on God. She didn't believe. But she swore. Oh God. For Christ sake. When you say things like that, you're acknowledging God, Harry had told her. God damn him.

She glanced up the canyon. She couldn't see Harry's car, only the trail of dust it left behind.

She turned to the bridge that now seemed to be rising toward them out of the ghostly winding sheets of mist that twisted up from the river. As another layer of mist peeled off, she saw the bridge as a casket opening to receive them. She imagined the station wagon imperceptibly slowing, coming finally to rest in the center of the bridge. The gossamer lid swirled over them. Shutting the coffin. Softly. Forever. She closed her eyes.

The soft thud of the front tires touching the uncertain planks of the bridge. The first clump of cold earth popping on the coffin that lowered her father into the canyon dug in the hard earth of a Connecticut cemetery a decade ago.

The last man died. And all the men since. The rattling of the bridge. What was it? Were there still trolley cars? Or the rattling of the subway as it broke from the tunnel at Cortelyou Road to climb the low embankments of Brooklyn. Her father taking her to walk the piers of Sheepshead Bay.

And then, on the closed lids of her eyes, she saw it. The low footbridge over the bay. A hump like a camel's back at one end for the small boats to pass under. The low wooden bridge that seemed a hundred miles long to the spindles that were her four-year-old legs. Where the bridge arced, her father would always sweep her up in his arms to carry her over. Over. A bump and her eyes were open.

They had crossed the bridge. Tipped backward as the car began its steep ascent, for a moment she could see only a patch of brown rock wall framed and veiled in the dust-filmed windshield.

Baria eased the car into a sharp left turn. They climbed the narrow strip of road carved into the rock. The dust raised by Harry's car, mingled with mist, fell like a thick shroud around them.

"It's like flying through a storm," said Julie.

With one hand she clung to the strap fastened to the door-frame. With the other she gripped the rubber bar on the dash-board. The wagon edged up the now invisible road. The windshield wipers flicked moist sand from the glass.

"Flying blind," said Baria. "I wish that energetic husband of yours had sense enough to drive with his lights on."

A breath of laughter flared through Julie's nostrils.

"If he had sense . . . Oh, well."

"We better stop," said Baria, "and let your husband's dust settle."

"Must you call him that?"

"What?"

"Your husband."

"But he is your husband."

"Poor Harry," said Julie.

"Must you call him that?"

"Don't make fun of me. He is poor Harry. Because of me. He'd be a lot better off without me."

"But you'll never let him know that, will you?"

"I don't know."

She watched him as he tapped the footbrake lightly, slipped the clutch in, eased the emergency brake on. She admired his concentration, the sureness of his hands. He raced the motor for a moment, turned the windshield wipers off but left the parking lights on. Finally, he shut off the ignition. She waited for him to speak, but he kept himself silent, his eyes fixed on the dust billowing over the road ahead.

"I guess I need Harry," said Julie. "Just the way he is."

"Why?"

"You know why."

For the first time, he turned to her. She had been studying the shaven, dark brown head. Round, strong. His cheeks, chin, forehead. His eyes, brown globes circled in white. The raw, pink patches flecked with purple that diseased the flesh of his face, his hands, his bull-like neck. Circles within circles. Like so many of his own paintings. Circles built upon circles.

Because he was so grimly conscious of the discolored spots, she never commented on them. Not even when he did. Now, as she let her glance linger on them, his eyes caught and held hers. It was his way of forbidding her to stare.

She tightened her grip on the strap and hand bar and forced a grin.

"You look so mean."

"I am."

"Why did you stop?"

"Because you want to."

"Do I?"

"Yes."

"No." She shook her head. "I don't."

"Oh yes," said Baria.

Harry slammed on the brakes. The small car slithered through the dirt but seemed to gain rather than lose momentum. They bounced over the railroad tracks with a jolt that rattled the car and all its contents.

The baby woke with a scream. Harry's foot was still hard on the brake when the car smacked down on the road on the far side of the tracks. The car shuddered, spun halfway round, stopped, and stalled.

"*Cas*, Harry. Please. *Cas bih cas.*"

Slow by slow. Slowly, Harry translated.

"Who put that railroad track there anyway?"

"The French," said Tesfaye. "*Zim bal*, little baby. *Zim bal.*"

Harry twisted around and knelt on the seat. He reached into the back and lifted the baby from his car bed. "There, there, fella.

What's the matter, Johnny fella? What's the matter, fella, huh? Oh-oh. He's wet."

"No wonder," said Tesfaye. "You scared the piss out of both of us."

Their breakfast at Awash had refreshed him. He at last felt fully awake and his mood had improved. He hoped he could improve Harry's.

"Stupid tracks stick so far up. They oughta level them with the road."

"The tracks aren't stupid," said Tesfaye. "In fact, as tracks go, they're very rational. That's the French influence, you know."

"Oh sure."

"And that bridge back there. The highway bridge the Italians built. Also a very intelligent bridge. It was a patriotic mistake to blow it up during the war. That bridge went over the valley. Built on strong stone towers. Not like that stupid *Habesha* bridge back there on metal braces. An Ethiopian bridge that trembles like a girl when you touch her and makes you go down into the valley till you're almost in the river before you can cross and crawl your way back up."

They had climbed far enough above the river valley that the mist had cleared. The sun was beginning to burn off the clouds and bake the earth.

Harry inspected the baby's diapers. "Not too bad. Guess he can wait."

Tesfaye's monologue somehow calmed both father and child.

"As for the tracks," he continued, "they just sit there, cool, serene in their narrow-gauge logic, perfectly equidistant apart, perfectly composed. French tracks too logical ever to meet except in the illogical eye of the beholder.

"But if an Ethiopian looks down those tracks, he will tell you they do meet. 'Where?' you ask him, and the silly fellow says, 'Just there. See?' "

"Oh sure," grunted Harry, still absorbed with the baby.

"You ask him to walk to the spot and, being illogical, he walks to the spot where his not very logical eyes and his all too common sense tell him the tracks meet. He walks through mountains and deserts all the way to Djibouti where the railroad ends by the docks on the Red Sea. By now the mirage of meeting tracks is so fixed in his mind that he follows the image right off the end of a pier. And drowns. Such are our illusions."

Harry lowered the baby back in his car bed, tucked him in, and quickly wedged a pacifier into his mouth.

"Some illusion," he mumbled.

"But you can't blame the tracks for the mistake made by the fellow who follows them off the pier. He's deceived by the appearances of Western logic."

"Some logic."

"It's a beautiful logic. That's the trouble with you Westerners. You don't appreciate the beauty of your own logic."

"If it's foreign it's got to be good, huh?"

"No, but there are advantages. You've been to Nairobi. Lagos and Accra are the same. Jewels of British imperialism. Even Asmara that the Italians had for sixty years or Dire Dawa that the French built along with the railway. Then look at dear, dirty Addis Ababa and think what a century or so of colonialism would have done for Ethiopia."

"For Ethiopia," said Harry, "or *to* Ethiopia?"

"You sentimentalists. Be serious a moment. Look what the British have done here at Tendaho. Hectares and hectares of cotton where there used to be desert. Or the Dutch sugar plantations we passed this morning at Wonji and Metahara. Nothing, nothing but nothing was there till they tapped the Awash, the same river the British use for irrigation at Tendaho.

"For centuries the damn thing has been flowing through Ethiopia and none of us ever thought to do anything with it except wash his feet in it or give his donkey a drink. Now the British come and we have cotton. The Indians and Japanese come and we have textile mills. The Dutch come and we have sugar and candy and a soft drink industry."

"And cavities in your teeth."

"And cavities in my teeth. I'm glad to have them. To you the cavities may look like a problem, like pollution in Addis Ababa. To me pollution isn't a problem. Smoke belching from factory chimneys or trucks or buses is beautiful. To me it means my country, at last, at last is making progress."

"Some progress," said Harry. "Out of the Middle Ages into the dark night of pollution."

"God bless pollution," said Tesfaye. He knew they should be moving, but he hated the foreigners' easy assumption that backward people were happy in their pristine poverty.

"You told me once," he said sharply to Harry, "that you

thought living in New York City was like living in hell. When I was there I thought it was wonderful. If you think New York is hell, try living in the Danakil on camel's blood and milk. Try the life of a laborer or street boy in Addis Ababa. Try being a tenant farmer in Tigre where famine comes so often we keep our people alive with surplus wheat you Americans don't know what else to do with."

"And so for a handful of porridge . . ."

"I know, I know. We would give up all that's best in our own culture."

"Exactly."

"Give it up and gladly," said Tesfaye. "I wouldn't condemn our people to a life of poverty so a fat handful of tourists will have something quaint and exotic and ancient to come and aim their cameras at."

"Some countries make a lot of money on tourism."

"And if they have any sense they spend the tourists' money to build factories. Harry, let's move."

"Okay. Except . . ."

"What now, Harry?"

"I think . . . I think I better change the monster. Can't you tell? He stinks."

"I know. It's one of the less significant forms of pollution."

"I better change him."

"Harry?"

"Yes?"

"Why doesn't his mother change him?"

"Why don't you change him?"

"I suppose I should be able to help with his nappies. After all, I've been through labor with him."

"Boy, now you sound more like his father than I am."

"It's a wise father, dear Harry, who knows his child."

"What's that supposed to mean?"

"Nothing. Just a misquote from someone. Come on. Let's change him."

Harry put the baby on the front seat and reached into the flight bag on the floor for a disposable diaper. He did the job quickly if clumsily, chattering all the while.

"And look at the church. How rich in tradition the church is. Compared to what we've done in the West. Made ritual rational. Made mystery mechanical."

"You're quoting yourself, Harry."

"I guess I did say that in my Kulubi article, didn't I?"

"You did."

"There. That's done."

The diapers were roughly secure. Harry picked the baby up. Tesfaye looked at the infant glumly, as Harry returned him to his car bed. Spittle dribbled down his still unformed chin. He wondered if the chin would stay underslung like Harry's. Poor Harry. Tesfaye glanced at him.

"Yes, he must be your son."

"Think he looks like me, huh?" Harry started up the car and the baby was soon again asleep. "He's got my forehead all right. And my complexion." He laughed fondly. "Swarthy little bugger."

"Watch the road, Harry. Let me take care of the comparative anatomy."

"He's darkening up since he was born," said Harry. "Going to be olive complected just like his daddy."

"Umm. It's true, though. I remember when you came back from your trip to Mombasa. You looked like one of us."

"I tan very fast. Olive skin. Two weeks in the sun and I'm black."

"Well, brown," said Tesfaye. "In the oven just long enough. Have I ever told you that story? About how God made Ethiopians?"

"I don't think."

"Well, it seems that when God first tried making man he took the dough out of the oven too soon. The result was the white man, a very soggy, inferior product. The next try, God went too far in the other direction. He left the dough in too long and it came out burnt. The result was the African, black as charcoal, tough as leather.

"Next time he hit the happy medium. Left the dough in just long enough. The result was the Ethiopian, light brown and very fine. A truly superior product."

"Oh boy. You mean you're one of these Ethiopians who still doesn't think he's African?"

"It's the way we're brought up," said Tesfaye. "Now it's just a joke. But to tell you the truth I never believed I was a black man till I went to America. We always used to tell ourselves we weren't African. And certainly not Negro. Our word for a black man, *shankila*, means slave. Our friend Baria, his name means the same."

"I know," said Harry.

"We even put them together. Like a kind of a curse. *Shankila baria*. It's our way of saying your word. Your word nigger."

"Not my word," said Harry. "I never use that word."

"You should. It's part of your language. The language of your people. That's what I found out when I went to the States. I used to think I'd been in the oven just long enough. Scholars tell us we're a Semitic people. Not Negroid. Maybe. Maybe I'm not Negro, but when I went to America I found out I was a black man."

"Americans usually treat Africans better than we do our own Negroes."

"Your own Negroes?" said Tesfaye. "What makes them yours?"

"You know what I mean."

"I know what you mean. And I know what I found out in the States. That makes me a brother to 'your' Negroes. Even if they aren't Africans. Even if I'm not Negro. We're brothers. I took my degree at Columbia in journalism. Not race relations. But that's what I really learned in the States. In my own black studies program. From the way your people treat us all, I found out I'm a black man."

Harry was silent. Good, thought Tesfaye. Maybe he'll pay attention to his driving.

The road to Kulubi, the new road, is 461 kilometers. From Addis Ababa to Nazaret it is paved and in good repair. For the remaining 355 kilometers, the road varies from a well-graded gravel-topped ribbon to a pockmarked, rock-strewn serpent spitting through riverbeds. The riverbeds may be bone dry or suddenly flooded by a torrent spilling down after a heavy rainfall in the distant highlands.

The worst section, from Awash Station to Miesso, is also the safest. Stricter than any law or patrol, it enforces its limits even on madmen and fools. It ruins many cars, wrecks a few but rarely kills, for its hazards make speed impossible.

Even Harry, after his encounter with the hard logic of the railroad tracks, soon learned to give the road its due. At least for a while.

He remembered how bad this stretch of road had been the year before. And what happened at Miesso. The incident had become part of the article he'd already written on Kulubi, even though it now embarrassed him to think of it. He wondered about the trip they were making. If in time it would become part of the book he wanted to write. The dead kudu they'd seen. The woman who had chained herself up to a flagpole. Like that old man in Miesso last year.

In his article he had written:

> Many potential pilgrims, particularly among the old and infirm, for one reason or another find it impossible to make the trip. Often other pilgrims on the road to Kulubi are stopped and asked to carry someone's gift to the saint. A story related by a group of journalists is typical. They were driving to Kulubi and had stopped at Miesso for refueling. The driver was stretching his legs when an old and poorly dressed man approached the car.
>
> The old man was soft spoken and shy. The driver caught only his pleading tone. Assuming the man was begging, he put him off with, "*Egziabehare yistot abate. Egziabehare yistot.*"
>
> "Let God take care of you, father. Let God give you."
>
> Patiently, humbly, the old man explained he wasn't asking for money. He was asking the driver to take money.
>
> "If you are going to Kulubi," he pleaded, "please take my gift to St. Gabriel. I am too old and sick to go myself, but please, take this for me. It is my *silet*."
>
> He handed the shamefaced driver two dollars. Clearly it was a gift that strained his means, for the man's poverty spoke from every bone of his body. The driver apologized and promised to deliver the gift. The old man kissed his hand and garments and backed away, bowing and softly intoning his blessing and thanks.

Harry didn't want to think about that old man at Miesso. He himself had been the driver. In his article he had made it appear that the driver was an Ethiopian who had eventually understood what the old man was asking. In fact, Tesfaye had had to intervene. And it was Tesfaye who had taken the brown paper bag with whatever it was the old man had wanted to fulfill his *silet* to Gabriel.

Even now Harry couldn't understand what had made him invent the detail of the two dollars. Tesfaye had steadfastly refused to open the bag to see what it contained.

"That's between him and Gabriel," said Tesfaye. Tesfaye the skeptic who scoffed at Harry's willingness to believe.

Harry wished he had known enough Amharic to have used the phrase Tesfaye had supplied for the article. This deception bothered him, too. The phrase was a cruel one. Let God take care of you, old man.

Before the article appeared, Harry had forced himself to memorize it. *Egziabehare yistot abate. Egziabehare yistot.* There was another word for old man. *Shimagele.* But Tesfaye hadn't used that. *Egziabehare* was God. He knew that. Every Amharic greeting included or implied the presence of God.

To say hello you said *tenastelign*—May He give you health for me. To say thanks you said may God give you for me. If you said you felt well you added—May God be praised.

The presence of God. In every phrase. It was what had first made him think about the meaning of casual swearwords everyone used. God damn. We drove all the way to Afghanistan for God's sake.

Egziabehare yistot abate. He knew God was *Egziabehare.* And *yistot.* He didn't know. *Abate.* He'd forgotten. Which was old man? Let God take care of you. It was what people said to send beggars away. Tesfaye had supplied the translation, too. Let God take care of me, thought Harry.

It embarrassed him to know so little. Eisler, his mentor at Stanford, would be ashamed of him. He hadn't wanted to think about Miesso. The old man hadn't been a beggar. Tesfaye had supplied the Amharic. He'd invented the two dollars. Not very scholarly. Not very religious. Not very honest.

Harry, lost in his thoughts, was unaware of the cloud of dust that now enveloped them. He hadn't seen the truck ahead of them that was raising the dust.

"Harry," said Tesfaye softly, "are you trying to pass that truck?"

"What truck?"

"Slowly," said Tesfaye. "Just slow down but slowly."

Harry took his foot from the accelerator.

"Nice. Now just let the car roll a bit."

They were starting up an incline and for a moment the cloud of dust parted.

"My God," said Harry. "There's a truck."

Fear paralyzed him . . . and saved him. His usual instinct would have been to hit the brake and twist the wheel to swerve around the truck. Now he clenched the wheel rigidly which steadied the car. His foot slid from the accelerator but froze above the brake.

The car was in third gear and stayed there. The incline slowed them. Unfed by fuel, the motor stalled. The car bucked, swerved a fraction, stopped.

When the cloud of dust lifted, Tesfaye saw a wall of solid rock to their right. A sheer drop of two hundred meters to their left. They'd been traveling through rocky scrub desert but a wide patch of land below, apparently irrigated and well fed with water from the surrounding slopes, was lush and green.

"That's cultivated land down there," said Tesfaye. "We would have made good fertilizer."

"We could have been killed."

"Harry, didn't you see that truck?"

"Who could see? With all that dust."

Tesfaye glanced back at the baby. Blissfully, he hadn't awakened. But there's another fine reason, he thought, to stay single.

"Poor child," he said. "Should be home where it's safe with his mother."

"Oh sure," said Harry. "Woman's place is in the kitchen with her babies."

"Barefoot, pregnant, and tattooed," said Tesfaye.

"Nothing I like better than hearing bachelors lecture on how to handle a wife."

"No one knows better."

"Like that proverb of yours," said Harry. "Women and donkeys need the stick."

"Not always," said Tesfaye. "This woman coming doesn't need the stick."

"Huh? Where?" Harry turned and saw a woman approaching along the road. She wore rough leather rags and was bent low under a load of firewood strapped to her shoulders.

In the cities men, most of them Guarages, were often seen both alone and in teams carrying everything from grain and furniture to small houses, but rarely firewood. Carrying firewood was the work of women and donkeys.

The woman they encountered now carried not the long-branched eucalyptus transported by Amhara women of the highlands but short sticks hacked from the hard thorn trees of the scrub.

She looked eighty, but Tesfaye guessed her age closer to thirty. She scowled as she passed them.

"A Danakil," said Tesfaye.

"How can you tell?"

"A good question," said Tesfaye. "Since we all look alike."

"That's not what I meant, and you know it."

"But we must look all alike to you. I know I can never tell one Swede from another. And I even have trouble with some Germans. It's hard for me to tell people apart if they're too blond."

"You're putting me on," said Harry.

"I'm not," said Tesfaye. "Haile Selassie *yih muwt*. May that old man die if I lie. And for me to tell if one of you is a Swede or a German or an American, it's beyond me. But with another Ethiopian, that's easy. There are so many things. Hair style, clothes. Physique, features, color. The kinds of weapons or beads they have. Many things make a Danakil look different from a Somali, or a Somali from a Galla. Or even a Galla from one region different from a Galla from another region. Even for you it shouldn't be hard. You can apply the animal test, for instance."

"You are putting me on."

"Ai, Harry." He laughed. "But it's true. It's not always a perfect test, and it changes for different sections. But in this part of the country, if you see a man with a donkey, you can be pretty sure he's a Galla. In Arrusi, the Galla would have a horse. In this region if a man has camels, he's a Danakil. If he's herding cattle, he's a Somali."

"And if he's an Amhara?"

Tesfaye smiled. "I was hoping you'd ask that. If he's an Amhara, he has a Volkswagen."

The Danakil woman had stopped just beyond the car to stare at them. Now she frowned at their laughter and moved away.

"And if an animal has a load of wood on its back," said Tesfaye, "she's a woman. Some day I must write an editorial about the human being as a beast of burden."

"I wonder where Julie and Baria are?" said Harry.

"Somewhere between Awash and Miesso. Just like we are. Don't you think we should get moving."

"You're right," said Harry. "I just hope nothing else happens."

Harry wasn't in the habit of using his rearview mirror. He was unaware that Baria's station wagon had overtaken him until he heard the blaring of the horn. He turned half around in his seat. Tesfaye covered his eyes as the car veered to the left. Harry fought it back to the middle.

"This road," he muttered. He glanced in the mirror, recognized the station wagon and stuck his left hand out of the window to wave.

"Two hands, Harry, please."

"I don't need two hands to drive *this* little car," Harry answered. He waved again, a vigorous up-and-down motion like an injured bird flapping its one good wing.

"Baria will think you're signaling him to jump off the road."

"I wish he would," said Harry. "And get off my tail."

Baria began weaving the station wagon back and forth across the road. He accompanied the movement with a rhythmic braying of his horn.

"What's he *want?*"

"It's a mating dance," said Tesfaye.

Baria pressed the station wagon closer. The horn blared.

"Good grief. We just better not lock bumpers, that's all."

"Uh," grunted Tesfaye. "That would be all."

"He's got his lights on," said Harry.

"Not a bad idea when there's this much dust to see through."

"In the daytime?"

"Even if it doesn't help you to see, it helps other people see you."

"Well, that truck didn't have any lights on. He's flashing them."

Tesfaye was used to Harry's jumps in thought. He knew Harry meant that Baria, not the driver of the truck, was flashing his lights. "That truck," he said, "probably didn't have lights."

"Maybe it is a good idea," said Harry. He pulled on his parking lights. Baria sounded a salute on his horn.

His sudden intimacy with the station wagon had made Harry's foot heavy on the accelerator. He was again catching up to the truck, but this time he noticed it.

"Look," he said. "Dust over that next rise. Must be that truck again." He eased his foot up on the accelerator.

"You're learning," said Tesfaye.

"Listen, I'm a pretty fair country driver."

"You must be. We've driven many kilometers together and despite everything I'm still alive."

When they reached the crest of the rise, Harry could see only the sacks piled on the top of the overloaded truck. The truck itself was swathed in layers of dust. "It is the truck," he said. He slowed down even more. Baria's horn pulled his eyes to the mirror. Again the station wagon hovered on his bumper.

Tesfaye was laughing, shaking his head, his hands clasped together between his legs. "Ai, Harry. You know, this reminds me of the story of the man in Addis who was driving behind a *siecento* taxi when he noticed there was an army jeep right in back of his car."

"I know, I know," said Harry. "So he jumped out of his car because he knew the *siecento* would always stop and the army jeep never would stop."

"Correct."

"Well, that truck's no *siecento*," said Harry. "And Baria's no jeep."

"Don't be too sure."

"Huh? Well, don't worry. I'm not jumping out of my car."

"You're not," said Tesfaye. "But I may."

Baria pumped his horn and again flashed his lights.

"Now what's he want?"

"He wants to pass."

"On *this* road?"

"Well," said Tesfaye, glancing at his watch, "we're now doing a bit less than thirty kilometers an hour. At this rate we should reach Kulubi approximately sometime next month."

"Before you said I was going too fast."

"Times change."

Baria edged the station wagon out to the left, pressing close to Harry's flank.

"Oh my God. He is trying to pass." He leaned on the gas pedal and accelerated down the incline.

"Very good," said Tesfaye. "Don't make it too easy for him. Speed up. Kick dust in his face."

"Yeah."

"Arouse his competitive instinct. Show the flag. Throw down the gauntlet. Let him know what Americans are made of." He rocked back in his seat with laughter. "Ai, Harry, I love you."

The car rattled furiously, rocking from side to side. The baby woke up. Baria's horn howled in Harry's ear, and the baby wailed like an echo of it. Harry wrestled the wheel, pinning the car to the middle of the road. The baby's head bounced like a ball.

The horn kept tapping against Harry's mind. They were just at the edge of the wake of dust left by the truck. Slowly, imperceptibly, Harry edged the car to the right. They had begun to climb. Harry forgot to change gears. The Volkswagen shuddered. Even as he fed it more gas, it slowed. Harry cursed. Baria pulled the station wagon abreast of him.

"Passing on a *hill*," screamed Harry. He glanced to his left. The car veered in the same direction. Tesfaye groaned. Julie was waving at them.

Baria glanced over at Tesfaye. His eyes bugged out in mock alarm. The station wagon had edged ahead. Baria rammed it into a lower gear. It mounted the incline at an increasing speed. Harry faltered, fell behind.

The jarring of his motor got through to him just in time to shift down to second before it stalled. Baria shot ahead. In another moment he ducked in behind the truck. Then, on a relatively straight stretch, he pulled out and quickly passed.

"They'll be killed."

"But not by boredom," said Tesfaye. He was nearly breathless with laughter and suppressed fear.

The baby's cries reached a crescendo. Abruptly, Harry braked the car to a halt.

"Wow."

"Harry?"

"Yes?"

"Why are we stopping?"

Harry still clung to the wheel. He stared out over it at the dust-shrouded road ahead.

"I think . . . I think I better change the baby again."

The white minaret of Miesso poked its green-domed head up over the next brown hump in the twisting road. Baria slowed as they descended to the concrete trough at the base of the hump. The minaret sank into the landscape.

Baria eased off the brake, angled over the dip into the dry riverbed and, with only a slight jolt, gunned the wagon up the steep incline. The minaret popped back into view. They could see only the top half of the shaft, the slender balcony and the green conical dome.

"It looks circumcised," said Julie.

Baria assented with a tight-lipped "Mmm." He studied the distinctly phallic minaret with the balcony not unlike the ridge of peeled-back foreskin.

"Phallic yes," he said. "Correct. Obvious, but it also aspires to heaven." He glanced at Julie. "The Muslims are right about women."

"What do the Muslims say about women?"

"I wouldn't know. I don't speak Arabic. But the shape of the mosque shouldn't surprise you. After all, we're all circumcised here."

"I know," said Julie. "Even the girls."

"Some of the girls."

He cut rather sharply into a descending curve that swept to the left. The rear of the wagon skittered slightly, scattering loose stones into the stunted sisal plants at the side of the road.

"Oh? Did I touch a sore spot?"

"A sensitive spot," said Baria. The minaret again disappeared.

"This Miesso is a very nasty little town, but when you come off this road . . ." His sentence trailed off as they went into another downhill curve which the heavy braking of skidding cars and overloaded trucks and buses had turned into a rocky washboard. Baria generally slowed before entering such rough spots, but this time their speed was too great. He geared down and gently tapped the brake, but the successive ruts bounced them like inexperienced riders on balky horses. Julie clung with both hands to the rubber bar on the dashboard.

"Heigh-ho, Silver," she mumbled between clenched teeth.

In a moment it was over.

"Yes. As I was saying, after this road, even nasty little Miesso is a pleasure."

Miesso proved the most dismal-looking pleasure Julie had ever seen. Everything in the village seemed the same dusty brown. Even the minaret of the mosque, which had looked so white in the distance, was covered with a dull, dusty patina.

The red *O* and the blue *M*, *B*, *I*, and *L* of the service station sign fought boldly to be seen through the desert veil that clung to it. Here, though the village did have a Christian church, even the Galla tribesmen were Muslim. Everyone knew at least some Somali and Afar, the language of the Danakil. A few people spoke Arabic and the gas station attendants knew the Amharic essential to their trade.

The service station men were busy hand-pumping benzine into a Land Rover. Several cars waited their turn. Except for a few wandering donkeys, no other movement could be seen in the town.

Baria stopped at the edge of the service station area in the shadow of an indifferent, stationary camel. He hunched over the wheel, peering at the people around the gas pumps. Julie began to feel the heat, and the funky smell of the camel assaulted her nostrils.

"Do we have to stop?"

"No," said Baria. "We don't need benzine, but it might be good to stretch our legs."

"Let's not," said Julie as she turned her eyes from the ravaged face of a tiny boy with a palm extended in her direction. Dozens of flies adhered to the open sores on his eyes and mouth.

"And we should wait for Tesfaye and your husband to catch up."

"At the next town," said Julie.

"Here. It's a rule of the road to make sure your traveling companions are safe."

"Is that why you nearly ran them off the road back there?"

"Nonsense. Just a friendly pass." He put a hand briefly on her knee and laughed. As he spoke, he didn't look at Julie, but beyond her, staring fixedly at something outside the car.

Julie turned and saw a classically beautiful Ethiopian girl. She stood among a group evidently waiting for the Land Rover slowly being filled at the pump.

In the now brilliant sun, the girl's dress, made of spun native cloth, seemed a dazzling white. Against her dress, her softly curled, shoulder-length hair was a black so rich it seemed a midnight blue. The gray metallic thread of the *shamma*'s embroidered border glistened like sequins. The dress was cut daringly above the knee. The matching *netela* was draped to make the most of a rather full figure.

The girl looked remarkably fresh for someone who had just traveled over the road from Awash. Automatically, Julie's hand went to her cheeks, which were grimy with dust, then to her hair, wildly disheveled despite the spray she'd applied to it that morning. She hoped Baria hadn't noticed. He continued to look beyond her toward the girl.

"Is that someone you know?"

"Mmmm. Don't you know her, too?"

"No."

"That's Zenebetch Desta."

"The girl who's on radio?"

"And television. A very famous personality. Do you know what her name means?"

"How would I know what her name means?"

"But all our names mean something."

"I remember your name means slave."

"Yes. Something the Amharas gave me." He forced a laugh. "Well, anyway, her name, Zenebetch, Zenebetch Desta. It means she rains happiness."

"Desta is happiness, isn't it? I know that from the candy. So Zenebetch means she rains. I always wondered. It's such a common name."

"But not a common girl. Many say she's the most beautiful woman in Ethiopia."

"And does she rain happiness for you?"

"Well, no. We know each other, but she rains happiness in somewhat different circles. Not among slaves. Would you like to meet her?"

"Not right now," said Julie, hand to her hair. "But you go ahead. I don't mind waiting." Her smile did not come easily.

He climbed out of the car. Julie watched him crossing to the girl in the dazzling white dress and her friends. It had taken her several months to learn to recognize the beauty Ethiopians considered most purely classic, but she could see that this girl had all the elements. Her lips were relatively thin, her nostrils, narrow. Her eyes were large. Her slightly hooked, Semitic nose would have been a mark against her by Western standards. Her complexion was the highly toned café au lait which Ethiopians termed "red."

Julie shaded her eyes. She realized she was squinting and wondered if she'd been doing so before, making herself look ugly before Baria and deepening crow's-feet for the future. She reached into the oversize pocketbook open on the floor between her feet and clawed out her sunglasses.

Tinted by Julie's dark glasses, the girl seemed less striking. The dress, like the minaret, must have its share of dust however pure it seemed in the distance. The smile she had turned on Baria was hard to fault and, for that reason, thought Julie, a bit ordinary.

Bright but not really gay, apparently warm and welcoming, yet not intimate. The smile of a public personality, not a person. Julie relaxed.

She glanced around the station. There were three young men and another girl near the Land Rover, apparently the rest of the party Zenebetch was traveling with. Julie barely noticed the men. The girl was as fresh looking as Zenebetch but in a totally different style. She was fine featured but slightly darker than Zenebetch. Slender and chic in beige slacks and matching blouse, she wore her hair cropped short and was casually smoking a cigarette.

By the standards Julie had grown up with, the girl in the slacks was far more beautiful than Zenebetch. She saw her call out and wave to Baria. He returned the greeting. His smile was thin, veiled. Julie looked back at the girl in slacks who had already returned to her conversation with the boys. She had altered her position and in profile Julie now saw that, despite her slenderness, the girl was shapelier than she'd realized at first.

One of the young men, tall and well built, wasn't bad looking. Julie guessed he was with the girl in slacks. He seemed to be defending his interest against the fast-talking young man in neatly tailored khakis. Festooned with cameras, wearing dark glasses and his hair in a modified version of an Afro, he looked like one of the many young Ethiopians who had taken to imitating American Negroes. The third young man was slight enough to look feminine despite his straggly beard.

The tallest of the three climbed into the Land Rover and eased it away from the pumps. A white Peugeot pulled into its place. The hipster in khakis pulled out a wallet and paid for the benzine.

Julie glanced at the service station sign above the dirt encrusted pumps. Mobil, she said to herself. If it were really mobile, it would move someplace else. She was amused at her pun, sad there was no one to share it with. But was there ever anyone? Baria, she assumed, wouldn't have understood it. Harry, she knew, would have explained it to death.

The slender girl in beige, the hipster, and the young man with the beard walked toward Baria. The tallest of the three young men parked the Land Rover at the far edge of the service station area and walked back to join them. The girl in the slacks and Baria shook hands. The girl in white introduced the young men to Baria. They bowed slightly, deferential, perhaps a bit awed at meeting the honored painter, the great poet. The globe of Baria's shaven brown head shone in the sunlight, the pink patches lit like wild flowers in the parched scrub of a sun-baked land. He spoke to the young men, not even glancing at the girls. But Julie guessed it was for the girls' benefit he spoke. They watched him with does' eyes.

She waited patiently. Greetings and introductions, she had learned, were slow and formal ceremonies in Ethiopia. But it soon became apparent that the formal exchanges were settling into conversation. She wore no watch but kept glancing at her wrist. The sun slowly made an oven of the car. No breeze stirred, and the heavy odor of the motionless camel surrounded her. A truck curved around the service station. The dust it raised hung in the air, a low, yellow vapor long after the roar of the truck had faded away.

Baria would not, Julie knew, bring the group to the car to meet her. They could see her sitting there in the front seat of his station wagon a few feet away, but he would not explain her.

They would wonder about her but—out of politeness—would not ask. This politeness would leave them free later to invent about her whatever gossip they pleased.

The scorching light of the sun didn't seem to bother the group chatting under its blinding rays. She wanted to join them. She told herself there was no reason to be afraid. Yet, she couldn't imagine herself joining those two girls, not looking the way she knew she must.

She twisted the rearview mirror and pulled off her sunglasses to study herself. Like a wide-view movie screen, it wasn't suitable for close-ups. She had to construct her face from a series of broad, narrow strips, hair and forehead, eyes and nose, compressed lips and slightly trembling chin. It wouldn't do.

She looked down at the sundress filmed with dust. Though she avoided the sun, the heat alone had freckled her bare arms. The unclocked time dragged on. She reached into the vast pocketbook at her feet and found a comb. She pulled it through her tangled, sticky hair. The effort made her even more aware of the heat of the car. The air was desert dry. Even now she wasn't perspiring, but she felt stifled.

The camel, close to the door on her side, seemed to be edging even closer. When she finally scrambled over the gearshift and jerked the door handle down on the driver's side, it was less a decision to join Baria's circle than to escape the camel and the baking walls of the car.

Her mind, empty as she left the car, now filled with the

struggle to find something to say as she approached the wall of backs before her. Hi, she might say simply, or, perhaps more flip, Since the circle won't come to Mohammed, Mohammed . . .

She was unaware of the approaching Volkswagen until it braked a few feet behind her. She turned. Tesfaye was driving.

"Good God, where have you been?" Harry bellowed at her. He seemed to have emerged from the car with magic swiftness. He held the bawling, soaking wet infant stiffly at arms' length before him. "Your son has been screaming."

"What . . . what do you mean?" stammered Julie. "He's your son, too."

"But at a time like this . . ." said Harry.

Julie took the baby from him. "You could have changed him."

"I did change him. Twice."

"Three times," said Tesfaye, who had shut off the car motor and joined them. He spoke so softly no one heard him over the baby's cries. He left them and went to join Baria and the others.

The infant's diaper sagged almost to his knees. His cotton shirt was soaked. Julie craddled him in her bare arms, slightly away from her body. She could change his diapers, but she couldn't easily change her dress.

She turned away from the group she'd been approaching and went to Harry's car. He plodded after her. The door on the passenger's side swung half-open. Julie pushed it wide with an elbow and stretched the infant out on the seat. Sweat broke out on her now. And tears.

"Can I help, hon?"

"Drop dead, you bastard."

"What . . . what's wrong, hon?"

"Just look at them. And what do you do? You humiliate me. Just turn around and look at them."

"At who?" He turned around helplessly. He flapped his arms.

Julie leaned farther into the car to reach the diapers. The short dress hiked.

"At who?" Harry repeated. "I don't see . . ." The wrinkled backs of her pink thighs were bare to the white line of her girdle.

"I've never been so humiliated."

"Julie, that skirt's too short."

"Oh, sure." Tears streaked her face as she tugged at the soaking diaper around the baby. "You want your frump of a wife to look like even more of a frump in some baggy long dress. Why don't you go back and talk to your girl friends."

"What girl friends?" Again he turned and adjusted his glasses. "Them? Do I know them?"

"Some day . . . You drive me right up a wall."

"Ah, hon. Please."

"Some day you'll drive me too far." She stared down at the baby. "You and your damn miracle."

"Please . . ."

"You'll drive me too far. And I swear I'll cut you up into little pieces."

"Ah, hon. Cut me up into little pieces." He tried to laugh. "I'll go buy you a knife."

She was staring down at the baby. He saw her fists clench. "I've got a knife," she said. "And some day you'll drive me too far."

The girl in the beige slacks had been watching them. Now she approached the car. Harry turned. He tried to remember where he might have met her. No name would register. All he could think of were the words Julie had spoken. Cut into little pieces.

The girl circled beyond him to Julie. "Can I help? I grew up in a family of eight. I'm good at this sort of nonsense."

"Oh, that's all right," said Harry. He was confused, grateful. He wanted desperately to forget what had happened.

Julie blinked up at her. "He's crying so."

"The road must have been rough on him, too," said the girl. Her English had an American accent. Julie stepped away from the car door. "What's his name?" asked the girl, edging past her. Without having to unpin them, she slipped the soggy diapers down over the baby's knees.

"Jonathan," said Julie. "It was my father's name."

"We were going to name him Menelik," said Harry. He stared down at the rounded behind in the tight beige slacks. "But Julie thought . . ."

"Is there powder?" said the girl. "His bottom's all red."

"It must be in the back," said Julie.

"I think I left it in the front," said Harry, leaning closer to the girl.

"I found it." The girl eased back out of the car, holding the powder and the soggy diaper. She handed the diaper to Harry. "If you have cotton ones it would be better for his bottom than these."

"Just these," said Julie. "But there's liners."

"Wait. I have something." The girl went back to the Land Rover. She returned in a minute to a silent, motionless Harry and Julie. She carried a wet washcloth and a square piece of homespun cloth. "Let's use this," she said. "It's soft. I brought it to cream my face." She improvised a diaper from the cloth and had the baby wrapped in a matter of seconds. He had quieted during the process, watching her with eyes that crossed when they tried to focus.

She took the used diaper from Harry without a word and stuffed it and the baby's soiled cotton shirt into a plastic bag Harry had hung from the inside door handle.

"Is there another shirt?" she asked Julie. "He'll be needing it soon. From here you'll be going up into the mountains." She turned to Harry. "Why don't you join the others. This is a woman's world now."

"Oh. Oh, sure," said Harry. "I'll just be going. Going along. Are you all right, hon?"

Julie studied him. She didn't answer.

"I'll be over there," said Harry. He joined the others.

"You know," said the girl, "I'd like to have children. But I'm not sure I'm ready for husbands."

"I know what you mean," said Julie. She smiled. "And thank you."

"My name's Helen," said the girl. She held out her hand in an abrupt, masculine fashion.

"Julie." They shook hands. "You did say Helen? You must be American. I thought you were Ethiopian."

"Well, it's Eleni. I am Ethiopian. But I prefer Helen. Especially since they started calling these cigarettes they're selling Eleni."

"*Ishi*," said Julie. "Helen's fine with me."

"Good." The girl's features did little more than hint at a smile, but there was warmth in her expression. "You know, you really ought to travel in a Land Rover. It's not exactly comfortable, but there's much more room for everything."

"Well, we're sort of traveling in tandem," said Julie. She nodded at the Volkswagen. "And we have the station wagon."

"That thing? It's just another Volkswagen. Come and see the setup Zenebetch and I have. It's a regular little beauty shop."

"Really?"

"You need it on a trip like this." She lifted the now quiet infant from the car seat. He curled up in her arms the way Julie had seen him do with their servants. The girl kicked the car door closed with her foot. Julie thought it a most un-Ethiopian gesture. "Come on. The way we have the back of this Land Rover set up, it's a girl's world. We just have the boys along for the driving."

When they returned to join the others talking by the gas pumps, Julie was transformed, not beautiful, but cool and fresh as the girl she walked with.

"Gosh, hon, you look a whole lot better," said Harry.

"Thanks." Ordinarily she would have snapped it at him. Now there was a gentle, if mocking, smile on her lips. Helen, who held the now sleeping baby easily against her shoulder, took Julie by the arm and introduced her to the others.

Zenebetch, the girl whose face and voice were so familiar from radio and television and magazine covers. Hagos, the tallest of the young men. The bearded, slightly built Makonnen. And Claude, with cameras, Afro, and dark glasses and a name, Julie assumed, that must, like Helen's, be a Westernized version of his real name.

"And this is Julie," said Helen. "She's had a rough trip. Traveling with a little baby is no picnic."

Tesfaye caught Harry's eye. They exchanged a shrug.

Julie knew she was being handled with tact. But she didn't resent the handling. And she appreciated the tact. Helen's beauty shop had been exaggerated, just a makeup kit with a mirror propped up on some boxes of food in the back of the Land Rover. But it was a well-supplied kit. Helen was efficient at finding things and helpful enough even to comb out Julie's tangled hair.

To Julie, Helen was a marvel. Handsome but apparently hollow Ethiopian girls like Zenebetch left her cold, but she admired the few she had met like Helen who combined beauty with brains and a flair for style with a sense of independence. She'd learned as Helen labored over her hair that the girl worked in the secretariat of the Organization of African Unity, apparently in a position of some responsibility involving the liberation committee.

"Don't get it confused with your women's liberation committees," Helen had said to her. "For the OAU, liberation is for people who really need it. South Africans. Angolans. Zimbawbe. Namibians."

Julie had been forced to admit she knew very little about the OAU. "But then I don't know very much about women's lib either."

"I'll teach you," said Helen. "About both." She tugged the comb through a knot in Julie's hair. "Is Baria your man?"

"Ouch."

"Sorry. Your hair's all tangled."

"I know. But . . . but I thought you could tell. That other one. Harry is my husband."

"That's not what I mean," said Helen. "But never mind."

Now, as they stood among the others, Julie wondered if there were anything between this girl who held her arm and Baria.

Harry, like a nervous hummingbird at the mouth of a flower, again hovered close to Helen. "Here," he said, "I can take the baby."

"It's all right," said the girl, looking past him.

"Sister Eleni," said Tesfaye. "You'd make a wonderful nurse."

"No," said Helen, "but a good mother." She glanced at Baria. "Don't you agree, slave?"

"What, you call me slave?" His voice was theatrically mocking. He put a hand to his chest and bugged out his eyes.

"I don't," said Helen. "But someone did. Why don't you change your name?"

"To what?" said Baria. "Arraya? I hate you Amharas and Tigres." He rarely alluded to the fact that he was a Galla. He and Helen spoke in English out of politeness to the foreigners, but their conversation swirled past Harry and Julie.

"Baria. Slave. It just isn't a good name for an African," said Helen.

"But I'm an Ethiopian," said Baria. His voice was still mocking.

"Ah, yes. All you Gallas who wish you were Amharas insist on being Ethiopian."

"My culture," he said, "Ethiopian culture, is very important to me."

Julie noticed the mocking tone had gone out of his voice. But she could never tell when, if ever, he spoke in earnest. The taller of the two boys said something to Helen in Amharic.

"*Y'faranj joro indizzih fehwata tiro aydallam.*" She ignored him.

"You may consider yourself Ethiopian," she said to Baria. "Myself, I'm an African. Ethiopian comes second."

"Yeah, I used to think I was a African, too," said the young man with the arsenal of cameras. "I thought I was till I got to Africa."

"Oh," said Julie. Her surprise brought her out of her silence. "I thought you were Ethiopian."

"You did, huh?" Without quite moving, Claude managed to give the impression of a fighter bouncing lightly on the balls of his feet. "You did till I opened my mouth."

"I'm sorry," said Julie.

"Okay." His manner suddenly changed. The aggressive bouncing stopped. He smiled gently. "I should have used my Princeton accent. You might still be guessing. But you're right. I'm from the States."

"You're an African, too," said Eleni.

"Not me," said Claude.

"Yes. We all are. That's why I prefer being called Helen."

"Ah, yes," said Baria. "Helen. As I recall it, before you went to school in America, you were called Eleni."

"Speak it, brother," said Claude, reverting to his street jargon. "I knowed a chick back in the States her real name is Helen Brown. Now she call herself Ogadinga Shabaz."

Julie studied him. For all his hipster assurance, there was something restless, uncertain in his shifting poses. He caught her eye.

"You still try-na figure me out, huh? Don't sweat it. That makes two of us." He grinned and turned back to Eleni. "See, I hadda go to Princeton to find out I was no button-down white Nee-gro. But I was still dumb. 'Cause then I decided I was like you just said, a African. So I hadda go to Africa to find out I wasn't that either. Maybe my friend Ogadinga Shabaz come to Africa she'll find out the same. 'Cause see, with her Helen is her real name. Not somethin' she picked up on some other place."

"All right," said Eleni. "You're as bad as Baria. I admit I started using Helen for my name when I was in America. But the difference between me and your friend Ogadinga is that in my case I really am an African. Only here in Ethiopia could I be Eleni. Helen isn't especially an African name. But I could be called Helen almost anywhere in Africa."

To me you're Eleni, thought Tesfaye. But he said nothing. He knew how strongly she felt. He understood why.

"Ah, I was only jivin'," said Claude. "I don't know no girl named Helen Brown Ogadinga. I was only jivin' you."

He stared down at his shoe tops. One foot kicked up a small puff of dust. He senses it too, thought Tesfaye. In New York he'd met many black Americans who wanted to be African. But weren't. Eleni's the same. She wants to be African. Not just Ethiopian. We all do. But she knows she's Eleni.

The tall young man, Hagos, spoke to Helen in Amharic. Julie noticed that he called her Eleni. The girl turned to her.

"You see what I mean? Not for husbands."

Julie laughed. "I think you'll have to explain it to me later."

"At Kulubi, then," said the girl. "We won't be seeing you again on the way. You'll be taking the high road." She jerked her thumb over her shoulder. "We'll be taking the low road."

"Ah," said Baria, recovering his mocking tone and bowing low. "Not Helen, but Mary Queen of Scots."

Tesfaye noticed Julie looking perplexed. He rarely spoke to her but did so now.

"Don't be puzzled, Mrs. Comfort. It's the fault of our education at the hands of foreigners. All our allusions are European. Only our illusions are Ethiopian."

"Ai, Tesfaye," said Helen. "You don't say much."

Zenebetch hadn't understood Tesfaye's remark. Silent till now, content to be the most beautiful woman in Ethiopia, she suddenly felt compelled to say something. "But when he does speak, he says too much." The others laughed. Tesfaye, shriveled with embarrassment, vowed to say nothing more.

"But why take the old road?" said Harry, still trying to draw Helen out. "They say it's almost im*pass*able."

"If not im*poss*ible," said the mocking Baria.

"That's why we want to take it," said Hagos. It was the first time he'd spoken in English. His face bore two parallel scars near his right eye. *Asira-and*, thought Harry. Eleven. It was the name other Ethiopians used for Tigres because of the parallel scars shaped like an "11" near their eyes. Harry braced himself for the worst. He knew that when a Tigre had anti-American feelings, they were often particularly strong. And he knew why.

Hagos's veiled, long-lashed eyes were normally a quiet, clear brown. But now, as he fixed them on Harry, they had a black, cutting glint.

"We want to take the old road because it is the hard way. A true Ethiopian road, unimproved by the American Highway Authority."

"Now look," said Harry, raising his pink palms. He smiled and took a step back. "I mean just a minute. I'm no gung ho American, so let's not get started that way."

"I never accused you," said Hagos. "I only meant that I'm sure you know how we Ethiopians like to do things. Surely you know that joke. How an Ethiopian ties his shoe?" He walked over to the Land Rover and placed his left foot on the bumper. He mimed the motions of bending to tie, not the left shoe conveniently raised to the bumper, but awkwardly all the way down to the right shoe on the ground.

Everyone laughed but Harry and Hagos. The young man walked back, unsmiling, to rejoin the group.

"Yes, I've seen that one done," said Harry.

"Of course. You Americans tell it to each other at your cocktails."

"Look, I'm no gung ho American."

"What does that mean, this gung ho?"

"Look . . ." Harry couldn't remember the young man's name. It had been mentioned twice in the introductions, but now he couldn't summon it up. "Oh, never mind. Just I don't think jokes like that are so funny."

"Don't let this '*asira-and*' upset you," said Baria. "He's like me. Because we're not Amharas we think we have to be even tougher Ethiopians than the rest."

"You mean you admit that?" said Helen.

"Of course. And besides, Hagos knows these Americans support your feudal Amhara regime that suppresses the rest of us. And they build their military bases in Hagos's country and corrupt his cousins by giving them jobs."

"It's true," said Hagos.

"But don't you worry," said Baria. "One day we'll get together. Gallas. Tigres. Somalis. Barias. Shankilas. Guarages. Falashas. Danakils. All the tribes. And we'll drive out these Americans and their Amhara lackeys, isn't it? But meanwhile, you shouldn't attack this poor fellow. He isn't like that."

"He's an American," said Hagos. He again turned to Harry. "Aren't you?"

"And we're all alike," said Claude.

"Amen," said the bearded Makonnen. He'd been standing on the edge of the group, his thin arms folded across his concave chest. "You Americans are all alike. Black. White. Striped. Very aggressive. All of you."

"Better believe it," said Claude. "And watch out." He nodded at Harry. "Don't let 'em get ya down, Jim. Ever since I left home I been havin' to convince people, one, I ain't never been in no chain gang and, two, I didn't start no war in Vietnam."

Laughter broke the tension. Helen and Zenebetch busied themselves knotting a rope of conversation around the stiff and silent Hagos. Baria and Tesfaye consoled Harry.

Claude watched them all. Julie suddenly realized he had been casually snapping photographs. Not focusing, barely even aiming his camera. As though his own eyes weren't enough to take in what he saw without the third eye of his camera. Maybe that's what he really is, she thought. Not a Princeton man. Not a street boy. But a photographer. She thought it was a shame he couldn't get himself into his pictures.

Baria steered Harry to the Volkswagen. Julie volunteered to take the baby with her in the station wagon. With Helen's assistance she began transferring bottles and diapers. Hagos finally let himself be led off to the Land Rover. Claude tagged after the four young Ethiopians.

"It's best to stop for benzine in Asba Tafari," Baria crooned mechanically to Harry. "It's not very far up and it's cooler there. Then we'll be stopping in Mota to visit Tesfaye's father."

"He's a wonderful old man," said Harry. "We stopped there last year, you know."

"Yes, I know. You told me. Many times."

"A wonderful old man." He looked toward the Land Rover where Hagos was now behind the wheel. "I can't stand little punks like that. Who does he think he is, anyway? Little racist."

"Oh, come now, dear Harry. You know there isn't much racialism here. If anything it's the uneducated Amhara looking down on what he considers to be black people."

"Sure," said Harry. "And educated Ethiopians like that one hating white men."

"Don't be misled," said Baria. "He just doesn't like Americans."

"Oh. Is that all? Huh."

"Of course. Russians are just as white as Americans, but he wouldn't hate you if you were Russian. It's a question, you know, of ideology. Some of us, because of our ideology, we don't like Americans. We have to make exceptions when we get to know Americans like you."

"There are millions like me."

"Yes? Well, we haven't met so many."

"There aren't millions of us over here."

"There are enough."

"I can't stand . . ." His arms flapped. "The uninformedness of it all." He plunged into the car, squeezing himself in behind the wheel.

Baria propped his hands on the roof and peered through the open door.

"You really should get a bigger car."

"Oh sure," said Harry. "Something more American."

"You must remember, dear Harry, there are many of us here, we make an exception for you, our friend, but really we would like to see all of your Kagnew Station soldiers, all your Mapping Mission spies, and all your military advisors and your CIA and Peace Cores . . ."

"Peace Corps," corrected Harry.

"I was using the plural," said Baria. "My English is not so poor. Anyway, they can all go home."

"Yeah. Sure. I notice you didn't mention all our millions of dollars in aid."

"That, too," said Baria. He gently but firmly closed the Volkswagen door, then bent again to peer through the window. "You see, your America is arming Ethiopia. Or the present regime in Ethiopia. Russia is arming our Arab neighbors. China is equipping our Muslim rebels in Eritrea. But we don't want to be your next Vietnam. So all that, too, all that millions of dollars of aid, that, too, can go home."

He pushed himself away, and Harry watched him cross to the station wagon where Julie and the baby were waiting.

"Well maybe," Harry called after him, "maybe that's just what we should do." Baria didn't turn. Harry's words faded in the heat. "If we're not wanted," he muttered to himself. He gripped the wheel of the car and then thumped his hands against it. "If I had my way . . . Maybe that's just what we should do."

The baby had stirred only slightly when Julie took him from Eleni's shoulder. But now he was awake, pushing his bottle away and moaning softly on his mother's lap.

"Madonna and child," said Baria as he climbed into the driver's seat.

"Will you paint us?"

"I will."

"Been telling Harry the facts of life?" said Julie.

"Only a few."

Tesfaye waved as he walked by, passing from the Land Rover where he'd been talking to Helen to the Volkswagen where he slipped in beside Harry.

"Don't you want to ride with your husband?" said Baria.

"It's enough I took the baby."

"Quite so."

The Land Rover roared off, veering left to the old road.

"They're in a hurry," said Julie.

"Hagos is in a hurry."

"That's the tall boy?"

Baria nodded. "A very brilliant young man. Or so they say. I don't know him myself, but they say he's a very brilliant young man. Of course, we say that about all our young men who have a degree from abroad."

"He has a degree?"

"From America. He teaches at the university."

"Really? He looks so young. I would have thought he was a student."

"Perhaps to you he looks young, but he teaches at the university. A very brilliant young man. But why is it that all our brilliant young men who go to America come back hating America and all our young men who get their degrees in Russia come back hating Russia? If your countries were wise you would stop giving us scholarships to go and learn how unlikable you are. It is so much easier to admire your men on the moon when we don't have to meet your men in the streets. And in restaurants. And schools."

"But you liked Germany."

He shook his head. "Only the girls. And a few of the men so

soft and womanish they don't care what you do with their girls. Your husband's a very nice fellow."

"Not so nice. I don't think your brilliant young man likes Harry."

Baria started up the motor. "He doesn't know Harry."

"He's lucky." The baby, his eyes shut tight against the glare of the sun, began softly to cry.

"There, there, baby." Gently she began to rock him.

Harry's Volkswagen arced to the right. Baria followed, heading up to the Chercher Mountains where clouds like snow capped the peaks.

At the first bump, the baby's eyes popped open and fixed on Baria. He began to scream. His legs kicked and his tiny fists pummeled the air. The eyes stayed open, slightly crossed, staring in Baria's direction.

"I don't think he likes you," said Julie. "It's only Baria, honey-baby." Her rocking motion accelerated. "You know Baria." With an angry snap, Baria readjusted the rearview mirror.

"I wish you wouldn't use this for making up your face."

"I wasn't making up my face."

"Or combing your hair. Anyway, getting the mirror out of line. It's an irritating habit."

"Harry doesn't mind. He never bothers looking in it anyway."

"Your husband and I have very little in common."

"Just a few things," said Julie.

The baby went on staring at Baria. And screaming.

"There, there, baby," crooned Julie. The crying crescendoed. "What's the matter, honey? Don't you recognize your daddy?"

She glanced at Baria. His eyes were fixed on the dim outline of Harry's car beyond the cloud of dust it raised. She hugged the baby. She was afraid to say more.

"You know," said Baria, "Tesfaye told me your husband made a vow at Kulubi last year. In jest. What we call a *silet*."

"I know," said Julie.

"For a son, isn't it? But people should be more careful. *Silet*, like most words in Amharic, also means something else. It doesn't just mean a vow. It can also mean the blade of a knife."

"It can mean knife? Really."

"The blade of a knife. They say people shouldn't joke with a *silet*."

"I wonder if Harry knows."

"Do you intend to tell him?"

"Someday, I swear, he'll drive me too far."

Baria was silent. He shifted into third gear as they passed the huge Imperial Highway Authority sign bearing the legend, in Amharic and English:

Yih Kulubi Menged Bezih No
This Is The Road To Kulubi

The longest road to Kulubi that year was walked by Wandimu Getahun. For years Wandimu's life had been marked by two unequal struggles. One with a single-bladed wooden plow. The other, with a short-necked cruet of *tella.* He had never been a winner.

He was a poor Amhara living in a region of equally poor Falashas and Kunfels. The scorned Black Jews followed the taboo trades of pottery and ironmaking. The once proud Kunfels were a branch of the Agaws who claimed to be descended from Moses. They once had ruled the kingdom but were now a dwindling clan.

Even compared to his outcast neighbors, Wandimu was considered shiftless and poor, but he clung to a tribal Amhara pride that sheltered him from shame. The priests, he told himself, knew the answers to it all. They knew who was descended from Moses and who, like Menelik and Haile Selassie, the true line of rulers, were descended as all Amharas were from Solomon and Makeda. And the priests surely knew how these Falasha Jews came to be despised, although both Solomon and Moses had been Jews. Wandimu didn't trouble himself with details. That was all right for priests and women, but it was too much for him. At least he knew his father's name.

He was Wandimu, a late son of Getahun the Prolific, a son who should have gone to the army or the church. He hadn't the patience for the church. Who could memorize all its psalms and secrets? A generation ago he would have done well enough in some big man's local army, but now the army was Haile Selassie's modern machine. He would gladly serve the Emperor, but he hadn't the discipline to be part of a machine. The last of seven brothers, he inherited the poorest seventh of his father's land. For two decades he had scratched at the soil, turned it, tilled it. And harvested little.

The land had been granted to their father by Emperor

Menelik II whom he'd served as a tax collector. The eldest brother, Habte, had inherited the tax collector's job. Habte paid no taxes himself and took what he considered his share of the taxes paid by others. His government service made Habte rich even though, like his brothers, he had only a seventh share in the father's land. Even that share in theory at least was owned communally. He could not sell his land and at any time the government could take away both his tax collecting job and all the land inherited from the father. Except for Habte, all the brothers were poor, but none lived so low as Wandimu.

Wandimu was a firm believer in the magic of names. His eldest brother's name meant "wealth," and he was convinced that his own name, which meant "his brother," had determined the course his life would take. When he was a child, he always stood on the fringe of the family circle. If a visitor would ask, "Who are you?" he would nod at his eldest brother and say, "I am his brother. I am Wandimu." His family would laugh at the joke, and the child would repeat, "I am nothing. I am only his brother."

Wandimu acquired a wife and in time two daughters but no sons. He had one goat, a few chickens, and a small ox as spiritless as himself. It wasn't unusual for a farmer to be lazy. His neighbors often agreed over *tella* or coffee on the truth of the proverb that, no matter how much a man plows, nothing tastes as good as *goman*, the cabbage that grows with no need for plowing or cultivation.

The land of the region was fertile and gave generously. Women and children did most of the real work. For the men three to four hours of effort a day was enough. And the endless succession of church holy days gave a frequent excuse for total abstinence from work. But even by the modest standards of his neighbors, Wandimu was considered a slacker. His harvests were so meagre that the church and the local governor often didn't bother taking the portions due them in taxes and tithes.

Then, one night on the eve of Gabriel's Day, in a drunken vision Wandimu saw the devil in the form of the giant, hairy Diablos with fierce claws stuffing the bodies of the damned into his mouth. Wandimu saw himself among them and woke screaming from his stupor. The next day he made his vow to Gabriel. And the miracle of Wandimu began.

From that day the strength of Gabriel inhabited his hands, his arms, his legs, his heart. He stirred from the bed of straw in his crude thatch hut before dawn to recite his prayers. His wife would already be up, and the sound of stone being dragged over stone to grind *teff* or barley was enough to wake him now that he no longer downed *tella* until he collapsed in the evening.

He religiously followed the fasts, and so, on more than half the days of the year, he yoked his tiny ox to the wooden plow with the single iron-tipped blade and went to his fields without breakfast. He sowed barley, wheat, and chick-peas in late September when the long rains had ended. Corn, beans, and peas were planted in May and *teff* for his *injera* in July.

He had ceased bothering to gather the *gesho* his wife had used in the old days to ferment his barley-based *tella*. He now grew his own *berberie* to spice his *wat* and even sold a small surplus. He acquired coffee bushes but only enough for his own needs. He was not such a fool as to think a poor man could grow rich on coffee. Plowing was nearly a year-round cycle for him now, with each patch to be turned over twice, once to loosen the ground, once to bury the seed.

In the past he had rarely bothered to prepare his land properly or to break in uncultivated grassland but went on wasting seed on the same overused plots year after year. Now, when the dry season came, he selected new patches and plowed the matted turf first in one direction, then again at right angles to the first and still a third time.

His neighbors marveled at his new energy, but when they would speak of the miracle of Wandimu, he would caution them: "Do not talk of the miracle of Wandimu. It is the miracle of Gabriel. I work with his hands."

With Gabriel's hands he piled the newly loosened earth he'd plowed into small mounds. Then, after giving them time to dry under the strong sun, he set them afire. Like a hundred little volcanos, they smoldered for days, killing off weeds that might otherwise strangle the crops he would plant.

He no longer went back to his mud hut for the midday meal and the start of *tella* drinking which often in the past had meant no return to work. Now his wife brought him his lunch in the field. Though rigorous in fasting, he no longer took advantage of the many holy days on which work was prohibited by the priests.

He also abandoned his old habit of making frequent trips into the village where he would join in the crowd where land cases were being heard by the court. He used to imagine that if he were a big man himself, he would spend all his time at the open-air courts. He even dreamed of taking his eldest brother before the judges to sue for all the land he believed was rightfully his. In his mind he saw how he would astound them all, brothers and elders, neighbors and strangers, priests and officials with his knowledge of the law and the scriptures and proverbs.

His tongue would be as strong as the iron tip of his plow. Yes, he, Wandimu Getahun, would astound them all and they would say, "No longer is Wandimu only 'his brother.' He is his own man now." But he always woke from his daydreams knowing he would have no chance against his powerful older brother who in the end would turn him out even from the meagre plot he farmed. He had to content himself to be a spectator on court days though he often interrupted to express his opinions on the proceedings or to turn the hearing into a debate on some other case still in dispute. They called him the clown in those days, but since his vow to Gabriel he no longer haunted the courts.

In the past he also frequented a drinking house in the village where there was a radio. He never had money but could often count on drinks from others. He loved to listen to the music and especially to the news and speeches telling how much the Emperor was doing to develop the country.

"If *Janhoy* is doing so much, why should Wandimu break his back? Another *tella*," he would cry out. "When Haile Selassie is finished building his dam and his factory and a new palace for African unity, he can come here and build a road to Wandimu's place and plow my fields. Another *tella*, my friends. Haile Selassie is at work building Ethiopia. Long live *Janhoy*. Our unfortunate fathers were not as lucky as we are. We can relax, my friends, more *tella*. Let Haile Selassie do the work."

They would laugh and bring him more *tella*.

But now the drinking house saw him no more than the courts. He was wedded to his thatch hut, his fields. When neighbors, wondering what had happened to him, came to visit, he would tell them, "I can't stop long."

He harvested his grain with a fine-toothed sickle which he now took pains to keep sharpened. He threshed his harvest under the hooves of his ox and winnowed it by tossing it into the breeze where it caught sunshine and fell with the softly golden grain blown from the brilliant yellow chaff.

Through the months of the long rains, Wandimu's plowing

went on. Then barley and later wheat were planted and a new cycle would begin. The year coming to a close had been the year of Mark and the lion, a year of war, and Wandimu, for the first time, had won his battle with cruet and plow. Now, the year of Yohannes and his ox, a year of plenty was about to begin, and for Wandimu, for the first time in his life, the year of plenty would have meaning. He and his family would not go hungry. He would not have to beg his neighbors for grain to keep alive. He would pay the local governor and the church their full portion of his crops.

He would have a small surplus to sell in the market. He could barter for more chickens and maybe a sheep. When the major feast days came, he would eat meat like his neighbors. In another year he could perhaps buy a cow. His neighbors still made fun of him but in a new way now. They called him *ahiya shankila* because he worked like a donkey. But Wandimu didn't mind. There was surprise, even a touch of awe, a hint of respect in their jokes. He was still a poor man but now even with his wealthy older brother he could hold his head up. He was no longer the clown, no longer the drunk. No more did he beat his wife daily, but only when she was contrary or slow. His daughters showed him the honor due a father and washed his feet every evening when his work was done.

The next year continued the slow fulfillment of Wandimu's narrow dreams. His harvest was such that his neighbors helped him build a small shed to store his grain. When he had finished his trips to the market with a donkey borrowed from his eldest brother bearing his crops, Wandimu was able to bury twenty Maria Theresa thalers, worth thirty Ethiopian dollars, in the earth floor of his *gojo*. He still had no trust in the government's paper money. He preferred the old silver thalers minted long ago in Austria.

"Let them be seeds," he said to his wife. "Next year, God willing and with Gabriel's help, we will harvest more."

"A good man earns more than his wages," answered his wife. Wandimu shook his head. He never found his wife's sayings quite to the point.

He was now in his fields from dawn till the last light drained from the sky. There was much to be done with the land. He patiently explained to his wife and daughters that soon they would have to carry on in his stead. In a few weeks he would be off with the tiny ox he had come to love to fulfill his vow to Gabriel of Kulubi.

For his *silet* had been that, if he achieved success in his fields, he would walk from his home to Kulubi and present his ox as a gift to Gabriel.

He had calculated carefully and sought the advice of priests who knew the power of the saint and old soldiers who were used to long marches. It was well over a thousand kilometers from his village to Kulubi. He would avoid the town of Gondar, the ancient capital where foreigners crowded the roads to stare at castles that no one even bothered to live in. He would stay clear as much as he could of major highways where lorries and buses would frighten his ox and where thieves lay in wait to attack the cars of the rich and to seize even the simple possessions of the poor. Even an ox dedicated to Gabriel these *shiftas* would steal.

He would avoid the new capital in the south where a simple man like himself, once entering, might never find his way out. It had been known to happen. The sons of many of his neighbors had gone to Addis Ababa never to return. No. Wandimu told his friends he was no fool. He would follow the old roads which went by the shortest way and where even in the desert a man might find dry riverbeds where he could dig for water.

When he told his neighbors his plan, his vow to Gabriel, they laughed. They said he was mad.

"How can a poor man give his only ox to Gabriel? With what will you plow your fields?"

"You have no faith in the saint," Wandimu answered. "How is it Gabriel who has given my wife a new husband, who has given us both a new Wandimu, cannot provide a new ox if that is what I will need? Or even a new plow or a new house if in his name I burn this one down for my *silet*."

They said he was a fool. They said he would die in the desert. They said Rayas or Danakils would take his testicles. Even if he lived he could never father the son he wanted.

"Gabriel will protect me. If it's to be a son, Gabriel will provide. Look at all he has given me these past two years. Can he not give me more? To so faithful a servant? Who keeps his word? I have made my *silet*. I must go."

He allowed two months for the journey. On Gabriel's day in the month of *Tikimt*, he walked to a small church dedicated to the saint on a hilltop near his home. The priest blessed him, and a *dabtara* gave him a scroll with a magical inscription to wear around his neck.

The *Ge'ez* words, he was told, included God's command to Gebre Manfas Keddus, the saint who had been led into Ethiopia by the Archangel Gabriel. "Dwell with the lions and panthers each sixty in number. If thou treadest the ground with thy foot, they will lick the dust of thy foot and will be satisfied until they obtain food." He was told that the words would protect him in deserts and jungles as Gabriel had protected Gebre Manfas Keddus and that he would arrive in Kulubi on Gabriel's Day in *Tahsas*, exactly sixty days later.

"I would like to get there in time for the eve," said Wandimu.

"Then walk faster," said the evil-looking *dabtara*.

He was forced to give the witch doctor some of the money he carried for his bus fare back home from Kulubi. But he didn't begrudge the money given to the *dabtara*. If he fell short, Gabriel, he knew, would provide.

And so Wandimu set out. His route took him east of Gondar. Then through Addis Zemen and Debra Tabor. He made his way along the old road through the highlands of Begemdir and Wollo to Magdala where the great Emperor Tewodros had defied the British for so long.

Tewodros was a personal hero for Wandimu. Ai, *shifta*, he said to himself as he walked through the region of Magdala. You showed them. From *shifta* to emperor. The others go from emperor to *shifta*, but you were different. The others when they get to be king become bandits and rob us, but you were the bandit who robbed them until you became our fairest king. *Ante shifta*, you were great.

There was little sign of Tewodros in Magdala, only the blasted-out rock fortress high on a hill where the British with their army under Napier had finally crushed him. He'd ended in suicide but first he had created an empire and challenged the greatest ruler of Europe.

To Wandimu, as to many Ethiopians, Tewodros was more idolized than the noble Menelik or the successful Haile Selassie. He started as nothing, like me, thought Wandimu. He wondered if Tewodros had prayed to Gabriel, too.

He enjoyed his long walk through the highlands though he was oblivious to most of the beauty around him. He admired the silver-blue glint of *teff* dancing in the windswept fields but took no notice of wild roses on the hillsides or purple clover and vetch in the pastures or tall blue delphinium by the rocky streams. He liked the translucent yellow green spears of healthy young wheat, the softer green of barley and the blue green tint of chick-peas in bloom.

But when he noticed the chattering starlings, the golden flashes of canaries and weaverbirds, or the russet of orioles, it was only to wonder what damage they might be doing to the crops. He noted with approval those fields where children perched on raised platforms called *mamma* and chased off birds and baboons with stones hurled from slingshots. He wished he had a slingshot of his own when he heard the harsh croak of the white-collared pied crow and the deep cooing of the pink-breasted dove and especially when he and his plodding ox were pursued by a pair of darting, diving, greenish bronze sunbirds.

Despite the birds, the mountains were pleasant and green. The air was fresh, the sun, warm. Water was plentiful, and there were always villagers and farmers quick to share the hospitality of their kitchen, especially when he told them he was a pilgrim walking across the empire to Kulubi Gabriel.

All through the highlands, Wandimu, the pilgrim, ate far better than Wandimu, the farmer, ever ate at home. Chickens and once even a sheep had been slaughtered in his honor. Fresh eggs, yogurt, and milk had been lavished on him. The large leather *agalgil* in which he carried his food was always full. Packets of dried meat and fried corn bread were pressed upon the willing pilgrim. Many gave him a gift to carry to Gabriel or asked him to pray to the saint on their behalf when he reached Kulubi.

He covered what he guessed to be five hundred kilometers, roughly half his journey, in only three weeks. His pace had been leisurely, and as he approached the capital of the province of Wollo, he was confident he would be in Kulubi well in advance of the sixty days the *dabtara* had predicted.

It was only when he actually entered Dessie that he had his first misgivings. The town was hateful to him. An out-of-season rain had fallen and the streets were thick with mud and foul smells. He covered his face with his *gabbi* to protect himself from disease. It was midmorning. Rushing, shouting people scuttled through the streets. The drivers of racing, horse-drawn *garis* and heavy, growling trucks cursed the confused peasant and his slow-moving ox. Here, for the first time, he found no kind words, no generous hands, no awe for his pilgrimage nor rest for his limbs. When he asked for shelter, he was taken into no one's home but was directed to a hotel.

He wandered through the oversized village for an hour, leading his patient ox. He decided he couldn't bear to stay in the town. He had to ask directions again and again before he could find his way out, following, for the first time on his trip, a major highway.

On the edge of town the road curved past an impressive mosque of dark brick and stone. Wandimu had never before encountered a mosque. He took it for a church of unfamiliar design. He asked a passerby what saint it was dedicated to and was amazed at the answer–Saint Mohammed. He passed a garbage dump that spilled down the side of a hill off the edge of the road. Human scavengers picked their way through it. He hurried by.

Beyond town, he braced his shoulders against his walking stick and draped his arms over it. From a distance he looked like a man crucified, but he carried his cross with him, moving slowly toward Kulubi.

The ox, untied, plodded before him. Wandimu, no less than the beast, was unaware of his surroundings. They walked along a highway. It might as well have been over a field. There was a yoke around the neck of the ox in case it proved balky, but there was no plow in Wandimu's hand. Yet, they made their stolid way just as they did through the fields at home. They had thirty kilometers of road to furrow each day until they reached the desert where they would begin to plow by night.

The road twisted steeply down. Wandimu began to feel the warmth of the afternoon sun. He slipped his heavy *gabbi* from his shoulders and wrapped it around his waist. With a lighter shawl, he covered his head to protect it from the sun.

Sheer rock walls scraped the side of the road on their right. To the left of the shoulderless road, sudden falls opened onto a lush river valley far below them. Wandimu wished they were walking the banks of the river rather than the road. Passing trucks frightened both him and the ox. Each time he heard the groaning of a motor Wandimu clubbed the ox to the rock wall and waited, man and beast trembling against each other, until the vehicle passed.

He'd set his mind on reaching Kombolcha before nightfall. He'd been told it was only twenty-three kilometers from Dessie and all downhill. Their way should have been swift, but fear slowed them. The sun was already setting when they reached the last long, level stretch before Kombolcha. The roofs of the town shimmered like a mirage in the near distance. Fields of sorghum flanked the highway. They were able to walk on the edges of the fields, safe from an occasional vehicle roaring by. They passed a gang of prisoners in chains, farm implements braced across their shoulders. The prisoners called out greetings to Wandimu and joked among themselves. Their armed guards watched with stony, silent faces.

Wandimu and his ox walked another hour, and, in the last light of day, Kombolcha looked no closer. It was full dark when they finally entered the town. Though neither as big nor as busy as Dessie, Wandimu wanted to put the place behind him before settling down for the night. He knew that from here he would start his descent toward the desert. He would again be forced to follow a highway used by heavy trucks and he wanted an early start.

He tied his rope of tightly twisted vines through the yoke to hurry his ox through the streets. At the center of the town there was a traffic circle around a monument with strange symbols he couldn't fathom and was too shy to ask about. Arrows on the monument pointed the way to various cities, but Wandimu could not read the signs. At a service station he timidly approached a beggar and asked which was the road to Bati. The beggar, shy as Wandimu, pointed the way.

Rather than approach a house in the town or even one of the clusters of huts at its edge, he decided to press on and sleep in the fields beyond. He had no need of these hard people of the towns. He was armed only with his *dulla*, the thick walking stick now braced against his shoulders, but he had no fear. Gabriel was with him, and around his neck he wore the *Aqabe Ris* prepared by the *dabtara* in his village. *Jib*, the hyena, came sniffing near in packs of three and four on their way into Kombolcha for a night's scavenging. They passed him by for the garbage of the town. He heard their cries through the cold, moonlit night. But he had no fear.

Let the lion come and the leopard. Gabriel's sword would protect him. He had his heavy white *gabbi* to keep him warm. Let the wind come with the panther. He had no fear of either.

His small ox grazed untethered in the fields while Wandimu feasted on dried meat and *injera* and chicken *wat* from his leather-covered basket. There was even an egg. When they finished their evening meals, the ox and its master lay down a few feet from each other and slept. Before dawn they were up and on their way.

The road was a steep, twisting fall toward a gradually unfolding silvery dawn. They were still nearly two thousand meters above the floor of the Rift Valley and the air was chill and damp. Full dawn struck their faces as they approached the mouth of a short tunnel cutting through one of the hills. The ox and Wandimu hesitated.

The white, fiery globe of the rising sun seemed to fill the tunnel as they stared into its mouth. Thoughts of Diablos filled Wandimu's mind. Who but the devil could live down such a hole on top of this fiery white light? And who would dare to enter it? Using his walking stick as a club, he moved his ox to the side of the road, then squatted beside it, staring into the sun-blocked tunnel. He sat, mesmerized by the light at the base of the tunnel.

He had heard of volcanoes tearing such holes in a mountain, but he had never before seen one. The road ran straight into the crater like a funnel designed to pour lost souls into the jaws of hell. Surely this road wasn't the way he sought. The beggar who directed him must have been a guide of the devil.

He heard a truck roaring its way down toward them. He watched it disappear into the tunnel, blocking out the fire of the sun. In a few moments, its sound was muffled, swallowed. And then the melting white light was there again. Wandimu shivered and went on staring into the mouth of the tunnel. He had no thoughts. His mind was a blank, waiting. He could feel a warm breeze rising from the tunnel, like the breath of a devil. Soon, on the warm breeze, he caught a more familiar scent. Donkeys. A few minutes later he watched them emerge like shades from the underground.

There were twenty, loaded down with cylinders of salt carelessly wrapped in palm leaves. Four Galla men guarded them. Long, curved swords were tied to their waists. Three had heavy sticks with which they whacked the reluctant donkeys up the steep grade. The fourth held a rifle. Wandimu gulped. They weren't Raya Gallas, not in this area, but perhaps these, too, took trophies from between a man's legs. They glanced at him. He didn't speak.

Then, to his surprise, one of them called out a greeting in Amharic. He answered:

"I am well, thanks be to God."

"May God give you health. How did you pass the night?"

The exchange of greetings forced him to stand. He nodded at the tunnel and called out, "Is it safe?" The men didn't slacken their pace.

"Of course it's safe," answered the man who had spoken in a harshly accented Amharic. He touched the handle of his sword and crossed himself.

Thank God, thought Wandimu. The man is a Christian.

The Galla nodded back at the tunnel. "This hole leads straight down to hell." He laughed. "It's safe if you want to go to hell. Just follow it down. You can't go wrong."

The other three called out in a Babel of Galligna. They hadn't understood. The Galla who spoke Amharic explained his joke to his friends in their own language. All four looked at Wandimu and laughed. They shouted back at him words he couldn't understand and passed on, beating their donkeys up the sharp incline.

Wandimu turned away and stared again down the gaping mouth of the tunnel. The rapidly climbing morning sun had shifted. It's fire still dazzled him, but it no longer completely filled the tunnel. "It's a lie," said Wandimu aloud. To himself he repeated, It's a lie. Does salt come to us from hell? Would a truck loaded down with goods be going to hell? It isn't true.

He cracked the ox sharply across the rump with his heavy stick. If trucks go in and donkeys come out, it must be safe for us. He thumped the ox toward the tunnel. He didn't brace his walking stick behind his shoulders. He held it raised in his hand, like a sword, ready to strike.

The tunnel proved even shorter than it looked. Nothing stirred in its depth except a trickle of water somewhere and the soft footfalls of himself and his ox, punctuating the silence. They hurried through it in less than a minute. At its far edge, the ox hesitated again. Wandimu struck him smartly on the ribs, and they stepped out into full sunlight. Wandimu blinked, shielded his eyes, and looked down the sheer face of the escarpment toward the lowlands shimmering below them.

They stood for a moment, then continued their descent to the east. They passed through cultivated fields and among low hills covered with green thornbush, acacia, and towering euphorbia. Wandimu had never seen such plants before. He gave the ox a long midday feed here where the grass was still tender and green. Ahead, shrouded in haze, he could see the final foothills of the escarpment.

Gradually, as they continued their way down, the scrub and acacia turned brown, then gray. Trees were stunted; bushes, burnt. Even the cactus looked parched. Despite the growing heat, the pace of their descent was swift.

That night they rested on the slope of the escarpment. The air was again surprisingly chill. Wandimu's own food supply was getting low, but at least there was some remaining scrub for the ox.

People had told him that the desert was no place for an ox, and now, as they hung over its edge, fear of the dry, baking lowlands tingled on his flesh. But cutting across the desert would save nearly four hundred kilometers over the only other route they could take. The longer route would also have exposed them to the dangers of the most heavily traveled highways, crowded cities, and one long stretch of lowlands nearly as forbidding as the Danakil itself.

There were streams and rivers, including the mighty Awash, along the way he had chosen. And an old desert campaigner had taught him how to dig for water even in dry riverbeds. He told himself they had nothing to fear as he shivered in the cold wind that whipped across the face of the escarpment. In two or three days they would be in the desert itself. He wondered if the Gallas they had met at the mouth of the tunnel might not have been right. Perhaps this was the road to hell.

The dawn was pale gray. Wandimu and his ox walked swiftly into the stare of the white, rising sun. They encountered occasional groups of Kirayu Gallas, usually leading donkeys, and densely black Danakils with clusters of mean-faced, musky camels. The Danakil women were bare-breasted, which neither surprised nor shocked Wandimu. They weren't Amharas; they weren't even Christians. What did it matter if their women went naked?

The clusters of travelers on the road grew denser. When they reached Bati, Wandimu saw why. It was a market day. In Bati, still only halfway down the escarpment, this meant a wild array of the sparse goods of the desert on display for exchange with the riches of the highlands and the world beyond. He followed the flow of the crowd up a narrow street off to the right of the main road and into the vast market area.

Wandimu had never seen such crowds, heard such noise, nor been assaulted by such smells. He stood on the edge of the scene, frightened and fascinated.

The market was spread over a series of low slopes on the edge of the town. There was no way of counting how many people had gathered, how many camels, donkeys, and lorries. Wandimu wondered how even the famous *mercato* in Addis Ababa, which people said was the biggest in Africa, could possibly rival the scene before him.

He had heard that the leather skins available at the market in Bati were the finest in Ethiopia, and now he noticed shrewd Arab traders carefully making their way through the crowds, sharply judging, belligerently bargaining.

Apart from the skins, the main items offered by the lowlanders were salt, incense, and butter. Grains and cloth and metal goods had been shipped down from the highlands. Here, bars of salt known as *amole* were used as currency, for the Danakils trusted neither Haile Selassie's paper dollars nor even Maria Theresa's silver thalers. Beads and bracelets and knives were being freely traded, but all were so strange to Wandimu he couldn't tell what had come from where.

There were a few Amharas and even some white *faranjoch* in the mob, but Wandimu for the first time in his life felt completely alone. He could not still be in Ethiopia, he told himself, here among these desert savages. And God, how they reeked. He was sure they never bathed.

Nearly all the women were half-naked, and the men without exception were armed. The Gallas had spears and long curved swords. The Danakils had their huge oddly shaped knives and an occasional rifle. Both the nakedness of the women and the knives of the men filled him with terror. A gallows stood in the midst of the market, a mute reminder of Amhara law. Wandimu hoped these wickedly armed wildmen would heed its message.

He looked away from the men and was struck by the animal danger he sensed in the Danakil girls. Their glistening skins smeared with butter or oil turned rancid in the heat. Firm breasts pointed to the sun. Even their smiles frightened him, teeth like tiny knives made of ivory against their skin. They were black as any sin a man could think of committing. Graceful as gazelles. Quick as leopards.

Others, who seemed only a few years older, were withered hags. Breasts drooping to their waists. Arms stringy as vines. They were as frightening as the men.

And, evil as the Danakils looked to him, the escarpment Gallas were even worse. Bigger, more muscular, no less mean as they squinted in the sun. The hostile tribes mingled freely and, despite their ferocious appearance, acted peacefully enough. Yet, Wandimu wondered how tiny a spark it would take to turn this market into a battlefield.

You could live untroubled among such people for years, he told himself, and then suddenly find yourself without tongue or balls. Or life itself. He wanted to flee, but he despaired of finding his way through the market's maze and away from town. The sun was already high, held to the sky like a burning shield. He needed to rest. He wanted to hide.

He edged his way beyond the outer circle of the crowd. He settled himself on a low knoll and sat in a patch of shade cast by his ox. He felt as he often had as a child, hovering at the edge of his family. But now he was not even Wandimu. Not even "his brother." Here he was no one.

An umbrella of clouds descended from the mountains and sheltered the escarpment from the sun. Wandimu welcomed their cool relief. Still fascinated by the busy market, he picked at the shrinking supply of food in his *agalgil* while his ox nudged his back. The dusty open market area provided no forage for the beast. Wandimu knew they should be moving but still sat, immobilized by vague fears of what he would encounter after Bati.

Slowly, the market began to break up. He stared over the littered expanse. The Danakils were packing their belongings onto their camels. The hoops and grass mats, which here had been market stalls and somewhere on the desert would be unpacked to become homes, now flared up over the backs of the camels like the masts of a fleet of ships.

Wandimu knew he must move on. Darkness would fall and *jib* would be coming to clean the market, hyenas by the hundreds to scavenge on the refuse of a long day's buying and selling and feasting. He knew he must find someone who spoke Amharic and replenish his supplies. With the people gone, the air began to clear. But lingering smells of burnt incense, coffee, and dust mingled in his nostrils.

He stood and looked back the way he had come. He could see the glow of the sun fading into the highlands. He couldn't see the mountains. He turned and looked toward the darkening desert. From now on he knew he must live like the nomads and move by night. His throat was dry. His stomach churned. His bare, hardened feet twitched on the unfamiliar ground. He knew he must be moving.

He wished he could follow the setting sun and retreat back to the highlands he knew so well. But he was already halfway down the escarpment, suspended above the edge of the desert. His only way to Kulubi now was to follow the rising sun. He crossed himself three times and invoked the blessing of Gabriel. He touched the magic scroll around his neck. He picked up his walking stick, but this time he didn't strike the ox. He merely placed the stick across its rump and said, "Move." The ox shuffled forward. They started back down from the market area to the town. The narrow lanes were already dark. He had lingered too long.

They came back to the main road near the tiny wood frame house that served as the post office. Three men and a girl lounged on the porch and, on the soft evening air the familiar sound of voices speaking Amharic carried to Wandimu. He approached and greeted them.

"*Tenastelign. Indemin nacho. Indemin ameshu.*"

His greetings were returned.

"Is it possible you speak Amharic?" he asked.

"Why not, old father?" said one of the men. "There are many of us now in these frontier outposts. And you? You must be far from home yourself."

"I am from Begemdir," said Wandimu, "walking to Kulubi to fulfill my *silet*."

"*Wei good*," said the man. He turned to repeat to the others what Wandimu had said as though they could not have heard such strange news. He glanced back at Wandimu. He was a stocky, fairly young man casually dressed in sweater and khakis. He stood at the top of the three steps leading up to the low porch, his arms sternly folded across his chest.

"But that's impossible," he said. "You would have to cross the desert, days without water. There's only one track and that you can't follow easily. You have to cross the Awash and that can't always be done either."

"But they told me there's a bridge over the river at Tendaho."

"There is, but wait. Don't ask me. Let this fellow tell you. He works at Tendaho."

A young, slenderly built man leaned back in his chair against the wall of the post office. His hands were folded at his belt. In the uncertain light spilling from a service station across the street, Wandimu could trace the flicker of a smile.

"There's no way," said the voice behind the smile. "We have a very fine bridge over the river, but from Tendaho you have not only desert but mountains, the Maghenta range, to cross. A real caravan maybe could do it, well equipped, well financed, strong camels, good guides. And then it would take more time than you have. It would take months if it could be done."

"But I was told there's a road from Tendaho straight to Dire Dawa. They say all the maps show it."

"The maps have a good imagination. I've worked at Tendaho five years. I know the area well. The maps don't know it at all. Let me tell you. The maps show a town they call Tendaho right on the highway. There is no such town. There's Loggia. There's Dubte. They're towns on the highway but the maps don't show them. Tendaho is the name of the region and the name taken by the cotton plantation where I work. But if you look for a town called Tendaho on the highway you'll look for a long time. These same maps show the Awash River coming no closer than twenty kilometers to the highway. But at Loggia you could throw a rock from the highway and watch it splash in the river. And these are the same maps that show a road from Tendaho to Dire Dawa. The Highway Authority map even gives it a number. Highway Number Twenty-six I think it is. Joke Twenty-six they should call it."

"But then how do I go?"

"You don't," said the slender young man, hooking his thumbs into his belt.

"There is a way," said the man on the steps. He unfolded his arms to gesture down the road with his thumb. "From a place near here called Eloha. But you could never follow the track by yourself. There's no real road. Just a way you have to know. The Afars know it, but they won't show you. And even if you could find it, once you're beyond the Awash without an Afar you could never find water."

"Afars?" said Wandimu. "What are Afars?"

"One of the tribes that strangers to this country call Danakils."

"I won't go with a Danakil for a guide."

"Some of them aren't so bad," said the slender man on the chair. "I know some good ones we use at the plantation, not as laborers you can be sure, but as guards. That they're good at. They don't like work but being a guard gives them a chance every once in a while to shoot somebody. That they like."

The third man, who leaned with the girl against the rail, had been silent. When he spoke now it was with a voice so soft that Wandimu could barely hear him.

"Go home, old man," he said. "There's nothing for you in that desert but death. Even if I could find you an Afar who knew the way, you couldn't trust him not to kill you for your ox. And even if he did decide to help you and show you the way, he could only take you partway because then you would come into Issa country where the Afar himself couldn't go because the Issas are his enemy and surely would kill him—and you for being with an Afar."

"Issas? What are they?"

"Danakils. We call them all Danakils because until you live where they are you don't know any better."

"He's the police major here," said the man on the steps. "He used to be down at Erer Gota where they use prisoners to work the Emperor's farm. Here he knows the Afars. Down there he knew the Issas. He knows them all."

"Down there," said the soft-voiced major, "there are many bad men, murderers who have fled their own regions to hide in those jungles. If you get that far alive, which you won't, there surely you would be killed."

"Best come to the bar where I work," said the girl next to the major. "You can see it by those blue and red lights up the road. We can feed you there and you can sleep in the back and tomorrow morning start for home."

"But I have a vow to Gabriel," said Wandimu. "If I don't fulfill my *silet*, Gabriel will strike me down."

"And that ox you're leading," said the major. "Is he part of your vow?"

"He's pledged to Gabriel," said Wandimu.

"No ox will survive that journey."

Wandimu had heard that judgment before. From other people who had no real faith in Gabriel. But he knew better than to argue with a major of the police. He must seem to agree. Then find some way to escape and make his way to Kulubi.

"Very well," he said. "Let my ox and myself find food. Then rest. In the morning we will go."

"I will be there," said the major, "to make sure you get the right way. Take him with you," he said to the girl. "Feed him. Have his ox taken to that field above. Leave word that in the morning his *agalgil* should be filled with food, his jugs with water.

Take no money from him. We will pay you. Go now. I will be coming to you later."

The girl stood and came down the porch. The stocky man stepped aside to let her pass. Behind them, in the half-light, Wandimu thought he again saw a smile flash across the shadowed features of the man in the chair.

The shabby, barefoot peasant leading his tethered ox followed the long, swaying skirts of the attractive bar girl back up the highway. She led him around to the back of the bar. He ate on a bench outside the cookhouse. As he downed his meal of *injera* and goat meat, he had to tell his story to the fat madame of the house, several of her servants and girls and a few idlers who strolled out from the bar to listen to the mad pilgrim. Some warned him against breaking a vow to the saint, but most agreed he and his ox could never survive a journey through the arid land of the savage nomads.

"If you try to complete your journey, the Afars will kill you," said the fat madame. "If you don't, Gabriel will punish you for breaking your vow. Either way you are doomed."

She shrugged her fleshy shoulders and returned to the bar.

The girl who had led him from the post office pointed the way to a field above the bar where Wandimu left his ox on a long tether to graze on the short grass. He settled himself to rest, wrapped in his *gabbi* on the dirt floor of a storage room next to the cookhouse. With his stomach full and his body warm and secure in the *gabbi*, it was difficult to fight the temptation to sleep. He was sure the police major would be coming, no doubt to spend the night with the bar girl. He knew he must stay awake till he was sure the major was sated and asleep. Then he could escape with his ox. He sat up listening to the strange music that pounded through the walls of the bar. The words were Amharic but so garbled he could not understand them. And the music was not Ethiopian. He had never heard anything like it.

From his room he could see the back door of the bar. He knew that soon the major would come through that door and accompany the girl to one of the other rooms behind the bar. He watched the door, keeping himself awake with grim thoughts of what lay before him. He tried to remember the name of the place where the track turned off that could take him to Dire Dawa. What had the man on the steps of the post office called it?

Filwoha? No. But something like it. However difficult the way, he must find it. And be at Kulubi in time for Gabriel's day.

He suddenly woke with a start. The bar was quiet but in the open doorway he could see the tall form of the major silhouetted. The girl pulled at his wrist, laughing. Wandimu cursed himself for falling asleep. He could have slept till dawn and been trapped by the major. Now he watched as the girl led the major across the yard to another group of rooms in a long, low building opposite the cookhouse. They entered one of the rooms. Wandimu watched the door close behind them. A light went on. Briefly. Then out. Other lights in the bar were going out, and someone closed the back door from inside.

The silence and darkness seemed to deepen around him. He stood and unwound his *gabbi.* The air was cooler, but he no longer trusted himself to wait in comfort and warmth. The girl's laughter carried from the room. He would have to wait longer. He cursed the time, and then, only a few minutes later, he impatiently folded the *gabbi* under his arm. He was about to step out into the night when he saw a thin smile flicker in the doorway of the room. It was the young man who'd been sitting on the porch of the post office.

"So," said Wandimu. "You've been sent to guard me."

The young man raised his hands to silence him. The sound of a girl's laughter from one of the rooms opposite turned them.

"The major still at play," whispered the young man. "Not a sound. Follow me."

He led the way up to the field where the ox was tethered. Not till they were safely away from the bar did he speak.

"Listen to me carefully, old father. I want to help you. You were planning to fool the major and get away tonight, weren't you?"

Cautiously, Wandimu said nothing.

"Never mind. I could read your thoughts when you told him you would sleep the night and then return home. He suspects the same, but he knows you can't get away. There are police checkpoints on both ends of town. You don't know the area. The only way you could find a way out is to follow the highway, and you'd be stopped."

"There must be footpaths."

"There are. But how will you follow them? Or find your way

back to the highway. Besides, you would be two days on the highway just walking to Eloha. It would be easy to pick you up. No, listen to me. I am going back to Tendaho this night. I had planned to stay here with that girl. But the major has taken her. Just to spite me. He can have her any night he wants. I only get here rarely from Tendaho. Besides, he has a wife of his own."

"Then it isn't good," said Wandimu.

"Never mind. We'll have our little trick on the major. There's your ox. Now, down there, behind that other building, you can't see it in the dark but my truck is parked there. I'm taking a nice fat highland sheep back to Tendaho, but there is room in the back of my truck for your ox as well. I have special papers with permission to get us by the checkpoints, and besides, the police all know me. It won't be a problem. Now get moving. Lead your ox down that other slope. I'll be waiting behind that building for you. Quiet, but hurry."

"But how can I ride with you in your truck?" said Wandimu. "I have vowed to walk the whole way to Kulubi. You say it would take me two days to walk to this place, Eloha. How will Gabriel judge me if I ride in a truck and steal two days of walking from my vow?"

"Leave that, old father. Gabriel will understand. To keep your vow now you must be cunning to escape the major. Get your ox and move quickly. I'll be waiting below."

Wandimu did as he was told but with a troubled mind. He found the young man at his low-slung rack truck with two planks already in place leading down from the back to form a ramp. Wandimu was afraid his ox might balk, or bellow, but he patiently allowed himself to be led up despite the bleating of the sheep who was crowded to the side. Somewhere a dog began to bark and soon was joined by a chorus of others. Hyenas filtering through the marketplace raised cries of their own.

"Good," said the young man. "This town is used to hearing dogs and hyenas. You stay back here. After the checkpoint, you can come up front with me."

In twenty minutes they were beyond the town. There had been no trouble with the police. Wandimu, frightened by the roar of the truck, sat stonily silent in the front trying to pay attention to the monologue the young man kept up.

"No, old man, I, too, have faith in Gabriel. And a simple man like you, the Afars may let you go in peace. I may be sending you to your death, but for some reason I have faith in you. I think you can make it."

"Don't have faith in me," said Wandimu. "Have faith in Gabriel."

"Exactly said. Have faith in Gabriel. And listen, old father, when you get to Kulubi, if you get to Kulubi, I want you to pray to Gabriel for me. I want to get out of this damned Tendaho where I've been sentenced for five years. All my friends that I finished the agricultural college with have nice jobs in the ministry in Addis Ababa. Their salary may be no better than mine, but at least they get to live like normal human beings. Not sentenced to a plantation in the desert like I've been for five years, living among crazy Englishmen and savage Afars and Gallas.

"Listen, I have a degree from the Alemaya Agricultural College and now at Tendaho I do the work, the very same job, that up to a year ago a Britisher did. And that man, who didn't even have a degree, they paid him three times what I am given. No, let Gabriel get me to Addis Ababa and into a job I want at the ministry, and next year I'll come to him at Kulubi. I'll walk from Dire Dawa with a gift of a hundred dollars for his church. Just let him get me to Addis where I can work with my feet on a desk and a government car of my own to drive—and not this damned plantation truck. Tell Gabriel that and pray for me. He'll listen well to your prayers after what you're doing in his name. If you get there alive."

The young man drove swiftly over the rough, unpaved road. Wandimu braced himself against the dashboard. They drove for more than an hour with no letup in speed or in the flow of the young man's conversation.

"It's a shame you're not making this trip a year or two from now. Then it would be easier for you. The Germans have started building a road from Awash Station up through Gewani to meet this road near the Mille River. But it won't help you now. They haven't even gotten to Gewani yet, and of course there's still no bridge over this end of the Awash. That may be your worst part, getting over the Awash. This track I'll show you is supposed to ford the river at a place further south where the banks are low. I don't suppose you can swim?"

"No," mumbled Wandimu.

"Nor the ox either, I'm sure. Well, maybe you'll make it somehow. At least we put one over on that bastard, the major."

They drove another ten minutes before the man at the wheel began to slow down.

"We must be getting close," he said. "Listen, I want to tell you what to do when we get there. I've got it all worked out in my mind, so listen. When we get near enough to Eloha, I'll stop and let you out. There's another police check at Eloha. There's no real village. Just some shacks and a place for truck drivers to eat and sleep. And a place for the police. If they see me with you, word may get back to the major. He's a friend of mine, but he might decide to make some trouble for me."

"Never trust a friend," said Wandimu simply.

"You're right. It is useless to trust in man. My mother used to have a rug with that saying woven into it."

"Yes," said Wandimu.

"Anyway, after I drop you off, you follow the road till you see some shacks. That will be Eloha. Luckily the track you have to follow cuts off just before you get there. People have pointed it out to me, but it isn't easy to find. So don't take a chance on getting lost before you even get started. For tonight, just get off the road. When you see the shacks, go off the road to your right. Remember. To your right."

"My right," echoed Wandimu.

"Walk a good ways then find a place where you can sleep out of sight. If the police spot you, they'll want to stop you just like the major did. They don't want an Ethiopian getting killed out there among these damned Afars. But never mind that. At first light, get up and start looking for the track. You may get lucky and spot some Afars moving along it. Then you'll know where it is. Maybe you'll be lucky and find some friendly ones who'll show you the way."

Wandimu was silent. He was determined to find his own way and not trust infidels.

"We must be close now. That looks like a tin roof in the moonlight ahead. That would be the police building. I better let you off now."

He stopped the truck in the middle of the road.

"Come on. Let's unload your ox."

The ox proved stubborn going down the ramp. Wandimu beat him unmercifully with his stick and shoved while the young man pulled at the vine rope from the ground. The ox trumpeted his protest until the young man, fearful of arousing the police at

Eloha, finally thought to wrap Wandimu's *gabbi* around the beast's eyes. Blinded, the ox went down gently.

"Before we part," said the young man, "I have something to give you. Come."

He led Wandimu back to the cab of the truck. He reached under the driver's seat and pulled out a curved Danakil knife in a leather sheath.

"It's one of their knives. I bought it from an Afar who works as a guard at Tendaho. They like seeing other people with their knives. As though you're some sort of brother. There's a belt. Wear it where they can see it. And wait. Take some of these as well."

He climbed up into the cab and opened the glove compartment. He handed Wandimu a half-dozen empty rifle cartridges.

"They like to have these things for some reason. Sometimes they wear them as beads. Maybe they use them for money. I don't know. But if some of them do you a favor, show you part of the way or get you food or help you over the river, give them one of these as a gift. It may help. God knows. You'll need all the help you can get."

The two men then parted quickly. Wandimu's mentor seemed anxious to be off. And Wandimu had no reason to delay him. He was glad to be alone again with his dumb ox, listening to the fading roar of the truck. He'd had enough of talk and of civilization. He even welcomed the desert that had frightened him so much. But he was weary from his long vigil in the room behind the bar and the loud ride in the truck.

He led the ox a short way off the road, then slumped down behind a jagged heap of lava that he took for rocks. The dawn would be on them soon enough. Then he could worry about the track he must find, the police, the Afars, the desert. Now he must sleep, but sleep eluded him. Oil trucks from Assab thundered by in convoy, taking advantage of the cool night air, shaking the ground beneath him. When the highway was quiet, the unfamiliar sounds of the desert intruded. He had been glad a few minutes before to be getting away from civilization. Civilization roared past on the highway, still near at hand, but already he was beginning again to fear the desert.

He slept fitfully, tortured by a growing doubt. He had vowed to walk the whole way to Kulubi. But he had just cheated by two days. He thought of retracing his steps to Bati. He knew his *silet* must be kept pure. But to return to Bati would put him back in the police major's hands. He vowed to find some other way to pay back the two days he'd stolen.

He was up at the first light, long before the sun emerged from the desert floor. There was no grazing in sight for his ox, but Wandimu ate well from the *agalgil* that had been filled the night before at the bar in Bati. He drank greedily from one of his two bottles of water, nearly emptying it before replacing it among the provisions he again secured to the back of his ox. He looked down at his flat, broad feet. They seemed to him suddenly naked, defenseless on the rocky desert ground around him. He pulled his one pair of sandals from the pack of his belongings and put them on. He had expected a desert of sand. He had found a place of rocks. He hoped his sandals would protect him.

He looked about for some sign of the track. He saw none. He knew he must avoid both police and Afars. He wondered how, with no one he could rely on, he would ever find his way. The sun was now beginning to rise beyond the shacks of Eloha, a curved sliver of white on the distant edge of the desert. He turned slowly in a full circle, straining his eyes in every direction, but could see no sign of life. The highway and the shacks ahead seemed as abandoned as the desert. He decided to strike out on his own, turning south, to the right of the rising sun, for he thought that was roughly the direction he should take.

Gabriel protect us and find us the way, he prayed. He touched the sacred scroll at his neck, prodded the ox with his walking stick, and set out. The land around him was ghostly. Vast outcroppings of lava littered the desert. Wandimu wondered what giants could have hurled such boulders across the face of the earth, building mountains in some mad game of their own. He stumbled among the lava for an hour before a high, unfamiliar braying cut across the desert.

He circled some boulders. Then, off to his left, he saw a family of Afars coming up from the south leading a half-dozen heavily loaded camels. He gave swift thanks to Gabriel for showing him the way. He waited till the Afars had passed, then set out in the direction of the track they'd been following. He found the track, more clearly marked by recent, unfamiliar droppings he knew must be camel dung. "Or Afar shit," he said aloud to his ox, much pleased with his joke. He started out, carefully, slowly making his way along the ill-defined track, moving in the direction from which the Afars had come.

He managed to walk for only a few hours, descending steadily deeper into the lowlands, before the heat of the rapidly rising sun forced him to stop. The rocky desert floor had become a grill, bouncing reflected heat back up, creating mirages that beckoned in the distance. Wandimu was grateful for his sandals and the thin cloth with which he had covered his head. He halted his morning march at a spot where the road crossed a sandy riverbed in which the soil seemed a bit darker than in others he'd passed.

Leading his ox, he followed the stream for a few hundred meters till he found a rocky depression where the sand was a dark, moist stain. He pulled up rocks and dug with his bare hands till he reached wet, slimy mud. He pitched up mud for the ox to lap what moisture he could.

Wandimu had no can. A few meters off in the scrub he spotted a cactus with long, pendulous gourds. He tore his hands and arms on the cactus needles cutting loose a gourd which he then split open with the Danakil knife he'd been given. He scooped the gourd out with a flat stone. He went back to digging in the riverbed with the gourd.

Slowly, as he went deeper, the wet mud became muddy water. He stripped himself naked under the broiling sun. He built a makeshift pool with stones and went on digging, scooping brown water into the shallow, porous pool for his ox. He did not drink but drenched his body with water, then wrapped himself in his *gabbi* and slept in the shade of an acacia. He let the ox graze where it could. He knew the beast would not wander far from the muddy rock pool.

When the sun began to enter the earth in the haze to the west, Wandimu and his ox set off again. He was proud of the courage that had brought him this far into the desert. He walked jauntily through the cooling evening air, prodding the slow-moving ox to move faster before him. He paused at sundown, again without finding forage for his ox, but eating well from the now diminishing supply of food in his *agalgil*. But his spirits sagged when darkness fell. He heard a lion roar. He heard swift, unseen animals pad by. He had to wait for the light of a late-rising moon to guide him through the night. They made fair time till the moon went down. He then had to pick his way slowly, tugging his suddenly reluctant ox behind him.

Hyenas howled in the distance. The yapping of jackals sounded much closer. Once there was a low growl so close that Wandimu jumped with fright and the ox lay down in its tracks.

There were scattered low hills with outcroppings of rocks from which the barking of baboons could be heard. And once a pack of the dog-faced creatures pelted them with dung as they passed. Most troubling of all was the screaming of frightened birds mixed with a sharp, cackling gluw-gluw sound he had never heard before. Finally, at a rocky water hole, he found the cause: guinea fowls lured by their thirst to the rocky pool and caught in the jaws of hungry snakes. The ox was too frightened to move, Wandimu, too frightened to stop. They struggled on.

When the white light of dawn finally broke in the east, Wandimu's eyes blinked with fatigue. He wanted to press on till the heat of the sun forced him to halt, but both he and the ox were exhausted from their long, tense walk through the night.

Suddenly he stopped short, blinded by a glint of sunlight striking something silvery in the rocks to his right. When he opened his eyes, he saw what he first took for an old man crouched, knife in hand, by the edge of the track.

He blinked again and saw that the crouching man was not so old. Though his sparse beard was gray, his woolly hair was still black and his slender arms were veined and muscled with the strength of a warrior.

Diamonds of early morning sunlight danced off the polished brass bracelets above his wrist and elbow. The wickedly curved knife he held was a silvery gray like his beard. The Danakil, whose lips parted narrowly in a thin smile, was whittling a small twig with the oversized knife.

There were sharply etched frown lines between his eyes as he squinted in the sun. One of the lines lengthened into a scar above his left eye. He squatted low on his heels, and the knees of his long, spindly legs were higher than his shoulders.

Wandimu noticed that he held the knife in his left hand. He thought of Mohammed Grayg, the fierce, left-handed warrior chief who had devastated highland Ethiopia, burning churches and slaughtering Christians centuries ago. He was convinced that the gray-bearded apparition which had suddenly emerged from the desert rocks was the ghost of the ancient pillager.

His hand went instinctively to the handle of the knife he'd

been given the evening before by his young friend from Tendaho. The graybeard stopped his whittling and held his own knife up, turning it over and nodding at Wandimu's sheathed blade. His smile broadened. Dimples flashed under his high cheekbones.

The ghost believes I'm a Danakil, thought Wandimu. Because of my knife.

"*Selam*," said the Danakil.

"*Selam*," answered Wandimu.

It was a word in both their languages. In Amharic it meant peace. Wandimu hoped it meant the same to the Danakil. He knew that Muslims of all tribes, including the Danakil, used it as a greeting, and so he repeated, "*Selam*."

"*Selam*," echoed the Danakil.

"*Indemin aderu?*" tried Wandimu. How did you pass the night?

The Danakil replied with a string of words Wandimu didn't understand though he heard *selam* once again. The Danakil fell silent and went back to his patient whittling, his eyes flickering from the twig to Wandimu.

We have peace now, thought Wandimu, but what happens if I try to move on? He has his knife in his hand. Mine is in its sheath. I have my stick and it's bigger than the knife. But if we fight there may be other Danakils to appear from the rocks as this ghost of the left-handed Mohammed did.

The two men studied each other quietly as the soft dawn swiftly hardened into a bright desert morning. Color faded from the yellow rocks among which the Danakil squatted. The ox nudged Wandimu's back with his muzzle. Wandimu cracked him between the horns with his thick *dulla*.

The Danakil grinned and went on with his whittling. The dun-colored cloth wrapped tightly around his thighs and hips and draped over his right shoulder seemed to merge with the rocks and sand. The dark brown of his limbs glistened in the sun.

I can't offer him food, thought Wandimu. When he sees it and smells it, he'll know I'm a Christian. Water . . . I can offer him water.

But before Wandimu could reach for one of the water bottles strapped to the ox, the Danakil spoke. It was a question.

What does he want? thought Wandimu.

The question was repeated with a nod up the track.

Wandimu shook his head.

Again, the Danakil questioned him. Some of the words sounded the same. Some were different.

Again, Wandimu shook his head.

The third time the question was repeated, Wandimu recognized two words.

Dire Dawa.

"*Awon,*" he answered with a nod. "Yes, Dire Dawa."

The Danakil smiled and stood. It was as though a grasshopper had become a tree. Wandimu inhaled sharply. The Danakil had looked tiny crouched among his rocks. Now he stood a head taller than Wandimu. He casually tossed aside the tiny twig he'd been whittling. The knife flashed in the sunlight, but the Danakil secured it in the cloth sheath tied to his waist.

Wandimu's lips parted slightly as the breath he'd been holding escaped in a long, silent sigh.

The tall Danakil started up the track in the direction Wandimu had been heading. Wandimu stood mute. The Danakil looked back over his shoulder. With a jerk of his head, the desert nomad beckoned the highland peasant to follow.

Wandimu stumbled forward, caught his balance, and followed. For a moment, he forgot the ox. When he looked back he saw the beast standing motionless, his head bowed.

"Come," called Wandimu. "Come quickly." What choice have we, he thought, but to follow this left-handed ghost? "Come." The ox looked up. Wandimu brandished the stick. The ox lowered his head and shuffled slowly forward.

Wandimu followed the Danakil, his eyes mesmerized by the glinting shafts of light cut from the man's bracelets by the sun. The Danakil walked on the balls of his feet with the spring of a leopard in each step. Wandimu padded after. The ox, even more stolid than his master, plodded behind. As they walked, the distance between them widened.

An hour's march brought them to a dry riverbed fringed with flat-topped acacias, shriveled fig trees, and desert palms. A thin track branched off to the right from the path they'd been following. The sun was now a high, white-hot ball in the pale blue sky. Wandimu's muscles were stiff with tension. Still suspicious, he was too tired not to welcome the prospect of rest in the feathery shade. He dropped his stick, wiped his face with his shawl, and kept an eye on the Danakil as he unstrapped a bottle of water from the back of his ox.

He offered the first taste to the Danakil. The man smiled and shook his head. Wandimu offered the bottle again and again the man refused. The third time the proffered bottle was taken, but the Danakil barely touched the water to his lips.

Wandimu watched him closely. He takes my bottle but doesn't drink. A bad sign. He himself took a long gulp. His stomach growled with hunger, but he dared not offer the man a Christian's food, and he could not eat without offering to share.

Again, he gestured to the Danakil with the bottle of water. The Danakil shook his head. Wandimu drained the bottle.

He studied the dry riverbed. Spots looked promisingly dark. He replaced the now empty bottle among the provisions tied to the ox and drew out the gourd he had hollowed out the day before. He indicated his intentions to the Danakil who nodded his approval. Wandimu scrambled down into the wadi, picked a spot, and started to dig.

He was soon forced to stop. His stomach was cramping violently. He realized he had drunk too much of the water too quickly. He dropped the gourd and hunched himself up at the edge of the wadi in the shade of an overhanging acacia.

The Danakil, who'd been squatting on the roots of a fig tree, whittling on a twig and watching Wandimu dig into the sand of the riverbed, now stood, sheathed his knife, and hopped down into the wadi. If he strikes now, thought Wandimu, I won't be able to defend myself.

The Danakil picked up the gourd. He glanced at Wandimu, then went through the motions of taking a long drink. He lowered the gourd, clutched at his stomach, shook his head, and waved a finger at Wandimu.

"*Awon*," said Wandimu. "Yes, it's my stomach that hurts." The evil eye must be working, he thought. "Your evil eye," he said aloud.

The Danakil nodded and set to digging where Wandimu had left off. Soon the ox was lapping at moist mud tossed up by the lean nomad. Wandimu watched him. This Danakil is not a bad man, he thought. Or does he do this to trick me? Waits till I relax, perhaps till I sleep in this heat to strike me with that knife.

I must be careful. He struggled to keep sleep from closing his eyes while the Danakil dug.

He noticed that when the nomad had gone deep enough to scoop up muddy water, he hadn't paused to build a trough of rocks to preserve water for the ox. He simply dumped the water out in muddy pools which seeped quickly back into the sandy soil. These people are wasteful, thought Wandimu. No wonder they can't tend crops like us.

The Danakil looked up. He stood shin deep in the muddy pit. A grin cleft his cheeks above the scraggly beard. He gestured at the pool of mud he'd created for the ox. Wandimu nodded and raised his palms before him. Yes, it was enough. The Danakil climbed out of the mud pit and wiped his hands on the cloth at his hips. Two long steps carried him up out of the wadi.

Wandimu twisted around. The man stood above him with his knife drawn. A spasm of terror knotted his stomach, but the Danakil merely glanced at him, turned, and walked away.

Wandimu watched him climb catlike up into the branches of a fig tree which he proceeded to hack away at with his knife. Wandimu gently eased himself around and drew his knees up, relaxing the cramps in his stomach. In a few minutes, the Danakil returned with a handful of withered figs which he held out to Wandimu.

He had never cared even for the ripe figs of the highlands, and these twisted old men looked as though they'd been shriveled by the poisons of the desert. But his hunger called out louder than his cramps, stronger than his dislike for figs. He didn't bother with the ritual of refusing twice before cupping his hands to accept.

The Danakil poured the figs into his upturned palms. Their hands didn't touch. The Danakil held up a cautionary finger, but Wandimu had already crammed a fistful of figs into his mouth. He gulped them down greedily, pits included. His offended stomach reacted immediately. He gagged, pitched forward on his knees, and retched.

He vomited the figs, the water, even what felt like the last gasp of his breath. His throat was raw. His ribs ached. He pulled the hot desert air into his lungs in short sobs. His eyes teared. When he blinked them open, he saw the sandaled feet of the Danakil. Why should this nomad have shoes, he thought, when so many of our own people go barefoot. He pushed himself up and looked into the face of the slender Danakil. The nomad's eyes seemed to question him. Wandimu shook his head. He couldn't name the question. He had no answer.

He washed himself in water from the muddy pit, giving special attention to his burning feet. He filled the gourd with water, then let it sit for the mud to settle as much as possible before refilling the water bottle he'd drained. The two men sat for hours in the shade of the trees, letting the heat of the day pass while they watched slender, bare-breasted Danakil girls who brought a large herd of goats to the edge of the wadi for grazing on the green thornbush and scrub.

Wandimu lost track of the nights and mornings and evenings he marched with the tall Danakil. They passed the base of a volcanic mountain the Danakil said was called Askoma, where they found a stream with good water and multicolored honeycombed lava scattered like jewels around the flat-topped mountain that rose starkly from the desolate plain. Much of the ground they crossed was clay, sometimes with a thin covering of sand or fine gravel and pebbles.

They went through regions so barren they saw no game, nor even birds or insects, and regions only slightly higher and cooler where great swarms of horseflies fastened themselves to the ox, sucking its blood, attacking the men who fought them off, then fastening back on the defenseless ox. For one whole morning they trekked through a dry riverbed that passed between two hills, finally stumbling up its rocky edges as stones slid out from under their feet, one man dragging, the other shoving the reluctant ox.

Often the Danakil paused to point to the triangle of a distant mountain he called Ayelu, an Amhara name.

"Ayelu, Gewani," he repeated again and again.

Wandimu knew the name Gewani. It was a village a few days north of Erer Gota, and Erer Gota was only a day's march from Dire Dawa. The mountain called Ayelu must be near Gewani, but behind them they could still catch glimpses of the volcano called Askoma. They had not come far. They still had far to go.

They passed through only a handful of villages, though at each his tall guide insisted they stop for hours on end, giving his fellow tribesmen a chance to sniff at this stranger he had brought among them. The young warriors would stand, leaning on their spears, one leg twined around the butt, or squatting in a circle around him, staring hostilely, spitting fiercely at regular intervals.

His guide would talk to them patiently, rubbing hands with the headman and repeating over and over again, "*Mane, mane, mane.*" Wandimu had no idea what the word meant, but he learned to say it, but only after the hostile, suspicious stares had given way to smiles and comments on the Danakil knife he wore.

It was even rarer that they encountered nomads along the track. Sometimes greetings were exchanged, sometimes the two groups passed each other with averted eyes and total silence. One day, after their long rest through the warmest hours, the afternoon sun was just beginning to fall when Wandimu heard, faintly at first, the sound of hooves thumping rapidly up the track which led off to their right. Horses? How could there be horses, though he had heard that the Danakils did keep ponies for their raids against the Kirayu Gallas. Then he caught the odor he had learned to recognize since he had begun his descent from Dessie, the musky, heavy odor of camels. It was another moment before he saw them and quickly scrambled to his feet.

There were a dozen: six camels with armed riders; six on leads lightly loaded with skins, mats, and frames. When they saw their tribesman and Wandimu, the riders reined in their mounts and tugged at the leads of the pack animals. The twelve beasts came to an ungainly clomping halt. Their mouths foamed. They bared their teeth and pinkish gray gums. Their eyes shot wicked glances from the sides of their heads.

Wandimu was too busy with his critical study of the animals to register fear at the sudden change in his predicament. He had come to hate camels since first encountering them at Dessie. Now he looked with distaste at these ugly beasts as their riders beat them down to dismount. Only when the six men were on the ground did the squatting Danakil with the scraggly beard rise.

The riders briskly greeted the graybeard, then turned to Wandimu and began questioning their tribesman about him. Their voices were loud, demanding. Wandimu still ignored them as he studied the foul-smelling camels that had struggled to their feet and again towered over him. The thin, knobby legs which splayed out to the sides when they weren't in motion seemed barely able to support the awkward, bulky bodies.

Two of the camels on long leads had already begun to graze on the tops of the stunted, thorny acacia. Wandimu shook his head. No wonder they're so mean. They live on thorns.

When he finally turned his attention to the new arrivals, he found they were studying him with as much interest as he'd devoted to their camels. The Danakil he'd been traveling with was talking now, patiently, slowly, with many shrugs of the shoulder and a steady, soft smile. As the others listened, they stopped spitting and their hard features began to relax.

But Wandimu was only beginning to realize his plight. Instead of one, lightly armed, apparently gentle Danakil, he now faced seven, six of whom had rifles.

And then he saw them.

Several of the men wore trophies tied to cords around their necks. Ears, fingers, testicles, a tongue. Shriveled but still recognizable remnants of human beings. Two of the riders wore white feathers in their bushy hair. He had learned that this was the sign of a kill made within the year. He searched the faces of the riders. He read no mercy.

Only one of them, a boy in his teens, wore no trophy of the kill. Wandimu studied the boy carefully. He had heard that the Danakil, before he can take a bride, must present her some proof of his manliness. The skin of a wild animal he'd killed would do. The testicles of a human victim were preferred.

He wondered if the boy was ready for marriage. He took a step backward. The boy's eyes were on him like coals. His skin seemed even blacker than the others'. Though lean in the Danakil manner, his muscles were as full as the most mature of the men he rode among.

Forget the lion, old Wandimu. Forget the leopard. Here is your death.

Gabriel help me.

He prayed, counting his prayers on the fingers of numbed hands.

The man went on talking. Soon it was apparent they were ignoring him, even the boy. Though their talk formed a circle among themselves, Wandimu was sure he was the center of it.

In a few minutes the man who appeared the oldest among the riders turned to him and spoke. Wandimu caught the words Dire Dawa.

"*Awon*," he said. "Dire Dawa."

The man nodded. He gestured to the boy and spoke. The boy turned to Wandimu with a smile. The peasant felt weak. He stiffened his legs but couldn't keep his knees from trembling. The boy waved his hands at Wandimu and smiled again. He pointed back and forth between Wandimu and himself with one hand and with the other pointed up the track Wandimu and the graybeard had been following. He spoke words which again included what to Wandimu had become a magic formula—Dire Dawa.

"Dire Dawa," muttered Wandimu. The only words we can exchange, he thought. And then he remembered—peace.

"*Selam,*" he said. "*Selam, selam.*"

The boy's eyes brightened. The circle of men around him laughed.

"*Selam, selam,*" cried the boy. He joined the laughter, then let loose a torrent of words in which Wandimu distinctly heard, "Allah . . . Muhammad." How does he greet me, a Christian, with such heathen words? I will kill him, thought Wandimu.

The bearded Danakil he'd met that dawn came closer and touched the handle of the knife Wandimu had been given at Tendaho. Graybeard glanced at the boy who smiled and touched the handle of the knife sheathed at his waist. He drew the knife.

So then, we'll fight with Danakil knives, thought Wandimu. He worked his own knife free from its sheath. But if I kill the boy, the others will kill me. So be it.

"Very well, then," he said aloud, flexing his arms. "Give us room."

But, as he watched, the boy replaced his knife in its leather covering.

Ah ha, thought Wandimu. You are wise beyond your years. If you had dared to fight me, your blood would have watered this desert. He puffed out his chest and stomped his foot. The Danakils smiled and nodded in a way he took for approval.

I have won, thought Wandimu. I have won.

The apparent leader of the group took the boy aside. The Danakil with the gray beard joined them. They shouldn't be too hard on him, thought Wandimu. The boy showed wisdom. The three Danakils stood at the edge of the track to Dire Dawa. The others went off after the ox which had wandered along the banks of the wadi in search of grazing.

Wandimu watched as they retrieved the ox and began lashing his possessions to the back of the patient beast—his *agalgil,* his bottle filled with muddy water, his heavy cloth *gabbi.*

Now they act as my servants, thought Wandimu. They recognize their master now. But that's as it should be. For all the heathen tribes of Ethiopia know the Amhara is their ruler. Politely, with just a touch of disdain, he thanked them.

It all happened so quickly Wandimu barely had time to understand. He and his ox, the young boy, and one of the camels were set out on the track heading south. Treachery. Treachery, thought Wandimu. They act as my servants only to send me off with this boy. To give him another chance to kill me.

Well, we shall see.

He turned to see his bearded companion of the dawn waving to him. His bracelets glinted in the light of the now declining sun. Betrayer, thought Wandimu.

The others had already set off, heading north. They carry their skins to market, thought Wandimu. And what of me? They expect my skin to rot in this desert minus its jewels and maybe an ear and some fingers. They expect this boy to prove himself on Wandimu.

Well, we shall see.

There aren't seven of you now, my Danakil friends. Only one. My knife is as sharp as yours, small child. And my stick can cut the air more quickly than you can fire a bullet from your gun.

We will show you the cunning of the Amhara.

It would soon be dark. He resolved to kill the boy that night.

Yes, thought Wandimu. Gabriel watches over me. The Christian will cut the heathen down. And then I shall be able to make my way to Kulubi—in peace.

"*Selam,*" said Fikr as he climbed back into his bus. "Our next stop is Kulubi."

It amused him to use the Islamic greeting to his Christian passengers. In the cities some of the young people had taken to using *selam* as a greeting among themselves. For many it was only a fad. Others viewed it more seriously as their way of expressing the unity, not only of all Ethiopians, but of all Africans. And it was their way, too, of turning their backs on the official church that had so long dominated the people.

But what would this busload of superstitious fools know of all that? thought Fikr as he settled himself behind the wheel. He wished there were someone to talk to, someone of his own intelligence.

The Englishman in the sun helmet, perhaps. But no, the man was mad. Fikr watched him approaching the bus door, his arms loaded down with bottles of mineral water, his shoulders strapped with cameras, a canteen, and an *agalgil* freshly filled with *injera* and *wat* from the kitchen of the Rocket Hotel.

Fikr had driven the eccentric Colonel Wilson once before on a trip to Jimma in the coffee country. He remembered the colonel, but the colonel, of course, had forgotten him.

Fikr offered to help him up the steps with his burdens. "*Gedyelyam*," said the colonel. "Assistance is not wanted." His Amharic was facile but bad. "However, I do want to congratulate you. You must have been raised by Englishmen."

"No, sir," answered Fikr in English. "I was raised by the Italians."

"Impossible," said the colonel, still in Amharic. "You can not possibly have been raised by Italians. You drive like an Englishman."

"Yes, sir," said Fikr.

"I could tell it immediately. That's why it's a pleasure to drive in Nairobi and a terror in Addis Ababa. Can't blame your average Ethiopian for being a bad driver. Or praise your average Kenyan for being good at it. Question of influence. Kenyans drive like Englishmen. Ethiopians, yourself excepted, drive like Italians."

"Yes sir. I never been to Nairobi."

"Ah, you speak the Queen's language. My congratulations. Ha ha." He managed to shake a finger of the hand that held two bottles of mineral water. "You see? I knew you couldn't have been raised by Italians." This time he did Fikr the honor of speaking to him in English.

"Yes sir," said Fikr. His shrug was barely perceptible. Who am I, he thought, to contradict an Englishman?

The colonel turned up the aisle but paused by the young mother sitting with her infant in the first seat.

"And you, madame," he intoned in his wretched Amharic, "are the fairest flower of Ethiopia. My congratulations." He marched up the aisle to his seat at the back.

Fikr had turned round to watch the exchange. The young woman looked at him in astonishment. She hadn't understood a word.

"He says you're pretty," Fikr told her.

She glanced back at the Englishman, then smiled at Fikr and cast her eyes down.

Yes, thought Fikr. Well, here is someone I can talk to. But what would it mean? The Englishman might be intelligent, but he was mad. The girl might be sane, but she was sure to prove stupid. They could talk of her region, of the festival at Kulubi, of the crowds, her family. Small things only. Her talk would be boring.

Because of the baby she was nursing, he had helped her board the bus back in Addis before the other passengers. She had chosen the seat behind and across the aisle from his. He knew she wanted to talk, but what was the use? He glanced at her image in his mirror. It was better this way.

Her face was pretty enough. It was better to glance at her once in a while to enjoy her beauty without wasting breath on foolish talk. The white of her freshly washed *tibeb* set off the café au lait glow of her face and her blue throat tattoos. She was from the province of Gojjam. He knew that from the purity of her Amharic when she thanked him for helping her on the bus. But the style of her tattoos was exceptional.

Etched like stylized waves in three bands, they went precisely halfway round her sturdy, unlined throat. As she aged, the folds of the skin would merge into one mass of flabby blue. But now they formed a perfect necklace more cunning than any a jeweler could fashion.

Even more to his taste, there were no other tattoos to distract from the beauty of the throat: no cross on the forehead, no radiating suns or circles on the backs of her hands, no dimple cut into her chin, no band looking like an unfeminine blue beard along her jaw. No, the necklace was alone, simple, perfect, a tribute to someone's taste.

Like her Amharic, it was a sign of an educated family. Possibly a priest's, but a priest surely would have put some cross on her. He was about to look away and start the motor when the girl spoke.

"You shouldn't watch us."

She'd caught his eye in the mirror. For a moment he was too startled to answer.

"Why not?"

"You're too proud to speak to us. You shouldn't watch us either."

He swung around in his seat. "But I have to look after my passengers. It isn't just driving the bus. My job, you know."

"Oh, you're too good for us," said the girl. Her gums were gray. He knew it was deficiency in the diet, but he found it attractive. He smiled at her.

"Why do you say that? Didn't I help you and the baby first on the bus?"

The old woman who had squeezed herself into the window seat next to the girl glared at them.

"It's the old ones you should be helping. Not these young chickens. What help does she need?"

He turned his back on them and started up the motor. He gunned the engine fiercely while he scanned the passengers in his mirror. There were still some stragglers in the aisle.

"Everyone in this bus be seated."

His sharp tone got results. Automatically, he checked the two outside mirrors. The street behind him was clear. He eased up on the accelerator, clutched, and pushed the gearshift into low.

"The next stop on this bus is Kulubi. All passengers please remain in your seats."

The girl with the neck tattoo was watching him in the mirror. He nodded at her.

"Kulubi next stop."

He started the bus up the road, then swung wide to arc up the narrow street that led back to the highway. The girl had unnerved him. For one thing, she had spoken too boldly. All the way from Addis to Asba Tafari she had sat quietly, shyly without a word. He had enjoyed watching her nurse the baby and had even adjusted the interior mirror to see her better. Her shapely breasts were swollen with milk but didn't sag. It had been fine like that. Watching a shy, pretty girl nurse her baby. He wished she hadn't started talking.

He paused at the edge of the highway to let a Volkswagen and then a station wagon go by. He noticed a *faranj* was at the wheel of the little car. Each year more and more foreigners made this trip to Kulubi. Some even walked from Dire Dawa. He couldn't understand why. He expected more intelligence from foreigners.

He gunned the big bus up onto the highway, angling it to the left and up the road into the cool green hills. She shouldn't have spoiled it, thought Fikr. He decided the girl must have taken some *tej* at the hotel. He glanced at her reflection in the mirror. That was it. Her cheeks were flushed.

The baby in her arms whimpered softly. She loosed the folds of her dress and drew out a firm, brown breast. Such lovely red nipples, thought Fikr. Ai, lucky baby. With a *tut-tut* like that to feed on you'll never scream for a bottle like the *faranj* brats. He wished the mother had stayed quiet like the baby. I could have just watched her like I watch the road and gone on with my thinking. I don't have to talk to the road. But now that she's begun I'll have to talk to her again or she'll think I'm too proud, like a Gondare. But how can you say to a woman, or even a friend, the things you can think to yourself?

Her eye caught his.

"Anyway," he said, "that's what this one is for. This mirror. To watch you passengers. Make sure you're all right. I use the outside mirrors for the road behind me. Not that it does much good to watch the road behind me in all this dust, but I watch it all the same."

The girl took her eyes from the mirror and nodded at the windshield. "You should just watch the road ahead."

"Are you joking? I always watch the road ahead. When I look in the mirror, it's just a glance. Thirty times a minute, maybe more, my eyes go from one to the other.

"The road ahead. The left mirror. The road ahead. The right mirror. The road ahead. The inside mirror. The road ahead. Huh. You won't find a safer driver in all Ethiopia."

"He better watch the road ahead," said the old woman by the window. "He better watch the road ahead or we'll all end up at the bottom of one of these hills and never get to Kulubi to see Gabriel."

"If we end up at the bottom of one of these hills," said Fikr, "you may see Gabriel sooner than you think."

"Never mind. Just watch the road."

Now there were two of them. Having to talk to the girl was bad enough. But now, whenever he spoke, this old hag would butt in. He glanced at the girl in the mirror. Such lovely breasts. He shook his head. If only I could just look at her. And study the country. And remember.

As the jaws of the huge bus slowly chewed at the tough strips of highway that curled through the mountains, Fikr liked to let his mind roam from the road he was driving to all the roads he had known. It was said that only the Emperor really knew Ethiopia.

But the Emperor had only recently made his first visit to the vast province of Gemu Goffa, and there were many regions still untouched by the imperial presence.

Fikr had never spoken the thought, but he was sure he knew Ethiopia far better than any number of emperors ever could. There was hardly a road or a track that a skillfully driven bus or lorry or Land Rover could negotiate that he had not traveled.

Unlike other drivers he knew, Fikr studied as he went. The people, the towns, the villages, the road, the mountains, the river valleys, rain forests, and deserts were maps drawn and retained in his mind. As he drove he remembered and compared places opposite and similar. Incidents and characters helped him trace the web of reflections he could summon up after thirty years on the road for a dozen employers.

He had begun as a boy when he fled the beatings of a drunken, sadistic father. During the war against the Italians, he had prayed to Mariam that his father would be killed. But that terrified recruit had fallen in a drunken stupor on the plains of Maichew and slept in the shadow of a rock while his brothers were being slaughtered by the fascists.

At Maichew the Emperor himself, according to legend and heroically captioned propaganda photos, had manned an antiaircraft gun against Italian bombers. But neither heroism nor prayers prevailed that day. The mechanized Italian forces massacred the ill-equipped Ethiopians, and, when the battle was over, Fikr's father picked himself up and went home.

When the survivor returned to his rocky hillside farm a few days later, young Fikr fled down one slope while his father stumbled up the other. The young boy joined the victorious Italian army on its march south. He attached himself as an all-purpose errand boy to the driver of a supply lorry.

War was a game, but neither as exciting nor as brutal as *genna* or *kuskus*, the rough holiday games his father pushed him into each year. Ethiopian warriors melted like butter under the savage sun of Italian planes dropping fire bombs and poison gas and armored vehicles spraying machine gun bullets and cannon shells. Bad roads and rugged terrain were more of a barrier than the defending armies.

Fikr, then an undersized boy of twelve, got to know these natural defenses well. He rode the lorry on top of the rope-secured canvas which covered the cases of pasta and other food the Italians carried with them to supplement the sheep and cattle and grain they stole from the peasants they killed. Though he had good reason to admire some of the roads the Italians built during their brief occupation, Fikr knew their main contribution to the country had been death.

Herod in the Bible had ordered the slaughter of the innocents, killing all male infants in the land. Graziani, the fascist butcher of Ethiopia, spared the innocents but massacred all males he could find with an education above the elementary level. In those days Fikr had blessed his ignorance. He had never seen a school. The Italians were good to him. From them he learned the trade he had followed ever since and would cling to as long as his eyes were able to describe the road to his hands.

Like a man with an ungainly dancing partner, he twisted the heavy bus into a series of ascending curves. He sounded the enormous howler of a horn mounted above his cab, not just to warn every living creature out of his way, but to hear its music above his head and to let the mountains and all their rocks and trees and flowers know that Fikr and his bus were wailing on the highway. There were times as he drove that he wanted to sing, but he let the Klaxon do it for him.

"He drives like an Englishman," said Colonel Wilson to his seat companion at the back of the bus. "He drives like an Englishman, but he sounds the Klaxon like a bloody Italian."

Like most Ethiopians, the old peasant sitting next to the colonel was unused to hearing foreigners speak Amharic. He understood only a few of the Englishman's mispronounced words. He laughed at the way the *faranj* abused the language. The colonel took the laughter for appreciation of his humor and praised the peasant for his understanding.

"Oh, it's true, true," he said, taking a swig from his bottled water. "I've been here a long time. Know the country. Know the language. Know the people. Love it. Love it."

He pressed the cap back on and secured the bottle on the floor between his heavy boots. He readjusted his camera straps and briefly lifted his topi to wipe the sweat from his forehead.

"Till the day I die," he said. He sat upright, hands on his knees, and went on talking to the peasant.

"Yes, made me laugh, they did. At Africa Hall. One of those ruddy OAU conferences. Getting my press credentials, I was." His

Amharic vocabulary was so limited that nearly half his words were in English.

"Had to fill out this ruddy questionnaire. Usual stuff. Then came these two questions. How long have you been in Ethiopia? How long do you intend to stay in Ethiopia? Huh. For the first one I put down, 'Since the day we drove the bloody fascists out.' Second one, 'How long do you intend to stay in Ethiopia?' I put down, 'Till the day I die.'

"Made me laugh. But I told them. Till the day I die. Oh, yes, make no mistake. I love this country. Love it. I came out with Sanford, you know." He half turned to the old peasant. "Old *Janhoy* himself was with us clear from Khartoum. Every inch a king, that one. Not many inches of him, but every inch an emperor."

The peasant watched the foreigner sitting there, speaking a strange language with a few words he recognized. At first he had thought the man with all the straps and bottles was speaking Amharic. Surely some of the words sounded like Amharic, but now he thought it must be some other tongue. The *faranj* didn't look like an Arab, but the old peasant had heard Arab traders speaking their own language. There were always some words the same as Amharic. What had the *faranj* just said? *Arbegaw Ye Etiopia negne . . .*" What did he mean? The liberator of Ethiopia. Himself. This *faranj* was saying he was the liberator of Ethiopia. Who is he? wondered the peasant. This man who sat there like a king, wearing a sun helmet like the Emperor's. Speaking a language like the Arabs'. Claiming to be the liberator of Ethiopia.

He had seen Arabs who were as fair-skinned as this man in the sun helmet. Could this be some Arab, like a latter-day Mohammed Gragn, come secretly in a bus to conquer Ethiopia? He now hung on every word. If his suspicions were confirmed, he would report the invader to the police at the next stop.

"Yes, we were the liberators of Ethiopia, British regulars under Brigadier Sanford. Can't boast myself. Wasn't much of a hero." The colonel lapsed more and more into English as his memories carried him back to his days with the army of liberation.

"Didn't have much chance to be heroes. Italians wouldn't stop to fight. Best damn runners in the world, Italians." He glanced at the peasant. "Your boys, Abebe Bikila, the lot, they may win the marathon time after time at the ruddy Olympics, but they can't hold a candle to Italian soldiers on the run. Ruddy Italians can outrun even an Egyptian with a Jew at his heels."

What had this stranger said now? An insult to Abebe Bikila, a hero second only in reverence to the Emperor himself. And something about Egyptians. Ah ha. Now I see it, thought the peasant. An Egyptian agent was what the infidel was.

"Well, I told them at the OAU, I told them right out, I was fighting to liberate Africa from ruddy European colonialism when you fellows were just ideas in your fathers' loincloths. Take no nonsense from 'em, wherever they are. Your black bureaucrats are no better than your white.

"Stayed on, I did , with ol' Sanford, administration right through the war and after. Right-hand man, I was, or close to it. Still see the old boy now and again out at his Mullu Farm with his strawberries and roses. Bit dotty, he is, these days, but the old woman's sharp enough. Eighty if she's a day. They love the country, too. Like me. Be here, they will, till the day they die."

He rambled on, as much in English as Amharic now, all but oblivious of the peasant.

"Turned a hand to farming myself a time or two. Still raise chickens down at Bishoftu, I do, but administration's my game. Worked in half the ministries in Addis Ababa one time or another. Love old Addis, I do. Saw it grow. From six mud huts and a tree to what it is now. Finest city in the world, our Addis. Stinks a bit toward the end of the dry season, but the rains always wash it clean.

"Finest city in the world. Thank the old man for that. Every inch a king."

He lifted the topi again to wipe his brow. Why is he wearing that helmet? thought the peasant. Just like the helmet the Emperor wears.

The colonel noticed the close attention the peasant was paying to his sun helmet.

"See this topi, do you? Mark of honor here, it is. Indeed." He puffed out his chest. "Not like the rest of Africa. You wouldn't know about that, of course. Dare say you never been out of Ethiopia. But you go to British East Africa. You go to the Gold Coast, Nigeria. Anywhere the British raj has been. You won't see the topi any more. Rest of Africa, India, too, this old helmet meant the colonial boys, white man's burden, agonies of empire. No such thing here. Proud country. No white man in his topi ever conquered here. Old Menelik drove the Italians out when they tried. Drove 'em out no holds barred back in ninety-six. Proud day. And when Haile Selassie came back to run the Eyeties out again in forty-one, he was wearing a topi himself. Same as Sanford, Wingate, myself. Wears it till this day, ol' Haile does. Doesn't mean colonial days here, the topi." He removed the helmet from his gray head and held it before him. "Here it's like a crown, see. Crown of freedom. Liberation. Proud hat, this." He placed it solemnly back on his head.

So that's it, thought the peasant. Now this Arab has crowned himself king of Ethiopia. Well, we shall see. We shall see, you dog of an Arab.

"Old Haile, every inch a king and clever as a fox. Let the Italians stay on after the war, what was left of 'em. Myself, I'd of hung 'em to a man. But ol' Haile, milk of human kindness and clever as a fox, knew he needed every European he could get to rebuild the country and those Italians, some of 'em, once they stopped running, could turn a fair hand at plumbing and lights, construction, build a road, shoe repair, drive a truck. With British to run 'em, your Italian's not a bad hand at labor. Still here, what's left of 'em. Specially in Eritrea. Thirty years and more in the country and still can't speak the language. No gift for language, your Italian. Not like us British. Had a bunch of 'em myself building roads out to Jimma one time. Not a bad lot, your Italians."

So. The Italians are in it, too, thought the peasant. Arabs and Italians trying to conquer Ethiopia again. By the sword of Gabriel, they'll be stopped. He hummed a few phrases from a popular war song. By the sword of Gabriel, he vowed, we'll slaughter you again.

"Oh yes," said the Colonel. "I was in construction awhile, too. Helped build this ruddy country, I did. Helped 'em with their newspapers, too. Back when they started putting out the English one. Advertising, that was my game. Circulation, too. Till they accused me. Humph. As if an Englishman would steal. Wanted to run me out of the country, they did. But I had my connections. People I took good care of. Helped me open the casino after that. Ministers and all used to come. But mostly your Germans and Greeks and Armenians and, oh yes, our Italian friends, too. Love to gamble, your Italians do. Some ladies around, of course. Always had some ladies around for them that fancied the bed more than the tables. Went right well, the casino did, till your ruddy CID came and accused me.

"Humph. As if an Englishman would cheat."

He took another swig of his mineral water and, without looking at him, offered the bottle to the peasant. The peasant shook his head in refusal.

"Anyway, I've still got my house, fine old house, and my chickens down to Bishoftu, and always some ladies around. Some, well, they come and go, but some have been with me off and on ever since the old casino. Finest ladies in the world, your Ethiopian ladies. Some worked for me when I opened the agency, advertising, import, export, factors of every damn thing. Sold encyclopedias to every damn illiterate with a dollar. Fine business it was till some of your Armenians ganged up and accused me.

"Humph. As if anyone could steal money from an Armenian. Yes, we've got all kinds in Ethiopia, good with the bad. Most fascinating country in the world.

"Stay here, I will, till the day I die."

May Haile Selassie die, thought the peasant, if I don't bring this dog to justice this day.

"It's good to have someone to talk to," said the colonel. "A man of understanding like yourself to talk to now and again." He stared ahead for a minute, then sadly shook his head.

"I'm not as active, no, not as active as I was back when. But not to worry. I've still got the old house and I do my writing and file a story now and again for the *Telegraph*, *News of the World*, what I can, and a bit to do here and there. A bit of this. A bit of that. And always some ladies about the ol' place. They come and they go. But they always know there's a bed and a meal when they're in need. They know the old colonel's always good for a cot and a meal when a friend's in need. When they're out of a job or whatever. And if they lose a husband, well, one or two have come back when they lost a husband or until a spat blows over or whatever and stay till they find a new man or a new job. Or whatever. They know the old colonel's always a soft touch for a cot or a meal. When they need.

"Finest women in the world, your Ethiopian women. But no. I'm not so active no more. No need to lie. No need to lie about that. Be meeting one of my old friends at Kulubi, but . . .

"Humph. Well, no more o' that."

He reached for his bottle of water and took a gulp. This time he offered none to the silent peasant beside him. Instead, he held the bottle before him as though offering a toast.

"Yes," he said. "Till the day I die."

The shortest road to Kulubi, favored by the pious, prodigal pilgrims of the capital, begins with a quick drive along African Unity Boulevard to Haile Selassie I Airport. From there the way continues via a forty minute flight in a DC-6 to Dire Dawa. The passengers are mostly women, some with young children. Their musical chatter fills the aisles with softly accented Amharic.

Tiruwork, still slender, lovely and publicly shy despite four children under the age of six, traveled with four friends, loud, voluptuous, and vulgar, though none had more children and only one was older than their quiet companion.

Alganesh, Tiruwork's special friend who sat by her side, loved to joke about the meaning of her own name. " 'You're a bed.' Everytime somebody says hello to me, they say '*Tenastelign, alganesh.* You're a bed, Alganesh.' *Wei-good.* So that's me. Alganesh." She patted her enormous breasts. "Not a thin bed. Hey, not a cold bed. Me."

The five matrons sat across the aisle from each other. Each had a vow to walk the more than fifty uphill kilometers from Dire Dawa to Kulubi for each had a *silet* to Gabriel and a rendezvous to keep. As Alganesh roared on, the other ladies laughed, then lowered their eyes, remembering that the plane somewhere had its share of men. But the noise of the jet engines and the plane's high seat backs isolated them. Alganesh grew bolder and their laughter was louder. Their eyes danced, wondering how Alganesh could be so daring.

"It's all right for you ladies to be so Ethiopian. With a name like mine you can't pretend to be shy for long." Again she patted her bosom as though that fleshy pillow were part of the name. "With a name like mine I might as well be an American. *Ye Selam Gwadhesh.*" The pun was complex, "You are a body of peace," a play on the Amharic word for Peace Corps. The Peace Corps girls had a notorious reputation among Ethiopians for their availability.

"*Ye Selam na fikr gwad,*" said another of the ladies—the peace and love corps girls, punning on a modern salutation, peace and love. Alganesh kept it going. "*Ye Selam Gwadoch,*" turning the plural into another pun—the friendly peace bodies. "But not one of them is a piece of flesh like Alga-nesh." Their laughter grew louder as the plane rocked them toward Kulubi.

A stewardess isn't supposed to get airsick, Zewditu said to herself. But I'm airsick. She was stacking used plastic snack dishes in the galley while two other hostesses hustled soiled trays back up the aisles. She remembered what their aging American pilot had once said—a hostess is just a waitress with her ass in the clouds. No wonder I'm airsick, she thought. Or something.

She had been pulled off an international flight to work the special jet service to Dire Dawa for the festival. Normally, the provincial town was served by DC-3s, half hollowed out for cargo. For the festival as many planes as possible were pressed into service, shuttling back and forth several times a day. Minutes after takeoff, the hostesses had speedily racked up coffee, tea, sodas, and cakes for the entire economy section. The remains of the snack had barely been cleared away when the buzzers started. Zewditu steeled herself to return to the battle. There go the whores again, she thought, wanting to know why we don't have any gin.

"Thank God we're only flying them to Dire Dawa," she said to one of the other hostesses. "Can you imagine a planeload of these *shermutas* all the way to Rome?"

At the front of the second class cabin, Fat Margaret, a homely but much-sought-after half-caste, sat with her friend, Addis Ababa's most illustrious madame Shi Samanya, One Thousand Eighty. She'd been given the name long ago because of the stone highway kilometer marker opposite her house which recorded the distance from Asmara.

The house was in a small, quiet, high-fenced compound near the British church. It had none of the obvious markings of the city's thousands of *buna bets,* coffeehouses where whisky and women but rarely coffee were sold.

There were no neon signs, loud music, no lovely young girls in provocatively open doorways or weary harridans shrouded in shadowy interiors. It was just a house, more modest than many of its neighbors, in a residential section. The stone and glass villas of well-to-do foreigners on the slope on one side of the road looked down on the windowless mud and straw *tukuls* and tin-roofed shacks in the ravine beyond the opposite side of the Asmara Road.

The house of One Thousand Eighty was halfway between. It stood on the "poor" side of the street but level with the road and well above the ravine formed by the Kebbenna River. It was a *chika* house, mud walls plastered over and painted. Its tin roof was shaded by the trees and vines of the compact and well-kept compound.

Its existence was known to a fair-sized minority. But its clientele was much more restricted. The compound could accommodate only two or three cars, including the owner's chauffeur-driven Peugeot.

The men who came in black Mercedes, usually with white, government license plates, were mostly of ministerial rank. One Thousand Eighty, herself middle-aged but still fair and pleasant, and the surly but strangely popular Margaret were always on hand. But there was no resident supply of young beauties. Experience had taught her such girls couldn't be trusted and, for her visitors, girls who could be trusted were essential.

She allowed her guests to bring their own girls when they wanted, usually secretaries, sometimes a lesser-known actress. Occasionally, One Thousand Eighty would provide a girl who would be guaranteed to make up in ignorance what she might lack in discretion.

For the most part, however, her house served as an informal club. Men of importance could have a relaxed conversation in the gay and intelligent company of the lady of the house with mildly provocative asides from Fat Margaret.

Only one of her regular visitors knew she was paid a hundred dollar weekly retainer with frequent bonuses far in excess of that by the Amharic-speaking cultural attaché of the Russian Embassy. The one visitor who did know was head of security in the Emperor's private cabinet.

One Thousand Eighty was a Galla, but her profession was rare among women of her tribe. Most of the country's countless prostitutes were recruited from among the Amhara and Tigre Christians of the highlands. But the pattern which brought One Thousand Eighty to the life was a familiar one.

As a child bride, she had been brought from her remote countryside village to live in the fair-sized village of Lekempte. She was an adolescent mother used to town ways when her husband died. Unable to readjust to village life and with no way to earn a living in the town where she was known, she sent her two infant children to her parents' village and fled to Addis Ababa and the relative anonymity of its bars.

Her life changed again when an influential Galla of high rank in the military became her protector. He was as rare in the influence he held in the Amhara-dominated government as she was in her Amhara-dominated profession. Since his death, her own circle of influence had broadened.

Over the years she had acquired extensive land in the coffee areas of her native Wollega and several plots in Addis Ababa on which she had built expensive villas to rent to foreigners. But the homey *chica bet* which was no longer the main source of her income was still the focus of her considerable influence.

At present, her closest alliance was with another military man, General Tadesse Adera, the aging but still vigorous and constantly conniving head of the territorial army. General Tadesse discussed his schemes with her and often reshaped them on the basis of her shrewd suggestions. In the Byzantine world of palace intrigue, he had developed a technique of encouraging plots which he himself then exposed to the Emperor. He covered his own tracks well, and the Emperor's gratitude made it difficult for his enemies' accusations against him to win an audience.

A few months before he had sold weapons and explosives for use in a terrorist campaign waged by the Galla political movement known as *Metcha Tuluma*. Several meetings of the group were held at the house by the kilometer marker on the Asmara Road.

General Tadesse then informed the Emperor of the plot. And two days later One Thousand Eighty earned a generous bonus from her Russian friend for the same information. The general saw to it that the two men who could link him to the scheme were killed when police went to their homes to arrest them.

One Thousand Eighty resisted the temptation ever to expose the general to her contact in the private cabinet. She knew that behind his back he was called the hyena, but she was confident no one knew how close her own relationship with him was. And it was far too profitable a relationship to jeopardize.

The general cautiously visited her only in the mornings—at times when she contrived to make sure Fat Margaret was out. Fat Margaret had come into her life soon after her original Galla protector had died. They met at a beauty parlor. Margaret told her she had recently left her husband in Ambo.

"He was always trying to beat me. I didn't mind that so much, but he wasn't big enough for the job." She had a small amount of money of her own and was living in a hotel. "But soon I'll have no money, and I'll have to go back to the little man."

Instead she had moved in with One Thousand Eighty. She liked to drink and talk and adjusted to the life easily. Though she was outspoken and sullen, most men found her amusing and a few considered her a challenge. Except for her mentor, however, Fat Margaret's charm was lost on other women.

It had been Margaret who pressed the buzzer which Zewditu answered. The hostess managed, just barely, to smile as she hovered over their seats and released the call button.

"Can I help you, ladies?"

"You still don't have any gin?" asked Margaret.

"No, I'm sorry. No alcohol on domestic flights."

"Well, I suppose it can't be helped," pouted Margaret. "Bring us whisky then. With ice and Ambo water."

"I'm sorry." Zewditu glanced at One Thousand Eighty who looked a shade more intelligent. "We have no whisky, no brandy, no wine, no beer, and no gin. No alcohol at all."

"Never mind, dear," said One Thousand Eighty. "Just bring us two Coca-Colas."

"I don't want Coca-Cola," said Margaret. "It makes you fat."

"Would you like Sprite?" said Zewditu. "Mineral water? Fanta? Coffee? Tea?"

"I'll wait for gin," said Margaret.

"Then you'll wait till Dire Dawa," said Zewditu.

"What's Dire Dawa?" said Margaret. "A little town not much bigger than Ambo. We could get all the gin we wanted in Ambo. They had gin on that flight we took to Asmara."

"That would have been an international flight," chimed Zewditu.

"It certainly was," said Margaret. "We got all the gin we wanted."

"Never mind, dear," said One Thousand Eighty. "Just bring us two Coca-Colas." She patted Margaret's plump hand. "When we get to Dire Dawa, we'll buy you a nice gin and tonic at the hotel."

Zewditu glared at the passenger by the window. She'd been right. This one was smarter. Smart enough to be a bitch. Whores were all alike. Except you could never be sure. This one might be a general's wife.

She turned back up the aisle to get the Cokes.

Hilary Blankenship looked down at the train winding its way over the hot plains to Dire Dawa.

"They say the Emperor's taking the train this year," he said to Negussie, who was at the controls.

"The old man is tough," said Negussie. "I wouldn't take that train if you paid me."

"He's got his private car," said Hilary.

"It isn't air-conditioned," said the younger pilot. "Eight, nine hours that train takes to Dire Dawa, and you know it's hot down there."

"I know," said Hilary. "I've been hunting down there." He heard voices behind him and turned in his chair. It was Zewditu, one of the best looking of the hostesses, collecting empty coffee cups from the flight cabin.

A waitress with her ass in the clouds, thought Hilary. But what a splendid way for a waitress to be assembled. She laughed at something the radioman had said. She saw Hilary watching her and came forward. He handed her their cups.

"Hello, beauty."

"Hello, dirty old man."

She glanced at Negussie. Negussie kept his eyes ahead. Neither spoke. Hilary had been aware of this tension between them since their flight had begun. Aware and puzzled. Zewditu turned and left the cabin.

"She's a beauty," said Hilary.

"A beauty," agreed Negussie.

"I must admit though, that's one pitch where old Hilary struck out."

"Really."

"Tried more than once. No go at all. I've heard it said by some jealous minds that young Negus has been there, but that's only rumor."

"You can't believe every rumor you hear."

"True. Anyway, I'd be willing to believe the fair Zewditu isn't as available as some of our other playmates."

"That's what she tells me, too," said Negussie.

"Oh? Careful there, Negus. That could be serious."

Negussie tapped the flight controls and smiled. "You taught me everything I know, old Hill. I try never to get serious. Except about flying."

"Yes, well, flying's one thing. But sometimes the other serious catches up on you. Without your ever knowin'. Till it's too late."

Negussie didn't respond. Hilary let it drop. He was curious but knew better than to meddle too far into other men's affairs. He had enough trouble with his own. And the trouble was getting worse. For twenty-five years he'd been having an affair with Ethiopia.

He was one of the last of the original TWA personnel who had helped set up Ethiopian Airlines shortly after World War II. He contrived by every possible means to stay on despite age and vision that was no longer perfect. He had long ago memorized every conceivable eye test and had used his popularity with both TWA and Ethiopian officials to stay on.

His wife, Madge, harbored a hatred for Ethiopia directly proportional to Hilary's constantly growing affection, and for the same reason. Though he was sentimental about many aspects of the country, Hilary, above all, was in love with Ethiopian women.

He had come to enjoy Ethiopian food with its hot spicy stews scooped up in pieces of flat, sour bread, its liquors brewed from honey and *gesho*. Its landscapes of steep escarpments, fertile plateaus, soaring mountains, sprawling savannah and arid bush. Its western jungles and eastern deserts. He had come to love its varieties of people and its casual ways. The excitement of its modern, mountainous capital and the indolent ease of its steaming coastal ports.

He knew none of its countless languages and dialects well, not even Amharic, but could get along in five or six when he wanted to get along. He had learned his smattering of languages from a variety of women. In the same style, he had ignored the local food until from the hands of an attractive young matron he had savored his first *gursha*, a serving of strongly peppered *wat* daintily wrapped in a strip of pancakelike *injera*, placed in your mouth by another as a sign of affection or hospitality.

He soon yearned for *wat* made from chicken or lamb or beef at every meal and began to regret dinners at home or meals in hotels and restaurants on his flights to Europe. A Guarage girl who took care of his five children introduced him to *kitfo*, chopped beef and peppers taken raw or lightly cooked in thick butter. He had sampled it first late one night in the servants' quarters behind his ten-room villa.

At the wedding of a hostess he'd been dating, he had first dared *brundo*, the raw meat of a freshly slaughtered bull hacked still warm from sides of the flesh carried among the guests on poles by servants. A secretary from Gojjam brought him his first taste of a white liquor called *katikala* in a flask prepared by her mother in the countryside. The daughter of a restaurant owner taught him to forsake beer for *tella* and *tej*.

Though competent at the arts of relaxed and costly seduction, Hilary was honest enough to admit to himself that he was not a great lover. He held none of his exotic women for long. As he aged, he tried to tell himself it made no difference, that he was content to play the promising field. What a married man sought outside his marriage was variety. He insisted it made no sense for a man already tied to one woman to tie himself to another. Yet, he wished there were another tied to him. Or that one at least among his legion of lost women carried a still flickering torch for old Hill. None did. He knew it, and it hurt.

"You'll be seeing Abebetch?" asked Negussie, breaking his reverie. They were over Adefo, a parched lowland village on the railroad.

"No," said Hilary. "No more Abebetch. She got married a couple months ago, believe it or not, to some Russian."

"A Russian?" said Negussie with a laugh. "Poor Hill. That's not only disloyal. It's unpatriotic."

"That's what I thought," said Hilary. "Some guy who'd come up from Assab, you know, some oily technician from that refinery the Russkies built. It's so hot down there in Assab that Dire Dawa is their idea of someplace to come up to and cool off. He met Abebetch there and it didn't take long. We had one last weekend before the marriage. She told me to stay away after the wedding. She means to be the faithful wife. So now they're down at Assab, pumping oil and each other. Another well gone dry for old Hill."

"Abebetch settling down."

"It happens to the worst of us," said Hilary.

"But not to old Hill."

"I love you, Negus. No. Not yet. Settling down hasn't happened to old Hill."

He wished it would. He hoped he would settle down before it

got much worse. He hadn't tired of the pace. It was the change in course that worried him. It wasn't just the usual story—a man of forty fixated on girls of twenty. And growing older and at forty-five replacing a vanished mistress of twenty with a girl of nineteen. His problem had become far more acute.

Each year the girls his eyes selected, his thoughts followed, and his lust pursued were younger and younger. In Addis he often stopped his car to offer a lift to high school girls waiting a homeward bus. A surprising number accepted. A few were eventually seduced.

For several months he had been involved with a teen-age shoplifter, queen bee of a small group of girls whose well-to-do provincial parents had sent them to a private school in Addis. Their innocence had been their protector as they rifled Piazza stores for the latest European fashions. They lived in a strictly run Christian hostel for girls, but found enough free time for their shoplifting and—in the case of Sophia and one of the older girls—for their affairs.

He took a small, out-of-the-way house in Seratagna Sefer just below the Piazza. It became a drop for the girls' shoplifted goods and a haven for matiness for Hilary and the slender, elegant Sophia.

Five years ago, he told himself, I wouldn't have touched a girl under twenty. Then it had begun with Abebetch when she was only nineteen. His next girl had been eighteen, an EAL typist just out of the Commercial School. Then seventeen. Then Sophia the shoplifter at sixteen. Good God, sixteen.

Old Hill, if you're like this at forty-seven, what kind of clean old man will you be at sixty? The question hung in his mind as they began circling for their landing at Dire Dawa.

"*Kiburatina kiburan ahun kebetoachihun tateku*," Zewditu instructed over the plane's intercom. "Ladies and gentlemen, fasten your seat belts please. *Mesdames et messieurs, veuillez attacher vos ceintures de sécurité, s'il vous plaît.*"

Tiruwork needed Alganesh's help.

"You're so new at this, girl," said Alganesh. "Let the mistress of the bed help you." She picked up the metal couplings of the seat belt. "See, you slip this one into this one, see? Just like, you know." She laughed. Tiruwork smiled. "Then, when you hear it click, like this, you know he's in good and tight. Then you just sit back and leave the rest to God." The fair Tiruwork blushed. The next day she would meet him, the man, at Kulubi. Then she would relax and leave the rest to God—and to Gabriel.

For One Thousand Eighty, Kulubi was for business. She planned as she did each year to walk from the hotel in Dire Dawa to the church in the mountains. That was for Gabriel and for God.

But in the lobby of the Ras Hotel and in the bar run by her friend Kalamawork in the park two blocks away, One Thousand Eighty would be at work. All the famous madams and available entertainers of Addis would gather at Kalamawork's bar. The important men of the capital would circulate in the lobby of the hotel.

In both places, One Thousand Eighty would be doing business. At the bar she would be honored by the others in her trade as their queen. They would offer her their chairs and buy and carry drinks to her table. They would smile, take her hands, and address her in the familiar second person singular as they would in their own homes.

At the hotel, she would be greeted by ministers and generals. They would address her in the polite form. This annual public acknowledgment was part of the price they must pay for even potential entry to her very exclusive club.

At the level at which she practiced her profession, status was important. And at the feast of Kulubi Gabriel, from the peers of the realm and from her peers in the trade, One Thousand Eighty took care of the business of status. As she fastened her seat belt, she turned from Fat Margaret and glanced down at the buildings of Dire Dawa. She looked forward to the nights that were to come.

But as they circled the city below, she felt a vague sense of anxiety. She thought of a hyena circling its carrion. She thought of her general and his latest scheme. She had warned him it was too much like his last.

"A good poet," she had told him, "a good maker of poems, doesn't repeat the last line of a word in rhyming. He won't even use the same word twice in his poem."

"But this is a new poem," the general had said.

"It isn't," she said. "It's the same poem. And someone will catch you out. Repeating yourself."

She thought of his shuffling walk. It was true. He moved like a hyena. As their plane circled, she felt her stomach sinking.

The winds at Dire Dawa were often tricky. Warm air blew in off the desert, struck the mountains beyond the city, and clashed with the cool currents from the highlands. There was a sharp updraft as they came in, But Negussie circled into it and rode it down. His landing was perfect.

"Well done, young Negus."

"Thank you, old Hill."

Major Shiferaw Asfaw was pleased. As he reviewed them, all three of his purposes in going to Kulubi promised to work out well. He would profit financially; he would gather fresh ammunition to use against Tesfaye Tessema, the most troublesome of the journalists for whose work the major was responsible, and he would pleasantly surprise his wife, the shy and innocent Tiruwork, who would not be expecting him at the festival.

The major retained his military title—Shaleka, head of one thousand—and it was the name everyone, including Tiruwork, addressed him by. There was a hunting rifle in the government Land Rover in which he was being driven to Kulubi. And, as always, there was a .38 caliber revolver in the jacket pocket of his dark blue suit.

Though he shared the Ethiopian love of titles and guns, Shaleka did not play the game of being an old soldier. He liked to think of himself as a cog in the machinery of government, a thoroughly modern man involved in the development of his country. His guns were only for show. He himself was not a violent man. Cunning was his weapon. Persistence was his strength.

His motives for this trip to Kulubi were complex. A belief in miracles was not among them. Religion he left to his wife, who as she did every year, was flying to Dire Dawa with friends. But this year Shaleka, too, had an interest in Gabriel.

Twenty thousand copies of the pamphlet written by the American scholar Doctor Harriston Comfort and translated into Amharic by the journalist Tesfaye had been packed into the Land Rover. The Amharic version had been gathering dust in a Ministry of Information storeroom until the enterprising Shaleka had decided it could be profitably disposed of at the festival itself.

In his post as assistant minister of publications, it had not been difficult for him to have the pamphlets, which had been printed at government expense, loaded into a government Land Rover, which was fueled with benzine purchased by the government.

He planned to have the pamphlets sold at Kulubi for a dollar each. With scores of colored photographs, the pamphlets had cost more than a dollar each to produce, but Shaleka did not have to worry about cost accounting. The pamphlets had been earmarked for free distribution. There would be no auditors asking questions about the income from free pamphlets. There would be in fact no government accounting at all, for this was a purely private venture on the part of Shaleka.

Allowing for a certain *gursha* for his driver, a larger consideration for the National Lottery representative in Dire Dawa who was lining up street boys to peddle the booklets among the pilgrims, and an inevitable percentage for minor thieving, he was confident of a personal profit of at least fifteen thousand Ethiopian dollars.

Shaleka had already netted a three thousand dollar kickback from the Armenian printer to whom he had awarded the government contract for producing the Amharic and English versions. It was rare that Shaleka could profit so handsomely from a single pamphlet. The government seldom produced booklets that anyone would want to read, much less pay for. Most were dull compilations of inaccurate statistics laced with flowery tributes to the leadership of the Emperor in such fields as agriculture, education, public health, commerce, pest control, and highway development.

But *Kulubi* was different. This American friend of Tesfaye's had turned out an interesting little booklet, filled with historical information and alive with the color of the festival. There would be at least a hundred thousand pilgrims at Kulubi, each with a demonstrated interest in the subject matter. Shaleka knew he had a winner.

The pamphlet would take care of itself. What to do about Tesfaye was another matter.

In his present post, which included supervision of all the nation's newspapers, Shaleka had developed an intricate network of informers. Despite the formal absence of a system of precensorship, Shaleka was rarely caught by surprise by anything that appeared in the papers. His network of spies included typists, messenger boys, linotype operators, compositors, proofreaders, and at least one senior reporter on each of the papers.

He had made it a policy to make sure that the editor and assistant editor of each paper were men who neither liked nor trusted each other. In this aspect, Shaleka's own little empire was a mirror image of Ethiopia. The major had learned from a master, the Emperor himself.

In each ministry, in every military command, in the police and the various security branches, even in the church, the Emperor had carefully filled the top posts with men who could be counted on to keep an eye on each other. It was a remarkably effective system of checks and balances, not by institutions, but by personalities. The system, a sure guarantor of stability, also tended to produce stagnation. But men like Shaleka, more interested in survival than progress, found it to their liking and imitated it as best they could.

There was, however, a serious gap in Shaleka's control. Because of their fear of Shaleka, most editors and reporters had become their own censors. Tesfaye had not. As editor of the influential English-language daily, Tesfaye was developing an authority that was a threat, Shaleka knew, to his own. Tesfaye had even managed through his friendship with the Emperor's closest aide, Negash Mengistu, to have Shaleka's man rejected and for his paper to win the appointment of an assistant editor of his own choosing.

Shaleka had been plotting his revenge ever since. He had launched many rumors about Tesfaye, some of them mutually contradictory. He knew that lies did not always have to be believable to be believed. He recognized the deeply ingrained love of intrigue and storytelling in the Amhara personality.

His awareness of these tendencies was particularly acute because Shaleka saw them as an outsider diligently determined to cloak himself in the ways of Ethiopia's ruling tribe. Though his family had been Amharaizing itself for two generations, Shaleka was actually a Wollamo, one of the despised tribes from which until recent times the Amharas had taken their slaves. The military had provided upward mobility for other, more easily assimilated tribes like the Gallas, and it was this course that Shaleka's father had urged on his sons.

Even among his closest associates, there were none who knew for certain that Shaleka was anything but the Amhara he presented himself as. Though darker than most highlanders, Shaleka did have finer features than others of his tribesmen. A wound he'd suffered in Korea, a dime-sized circle below his right temple, was said by some of his enemies to be a Wollamo tribal scar.

He knew of the story. In fact, there was little that was said about Shaleka that did not eventually get back to him through his circle of informers. But he knew it was difficult to believe all he was told. He realized that some of his informers were capable of inventing rumors that maligned him, gossip which for his ears they would ascribe to enemies of their own. As a consummate inventor of lies, he was a fair judge of the probable degree of falsehood in what his informers told him.

Shaleka believed the Amhara love of lies and intrigue was built into the language itself. It was a language of ambiguities and puns. The tendency to say one thing while meaning another, sometimes playfully, sometimes deceitfully, was as natural to most Amharas as breathing. And, Shaleka was convinced, the tendency to look for the darker meaning in what one heard was just as natural.

The forms of polite conversation and the requirements of official propaganda both demanded a relentless commitment to positive statement. But whether in the subtle poems known as "wax and gold" or in the bland speeches of officials, the Amhara was gifted in searching for the hidden meaning. Almost by definition, the hidden meaning, the gold, was bound to be more negative than the visible mold of wax. The Amhara's instinct for such verbal play was a skill that Shaleka had to labor to develop.

Unlike many dishonest men, he was thoroughly honest with himself. In Tesfaye's case, he knew the young journalist too well to be fooled either by the lies he heard or the lies he told. Though he invented stories about Tesfaye's heavy drinking and neglect of his job, he knew him to be sober and uniquely devoted to the paper he edited.

This would not stop him from saying, "Well at least Tesfaye doesn't drink the way some of the other journalists do." Which his listeners would interpret as meaning that Tesfaye's drinking was far worse than his colleagues'. Shaleka might say that Tesfaye "usually shows up for work," which would be taken as a polite way of saying he hadn't been in his office for a month.

Shaleka, however, knew better. And that was what worried him.

For most of the journalists, work on a government paper just happened to be the particular civil service job they'd been assigned to by the government's Central Personnel Agency. They might as easily have been clerks in any other section of the government's all-pervasive bureaucracy. Which made them easy to control. To Tesfaye, as Shaleka admitted to himself, being a newspaperman mattered more than anything else in life.

He worked hard at all aspects of the job, from the frustrations of trying to gather publishable information in a closed and suspicious society to the equally frustrating task of seeing the news into print in a well-equipped but incompetently run government press.

Tesfaye was popular and respected among his colleagues. As an editor he had a knack of getting more work out of his staff than either their own initiative or Shaleka's fines would ordinarily produce. He had studied for his profession in America and wrote well in both Amharic and English. He did his best to stretch the narrow confines of freedom the government allowed its journalists. It was this last trait which brought him most frequently into conflict with Shaleka.

Alone among the editors, Tesfaye could manage to get stories into the papers without Shaleka's knowledge. He succeeded by being willing to work harder and longer than anyone else. He had developed a deeper understanding than Shaleka himself of the possibilities actually open to the press. A few weeks before Shaleka had discovered how sharply limited his authority over Tesfaye had become.

In the cemetery of Medhane Alem church, just beyond the university campus in Addis Ababa, a colony of lepers had made themselves a home in makeshift shanties tilting against gravestones. Tesfaye had long wanted to write about the colony. He knew the government was extremely sensitive about stories dealing with poverty, disease, and backwardness.

Most of the lepers supported themselves by descending with truncated limbs and fingerless hands to beg along the streets of the city. This, too, was an aspect of the story Tesfaye must have realized would be difficult to handle. He would have known that the photographs he intended to use would violate rules which prohibited pictures of barefoot children, much less of legless beggars.

Tesfaye's approach had been to treat the story of the colony in the cemetery as part of a two-page spread on the elimination of leprosy in Ethiopia. The lead story, fulsome in its praise, dealt with the pioneering role played by the Emperor in improving health services in general and the care of lepers in particular. Another story dealt with the impressive work done by German medical missionaries at a model farm near Harar at which six hundred lepers had become self-sufficient. A third described the work of an international leprosy research project conducted on the grounds of a sprawling leprosarium on the edge of Addis Ababa.

All of these "hallelujah" stories, as Tesfaye later described them to Shaleka, had appeared in one form or another often before. But now they were repackaged to give a respectable setting for the new story Tesfaye wanted to tell, the story of four hundred lepers living in an urban cemetery.

The story he wrote was detailed, accurate, objective. But Shaleka never would have agreed to its publication if he had learned of it in advance. But Tesfaye had saved this story for the very last. He typed it himself and personally carried it to a linotype operator he knew to be hostile to Shaleka. He did the proofreading himself, and, late one evening when he knew the major was attending a dinner at the Korean embassy, he supervised its final makeup on the composing room stone.

The story had caused considerable comment in the town. It was not the kind of material usually found in the rigidly bland official press. But except for some shouting by Shaleka, there was no protest from higher authorities. The liberal-minded minister of information even sent a note to Tesfaye praising him for the job he had done. Shaleka could do nothing but fume.

Tesfaye had used a similar technique to tell the story of the polite apartheid practiced by the Dutch at their sugar plantation at Wonji. That story, though framed by others about profits and progress, the creation of employment and the use of irrigation, had caused more trouble because several ministers had personal financial interests in the plantation. Shaleka was gleeful, but there was relatively little he could do. Civil service regulations made it all but impossible to fire a government employee. At worst he could be fined, suspended, or transferred to another job. But Shaleka knew that Tesfaye was too highly regarded for anything as drastic as removing him from his job. The Emperor or the Prime Minister could do it, but not Shaleka. He imposed a fifty dollar fine and wrote out an official reprimand. The next day the minister canceled the fine.

Tesfaye later told Shaleka he wouldn't have minded paying the fifty dollars. For the story led to improvements in the policies followed by the Dutch at the plantation. Things were changing, and Tesfaye knew he was helping. He had discovered that in recent years the ultimate authorities were reluctant to take punitive action over well-documented and objectively told stories in the papers. Trouble came when lazy journalists attacked without facts or when, no matter what the circumstances, the sanctity of the Emperor was in any way shadowed.

The relative easing of press restrictions wasn't something the government had granted. It was a victory slowly being won by Tesfaye and a few other newspapermen willing to work hard and test limits. Shaleka recognized the changes that were coming, but he also recognized that the changes would undermine his own position.

He knew he had not been chosen to supervise the press because he was an experienced journalist or a gifted administrator. He was in no sense a journalist. As an administrator, he tended to be careless. He was, however, cunning, suspicious, and deeply conservative. He could be counted on to keep young and potentially irresponsible journalists in line. But when editors like Tesfaye began to show they could be both responsible and hard working, Shaleka knew his own usefulness was reduced.

The more he began to respect Tesfaye, the more he knew he would have to cut him down. His methods were like a dark reverse image of Tesfaye's. Tesfaye as a journalist tried to test the acceptability of truth. Shaleka as an intriguer tried to test the believability of falsehood.

He might one day accuse Tesfaye of spending all his time drinking in the brothels of the city. The next day he might describe Tesfaye as a man who shuns prostitutes because he prefers to corrupt innocent young girls. To one audience he might describe Tesfaye as lazy and indifferent to work; to another, as diligent in digging up scandals to embarrass the government.

He had once told a contact in the Emperor's private cabinet that Tesfaye was working closely with the Crown Prince in a plot to force the abdication of Haile Selassie in favor of his son. He had told several people he knew were close to the Crown Prince that Tesfaye curried favor with the heir apparent only because he was a spy for the Emperor.

He had identified Tesfaye as a sympathizer with the Eritrean Liberation Front which was carrying out guerrilla warfare in the north and as secretly working with the Galla political movement, *Metcha Tuluma*, in the south. After Tesfaye accepted an invitation to visit Moscow, it had been natural for Shaleka to accuse him of being a Soviet agent. Virtually no one had been willing to believe this, which had given Shaleka his latest idea.

Tesfaye's growing friendship with the nervous American, Harry Comfort, was becoming widely known. Since most Americans were believed to be CIA agents, it was easy to assume that Tesfaye was being recruited. The fact that he had earned his master's degree in the United States seemed to Shaleka to make the story more likely. The idea had been in his mind for several weeks, but he had decided this time to put to use another lesson learned from Tesfaye. He would support his accusation with accurate details.

Tesfaye had been trying to persuade Shaleka to agree to the purchase of a tape recorder to use at press conferences and interviews. In one of their recent discussions, Tesfaye had mentioned that his American friend Doctor Comfort had recently acquired such a machine to help in his research. Also a photocopying device to reproduce library documents dealing with Ethiopian culture. Shaleka was sure the American must also own several cameras. Tape recorder. Photocopier. Camera. All the equipment of a spy. He knew that Tesfaye and Doctor Comfort were traveling to Kulubi together.

With all their equipment, he imagined himself saying. At Kulubi I saw with my own eyes . . . He hadn't yet formulated the rest of the sentence. But he was sure something would occur to him. I saw Tesfaye and this American agent. . . .

Tesfaye used the phrase "doing your homework" for his method of building up a file of information to detail a story. "When you do your homework," he had said after the appearance of the story on the lepers, "you don't have to worry about getting into trouble."

As the Land Rover he was being driven in made its way through the Chercher Mountains, Shaleka grinned and said to himself, Yes, this will be a good trip. We will do our homework, sell our pamphlets, and surprise Tiruwork. She'll be pleased to see me.

As they climbed deeper into the mountains, Tesfaye tensed with anticipation. He was home. Two decades before he had been a child growing up on the slopes of these hills. He was born the year the country had been liberated from the Italians, but his earliest memories were not of peace but of troubles.

During the war his father had led a guerrilla band that harassed the invaders for five long years. The British forces which fought their way up into the highlands from the deserts of Somaliland had named his father governor of this mountain district. But soon after the Emperor's return to power the hero of the resistance had been arrested and sentenced to the first of a series of imprisonments and exiles.

The old man and his legend had cast a powerful influence over Tesfaye's life. But the influence of the hills he had grown up among had been even greater. From the hills had grown his love of freedom and his love of the land and its people.

He learned nothing of love from his father, for his father had demanded fear and respect. Like most Ethiopian fathers of his generation, his rule was the rule of violence. But the old man was also passionately dedicated to an iron discipline of work, and in this he was unique.

Tesfaye remembered how they had often clashed. It had been hard to bear the sudden return of discipline whenever the old man was freed from prison or exile. For Tesfaye, his father's imprisonments had meant his own freedom in the lush hills of the Chercher Mountains and the fertile Galetta Valley beyond. The Chercher hills were not unlike the Shoan highlands around Addis Ababa. His adolescence at the Haile Selassie Secondary School at Kotebe and at the University College in the city had therefore been an echo of his childhood. He had grown up attuned to the cycles of the seasons and the feasts of the church. And now, though a man of the city contemptuous of the church, he was still tied by the rhythms of Ethiopian time and ritual.

He considered the European calendar and system of telling time meaningless. There was nothing new to hail on January 1 when most of the world which followed the Western calendar was locked in midwinter. What was true of the calendar was equally true of the clock. How could a new day begin in the dark middle of the night?

In Ethiopia the reckoning of the hours of the new day began at dawn. This close to the equator, an almost constant twelve hours of daylight prevailed the year round. What Europeans called seven A.M., the first full hour of sunshine, was accurately called one o'clock by Ethiopians. When the sun set, at six P.M. by European reckoning, Ethiopians said twelve o'clock, the last hour of the day.

Tesfaye argued that if Europeans were sensible about their

calendar, the new year would be marked at the first day of spring in April. Spring in Europe and America was the real time of beginning. In Ethiopia the equivalent season came when the long rains ended in mid-September. The Ethiopian new year appropriately fell when the first Maskal daisies rose golden yellow in the fields to meet the sun reappearing after months of rain clouds.

The Ethiopian calendar, like the Hebrew, maintained a respect for the seasons and the land that gave it birth. In both Israel and Ethiopia, the year began when it should, in mid-September when there was a new growth in the land and the spirits of the people.

For Tesfaye each *Maskaram*, the first month of the new year, brought a renewal of the meaning of his name—Tesfaye, my hope. It was a time of hope for the country and its people. The words were clichés he dutifully wrote each year in his New Year editorial, but he wanted the clichés to come true.

Each year, like a trap, hope flowered with the *maskal* daisies, splashing the green fields with sprays of gold while the cool breeze danced the petals, and grasses bowed in the brilliant sunshine. The *kosso* trees burnt into bloom with their pendulous red torches, and pale patches of vervain gave a purple, mystical touch to distant hillsides. Groves of tall, slender eucalyptus stood sentinel everywhere, erect as soldiers when the blue air was calm, sweeping across the sky like feather dusters on long poles when clouds gathered and the wind whistled its commands.

On New Year's Eve the three main theatres of Addis Ababa would be jammed with musicians and music lovers. Each year hundreds of new songs were introduced by scores of composers in marathon programs that lasted through the night. Tesfaye always went. This year he had taken Harry, and Harry, despite the din, had fallen asleep.

Tesfaye himself was often bored by the parade of songs but always hoped for that special moment when out of all the tired variations on old themes something truly new would sound out. When it came—a song so gay it made you want to stand up and dance or so moving that you would sit there and weep—Tesfaye felt the way he did on those special days when he was able to find and print in his paper a story truly new and significant.

Such stories did come, another form of the trap of hope sprung each new year amid the boundless fields of brief golden flowers and among the dreams of the composers of all the new songs. When it happened, Tesfaye could believe again in clichés coming true and wonder if this year—maybe this year—he could succeed in turning his government gazette into a real newspaper.

The new songs of the city meant hope, but in the countryside on New Year's Eve it was old songs that were sung. Children and *azmaris* would improvise but their inventions would be only new couplets for old songs. In each tiny village or in each compound of larger communities, small bonfires of reeds and tree branches would be lit and families would gather to sing and dance around them. There would be more singing the next day when groups of children would go from house to house begging for bread or money and presenting in exchange gifts of grass and flowers called *inkwutatash*, a name also given to the new year itself. And the couplets sung by the begging children would also be fit into the framework of traditional songs.

Unlike Addis, the countryside was not in love with the new. So much that was new in his country, Tesfaye realized, was shoddy. Poor imitations of the worst that Western civilization had to offer. In his student days, he used to scorn the reactionary older generation that turned its back on all change. Now, he sometimes thought the conservative peasants were right in their rejection of the foreign ways of Addis Ababa. But he knew it didn't require Western influence to spoil the old traditions.

Maskal proved the point. Both in the countryside and in Addis the feast of fire and flowers stirred even deeper feelings of renewal than did the day marked on the Ethiopian calendar as the first of the year. A fortnight after New Year, Maskal, and its eve, when giant bonfires were lit, honored the pious legend of the finding of the true cross. But Tesfaye recognized in the festival what he was sure was a far older pagan ritual marking the change of seasons.

He had always loved the wild beauty of the bonfires set at sunset, the torches carried by the young men, and the chanting and dancing of the people. But in recent years, even the lighting of the *demera*, the towering forty-meter bonfire in the capital's Maskal Square, was beginning to lose its appeal. Each year it became less a religious spectacle than a military parade.

Tesfaye would have liked to retreat to the countryside for such holidays, but his work chained him to the city. The Emperor was a ritual performer at such public ceremonies, which made them always major news for the government media. On Maskal Eve the old man himself would put the torch to the *demera* in Addis Ababa. Throughout the empire similar ceremonies would be held in every community where there were Christians.

Unlike the fires of New Year's Eve and other feasts which were primarily family affairs, the Maskal fire was communal. Tesfaye would have preferred to spend the eve in some unspoiled place like his father's village. As the great man of the community, it would be his father who would light the *demera*. All afternoon the giant pyramid would have grown as men and boys from the entire region came to add their long poles topped with bunches of Maskal daisies to the basic wood frame built by laborers from his father's farm.

Just at the moment Haile Selassie was lighting the bonfire in Addis Ababa, his boyhood friend would be lighting the *demera* in the village of Mota. In provincial village and capital city, bonfires and sunsets would compete. Surely, mused Tesfaye, at the moment his father must think of his old friend the Emperor performing the identical ritual hundreds of kilometers away. He wondered if the Emperor ever thought of his father.

The bonfires would be blessed by priests with incense and cross and ceremonially circled counterclockwise three times.

In the village young men with flaming *chibos* would race from hillside and huts to hurl fresh flames into the fire. "*Iyoha Ababaie Maskaram Tebaie*" and other Maskal songs would be chanted by everyone.

In the capital only those participating in the parade or graced with special passes would be allowed near the *demera*. The great crowds of people would be beaten back with police batons. Traffic would have been forbidden in the entire area since early afternoon. Wide streets radiating from the square would be white rivers of people dressed in the national costume. But the communal spirit of the village would be formalized here into a spectacle with gaudy floats. On one float the drugged lion Mekuria would be posed. Prodded on cue the aging lion would bow as the float he rode on passed the reviewing stand where the Emperor sat enthroned. The bow always drew a smile from the Emperor and applause from his courtiers. Military bands would play and endless columns of troops, punctuated by an occasional sports club or church society, would march by.

Once, as he was covering the event, notebook in hand,

Tesfaye heard an old man behind him in the crowd murmur, "At Maskal the priests used to carry the cross. But now *Janhoy* has the soldiers carry the torch."

Tesfaye could not explain his sadness. He believed Ethiopia's best hope for progress after the Emperor died would stem from the leadership of younger, hopefully liberal military leaders. He knew the church represented a backward aspect of Ethiopian society. He knew the old peasants and patriots, including the educated among them like his father, clung to the feudal past.

He knew all this and yet, as he saw the signs of the future in the torchbearing troops marching past the Maskal bonfire, he shared the unhappiness, even the bitterness of the murmuring old man behind him.

The peasants Tesfaye had grown up among lived in a world of locked circles. Their churches and the mud and straw *tukuls* in which they lived within compounds of thornbush were circles within circles. Priests and the pious turned three circles around octagonal churches. Within each church there was an outer circle open to all; then, an inner circle for communicants; finally, the inmost circle, the holy of holies which only the priests could enter.

The calendar ticked like a cyclical clock of the seasons. In the peasants' open air courts and in military camps, the circle gave shape to events. At festivals dancers leapt and strutted in circular patterns within circles of clapping onlookers. Tesfaye wondered if the circles could ever be broken.

As Harry drove in silence through the mountains, red aloes flamed from rocky crevices. Crops winnowed in the wind left mounds of brilliant yellow chaff among the deeper gold of the stubble fields. Slender eucalyptus with blue-tipped leaves bowed to the wind. Young boys hardly bigger than the goats and sheep they herded piped an eerie music on flutes made from bamboo cane. At times the roar of the car's motor was the only note of change in a landscape of Biblical sounds and ancient silence.

There were stretches of highway where the road was a narrow natural bridge across the tip of the hills. Great sprawling valleys stretched endlessly away on either side, lushly green to their right where chains of rivers flowed south, on their left fading to dun where bush gave way to scrub and scrub burned into desert.

On distant hillsides Tesfaye could see smoldering heaps of plowed and gathered turf. Seeing these new fields being prepared, a process begun earlier here than in the Shoan highlands around

Addis, made Tesfaye realize they were drawing nearer to his father's land. At a descending curve in the road, he noticed the surface change from brown crushed stone to a gravel almost white. After another curve he was able to see the road stretch out before him in a long, white downward spiral to the narrow bowl that cupped his father's village and farm. A dozen or more cars, heading toward Kulubi, dotted the road. The tin roofs of the village shimmered in the sunlight. Beyond them, the white ribbon of the road wound its way back up into the hills.

Mota, he thought to himself. He didn't want to say it aloud. He didn't want to speak. He didn't want Harry's questions walking on his thoughts. Mota. And my father.

Dejazmatch Tessema Bekele had been educated in czarist Russia. His son, Tesfaye, belonged to the second of three generations of children the old man had sired. The Dejazmatch, as a boy of twelve, had fought in 1896 by his father's side in the massacre of the Italian colonial army at Adwa. He was in his fifties when he again fought against the Italians, first as Haile Selassie's minister of war, then leading guerrilla bands throughout the five-year occupation that ended in 1941.

The old warrior now tended his farm with a seldom-used whip in one hand, a heavy staff in the other, and an ancient Colt revolver holstered to his hip. He was widely respected and feared by many. There were a few, like Tesfaye, who would have been willing to love him. If his father would have allowed love. Tesfaye was fond of taking people to meet the famous old man. His father was always a gracious host, and, like most legendary figures, expert at spinning stories out of his own fabulous past.

For Harry this would be a second visit to the farm. To him the old man represented all that was magic and noble in Ethiopia. Foreigners, even more than Ethiopians, were always impressed when they met the Dejazmatch.

His title, despite its ancient military connotation of "general that leads out of the king's gate," had been granted by the Emperor long ago, not for his contributions on the field of battle, but for his work in the secret councils of government. The Emperor since had had cause to regret the title he'd conferred on his old friend whose name, Tessema Bekele, meant "he is heard, he avenged." Over the years since the Italian invasion, the Emperor often had occasion to consider the name too apt by far.

"This is it," said Harry, coming down heavily on the brake as they entered the village. "Isn't this it?"

Tesfaye, wrapped in his own thoughts, grunted.

"Where do we turn? Where's the turnoff?"

"Ai, Harry." Tesfaye stirred himself. "Before we turn perhaps we should find the station wagon."

"Huh? What station wagon?"

"The one your wife is in."

"Oh. I'd forgot. I guess you're right. I was thinking about your father."

"So was I."

"I don't see them."

Tesfaye assumed that by "them" Harry meant Julie and Baria. "Straight ahead," he said. But Harry's mind had jumped again.

"Hey, isn't this where you turn? They must have turned off."

"They don't know the turnoff," said Tesfaye.

"Say, that's right. Baria's never met your father, has he?"

"Unlike you, my dear Harry, Baria has never had that particular privilege. But there's his car. Up ahead by the police station."

Harry recognized the black shape of the three Amharic letters on the sign. The same combination was used for the license plates on police cars. He pulled up alongside the station wagon.

"Hey," he yelled, leaning across Tesfaye. "You missed the turn."

Baria smiled at him blankly. Julie turned away. The baby, nestled in an improvised bed among the camping equipment in the back, was asleep.

"We have to go back aways. Follow me." Harry attempted to back the Volkswagen up, veering erratically from one side of the road to another. He had zigzagged only a short distance before getting tangled in oncoming traffic. The Klaxon of a bus howled like a hyena, leading a barking chorus of horns.

"Oh God," said Harry.

A wildly gesturing police captain came running out of the tin-roofed station. It took several minutes before Tesfaye's patient explanations, his repeated mentions of his father's name, and the unspoken authority of Harry's white face calmed the policeman. At Tesfaye's urging, the officer held back the other traffic long enough for Harry to sweat the Volkswagen through a U-turn. Baria had meanwhile swung the station wagon around.

Flushed with exertion and embarrassment, Harry finally managed to turn his car up into the rough rock road that led into the heart of the village. A curious, laughing crowd had gathered. Cries of *faranj, faranj* followed them up the narrow road between shops and bars. They veered left, climbed past a giant acacia the base of which was gardened with carefully placed rocks, then headed down another narrow street. At its foot, they found a cluster of workmen repairing a bridge over a shallow fast-running stream.

"Oh, no," said Harry. "The bridge is out."

"I'm glad you noticed," said Tesfaye.

He climbed from the car. The workmen were evasive. The bridge had become broken, they told him. How? Well, it had become broken. A flood? Well, yes, perhaps a flood. The ground showed no sign of recent rain. Well, no but perhaps in the hills above there had been rain and the water rushing down from the hills to the valley had flooded the stream. Such things had been known to happen. Or maybe old age. In any event, the bridge had become broken.

My language, thought Tesfaye. The bridge became broken. I got late for lunch. The examination failed me. Never I failed the examination. Grammarians must have a name for it. The conditional reflexive passive. Something. My money got spent. Not that I spent it.

Harry came up beside him.

"They say it may become repaired," Tesfaye told him. "Maybe by this evening. Perhaps tomorrow morning. Or after tomorrow, maybe."

Baria pulled the station wagon up behind Harry's car and joined them.

"What happened?"

"The bridge got broken," said Tesfaye in Amharic. The phrase sounded awkward in English. In his own language it was all too natural.

"I see," said Baria. He turned to Harry. "Perhaps it's just as well. Your wife, uh, Julie, says she can't be introduced anyway. In her condition. The baby, uh, fouled her."

"Oh." Harry turned back to the station wagon.

"Perhaps," said Baria in Amharic, "your father suspected you were coming. And bringing friends. And he got the bridge broken."

"Not a'tall. My father's famed for his hospitality. In any event, the stream can get crossed. It's shallow. And see? There are rocks. We can step from rock to rock and hold on to what's left of bridge."

"And then?" said Baria.

"Then walk up to the farm. See the house set back in the trees? It isn't far."

"It isn't near. And the lady?"

"How foul is she?"

Baria shrugged. "No more than usual. And there is that wet object, her child."

Tesfaye squeezed his arm. "The slave is strong. He can cart the child."

"Thank you, my master." He bowed. "But I'd rather court the lady."

"I'm sure."

They went back to the station wagon and joined forces with Harry to persuade Julie to join them. She finally agreed. The baby was changed and wrapped in a dry blanket. Baria carried him. Workmen plunged shin-deep into the stream, supporting the visitors as they stepped gingerly from rock to rock. The crossing wasn't difficult. The man who seemed to be in charge of the bridge repairs led them up the rutted dirt road to the farmstead. In his absence, all work on the bridge stopped.

There was a gentle breeze, and the climb wasn't steep. But the equatorial sun beat down directly on the unshaded path. Sweat broke out as they stumbled along. Their guide urged them to walk to the left of the road.

"All those ruts the trucks and tractors make during the rains. It's dangerous to walk in the road," he said to Tesfaye. "Walk over here at the edge of the field. It's safer."

Halfway up, Harry insisted on taking the baby. Baria did not object. Julie watched the exchange, then moved closer to Harry and took his elbow.

"I guess you'll have to support us both."

"Sure," said Harry. "Don't I always?"

"Yes," said Julie. "I guess you do."

A cluster of buildings made up the farmstead. There were storage sheds, living quarters, privy, cookhouse. It was hard to tell them apart. The roofs were thatched in the old style. The walls were mud, covered with skins of scores of animals: warthogs, bushpigs, hyenas, baboons, cheetahs, various gazelles.

"If we go out on the farm," said Tesfaye, "be careful where you step. There are traps all over."

"How cruel," said Julie.

"My father hates animals."

"But why?"

"He says he's a farmer and animals ruin crops. He won't have any. Not even chickens. He barters for his meat and eggs in the village."

"Or has his slaves supply him," said Baria.

Tesfaye shook his head. "He has no tenant farmers. He doesn't believe in that either. You'll see."

Questions to the house servants determined that Dejazmatch Tessema was somewhere in the fields. Several of the servants went off in different directions to locate him. More quickly than they expected, the man they'd met at the bridge reappeared at the crest of a low knoll and called out. He waved to them to follow.

"*Inn hid*," said Tesfaye. "He's off this way somewhere."

They hadn't far to go. In the shade of a giant cedar, the old man was stretched out on a dried animal skin. Sadly, as they approached, Tesfaye recognized the skin to be that of a kudu. *Et tu, abate?*

The Dejazmatch was propped on an elbow, watching the work of a dozen laborers breaking a small patch of ground with crude sticks. The old man wore thick boots, dirt brown jodhpurs, a shirt of indeterminate color, a coarse wool jacket, and a floppy, wide-brimmed hat. There was an enormous six-shooter in a cowboy-style holster on his hip. He didn't try to stand as they approached.

Tesfaye went to him, fell to his knees, kissed the mud-caked boots and said in Amharic, "Ababa. Father."

"Which one is that?" said the old man. "Tesfaye? Bringing foreigners as usual?" He smiled, but when he spoke again there was irritation in his voice. "You surprise me. I have much work today."

"My father having much work doesn't surprise me."

A smile again parted the thin, cracked lips. His teeth were yellow.

"Well, come sit by me. Come all and sit by me. Getting up is more of a struggle than war." There was a flat-topped rock nearby. He inclined his felt hat toward it. "For the lady."

"She's honored," said Baria. "It's almost a throne."

The Dejazmatch eyed him narrowly. His eyes, rheumed with age, had a bluish cast. His skin, despite long hours in the fields, was fairer than his son's.

Julie perched unhappily on the rock. Harry, still holding the baby, lowered himself stiffly to the ground. Baria knelt. Tesfaye squatted on his heels.

"So. What brings you our way this time?"

"Kulubi," said Tesfaye.

"Again?"

Tesfaye laughed. "Yes, again." He rocked on his heels. His hands were clasped between his thighs.

"What has old Saint Fraud of Kulubi ever done for you?"

"Didn't he defeat the Italians?" said Tesfaye.

"Hah," snorted the old man. "Him and the little king."

Instinctively, Baria looked around. He wondered which of the laborers worked for security.

"Gabriel with his holy sword and the other with his diplomacy," said the old man. "I know all about that."

"And the people with their fasting." Tesfaye wasn't bothering to translate. The references were too subtle for Harry and Julie anyway. It was better just to enjoy.

"And the priests with their fasting," said the old man. "They won the war, too. Some of us were too busy fighting to bother much with fasting. Some of us did not fast or go away for five year vacations over the waves instead of staying to fight the war." He nodded toward Harry and Julie. "Do they know about this?"

"You don't have to worry," said Tesfaye. "Talk freely. They're friends."

"Hah. I didn't worry then. I don't have time left to start worrying now."

Father and son shared a smile.

"Anyway," said Tesfaye. "Harry has heard. He was here last year. You remember Doctor Comfort."

"Which one is he?"

"Him," said Tesfaye, nodding.

"How could I remember? At my age . . . my eyes." He shook his head. "And anyway, you bring so many foreigners, and they all look alike. The only one I remember is that Russian."

"Yes. You liked him," said Tesfaye.

"He spoke Russian. Does this one speak Russian?"

"He's American."

"Then he doesn't speak anything. They don't even speak English properly. Not that my own English is much. Tell him I've never been in his country."

Tesfaye laughed. "I told him that last year." He switched to English. "Harry, you remember my father. Harry, Doctor Comfort. And Mrs. Comfort. My father, Dejazmatch Tessema."

Julie bowed. The old man returned the gesture.

"Mrs. Comfort," he said. "That means she's this one's wife?"

"His wife," said Tesfaye. "And this is Baria Medhane Alem."

"Baria? He's well named."

Baria's spine tensed but did not straighten. His fists were clenched.

"Don't mind me," said the Dejazmatch. "I'm an old man. All Ethiopians are one to me, *ante baria*." He said it with a smile. You slave. Baria was still tense. "Ai," said the old man. "Relax. Enjoy." He winked at Baria. "If we can't laugh and call each other slave, who can?"

"My lord," said Baria. "If I were to address yourself as slave . . ."

"I should have to say you called me by my rightful name. We are all slaves in Ethiopia. Shankila, Baria, Amhara, Galla, Guarage, Tigre, Danakil, Somali. All. God bless the little king. Oh, don't worry. He knows what I think. We have all come through Asba Tafari." He punned on the name of the nearby village where he'd once been governor. Tafari was the Emperor's given name; *asba* in Ge'ez meant "the usage." "Tafari uses what I think," said the old man. He glanced up into the leaves of the cedar.

"Well," he said, "I see the sun is high. You've managed to come just at lunchtime. You'll be wanting to eat."

"No, no," said Tesfaye. "Just to talk. We have provisions in our cars."

"Well, of course." He looked to the man who'd been directing work at the stream. "And is the bridge finished?"

"I had to leave the work, my lord. To accompany my lord's guests."

"Yes, I know. Well . . ." He pushed himself up to a sitting position. He reached behind him for the long, thong-handled whip made from the stretched testicles of a slaughtered bull. He handed the whip to the headman. "Take this. And see that the work here gets done. All must be finished by dark. All. The bridge, too."

"Yes, my lord. I know."

"Then do what you know." He glanced at Tesfaye. "We have guests coming tomorrow. Expected ones. Not like you. And now . . ."

He reached for his staff. The others stood. He pulled the staff closer to him and wedged one end into the ground. Slowly, painfully, he began to push himself up. None of the workers moved to help him. Harry took a sudden step forward, but Tesfaye put a restraining hand on his arm.

The old man's ascent was a slow, majestic struggle. As he rose, his legs seemed dwarfed by the enormous torso. All his weight was on the thick walking stick. The muscles of his arms and shoulders strained against the wool jacket. Halfway up, his legs still splayed out, he seemed to pause. Harry thought he would collapse. But again the thick, knotted hands tightened on the staff, and the old man forced himself up and dragged his legs under him.

Still bent, his weight on the staff, he took a shaky step. Another. He caught his balance. And straightened. He stood erect. At his full height, he was not much over five feet tall. His massive shoulders seemed nearly as wide. The round, wide-brimmed, flat-topped hat shaded his fair face. Julie looked into his bluish eyes.

"My god," she whispered to Harry. "He looks like a Russian."

Tesfaye turned to her. "He is a Russian," he said softly. "Come. You'll see."

The old man led the way. Once in motion, he moved with remarkable speed and sureness. Unused to walking even on city streets, the others were hard pressed to keep pace with him over the rough, unfamiliar ground. He paused occasionally to let them catch up so he could point out favored projects: an experimental patch of strawberries, a crop never before grown in the Cherchers; strips where new varieties of wheat were being tried; the grove in which he had grown Ethiopia's first avocados.

"And in this lot we are trying to find ways to improve our *teff*." Tesfaye was translating for him now. "The *teff* in this region is poor which means that for your lunch I can offer you but poor *injera*. I had these seedlings brought from Assela where the *teff* is good and the Swedes are teaching our people to grow it even better.

"Incredible." The old man shook his head. "Swedes teaching Ethiopians to grow better *teff* when *teff* is a crop that grows nowhere else in the world. *Teff*, the staple of our diet, and foreigners have to teach us how to grow it better. Incredible country. Tell your friend the Americans should do more the kind of work the Swedes do."

Tesfaye translated.

"I agree. I agree," said Harry.

"But the Swedes," said Tesfaye to his father, "may stop their aid to us."

"So I've heard," said the Dejazmatch. "Because of land reform."

"That," said Tesfaye, "and the Swedish press has been attacking us because of the killing of civilians by our soldiers in Eritrea."

"It's all very sad," said his father. "Our little king makes speeches about land reform and quietly makes sure there is no land reform. But never mind. We will change all that.

"Back up there and over in that field where you found me and elsewhere we're planting some new crops specially for our guests who are coming tomorrow."

"If they're for guests coming tomorrow," said Tesfaye, "they must be crops that mature very fast."

"Mmm," said the old man. "They give fruit in a flash. You'll hear about it in time. No more of that for now. *Allons, mes amis*. At my age, I hate to be late for a meal."

Lunch was vast. *Kitfo*, a chopped spiced raw meat which Harry likened to beef tartar, came first, served with a sour pot cheese made from yogurt. The servants then brought in *doro wat*, a chicken stew with whole boiled eggs in a sauce spiced with flaming *berberie* peppers; then a milder lamb *wat* called *allitcha;* then strips of beef and tripe with peppers and cooked greens.

The Dejazmatch was an aggressive host. He insisted his visitors eat heavily and rolled up neat morsels of *wat* in the dark, sour *injera* and fed his foreign guests with his own hands. There was no alcohol of any kind, not even beer. The Dejazmatch drank Coca-Cola. The others took Babile, a mineral water from Harar.

Harry and Julie swatted ineffectively at the flies that buzzed around their heads as they ate. Tesfaye and Baria shrugged the flies off. The old man ignored them.

In the shadows of the house, his eyes seemed less blue than gray. His hair and beard were sparse and white. The head, even on the enormous shoulders and thick neck, gave an impression of leonine mass. In the field, with his whip at hand, he looked very much the Russian kulak in the era before the serfs had been freed. Here, among his books and papers, the man of intellect and culture emerged.

They ate at a rough wooden table, sitting on benches in a multipurpose room. The whitewashed walls were lined with hand-hewn bookshelves. More than half the volumes were in Russian with a scattering of French, Italian, and Amharic. There was an English dictionary but, Harry noticed, even the Shakespeare was Pushkin's translation.

"Yes," said the old man through Tesfaye's translation, "Pushkin, like myself, was a Russian with Ethiopian blood. So my Shakespeare is Pushkin."

He was as courtly a host as he was generous. He kept the conversation going during the meal, eating relatively little himself.

"Surely you aren't really Russian," said Julie.

He seemed to understand without help from his son but answered in Amharic.

"But I am. With some Ethiopian blood. My mother, for example, was Ethiopian. My father was Ethiopian. But I am Russian. At least between the ears, where it doesn't show."

Except for beverages, the meal he served was traditional. When it was done, the Dejazmatch bent tradition again by serving tea and avocado flavored with lemon. Tesfaye had already warned them that his father would not tolerate coffee, alcohol, or tobacco.

The Dejazmatch recently had buried his third wife, but, as his house showed, he had always lived as a bachelor, accepting a succession of wives and children only on the edges of his private world. As a servant cleared the table, the old man thumped it with his powerful right hand.

"Yes," he said, "truly this board is my house. Not these walls or the roof. Just this board. Here, I eat. I sit here to read. And here I do my writing."

Baria expressed surprise.

"Oh yes," said the old man. "I still write. The bottom drawer of that old chest in the corner is my only publisher. For now. Some day we will be free. But for now my publisher sits there in the corner."

"What kinds of things is he writing?" asked Harry. Tesfaye translated the question.

"My books," said the old man. "I write in Amharic, you know, because I must if I want our people one day to read them.

But it's hard for me. It's a nice language for playing, our Amharic, but it is not a serious language. A good language for poetry and making love. But making poetry and love are not serious work."

Baria and Tesfaye laughed. Harry and Julie were puzzled when they were given the translation.

"Russian is my real language. I lived there a dozen years. From the time I was a small boy. Some of what I write even now I think in Russian and then—it is almost like translating for me to do it into Amharic. Whenever I have a serious problem, I think in Russian. I even dream in Russian. It's a language for me. But our Amharic, it's a language for women and priests."

Tesfaye had to rush to keep up with his translation.

"If it's a language for women and priests," said Julie, "Harry and I should learn it."

"Don't bother," said the old man. "No one needs it. Even in Ethiopia not even half the people speak Amharic. It has its own alphabet. No other African language does. But since hardly any of our people know how to read, what good is an alphabet? Especially an alphabet with more than two hundred letters. No. All you can do with our language is use it for a small elite to play games.

"In Amharic everything means itself and its opposite. How can you have mathematics or physics or even serious politics in a language that can't be precise? We have no politics in Ethiopia. Only intrigue. Our only mathematics is cheating. Science, we don't even know what it means. We think science is a branch of religion and our religion, like your Kulubi, is only superstition.

"On radio you have what you call a science program. Students write in and ask questions. 'How does a wheel turn?' 'God's holy will turns it,' comes the answer.

" 'How did the Americans put a man on the moon?' Our science expert on radio Ethiopia answers, 'They didn't, because it says in some holy book that God will not let man walk on the face of the moon.'

"That's Radio Ethiopia. Educating the people. That's what they give out for science at your Ministry of Vomit."

Tesfaye had to pause in his rapid translation to explain his father's pun. The word for information and the word for vomit in Amharic differ only in the letter *k*. The word for information is spelled with a guttural, explosive *k*. The almost identical word for vomit—*mastawokya*—is spelled with a soft *k*.

The old man grunted. "How can you communicate in a

language where the only difference between information and vomit is a catch in the throat? And that's only one example. There are thousands. You can choke on such a language, but to communicate is not possible. As a result my well-educated son here works for a ministry that gives the people puke instead of facts. Our only real means of mass communication is rumor and gossip. Radio is a joke. Our newspapers are rags for wiping up vomit. No matter what poor hope my poor son here may have for making them better."

Tesfaye laughed but didn't bother to explain his father's pun on his name—Tesfaye, my hope. To his father he added a joke of his own.

"And our news agency," he said. "We call it *y-Etiopia ware minch.* Ethiopia's source of rumor."

"Precisely," said his father. "We don't know the difference between news and rumor. Because our language gives us only one word for both. So what difference does it make which one we get?

"Listen," he said, rubbing the rough table with the palm of his hand. "Even if we try to talk about something simple like this table, we have to use a Greek word—*terapaiza*—to describe it. Because we don't have a table of our own. Can we discuss philosophy in such a language?"

"We could," said Tesfaye. "Philosophy is subtle. So is Amharic."

"Oh yes. It is a subtle language. Complex in its grammar. But try to discuss deeply and you get tongue-tied. In Amharic we can be sophists, my son, but that's the end of our philosophy. How many foreign words do I have to shove into Amharic even for a simple talk like this? Suppose we tried to have a really serious talk? What could we do? Speak French?"

"Perhaps Ge'ez," said Tesfaye. "I have a friend who says if we went back to our ancient language we could find ways to develop a language of science. Like the Israelis have done with Hebrew."

"Don't be foolish. I can't talk about Hebrew, but I grew up with Ge'ez. Before the Russians got me, my whole education was in priests' schools where they taught you nothing but Ge'ez. You can't make science out of a language of priests."

"What about Latin? That's a church language, too," said Tesfaye. "And for centuries it was the only language of science—and medicine and law as well."

"You're right," said the old man. "And look at the condition science was in back in those dark ages. Mystery and mumbo jumbo was your science then. The kind of science you get on Radio Addis Ababa now. In Amharic."

"Newton wrote in Latin."

"And we had to wait until Einstein came along, writing in German, to show us where poor Newton went wrong with his Latin. As for medicine and law . . . Surely you don't think lawyers are scientists or philosophers. They're cheats, and your priests' language I agree is good for cheating. And doctors, at best they dispense the drugs that real scientists invent. They use their Latin to fool the rest of us into thinking what they're doing is learned and difficult. The *dabtaras* in our church, our own witch doctors, use Ge'ez the way your foreign doctors use Latin. That's not science. It's a joke. Like the jokes we tell in Amharic."

"But, Father," said Tesfaye, "you remember when my friend Galakhov, the Russian, came here to visit you. He said Russian, too, is a language of puns and ambiguous proverbs."

The old man nodded his great head. His hands were clasped on the table before him.

"He said it, and he spoke nice Russian your friend. But in my day it was different. The Russians were borrowing many words from German and French to straighten themselves out. The same way we have to borrow from other languages now. Remember, the Russians had been a primitive people like us, but even then they had already spent a century or so learning from the rest of Europe. The great writers of those days weren't writing *pure* Russian. They were writing good Russian. Tolstoy went a bit off in his old age, getting mushy and mystical like us. But read *War and Peace*. Read *Anna Karenina*. Read Chekhov, Dostoevski, Turgenev, or our cousin Pushkin. Read the great newspapers and journals of those days. There were hundreds of them. Hundreds. And there was no doubt what they meant. Even though they had to get by censors then, too, same as we do now."

Tesfaye tried to catch Harry and Julie up on what his father had been saying.

"But the Russians, the Russians today have censors, too," said Harry.

As Tesfaye translated, a vague expression fell over the old man's face.

"What was it? There was something I wanted to tell you. I forget. It may come."

Tesfaye was worried they had tired him too much. Watching the old man struggle to collect his thoughts was for Tesfaye like watching him struggle to get to his feet, raising himself by brute strength in the field.

"Well, if I do forget some things there is still much more I can tell you. No matter how much I forget, I can still tell you more than you know."

He's almost on his feet, thought Tesfaye. He tried to help.

"When did you go to Russia? What year was it when you went to Russia?"

"Never mind. I can do. I remember what I was going to say. I was going to say that now, today, the Russians seem to be going backwards. The Russian language, I mean. When he was here, your friend, what was his name?"

"Galakhov," said Tesfaye.

"Yes, Galakhov. When he was here I asked him to send me some things to read. New things. He said he would, and, unlike an Ethiopian, he did what he said he was going to do. He sent me books, newspapers, magazines. Bad. They were bad. Their *Truth* is vomit. Like ours. Their *Pravda* is like our puke. Empty words. Government lies. The Russian you read in the things they publish today is not Russian. It's a government language. All government languages are the same. Bureaucratese. Vomit."

The fatigue, the vague expression were gone from his face. His conversation is like his walking, thought Tesfaye. Once he's underway, it's hard to keep up.

"When I read my Turgenev, when I read *Anna Karenina*, I'm not reading Russia a hundred years ago, I'm reading Ethiopia today. That makes us only about a century behind the Russians. That's what I wanted to say. And look where the Russians are now. There's hope for us yet. We may catch up."

"My Lord," said Baria, "have you read Haddis Alemayehu's book, *Fikr Iske Makabir?*"

The novel he referred to, *Love Until Death*, had become enormously popular. It had been written by a high government official and somehow, despite its critical depiction of social conditions, it had passed the censorship.

"Yes," said the Dejazmatch. "I read it. Not bad. He even tries to clean up our poor language. But no. The book is romantic, old fashioned in the worst way. Full of coincidence and the heavy hand of fate. Still, it's better than the one my son wrote. Not this son. That other. What's his name?"

"Getachew," said Tesfaye.

"Yes, Getachew. What's he minister of now?"

"They made him a senator," said Tesfaye.

"Ah, yes. A senator. Write a book and sooner or later the little king makes you a senator. Ha. People used to say I wrote that book myself."

"They say it still."

"Perhaps. But it isn't true. It is my story, but my son wrote it. I used to feel sad that people thought I could write so badly. Only my son would write that badly. He doesn't have me going to Russia, but only to France. As he did for his education. I went to France, but that was later. For the rest it's my story, but he left out the best part. He left out Russia.

"You asked me, you see, I remember, awhile ago you asked me when it was I went to Russia. Well, it was after we beat the Italians at Adwa. Someone told Emperor Menelik what a good little soldier I was fighting beside my father. Ras Makonnen was there, too, our little king's father. He was a great soldier, Ras Makonnen. Our little king, Tafari Makonnen, he was only a baby then, four or five years old. I wasn't much more myself. If he was four, I was twelve. They said I killed twenty Italians. I don't know. I wasn't counting. Anyway, I killed a lot more when the Italians came back and our little king ran. But I'll tell you about that later. You were asking about Russia.

"Well, we beat the Italians in 1889 . . ."

"Our calendar," said Tesfaye. He turned to Harry. "That would be 1896."

"It was a year later I went to Russia. There was a Russian, Count Rostov, who was Menelik's private physician. It was his family that took me to Russia. Menelik told them I was such a good little soldier he wanted me to go to military school in Russia. Well, I went. It was still the time of the czars. I saw great things, great changes in Russia. Even greater changes came later. But that's another story.

"For three years I lived in St. Petersburg with the Rostovs. I studied with tutors, concentrating on Russian. At sixteen I entered military school near Moscow. I was in the military school till I was what? Twenty-five. When I was finished I had a commission in the

Imperial Russian Army. But I wanted to come home. I had almost forgotten Ethiopia, but I wanted to come home to help my country.

"Well, I came home, but I didn't stay long. Oh, I was quite a favorite at court at first. They all made a big fuss over me.

"But then, well, Menelik, at least he understood. He was a modern man, but he was beginning to decline by then. The courtiers ran the court, and no one ran the country. They started to ask me questions. When would I build a munitions factory? How did you go about making cannons? I told them I knew nothing about making cannons or munitions factories. Then what had I studied? I had studied artillery. Then I must have learned how to make artillery. No, I told them, I had studied how to shoot artillery. What? I had studied artillery all the way over the sea in Russia for twelve years and all I had learned was how to shoot a gun? Why every Ethiopian who was a man knew how to shoot a gun from childhood. Hadn't we shown those Italians how to shoot at Adwa?

"I tried to tell them about ballistics, trajectory, about modern warfare, strategy and discipline and ordnance, and they laughed. I tried to tell them that when the Italians or the Germans or the British came back again with modern methods and modern weapons, they would slaughter us. They reminded me again of Adwa and laughed some more. They were still laughing thirty years later when the Italians came back with modern methods and modern weapons and slaughtered them. Great fools.

"When I first returned, that was what? Sixty years ago. I started to get to know my country. How poor we were. The problems we were having then were problems Europe had solved a century before. What we needed wasn't guns and well-trained soldiers. What we needed, really needed, was agricultural equipment and well-trained farmers. It's what we need still though our little king goes around the world asking for rockets and bombers and military advisers to train our soldiers. And to hell with our farmers. Ignore land reform. Let the Swedes withdraw their aid. We should make it our slogan. Billions for defense. Not one cent for progress. Look at our budget. Two thirds goes for defense and security. Whose security? The little king's security. Little for education. A pittance for agriculture. We haven't learned much these sixty years.

"I was a young man when I first came back from Russia. Sixty years ago. Just taking my first wife. Innocent as a baby, but it didn't take long to see that a soldier at court wasn't going to do this country much good. So off we went. There were children by then. I took them and their mother and back to Europe I went. This time to France. But this time I didn't study artillery. We didn't need men to go to school to learn to shoot up our country. It was devastated enough by ignorance, superstition, and the great fools at court. So I went to France. And studied farming.

"She died there, that first wife of mine. She died there in France, but there were more children by then. I stayed there, six, seven years, and at the end there was a French wife, too. But that's another story. I didn't bring her back.

"Strange. I went to Russia and studied artillery and came back and wanted to be a farmer. I went to France and studied farming and came back and what did I do? I became a soldier.

"Menelik at last was dead, and soon the war was on for who would succeed him. The grandson Lij Iyasu had been named to take his place, but the boy, Iyasu, was a fool. He couldn't keep the thing in his pants—Tesfaye, don't translate that in front of the lady—but the truth is he couldn't keep the damn thing in his pants long enough to get his mind straight. He wasn't much of a Christian. He was playing with the Muslims. He thought he could toss out Jesus and become Mohammed, so maybe he could have as many wives as he wanted. The fool.

"The priests didn't like that, of course. There were many others who didn't like Iyasu for that and other reasons as well. Including my old friend, Tafari Makonnen. Our little king wasn't much more than a boy himself back then, but he was the best we had. He was educated. He was modern. He had the royal blood. Lij Iyasu was worried about him and tried to kill him twice that I know of. Once he challenged him at Timkat to *feras gugs*. Tell them, Tesfaye, you know, what we do on horseback."

"Doctor Comfort has seen it," said Tesfaye. But he described to Julie the holiday sport of *gugs* in which men on horseback try to unsaddle each other with long wooden staffs in the manner of an old English joust. The old man continued.

"Yes. Well, Lij Iyasu had Ras Tafari's saddle cut. The saddle came off, all right, but Tafari stayed on. Takel, it's another of our little king's names, was always good on a horse, so Takel, his 'horse' name, suits him.

"Then another time, not far from here at Lake Aramaya, Lij

Iyasu scuttled his boat. The boat sank, but Tafari swam to the shore. He's tough, our little king. He can be kind up to a point, but when he gets mad, he can be very tough. And he was getting mad at this damned Iyasu.

"Soon we had another war on our hands. I fought by Tafari's side against Iyasu. We beat him, of course. This was 1916. All that's history now. Iyasu died many years later at Grawa. He wasn't chained to the walls like some people say. Just locked in. But he might as well have been in chains. He wasn't going anywhere. Some say old Zewditu, Menelik's daughter, hastened the end by supplying the fool with syphilitic beauties. It may not be true, but it's the kind of nasty story some of our people like to believe.

"Well, Iyasu was out, but even then we couldn't make our man Tafari emperor straight away. We had to settle for second best, sharing the rule with old Zewditu, that great cow. Fair enough. She was Menelik's daughter, and Tafari was only a nephew. But Menelik had been a modern man and Tafari was a modern man and Zewditu was everything that was wrong with our country. She was rich and mean and fat and superstitious, reactionary as death, hating smart foreigners and loving stupid priests, her big bottom stuck in the past and her eyes closed to the future. Tafari compared to her was like the sun to the dark side of the moon.

"Anyway, fat Zewditu may have been on the throne. But even then it was Tafari who ruled.

"Make no mistake. He was a man. I knew him well then. I've known him long now."

He paused and Tesfaye tried to catch up with his circumspect rendering of the story for Harry and Julie.

"Yes," said the old man when Tesfaye finished. He seemed to be looking over their heads at a place far distant in time.

"I knew him well. From the day he was born." He looked back at Tesfaye. "Did I ever tell you the story . . . it was me, you know, who fired the gun the day he was born. You know how we do it. When labor begins someone goes out and fires a rifle in the air. The mother starts screaming and the village starts gathering."

Harry cast a glance at Julie, remembering the screams of her labor. But Julie was absorbed in the old man's story.

"When the head shows," said the Dejazmatch, "you fire the

rifle again. By then there's a mob outside. When it's over you fire the gun again to bring down the placenta. If it's a boy they take the placenta outside and bury it under a tree. Don't ask me why. And then the feast starts.

"But wait . . . was it for him or when his brother was born that they let me fire the gun? My mind . . . no, it was at Ejersa Goro. I remember, so it must have been him. If I was eight then, I'm eighty and more now, but I fired the gun then, and I'll fire it again when he's dead."

A shiver went through Tesfaye. He didn't translate his father's last remark. He would caution Baria not to repeat it. Was his father cooking another of his plots? Impossible, Tesfaye decided. His father went on.

"After we whipped Iyasu, and Tafari became regent, I was his right-hand man. When old Zewditu finally died, I helped him climb up on the throne. He changed his name to Haile Selassie, and we all said hail to the King of the Kings of Ethiopia, the Elect of God, the Lion of the Tribe of Judah has conquered. I wrote him his constitution, the first one back forty years ago. Not the second. He had me in jail when they were writing the second one, but I'll come to that later.

"It was funny how I did the first one. I went around to what embassies and such as we had in Addis Ababa in those days and asked them to get me copies of their countries' constitutions. The one I used most was the Japanese because they had an emperor like us. The whole thing was my idea, and I had a draft all done before I even showed it to him though the books his parasites like to write say it was all his idea. I made lots of changes from the Japanese, mostly to simplify the thing and give the Emperor more power. He was going to need power because there were lots of backward old warlords still who would have to be cut down a peg or two.

"Well, Haile read it, and he liked it, especially the part that said only male descendants in the royal line could succeed. After Zewditu he figured Ethiopia didn't need another Empress.

"I served him well for twenty years after we whipped Iyasu, right up to the time I became a soldier again when the Italians came back. I became a soldier, and the little king ran away. Not at first, of course. At first he fought them, but after Maichew he wanted to run. It was sad. I told him he couldn't do it. He had to stay and fight. Hide in the hills like the rest of us and lead the fight, however long it took.

"He said, 'No.' He talked of diplomacy, winning world opinion, his precious League of Nations. He'd brought Ethiopia into the old League even before he was Emperor, and he thought the League would save us from the fascists. His wife, another fat cow, old Menen, was at him to run. She was another pious old hypocrite, as good as Zewditu, Menen was, and look at the pasty sons she gave him.

"I'd married again myself by then. She was my best wife, that one." He glanced at Tesfaye. "Yes . . . that one must have been your mother."

"Yes," said Tesfaye.

"She was the best wife I ever had. She fought right alongside us against the Italians. She was wounded twice. I don't think it was the wounds that killed her but the poison gas she swallowed when their planes caught us once in open bush and bombed us with poison gas.

"But wounds or poison, she went on fighting till the end. She died, isn't it, when . . . yes, she died when you were born."

"Yes," said Tesfaye. "She died when I was born."

"All the fighting she'd lived through, all the death, and then giving birth killed her. Giving birth and all she'd been through, mustard gas and wounds. It was 1941. The war was nearly over, and she died. That's why I called you Tesfaye. Tesfaye, my hope. She was the best wife I ever had, and when she died, you were my new hope. So we called you Tesfaye."

He caught his son's eyes, and in them he saw the wife he had loved most. He waved the image away.

"But leave that. We were talking about our king. Is it all right, my son?"

Tesfaye nodded.

"Yes," said the old man. "Our king. I had done a lot for him. Whatever he asked. Whatever he needed even when he didn't know enough to ask. But when the Italians came, I told him no. He couldn't run. He had to stay and fight. We broke on that. But I didn't give up. He was on the train going down to Djibouti to take his boat and escape. The Italians were letting him get away, but I had other ideas."

He looked around at his audience of four. He shifted his massive weight on the bench, and spread his palms on the table.

"Not many people know this story. You won't find it in your storybooks, but it's true.

"The Italians had crushed us at Maichew and were overrunning the country. I took myself back up here to these hills to gather an army of my own to keep the fight going where I could. Others were doing the same in different parts of the country. Then I got word that our little king was getting ready to leave Addis. Slipping out of Addis down to Akaki, then going down by the train to the sea like a merchant on holiday.

"Well, I wasn't having that. I took my men, and we went over the hills to the tracks beyond Adefo. We were too soon. We had to wait three days.

"I set up relays of runners between the camp we made in the bush and the station at Adefo. Meanwhile, we were cutting down trees. One old oak by a stream took us two days. It was big as a cannon, and that was what we called it. Our cannon. The cannon that was going to stop the king.

"When his train finally came and my men at Adefo made sure he was on it, they started the relay to get the message to our camp. On foot most of the way. One fast man after another. I had riders spotted where the bush was clear enough that a horse could make time. The last stretch wasn't a run or a rider, just a rifle fired three times from the top of a little hill.

"We got our oak tree, the cannon, down on the tracks in plenty of time and a few more good-sized trees as well. The little train didn't have any choice but to stop. There were troops on it, of course, but when they saw how many men and guns I had on both sides of the tracks, there wasn't any fight.

"We took the little king and his fat wife and the rest of his family up to our camp. I kept him three days. We treated him royally and why not? He was our king. The best we had.

"I tried everything. I begged. I threatened. I reasoned. I bullied. I talked about our boyhood. The battles we'd fought and won side by side. The government we'd created together.

"Nothing worked.

"I told him he was needed, not just to lead the fight, but to keep the country, the people together. He was our symbol, our hope."

So he is still, thought Tesfaye. But he knew better than to cross his father.

"He said it was up to me and the others to keep the war going at home. He was needed, he kept telling me, to fight what he called the 'diplomatic struggle' abroad. He said if he was captured or killed, the will of the people to fight would collapse. In exile, his chances were better, he told us, to survive as the symbol of the struggle.

"I saw then that it was his own skin he wanted to see survive. I knew then he was no more an Ethiopian. I knew then he was a coward."

Tesfaye was functioning now more as censor than translator. He didn't want his father's harsh words poured into foreign ears.

"What could I do?" said the old man. "I held him three days, but he was as stubborn as he was proud. I couldn't be bothered longer. There were Italians to be hunted down and killed. I had to let him go. He went, but as he climbed up into the train, he turned to me and said, 'I'll be back.' "

The old man fell silent. His two gnarled hands clenched into fists on the rough surface of the table.

"He did come back," said Tesfaye softly.

"Oh yes. He came back. An accident of history saw to that. Your world war saw to that. The books the little king has his parasites write like to say the great Haile Selassie won the diplomatic struggle, unifying world opinion against the Italians and persuading the British to help him liberate his country.

"The truth is something else.

"He skittered around Europe, made them weep and then sigh and then forget about him at the League of Nations. I must admit the League of Nations speech was a good one. Couldn't have been better if I'd written it for him myself. But it was Blattengeta Lorenzo who wrote it. He told them if they didn't stop the Italians in Ethiopia they wouldn't be able to stop the war that would come next in Europe, the war that would swallow them all.

"He told them the truth, but they wouldn't listen. They said what a brave little man he was and some of them wept, but they wouldn't listen. They let Mussolini and his Blackshirts chew up Ethiopia. Two years later the League did the same and let the Germans swallow poor Czechoslovakia. Someone's always swallowing it up. Now my Russian friends have done Czechoslovakia again. But leave that.

"Your history books will tell you World War II began in 1939. In Poland. But it didn't. It began right here in 1936. But nobody was paying attention. Or seeing it for what it was. The fascists went on and swallowed up the rest of them. And Europe stayed swallowed until the Americans and the Russians came and rescued them. And now, twenty-five years later, Europe is still trying to figure out how to get the Russians and the Americans out of their stomachs. They should have listened to the little king when he read them Lorenzo's speech.

"Anyway, after they ignored him in Geneva, the little king wound up in England where he was politely ignored again except for a few eccentric old ladies. He sat around like a vegetable for four years, just like my old friends from Russia who went to seed in London and Paris after the Bolsheviks kicked them out.

"Winning the diplomatic struggle, our little king called it. Hah. Hitler and our old friend Mussolini won the diplomatic struggle for him by going to war with England. Ethiopia controls the Red Sea, and the British needed the Red Sea to supply their North African army. Ethiopia was the soft belly where it was easiest to get the knife into the Italians. So the British came, and they brought an army in from India as well and another from South Africa.

"They chopped up the Italians pretty quick, but then there was still more chopping to do. Soon as the Italians were whipped we had revolts in Gojjam and Tigre."

"We still have revolts," said Tesfaye.

"True," said his father. "Gojjam again, Eritrea, Bale, the Ogaden. The list is long. As long as you have the mosquito you will have malaria as well. But leave that. I fought against the rebels in Tigre myself, but it was the British with their airplanes that won that little war for us, too.

"Well, we were rid of the Italians, and we'd put our own rebels down as well. But now we had the British to worry about. . . . There was a joke I remember . . ."

"About the peasant with the tapeworm?" said Baria.

"That's the one. He said he got the tapeworm from eating pasta, Italian pasta. A British doctor told him to take Epsom salts—British Epsom salts. Well, the salts cleaned out the Italian tapeworm all right. Quickly, too. But the peasant was still having trouble with his stomach. He complained to the doctor, 'Well, that Italian tapeworm is gone, but now how do I get your British Epsom salts out of my stomach?' "

Tesfaye had been carefully editing his father's remarks as he translated them. He gave Harry and Julie the joke in full, but he wasn't sure they understood it. His father had the same suspicion.

"Explain to them," he said, "that it turned out we had those

British salts in our Ethiopian stomach for nearly as long as we had the Italian tapeworm eating inside us. Just like the Europeans still can't get the Americans and Russians out of their countries. It wasn't until the war—their war with the fascists—was over and they didn't need us anymore that we finally got rid of the British."

"Even then," said Harry, anxious to impress with his knowledge, "the British kept Eritrea another ten years. Before the UN made them give it back to Ethiopia."

"Give it back?" said the old man. "I see your friend believes our fables. Eritrea was never ours in the first place. Even now we still have to fight the Muslims to make it ours. But we need it. So let the foreigners believe our fables."

"My father says you should be complimented on your knowledge of our history," said Tesfaye.

"Oh, thank. Thank you," said Harry. "*Batam existellign, getay*."

"I don't love Amharic," said the Dejazmatch, "but I do hate to see it murdered."

"He says your Amharic is also very good."

Harry beamed.

"But leave all that," said the old man. "When the little king came back, my friends said I should flee the country. They said he would throw me in jail for what I did when I stopped his train. But after the war there was too much to do for our country for a man to run away.

"Lorenzo who wrote his Geneva speech for the little king had been the contact man between himself and the rest of us who stayed behind to fight. He had the king's ear, as they say. So it was Lorenzo who went to him to beg forgiveness for me. Well, he forgave me. He's good at forgiving. He made me mayor of Addis Ababa, and then I went off to fight for him in Tigre.

"When that was over, well, it was exile for both me and Lorenzo. I forget what he accused Lorenzo of. He said I was plotting with the Tigres I went off to fight."

"Wasn't Blattengeta Lorenzo made ambassador?" asked Tesfaye.

"He was. It's one of the ways we exile people. Myself, I didn't wait for the little king to send me anyplace. At first we tried to hide out among some friends in Wollo. They caught us once. I got away, but I had to leave my children. I knew they'd be cared for, so I kept going."

"To Madagascar?" asked Tesfaye. He had been one of the children left behind. But his father had been right. They were cared for.

"Yes," said his father. "To Madagascar. The French had it then, and I found out one of my old friends from my days in Paris was there as governor. So off I went. I had some money. The French let me buy land, and at last I started to farm, a soldier no more. I might have stayed there forever, but then my son, that other one we were talking about, what's his name?"

"You've had many sons," said Tesfaye. "Do you mean Getachew?"

"Yes, that one. Getachew. He sent word to me that the little king had forgiven me again. There was a high post waiting me. And a grant of land as well. I was suspicious, but I missed Ethiopia. I was homesick and, yes, I guess I was flattered that the little king seemed to need me so much. I came back."

Tesfaye knew they had already stayed longer than they had intended. But he also realized his father wanted to go on talking. He couldn't suggest leaving. His father called for more tea and insisted they take another serving of avocado.

"I brought these back with me from Madagascar. Ethiopia never knew avocado before. Now even the little king grows them at his farm at Erer Gota. Yes, he is good at forgiving. In his own way. He'd confiscated my land at Asba Tafari. Rich, cultivated farms and more forests than you could cross in a week on horseback. The land he gave me was here. A generous amount, I admit, but it was nothing but scrub. In this place. Mota. It means 'he died,' you know. I didn't like the sound of that. Why name a village for death? I asked around. Who died here that they gave the place this name? No one seemed to know. Some great man must have died, they said. A long time ago. No one knew who. This was a poor village then, and the people were poor. What you see now I've done. All of it. You could call it Tessema's land reform.

"Men who were laborers for me when I first came back have farms of their own now. Land I gave them when they'd learned how to farm well enough to know what to do with it. No one here tithes me. I pay my laborers well and give land outright to those that deserve.

"The little king does things differently.

"They tell the story, you know, of the peasant stripped naked by the big landlord of his district. His cattle were taken, his land, the clothes he wore on his back, even his young wife, a wife as beautiful as mine, your mother that died. But leave that. He was left naked, this peasant, hungry, shivering with cold. The landlord had him sent for. The big man looked at the peasant and shook his head sadly. He told the peasant how he pitied his miserable condition.

" 'We are your father,' he told the peasant. He gave the poor man a blanket. Yes. To the peasant he'd robbed of everything, the landlord gave a blanket."

The Dejazmatch looked around his listeners. He knew the value of a pause in telling a story.

"And the peasant," he went on, "the peasant who'd been given the blanket, he was grateful. Do you like the avocado?"

"It's fine," said Harry. "It's fine. Best avocado I ever . . ." He caught Julie's sharp, sidelong look. He knew what she was thinking. It's fine. It's fine. That was twice. The best avocado I ever ate. That was three times. It was a tic with him, one of several Julie had all but given up trying to correct except with those glances that signaled despair out of the corners of her eye.

Repeating himself. Hesitantly balancing on one foot. His weakness for alliteration in his writing. His habit of locking a finger of one hand in the fist of the other. He started to make the gesture as he thought of it. He caught himself in time and instead put his hand under his thighs.

He wished he could be more like this tough old man who held them with his storytelling. He wanted his own book about Ethiopia to be as fascinating as the words the Dejazmatch spun out. Even in his eighties he displayed the kind of strength and certainty Harry longed to achieve for himself. He was sure Julie would be measuring him against Tesfaye's father. Old men were supposed to ramble, to repeat themselves. But there was little of that with Dejazmatch Tessema. He meandered a bit; he skipped in time. But there was directness, an economy of means in everything he said and did. Harry remembered the brute strength with which the old man levered himself to his feet in the fields. The Dejazmatch and Baria were now exchanging words in Amharic. Julie watched them intently though Harry knew their words were meaningless to her.

What held her interest? Strength, Harry told himself. He wanted to learn to be more like this forceful old man. He told himself he was still young. There was still time to shape his life into this kind of mold. He wished the physical discipline of his long climb to Kulubi were already underway. He was impatient to be on his feet. Undergoing the long walk through the night. Forcing himself to climb. Then the mental discipline of finishing his book. Walking the fat off his limbs. Trimming the flab from his mind. Like a boxer conditioning himself in the mountains. He wanted to be as tough as this old man. You would never hear this old man nervously say, It's fine; it's fine. Best avocado I ever . . .

Julie left her avocado untouched. She was frightened. There was something terrifying, she had decided, about Tesfaye's father. She watched him and Baria talking. They spoke in a language she did not understand. It made no difference. Men always thought that what they said to you mattered. It didn't. Let them talk Chinese. What counted was the sureness with which they spoke. The style of their strength.

She wondered if she would ever find the right man. Both strong and weak. She glanced at Harry. Poor Harry. He gave her so much of what she needed. He inspired no confidence, yet, he made her feel confident. Safely secure. A man she need never fear losing. No matter what she did. Harry would be there. To carry her baby. To lean on when she needed him. He could never control her. Make her be what she ought to be. But what she saw in Tesfaye's father was a brutal, domineering force. Such men would never let a woman be herself.

And Baria. He had the old man's strength. And a different brutality. A cold indifference. From Miesso to Mota he hadn't spoken a word in the car. She was sure he had guessed, suspected before, that he was the father of her child. But she had never told him till today. When she became pregnant, he had stopped seeing her. When she told him today that he was the father, he'd stopped speaking. His was a strength that controlled, not for a woman's sake, but for his own. To use. To exploit. She knew it, and yet she wanted him. His strength. His weakness. There was that other side to Baria. The poet. The painter. She studied the diseased patches of his skin. How sensitive he was to that. How afraid of rejection. How timid. Never offering his hand first, even in greeting a friend, for fear his hand wouldn't be taken. For fear someone would think he was a leper.

He masked his fear so well people thought he was arrogant. Aloof. Julie knew better. He had both weakness and strength. The combination she knew she needed. Yet, what was it? Somehow neither the weakness nor the strength came clear. One canceled the other, and, when she tried to be close to him, she was left with nothing.

Would there ever be a man, she wondered, the right man for her? Her father . . . The impossible man. He had been strong, but she could always have from him whatever she wanted.

Then. When she was his little girl.

But he left her. She wanted always to be his little girl. The perfect man. Weak and strong.

Tesfaye's words broke in on her.

"My father says . . . the Emperor was as good as his word."

She wished Tesfaye wouldn't bother translating. It was like someone trying to explain music. The power of the old man's voice, its bass rumbling, was all she cared about.

"What did he say?" asked Harry.

The old man worked Tesfaye like a ventriloquist. He spoke, but the words, their meaning, came from Tesfaye.

"He did give me land," said the old Tessema through the young Tesfaye. "Not the best, but our little king did give me land as he promised he would. And a post as well, not the highest, but a post in what we call our house of justice.

"Can you explain to them," he said to Tesfaye, "how we use the word *house?*"

The old man went on to explain himself. Tesfaye translated.

"He says we use the word *house* for everything–and in strange ways. A school is where teachers bully the students, but we call a school a *tamari bet*, house of students. We call a bathroom a piss house, excuse me, because that's what you do there. And a kitchen is a cooking house. But what we call a *buna bet*, which means coffeehouse, is actually, excuse me, a whorehouse where poverty, my father says, forces our women to sell not coffee but themselves.

"And what we call *fird bet*, which means justice house, is the place where the law persecutes the people. Excuse me. My father's very outspoken."

"Yes," said the old man. "Well, that lasted a year. My job in the house of justice. Then our little king had me put in jail. He didn't bother with any trial. Just put me in jail. They said I was taking bribes. You see, I'd let an innocent man go free. So I took the place they'd reserved for him in their jail. I was sixty-three when I went in. And seventy when I was let out. Forgiven again. Or my term was up. It doesn't matter which.

"I felt so good I got married. My third wife. Or fourth. Anyway, she died two years ago. It's lonely now. Even for an old man, being married isn't bad. It's nice to have new children. You forget the old ones, and being married is better than being in prison. Tesfaye, can you explain to them what the name of our prison means?"

"*Alem Bakagn*," said Tesfaye. "That's the name of our prison. It means something like 'for me the world is finished.' "

"Yes," said his father. "It's a good name for the place. But I was lucky. I did come out. He does know how to forgive. In his way. Not like me. I don't forgive. Old Haile doesn't forget, but he does know how to forgive. Me, I neither forget nor forgive."

Tesfaye edited his translation into praise for the Emperor's ability graciously to grant pardon.

"And then he really did give me a high post. The highest, the post of *Afa Negus*.

"Literally," said Tesfaye, "it means 'mouth of the king.' It's the title for chief justice of the high court."

"Since I knew what it was like, he made me his man in charge of the house of injustice. To send people to the house where for them the world would be finished. Our prison. Yes, we know how to name things.

"But I was a merciful judge. So I lost my job. I lasted four years. Then back to *Alem Bakagn*. That time I thought my world was really finished. He said I had been plotting against him. It was true, but it wasn't a very good plot. I deserved to go to jail."

"Was that during the coup?" asked Harry.

"No," said Tesfaye without relaying the question. "The coup was the year before."

The old man had understood. "No," he said, "not the coup. I wasn't involved in that one. I guess they thought I was too old. These young soldiers and officials, like the ones involved in the coup, they don't have much respect for us old men. That's why they always fail. Like your students now. Every year they tear up their textbooks and say down with the king, throw out the Americans, long live the Russians, land to the tiller, power to the people, and better dormitories and stipends for students. And then the police hit them on the head a few times, and the little king says, 'Oh, what ungrateful children. Don't you remember, my children? We are your father. When you were little children we used to come and visit you in elementary school and listen to you recite your lessons and give you oranges and presents. Now be good little children and go back to school.' And so they are good little children, and they go back to school until the next year when they do the same routine again, and meanwhile nothing has changed.

"No, it's not the youngsters who are going to do anything. It's us old men you have to watch out for. We've learned how to plot. We've been at it a long time.

"That's what was wrong with the coup. The men in it were too young. I had the privilege of being the judge when they were brought to trial. That was what? Nineteen sixty; sixty-one. The ones who weren't already dead. Interesting who they were. The head of the little king's personal security force. The head of his imperial bodyguard. His chief of police. It goes to show that those who know him best love him best.

"They were good men, but too young. They should have come to us old ones for advice. They struck when the little king was out of the country. That was a mistake. You can't kill malaria and let the mosquito live. He comes back and stings you, and you get malaria all over again. And that's what happened. They had the bodyguard, the security, the police. But the mosquito came back and got the army and the air force and stung them. They had forgotten the proverb, 'Kill the mosquito, and you cure the malaria.' "

"Father, you worry me," said Tesfaye. "You criticize our Amharic for not being a serious language, but when you yourself speak you make us laugh about justice houses and piss houses, about information and vomit. You give us puns and proverbs with double meanings and your talk is like the poetry you attack the old priests for writing."

The old man reached out and took his son's hand. The bluish gray eyes sparkled.

"I'm an Ethiopian, my son. I may say I'm a Russian, but you and I know I'm an Ethiopian. And like all good Ethiopians, I can't bear to say what's really on my mind. What can we do in a sad country but tell funny stories?"

Tesfaye didn't translate. He was fighting back tears. His father held his hand. It was the first tender gesture he could remember his father ever making toward him. His father was right. They shared a sadness that was Ethiopia. He wasn't going to weep. If he did, it wouldn't be for himself or the father he'd never had as a child. It would be for their country, Ethiopia.

He felt his father's hard hand on his, and he felt the truth of the old man's sad words. His father released his hand and swatted casually at a fly on the table. The fly just barely escaped.

"I missed," said his father. "But I bet I came close enough to worry him away for a while. Like the coup. It failed, but it came close enough to worry them for a while. Many things improved after that, didn't they? Changed. Were reformed. So even if we swat at the mosquito and miss, we may help the malaria a bit."

"Father . . . "

"Ai, don't worry. You're right. What can I do but make bad jokes? I'm an old man now, and so is he. Besides we've always been friends. In fact, he's coming to visit me tomorrow."

"What?"

"Yes. My old friend Tafari Makonnen. The little king, Haile Selassie. He is coming to visit us tomorrow."

"But that's impossible," said Tesfaye.

"Why impossible? You know he goes to Kulubi every year, though you don't know why. Well, this year instead of taking his jet to Dire Dawa, he's coming this way, by car, a whole caravan. And he's let me know he's stopping here for lunch, just as you did today."

"Father, I think there must be a mistake. He isn't flying this year, that's true. But he won't be coming this way by car. He's taking the train through the lowlands."

"Ai, Tesfaye. How would you know? These things are never announced in advance. Which way he's going or when. They're afraid someone will arrange too warm a reception."

"It hasn't been announced," said Tesfaye. "But I heard from a friend of mine, an official in the railway. They were preparing a special car for him. He was scheduled to leave Addis Ababa this morning."

"No, no. He's coming here tomorrow. This other is probably some story they've given out to confuse people. Or maybe he'll take the train as far as Miesso. Then come this way by car. But it's tomorrow. Not today."

Tesfaye knew better. He knew of the security arrangements that were being made at every stop along the railway. The extra train that would stay three minutes ahead of the Emperor's to make sure the tracks were clear. The helicopters with heavy-caliber machine guns that would hover above the route. Something was wrong, but he hesitated to contradict his father again.

"Perhaps that's it," he said. "Only as far as Miesso by the train."

"In any event," said the Dejazmatch, "I have every assurance he will be coming to us tomorrow. My friend General Tadesse has arranged it."

"The hyena?"

"Is that what they call him? Never mind. He's a good man."

"He's not a man to be trusted."

"Of course not. But the hyena only feeds after the lion has killed."

"Father, forget this."

"What?"

"Whatever you're cooking."

"There's nothing. I'm an old man. I've left all that. All I'm cooking is *wat* and *injera.* And you and your friends have eaten most of that. I'll have to cook more."

"Why this visit?"

The old man grinned, exposing his yellowed teeth.

"Who knows? Perhaps he wants to see if this land is worth confiscating now that I've developed it. No, don't worry. He won't be taking anything of mine tomorrow. It's just a friendly match, as the soccer players say. After all, we are old friends. Perhaps there are some people who want to bring us together. Who knows? Maybe the little king wants me to be his mouth again."

The old man raised a thick finger. His eyes hardened.

"But I am no more the mouth of the king. Now I am the mouth of the people." He relaxed and let his hand fall. "Anyway, he's coming."

"Father, if you are the mouth of the people, tell me. What are the people saying?"

"The people are silent. But what do the people know? That's why they need someone to be their mouth. You can take our people only so far. They can understand that some local governor is cruel or unjust. And that governor, they think, is to blame for their problems.

"But you ask them, 'Well, who appointed that governor?'

" 'Oh,' they say. 'Some minister appointed the governor.' Okay. You don't want to argue. You ask them, 'Well then, who appointed that minister?' Then they begin to get a glimmer, but they still try to hide. 'Well,' they say, 'nowadays probably the prime minister appoints that minister.'

" 'Good,' you tell them. 'And who appoints the prime minister?'

" 'Well, yes,' they say. 'The Emperor appoints the prime minister.' Then you can make them see that the mosquito causes malaria."

"You keep coming back to that," said Tesfaye.

"It keeps coming back to us," said his father. "But the people like their mosquito. Even if he does give them malaria."

Tesfaye had stopped translating what his father was saying. He told Harry it was a discussion of pest control on the farm, very dull.

"Well," said Harry, "in that case, I mean I don't want to change the subject or anything, but there was a question, a question I wanted to ask your father."

"Good," said Tesfaye. "What is it?"

"He said something before, something about Kulubi. He said there's a reason why the Emperor goes to Kulubi every year. Ask him what it is."

Tesfaye asked.

"He wants to know about that? All this important discussion, and that's what he wants to know about?"

"It's a fixed idea with him," said Tesfaye. "He thinks Kulubi is important to understand Ethiopia."

"Well, I suppose it's important to understand our superstitions, to understand what's wrong with Ethiopia."

"Exactly," said Tesfaye.

"Well, not many people know about it, and it isn't that important, but the church at Kulubi, the old church, of course, was built for him."

"For who?"

"For himself. Our little king. His father, Ras Makonnen, made a vow to Gabriel that if a son was born to him that year he would build a church for Gabriel at Kulubi. Menelik and Ras Makonnen had established a military camp there in 1882, our calendar, when they were conquering the Gallas and Somalis in the area. Ras Makonnen lived in the hills above the camp. His wife, what was her name?"

"Yeshimabet."

"Yes. That one. She didn't like Kulubi. There were all these Gallas around, pagans, and Somalis, who were Muslims. The Gallas always had some wild pagan ceremonies going. Beating drums all night, howling and dancing. There was an oak tree that they worshipped."

"They wouldn't have been worshipping the tree," said Baria. "The tree would just have been the place where they worshipped. The way Christians worship God at church. It doesn't mean that they worship the church."

"Some do," said the old man. "We Christians are no better than your pagans. The pagan can't tell the difference between God and a tree. The Christian, being more civilized, can't tell the difference between God and a church."

He looked at Baria and shrugged.

"Trees, churches, mosques. It's all the same. Anyway, this Yeshimabet from Wollo, she was only one generation out of the bush, but she considered herself a good civilized Christian, so no tree or mosques for her. She persuaded her husband to buy up the land and build a church. That way the drum beating would be done by Christians inside the church instead of by pagans around the tree. It wouldn't disturb the neighbors as much, and old Yeshimabet could sleep at night.

"So Ras Makonnen bought up the land. Forty head of cattle he paid for it."

"What's he saying?" asked Harry. "What's he saying?"

Tesfaye explained.

"My God," said Harry. "I've got to take notes on this. Where's my tape recorder? It all ties in with what that old priest told us last year.

"I remember," said Tesfaye.

"I've got to get this down for my book. Where's . . . Oh God. I left the tape recorder in the car."

"Don't worry," said Tesfaye. "I'll remember it. You can take it down later. Let my father tell his story."

"Yes," said the old man. "Well, when himself, our little king, was born at Ejersa Goro, Ras Makonnen was down in Harar. Menelik had only conquered the city a few years before, and the place was considered neither safe nor healthy. Yeshimabet insisted on going up into the hills when the lying-in time came. She didn't like Kulubi so she went up the other way, to Ejersa Goro where her family had friends.

"My father was part of the escort that took her up. He took me with him. So that's where they let me shoot off the rifle when the baby was born. Word was sent down to Ras Makonnen in Harar. He didn't go up to his wife and son. He went the other way to Kulubi. He was so sure the baby his wife was expecting would be a son that he'd started building the church months before and had a *tabot* brought from another church dedicated to Gabriel at Bulga."

Tesfaye translated, and Harry bounced up and down on his bench.

"It ties in. It all ties in. The *tabot* being brought from Bulga, just what they told us at Kulubi."

"Calm down, Harry."

"But how come that old priest didn't tell us about the church being built for the Emperor?"

"He wouldn't have," said Tesfaye. "Anything that personal about the royal family, he wouldn't have."

"But what a discovery about Kulubi," said Harry. "It's a piece of history. What a story you can write for the paper."

"No," said Tesfaye. "They only like official stories, not personal stories about the royal family."

"But the human interest . . ."

"You forget," said Tesfaye. "The Emperor is superhuman. Not human."

His father laughed. "*Ubermensch*," he said. "But he is mortal. We have to let people know he's mortal, though I sometimes suspect he forgets it himself these days. He believes those priestly flatterers who tell him he's God."

"There's a rumor," said Baria, "that they're going to rename Ejersa Goro and call it Bethlehem."

"It's possible," said the Dejazmatch. "But he wasn't always that way. You have to remember that in the beginning he was the best man we had. The only man. In all of Ethiopia after Menelik died there was no one more liberal, no one more modern, no one more brave. In those days it was he who fought the priests. It was only after he beat them down that they began to flatter him. And he began to believe them.

"He started to go bad during the war, when he let himself be talked into running away. When he came back and started listening to the parasites who told him he was a hero, a god, the rebirth of Christ, that's when he really went wrong. Then he started to turn into the people he'd defeated. He started to become greedy, superstitious, bloodthirsty, and afraid. He started to become as reactionary as the old stones he himself had overturned. It isn't the first time it's happened in history. Caesar, Nalopeon, Lenin, Nkrumah. Even our friend Mussolini. There have been hundreds. Liberators, becoming the tyrant."

Tesfaye was silent. Perhaps we need both, he thought. Liberators and tyrants.

"Is he saying anything more about Kulubi?" asked Harry.

"No," said Tesfaye. "Not Kulubi."

The Dejazmatch glanced at Harry. "Is that one still on Kulubi?"

Tesfaye nodded. Harry looked at his watch.

"Well," said the old man, "I should be letting you get on your way to Gabriel. I've kept you long enough with my talk."

"We enjoyed your talk," said Tesfaye.

"Uh, Tesfaye," said Harry. "Prob'ly we should be going."

"Yes," answered Tesfaye.

"I mean I don't want to interrupt or cut short our visit or anything, but if we're going to get to Kulubi before dark . . ."

Farewells among the Amhara are formal and slow, but Tesfaye now sensed that his father wanted to be rid of them. Still, he hesitated. Their conversation had troubled him.

"Yes," said his father, "be gone. You have your Kulubi to be getting to, and I have to finish my preparations for welcoming himself."

"Father, what preparations are you making?"

"What preparations? Huh. It's well you ask. You've already eaten some of them. Do you think I feast this way every day? No, that what you ate was for him. He eats always as I usually do. Some fruit, vegetables, nuts. A drop of wine."

"You seem to know his habits well."

"I've studied them long. He eats lightly, wisely for a man of our age. But the others with him will be looking to stuff themselves at my expense. So we've been preparing for two days now."

"Only food?"

"Oh, no. *Tella* and *tej* as well. I hate such poisons myself, but his camp followers will be looking for their drinks. And the little group of thugs that always precedes him with their automatic weapons. They'll be wanting to see what we've prepared."

"What will they find?"

"What you ate today. Don't worry. There's more of the same. Plus *tella* and *tej*. You never know how many to expect. I can't afford to feed them whisky though. They'll have to do without their whisky."

"It won't kill them," said Tesfaye.

"It's time for you to go," said his father.

As he turned to leave, Tesfaye noticed on the bookshelf the sharpened stub of a thick pencil placed in the empty cartridge of a heavy-caliber rifle.

"What's this?"

"Ah," said his father behind him. "You've noticed my little pencil holder. Strange, isn't it, how the sharpened pencil put inside like that makes the empty shell look like the full bullet."

"Yes," said Tesfaye. "It's strange."

He stood by the bookshelf, staring at the cartridge with the pencil that looked like a bullet.

"You know," said his father, "the first time I did it, almost by accident, placed the pencil inside the cartridge, I wasn't thinking anything about it. Then it made me see how the stub of a sharpened bullet and a pencil have the same shape. As they should. For they have the same use. Both are weapons. You can attack with a pencil—with words—as well as you can with a bullet."

"Unless you're censored," said Tesfaye.

"And when words fail, you can still get your point across," said his father. He picked up the cartridge. "When words fail, you can make propaganda with a bullet."

"You sound like our students," said Tesfaye. "Quoting Mao."

"I know nothing about Mao. But then I doubt that your students do either."

"Father . . ." Tesfaye turned his back on the others. Baria was already standing by the door which he'd opened. Tesfaye spoke softly.

"Father, he won't be coming here. He's on the train now. He'll be taking the train all the way to Dire Dawa."

"He'll be coming here. Don't you worry. He'll be here. Everything is arranged. But don't you worry. We're both old men, he and I. All our troubles are over. And now," the old man raised his voice, "your friends are waiting. You must go."

They finished their good-byes. His father kissed him, first on the left cheek, then the right. Tesfaye returned the embrace. Outside the house the man they'd met at the damaged bridge was waiting to lead them back to their cars. The old man followed them out. As they started down the path, he called out to their guide:

"Keep them to the right of the road going down. All those ruts after the rains, it's dangerous walking in the road. Keep to the right. It's safer."

The train had stopped at Adefo. Inside, behind protective steel plates, the Emperor rose slowly. The sad-faced minister of the imperial court pulled the footstool away from the Emperor's tiny feet. Using the strength of his wiry arms, the old man painfully pushed himself up from the velvet-draped chair.

He stared straight ahead, his back unbending as he forced his stiffened, arthritic limbs to function. Courtiers and aides watched respectfully. No one moved to assist him. It took nearly a full minute before the monarch was on his feet.

His uniformed aide-de-camp stood in the doorway, surveying the crowd and the security forces. The first car of the slender, toylike train was divided into three sections. The diesel engine was foremost, separated from what was normally a first-class compartment by a bathroom and storage section. The compartment had been specially fitted out with rugs, tapestries, fans in working order, steel security plates, and velvet appointments for the Emperor's chair which was forward on the right. Only half a dozen of his closest aides and three security officers shared this section with the Emperor.

At the rear of the compartment there was a refreshment bar and a glass door which led to the second-class section. Here a score of lesser members of the imperial party were accommodated.

The three remaining cars of the train, fitted with iron benches, were occupied by crack troops of the imperial bodyguard. The Emperor's aide-de-camp watched as the troops were deployed around the train. Some with automatic weapons mounted on the roof. A lean bodyguard major in immaculate, formfitting khakis and topi, paced the length of the train, then signaled with his swagger stick to the aide-de-camp that all was ready.

The aide-de-camp stepped down from the doorway and stood by the track. The Emperor moved into his place and, without smiling, accepted the cheers of his people.

As he stood in the doorway, waving to the dense crowd in the dusty marketplace, the Emperor looked up toward the low hills beyond. He knew that the village of Mota lay just on the far side of those hills. The hills were only a vague purple shape to his eyes. But he could smell the dust of the marketplace, the rancid butter the Kotu women had used in styling their hair, the acrid sweat of the half-naked warriors.

The smells triggered memories of three decades before. He had halted in this same village then, and, a few minutes after his train had pulled out, it stopped again. But that second time, the train had not stopped for a station. It stopped for a tree.

He had long known both the cheering of crowds and the plotting of his friends. But he could still be moved by the cheers and saddened by the plots. The Emperor, hatless and casually dressed in a gray business suit, waved a last time to the crowd and turned back into the car. The bald, jowled minister of the court stood by the velvet-draped chair, holding the tiny Papillon. Of a rare, ancient breed, the dog was cut to his master's scale. The Emperor was lightly framed and barely five feet tall. The brooding courtier by his side easily perched the Papillon in the palm of his hand.

Slowly, stiffly, but again without assistance, the Emperor lowered himself into his chair. The dog leaped from the courtier's hand into the lap of the Conquering Lion of the Tribe of Judah. The dainty Papillon peered into the face of the King of Kings. But the Emperor's thoughts were elsewhere. The dog hopped to the floor and made his way up the aisle in search of diversion.

He soon found it. His one real friend among the men and women close to the Emperor, Negash Mengistu, was sitting by himself, leafing through a folder of papers. The Papillon jumped up into the unoccupied seat beside him.

"Hello, butterfly," said Negash in English. The Papillon treated most ministers and courtiers with the haughty disdain of a monarch. Negash was different. He never tried to pet or cuddle the dog, and he never spoke to it in gibberish. Negash, like the aging minister of the imperial court, allowed the dog its dignity. But the courtier only tolerated the dog. The Papillon sensed it and responded in kind. Negash managed to be friendly without being fawning.

The dog balanced delicately on four slender legs, looking up at Negash. The handsome young minister dropped the papers he'd been glancing through into the attaché case propped open on his legs. He clicked the case shut but left it on his lap. The Papillon settled himself down in the chair beside Negash.

"Well, old friend," said Negash, "how are you enjoying the trip?" They studied each other. Though not yet forty, Negash was prematurely gray. His strong, rather dark face was lined with fatigue. He smoked heavily and was troubled by an almost constant cough. The ministry of interior was his official post, but the conduct of his country's internal administration was only one of his tasks. He was also the Emperor's closest adviser on foreign affairs. He headed the security section in the private cabinet and was often his country's spokesman with the world press.

The Papillon cocked his head at an inquiring angle.

"You're smarter than most butterflies, aren't you?"

The tiny dog's erect, heavily fringed ears, set wide on the sides of a small skull, resembled the wings of a butterfly. The French had given the breed its name because of those ears. Foreign journalists often made the mistake of describing the Emperor's dog as a chihuahua. As he looked down into the Papillon's dark brown eyes, Negash wondered if the dog would care.

It was only one of the many mistakes about Ethiopia which were fashionable among the foreign press. Negash considered the care and spoon-feeding of foreign correspondents the most onerous of his jobs. It took perhaps a twentieth of his time, but at the moment it was an important twentieth.

The larger task immediately confronting him was the orchestration of a series of events. There were two assassination plots to be suppressed. The backbone of student opposition to the government was to be broken through the arrest of several campus leaders, including the sons of two ministers. A novel by Ethiopia's most popular author, foolishly passed by the censors, would have to be confiscated at the printing press. And no hint of all this must appear in the foreign press.

In addition, the head of the territorial army, who was involved in both assassination schemes, was to be arrested with eight others on charges of embezzlement. Four Russians, including three alleged journalists, were to be expelled from the country for fomenting student unrest. These last two events were to be officially announced, and it was Negash's responsibility to get as much international publicity for them as possible.

He considered his task of repressing some and promoting

other news as complex, but not difficult. He had many tools of manipulation at his command.

The flamboyant Agence France Presse correspondent, despite his vaunted independence, was little more than an agent of his government. A call to his ambassador, and he did what was wanted. The American agencies, Associated Press and UPI, were served by local stringers, both of whom were employees of the Ethiopian government. No problem.

The Reuters correspondent, one-eyed, one-armed, and doddering, had once been a great journalist. But he had survived too many important battles around the globe to risk anything more in Ethiopia. He had come to like the country, the easy life it afforded him, and the absence of any real competition. He wanted to stay and was content to take Negash's well-written handouts as they came. In addition, there was the business of 38,000 pounds sterling owed to Reuters for wire services the news agency supplied to the government papers. Instructions from the home office in London said, in effect, don't ruffle any feathers; get the pounds.

The rest of the large foreign press corps were not journalists at all. Most were devoted wholly to serving as spies and spokesmen for their governments. Others, independent of any official ties, were dishonest only in their own behalf, posing as journalists while dealing in contraband goods, foreign exchange, and serving as "arrangers" for foreign businessmen entangled in bureaucratic red tape. From Negash's point of view, all had the saving graces of incompetence and laziness. They would rather curry favor by filing only stories that were officially released than court expulsion by digging for real news.

Little could be done about the occasional visiting journalists who swung through on their three-day tours. High-ranking officials could rarely be persuaded to talk to them. Which left them free to concoct their fantasy versions of quaint, savage, primitive Ethiopia. But the visiting journalists seldom left the bars of the modern hotels they stayed at and so inevitably missed the truly significant stories that might be breaking.

Though a fair number of stories did appear which upset some of his more sensitive colleagues, Negash was convinced that Ethiopia enjoyed a far more favorable world press than it deserved. He considered the most important aspect of his work with the foreign journalists to be the protection, not of his country's reputation, but of the Emperor's image. Since most correspondents considered the Emperor a nice old man who made colorful copy, the job was easy.

Negash found it a matter of surprise and relief that so few major wire services and no major periodicals maintained full-time correspondents in Ethiopia. Their absence made his own job simpler. But he considered it a slight on the importance of his country. Addis Ababa was headquarters for the Organization of African Unity, for the United Nations Economic Commission for Africa, and the regional center for a score of other international agencies. It was the stamping grounds for liberation movements from every part of southern Africa. There were embassies from more than fifty nations and espionage agents from all the major and many of the minor countries of the world.

Militarily its importance included control of the Red Sea "choke points" vital for access to the Indian Ocean and, if it ever reopened, for the Suez Canal. Ethiopia was also, as Negash often phrased it in his press conferences, "the last bastion of Western influence" in an area rapidly coming under the sway of Russia and China.

Negash was particularly surprised that American newspapermen showed so little interest in his country. The young minister held a doctorate in political science from an American university. He loved the United States. He had lengthened his stay there with a job in the secretariat of the United Nations and returned with a blond, angular American wife, a machine-tooled product of Vassar and Philadelphia's Main Line. He knew he was considered by his enemies to be an American stooge, but he considered his role to be quite the opposite: helping to make the Americans more useful to Ethiopia.

American investment in Ethiopia, both military and economic, was vast and growing. The government alone poured twenty million American dollars into his country each year, more than any other country in Africa received, and another seventy million were spent in trade between the two countries. More than six thousand Americans lived in Ethiopia, nearly half of them at the vital United States military communications base in Asmara, capital of the northern province of Eritrea. Russia, China, and several Arab countries were supporting a rebellion in Eritrea that could threaten the American base. An American diplomat and a television team employed by the Washington-based *National Geographic* had been kidnapped, and several American soldiers had been killed by Eritrean terrorists. Barely a word of this ever reached the American public. Negash considered Ethiopia second only to Israel as a potential battleground of Russian and American interests, and yet American journalists ignored his country.

"When you get around to closing Vietnam, we could be your next war," Negash had once told a briefly visiting *New York Times* correspondent. "We could be your next war, and your people don't even know we exist."

"Nonsense," the correspondent answered. "Southeast Asia is important to the United States. The Middle East is important. South Africa is important. But not Ethiopia. Ethiopia isn't important."

"Yes," Negash had said. "When I was at the UN in the 1950s, that's what American journalists and politicians were saying about Vietnam."

In truth, Negash wasn't sure how important Ethiopia was to the United States. But he wanted to make it important. He knew how desperately his country needed foreign help to break its endless cycle of poverty and ignorance. The planned expulsion of the four Russian agents had been decided upon for the Americans' benefit. They hadn't asked for it, but it was hoped they would be impressed. He knew no nation was more able to help, but he wondered how willing Americans would be to increase their assistance to a country unknown.

"Perhaps," he said to the Papillon sitting beside him, "if we had a communist government to overthrow . . ."

The dog stretched out, covering his eyes with diminutive paws.

The Honorable Senator Getachew Tessema, seated in the second-class compartment, wondered why he had been brought along on this trip. Still smarting from his abrupt dismissal as minister and his polite exile to the hollow chambers of the senate, he hadn't expected a special summons from the Emperor.

There was a barely perceptible jolt as the slender, diesel-powered train started up from the station. Amhara women in the crowd ululated shrilly, a high-pitched call somewhere between a yodel and a battle cry. The more numerous pagans and Muslims raised cheers of their own.

Getachew watched the crowd in the marketplace with distaste. He considered himself a socialist, the most radical minister the cabinet had ever known. But these unwashed, unlettered tribesmen filled him with a loathing he tried to conquer. He knew such instinctive reactions made him a caricature of the man he wanted to be. He blamed his upbringing, his Western European education. He often wished he'd been educated in Russia like his father.

The old man lived like a savage with his animal skins and his whip and his ancient revolver. Though his father had lived some years in France, his character had been formed in Menelik's Ethiopia and the Russia of Czar Nicholas II. He had not been scarred by the trappings of French bourgeois civilization. He could still live and work among animals like the crowd now running beside the slowly accelerating train, their wild shouts raising a last terrifying farewell to the great king who had deigned to wave at them a few minutes before.

The Danakils among them raised spears and rifles over their heads, but none dared fire a jubilant round into the air. Tense, armed troops still stood in every doorway and on the roof of the departing train. Getachew wondered at the extraordinary security precautions that had been taken. The window by the Emperor's velvet-draped chair in the forward compartment had been sheathed over with steel. There was also steel plating at the back of his chair and a steel partition in front of him.

Between stations the Emperor sat by himself in his steel cube. Yet, at every village at which the *littorina* stopped, he stood in an open doorway, exposing himself to crowds that at every station since Awash included murderous, armed desert tribesmen.

What was he afraid of, Getachew wondered, and what was he trying to prove?

The Emperor sat rigidly erect in his three-sided cell. There were cushions behind his back. His feet were propped on a low stool, for his legs were too short to reach the floor.

As the train moved on, he remembered that it had been somewhere here, somewhere just beyond Adefo, that his old friend Tessema Bekele had first raised his hand against his Emperor. He had no desire to see and recognize the spot. He was glad of the steel sheeting on the window. It had been more than three decades before, but the memory was still painful.

Of all those who had opposed him, betrayed him over the

years, none had saddened him so deeply as Tessema. And now the old bandit was at it again. They had been through so much together in the early days. Throughout so much of his long life Tessema had served the empire well.

A modern man, yet schooled in the ways of the old, Tessema had been vital to him in the early years of his rule and useful even later. But his strengths had been his weaknesses. Stubborn to the point where he would have had them all suffer a noble defeat and the death of heroes when the Italians came. Crafty to the point where he would use his intriguer's skills against the man who had loved him best.

As much as any man, as much as himself, Tessema was Ethiopia. Its weakness. Its strength. The secret Tessema had never learned was to let others see only the strength.

He turned to his deferential minister of court who sat with the aide-de-camp across the aisle.

"Bring Negash to us," said the Emperor.

The bald, sad-faced courtier rose slowly from his chair and went to summon Negash.

The young minister was standing at the refreshment bar at the rear of the compartment when the elder official delivered the Emperor's message. The courtier did not speak but nodded his head toward the front of the compartment. Negash snuffed out a cigarette in a red plastic ash tray advertising a local beer. He bent over the counter of the bar as a rasping cough racked his body. He straightened, swallowed half a glass of mineral water, wiped his lips with a white handkerchief, and went to his king.

The Emperor indicated the unoccupied seat beside him. Negash hesitated a moment, then sat.

"How is my son enjoying the trip?" said the Emperor.

"It's a warm trip through these lowlands," said Negash. His smile was boyish.

The Emperor looked at him. The trace of a smile played over his own lips. He turned his eyes back to the steel plate before him.

"This business saddens us," he said.

"Dejazmatch Tessema?"

"Yes."

"I'm sorry, Your Imperial Majesty."

"I know. I know." For a moment he was silent, staring at the steel. Then he said, "My son, there is something I must tell you."

"Yes?" Negash had to fight to suppress an attack of coughing.

"There are those who say you have been involved in this affair."

"Your Imperial Majesty knows the truth."

"Yes, and the truth is different. But your enemies are growing bolder. And more numerous."

"My fate is in the hands of my Emperor."

"But a man with too many enemies . . ."

"I understand."

"Are you still interested in being an ambassador?"

"When Your Imperial Majesty wishes it."

"It would be *shir* for you, not *shum*."

Negash smiled at the reference to the practice of *shum-shir*. It was a technique correctly attributed to the Emperor of keeping his subordinates in line by alternately promoting and demoting them, rewarding today to punish tomorrow.

"To serve Your Imperial Majesty in any capacity is always an elevation."

"Of course. Like our friend Tessema. From *Afa Negus* to *Alem Bakagn*. From the mouth of the king to the hole of a prison."

Negash was surprised at the unusual bitterness with which the Emperor spoke.

"Why is it that those who serve us best betray us most?"

"Ambition?" said Negash.

"Foolishness," answered the Emperor. "This demotion to ambassador, this exile to Washington would make your enemies happy. It is exactly what they want for you. And you want it for yourself."

"I want only what my Emperor wants."

"We appreciate the respect you show by talking sometimes like a courtier. You need not do it all the time."

He showed no trace of a smile. Negash remained silent.

"What your Emperor wants would be for you to be first among our ministers. But that day is not yet. Our country is old and conservative. If you were our premier, we, Ethiopia, would be younger, more liberal. But that day is not yet. We must go slowly. Like this train. It knows the way.

"Consider. Our premier is a handsome man, and his wife is French. You are handsome, and your wife is American. We have stopped teaching in French in our schools and have begun speaking English. But we must go slowly. The engine cannot outrace the train. We must bring the whole country with us."

"I understand."

"Good."

Negash waited while the old man stared with his magnetic eyes at the steel before him.

"Has Getachew been told?"

"Not yet. But all the arrangements have been made. He'll be driven to Mota tomorrow at dawn. I'll brief him just before."

"Very good. We have given you much to do. Not only because of our affection and admiration. But because there are so few who are capable. And none we can trust."

Negash was suddenly aware of perspiration in the pits of his arms, at the back of his neck. His palms were wet. He could not check a short spasm of coughing. He knew the Emperor considered his desire to return to America a form of betrayal.

"We have worked you hard," said the Emperor, "and we feel your health is not good."

Negash shivered as the Emperor pierced him with eyes that narrowed and darkened as they turned toward him. The eyes softened, then looked away.

"You have been our son and more than our son. You would leave us, and your enemies would like to see you gone. Your wife would also, I suspect, like to visit her country for a time."

"She misses it."

"I know."

Negash noticed that the old man for the moment had dropped that imperial first person plural when speaking of himself. He waited, expecting him to continue in a more personal vein.

But the Emperor remained silent, immobile. His mind was suddenly back in the camp where Tessema held him captive, begging him to stay. To stay and fight the Italians. The Italians had been his enemies. And they wanted him gone. And he had wanted to go and his own wife, Menen, had urged the same. He had no use for the love of a woman. Political alliances, spasms of pleasure, the need for children. So much for the love of a woman.

"We suspect your wife does not love us." His voice was chilly. The first person singular had turned back to the imperial first person plural.

"Her love for Your Majesty is very great."

"For our person, perhaps, but we suspect she does not love our country." He was silent for a moment, his thoughts again drifting to the past. Then he asked, "Are those magazines still published in her name?"

Negash was taken aback. It was a moment before he realized the Emperor's thoughts had turned to his own wife, the late Empress Menen. Two magazines, one in English, one in Amharic, had been named *Menen* in her honor.

"Yes, Your Imperial Majesty."

"They are magazines of news about Ethiopia. But a magazine that bears a woman's name sounds like a magazine for women."

"I'll suggest to your minister of information that he find new names for the magazines."

"Do it for him, my son, or it won't be done." He placed a bony hand lightly on Negash's knee. "One reason you have so many enemies is that we so often give you the work of our other ministers to do." He withdrew the hand. "You can't expect them to love you for it."

Negash laughed tensely. The laugh became a cough.

"A rest will do you good. We shall allow you to go to Washington when the time is ripe. But you must be prepared to return at our will."

"Always, Your Majesty." He choked down a cough.

"Do you know what I ask Gabriel for when we go to Kulubi?"

"No," said Negash, adjusting himself to another abrupt change in topic and tone.

"Each time we go, we ask for another good year. Not for ourselves. For the sake of our country. And for my *silet*, I promise to return the next year and give thanks. So far Gabriel continues to grant us more time."

"May he always," said Negash.

With more irony than Negash had thought him capable of, the Emperor answered, "*Haile Selassie yimut*. May Gabriel always help us. May Haile Selassie die if he doesn't."

The old man grinned broadly, a smile Negash had only seen him display when he was totally relaxed among his younger grandchildren. The moment passed quickly.

"Some of our police officials," said the Emperor, "are unhappy because it was you personally, not they, who have uncovered this latest plot against us. And because it was you, not they, who brought us evidence of what our Russian friends have been up to among our students. Some go so far as to say the evidence was manufactured for you by your friends at the American embassy."

"The old CIA story."

"One day I hear you spend all your time chasing ladies. The next, that you spend all your time plotting with the CIA. Knowing how busy I keep you, you must be very active in the few moments you have."

"An idle mind . . ."

"Yes, a workshop where rumors are manufactured. By people with nothing else they can do, or are willing to do. We have so few who are capable. You more than anyone know how difficult is our task."

In his mind Negash filled in the Emperor's unspoken accusation. And you, who know how difficult is our task, would leave us.

"We are not immortal," said the Emperor. Negash wondered if the old man really accepted the fact.

"You are our son," said the Emperor, "and more than our son, while our own son is less."

"The Crown Prince . . ."

The old man's eyes danced. He said in English. "The inheritor of the bed." It was the literal translation of the Amharic phrase for heir apparent.

A bed suits him, thought Negash. But not a throne. Yet, he felt the father must share the blame if the son was not prepared to rule. Now in his mid-fifties, the Crown Prince was always present at ceremonial functions as a corpulent shadow to his trim father. Negash thought of him as a kind of perpetual vice-president, always kept at a distance from the ruling councils of government.

During the abortive coup of 1960, the Crown Prince had read over Radio Addis Ababa a statement of the rebels. Since then his most important function had been the chairmanship of the Ethiopian Red Cross Society.

"Even our own son," said the Emperor, "has raised his voice against us." His favorite son, Makonnen, the Duke of Harar, had been killed in an auto accident in 1957. "But leave that." Another son had taken to drugs before his death in 1962. "We have not been blessed in our sons." None of his many grandchildren showed significant promise. "When they ask us what will happen after our time, we direct them to the constitution where the succession of the Crown Prince is clearly spelled out. But what is a constitution after all? What does it know?"

He stared at the bulletproof shield before him and tapped a bony knuckle against it.

"Look to the steel, my son. Look to the steel. *Aprés moi, les soldats*. When our time is done, it may be best for you to leave Ethiopia. The soldiers will come to rule, and they will not love you."

"I, too," said Negash, "will ask Kulubi Gabriel . . ."

"Leave Gabriel," said the Emperor. He said it abruptly, but softly. "As long as we are, you will be. We are your father and more than your father. But you would give us your back and go while our need for you is great."

"My father," said Negash impulsively, "let me be ambassador, not to Washington, but to the hand of my Emperor. I want no other post."

"Good," said the Emperor.

He nodded curtly. The interview was done.

Suddenly, Negash felt as though a fourth steel plate had closed around him. He realized this was what the whole meandering conversation had been about. He was trapped. He had committed himself to staying. There would be no restful ambassadorship. No return to his beloved America.

The old man had won.

As they curved up the white gravel road above Mota, his father's troubling, elusive words still echoed in Tesfaye's mind, rattling like the stones spun up by the tires that banged against the bottom of Harry's Volkswagen.

Kill the mosquito and the malaria will cure itself. Like so much of the foolish folk wisdom embodied in proverbs, thought Tesfaye, it simply wasn't true.

Kill all the mosquitoes in Ethiopia and half the people would still be suffering from malaria already contracted. Kill the mosquito of tyranny, and the country would still be infected with the malaria of poverty and ignorance. His father, like his half brother Getachew, fancied himself a radical. Getachew pledged allegiance to Soviet socialism. Bring in the Russians and all will be well. His father went no further than anarchy. Sweep away the feudal tyrant and all will be well. Simple solutions. The students were the same. Land to the tiller. Slogans were the proverbs of the young. Equally deceptive. Wisdom that went no further than the eardrum.

Both his father and his half brother would advocate land reform. But land reform, too, had become more slogan than solution. How do you reform land? Cultivating it would help. Land to the tiller. What did it mean? Every man his own half hectare? Or square meter?

Land to the tiller and kill the mosquito. His father and Getachew were men for quick solutions and radical change. Yet, they both had served the conservative king who alone had shown the ability to keep the country together and move it, however slowly, forward.

He might cast a cold skeptical eye on his father's words. He could not accept many of the old man's ideas. He even wondered how accurate his memories were. He remembered his father's momentary confusion when he couldn't be sure if it had been the Emperor or the Emperor's brother who had been born the day the young Tessema fired the rifle three times. He had heard other stories of the Emperor's escape by train to Djibouti, stories at odds with his father's.

But to Tesfaye the wisdom of his father's ideas, the accuracy of his stories, didn't matter. What mattered was the telling, the magical weaving of a legend, a myth. Let the facts be garbled, the details lost. His journalist's mind was willing to suspend its normal functioning when his father sat down to talk. He could decide for himself later about the moral.

But now in his thoughts, that moment had come. He thought of all his father had said and knew he rejected the lesson his father had been trying to convey.

Tesfaye could see nothing but chaos to come when the Emperor died. Separatist movements in several provinces, barely suppressed now, would flame out unchecked. Somali incursions in the Ogaden. Border wars with Sudan in the west. Tribes and regions and religions pitted against each other. Shrill echoes of Biafra, tearing his country apart. Priests and peasants pulling one way; students and intellectuals another. Conservative old generals and liberal young majors at each others' throats.

Haile Selassie aimuwt, thought Tesfaye. May he not die. Let him live forever. Beyond that, there was only one slender hope, embodied in one corpulent man.

Crown Prince Asfa Wossen was already in Dire Dawa. He had flown down along with his wife two days before. He wanted to escape the chill heights of Addis Ababa for a few extra days of warm desert air. He had invited the governor of the province for lunch in the modest, pink-walled villa he maintained near the French school. The middle-aged prince had a special affection for Dire Dawa. He often thought Menelik had made a great mistake in not making it his capital instead of Addis.

Their lunch finished, he strolled with the governor in the garden. They walked in the shade of flame trees now a lustrous green with great hanging pods that in another three months would break into red flower. Frangipani scented the garden. Poinsettias and bougainvillaea gave it color.

Asfa Wossen was sure he could have been happy living in this city. But as a young man he had been sent as nominal governor to Dessie, the dismal provincial capital of Wollo. It had been his younger brother, the favored Makonnen, whom their father had sent to Dire Dawa to govern the sunny and richly endowed province of Harar. But now Makonnen was dead, and his palace here stood empty like a shuttered mausoleum opposite the Ras Hotel.

At least I'm still alive to walk in this garden, thought Asfa Wossen, sadly content.

He and the governor, who had once been schoolmates, had eaten heavily. Their conversation was desultory. The Crown Prince suspected that the governor, like himself, had his mind fixed on the man both were expected to meet at the station when his train arrived that evening.

"My father will soon be with us," said the Crown Prince.

"Yes," said the governor. "His train should be here at five."

"Perhaps a little after," said the Prince. He was fairer than his father, an inch or two taller. In his round, double-chinned face, he resembled his mother. He had once affected a beard trimmed in imitation of his father's. The Emperor had not been pleased. He now sported a brush mustache.

"I expect my father will want to walk from the station to his palace."

"Perhaps," said the governor. He was a tall portly man with the pleasant face of a successful politician. "If he isn't fatigued."

"Even more likely he'll want to walk if he is fatigued. It makes . . . a good show." He spoke the phrase in English with a clipped, Oxonian accent.

"Good show," echoed the governor.

They lapsed into their separate silences. Outside the pastel walls of the compound, horse-drawn *garis,* which still served as taxis everywhere outside of Addis, clattered by, bells tinkling softly.

For whom the bell tolls, thought the Prince. Literature interested him more than politics, but politics, at the moment, was very much on his mind. He had heard of Dejazmatch Tessema's plot through informants of his own in the palace, men who anticipated the day when they might have a new emperor to serve. If the plot could have succeeded, he would indeed be emperor. But the scheme, he knew, had already been foiled. Like the coup. Like all such intrigues that might have put him on the throne. He had long since resigned himself to the possibility that he might be outlived by his father. With his fluttering heart and dyspeptic stomach, he was sure his health was not nearly so robust as his father's.

He was not anxious to rule, yet he sometimes dreamed that the crown might suddenly be his. It would be his father's final punishment. He was convinced that the old man would want him to fail. To fail as conspicuously as possible. Every step his father had taken seemed to assure that when he died, chaos would rule in his stead. Historians would be forced to conclude that only the great Haile Selassie had been powerful and wise enough to rule in this difficult kingdom. The last monument to his greatness would be the ruin of the country after he passed.

And probably, thought his sole surviving son, the old tyrant will have his way. As usual.

There still were moments when he believed that given half the chance he could rule far better than his father. But he knew he would need help. While his father still lived, he would need help to become more widely known, more highly respected. It would have to be done subtly, for this was precisely what his father would never allow. The prince troubled himself little about the mechanics of government. He knew his abilities in this realm were limited, but he believed his father's were, too. There had always been, there would always be, foreign advisers able and anxious to tell a king what to do. They were clever, and he would only have to choose among them.

He also felt he would need generous economic help from foreign governments. In this respect it was the Americans above all who could provide. But again his father had seen to it that he had little contact with influential foreigners. The only exceptions were the fluttery wives of various ambassadors, who, like himself, were sentenced to the charities of the Red Cross. It wouldn't do to approach an ambassador's wife about matters of state.

If only Negash could be trusted. He certainly had influence among the Americans, but Negash would run to his father.

Who else? The story he had heard about Tessema's plot had made him remember the Dejazmatch's son, Tesfaye. The young journalist could be useful, thought the Crown Prince. He had good reason to believe Tesfaye would be loyal and trustworthy. And Tesfaye, too, had friends among the Americans.

He and the governor had strolled into a patch of sunlight at the far end of the garden. Both men were wearing comfortable, tropical-weight suits, but, where there was no shade, the afternoon heat was oppressive. They turned back toward the house.

They had gone only a few steps, the governor slightly in the lead, when the Crown Prince, struck by a new fancy, stopped and called out to his old friend.

"Tell me," he said. "You've known me a long time." He clasped his hands behind his back and pulled in his stomach. He stood as erect as he could.

"Tell me frankly. What do you think of me?"

"Why, Your Highness," said the governor. "I think, I've always thought of you as the kindest, one of the gentlest men I've ever known."

"And my father?"

"Oh," said the governor. "His Majesty the Emperor is strong. Very strong."

"Yes," said the Crown Prince. He sighed and let his stomach go. "He's strong."

My *tut abat*, thought Tesfaye. Years before, when his father's first arrest seemed imminent, the old man had fled with his family to a remote part of Wollo. The Crown Prince was then living in Dessie. The Dejazmatch's whereabouts were easily traced. He was arrested and brought with his family to the provincial capital and held temporarily in the custody of Asfa Wossen. The kindhearted prince aided his escape, even supplying him with a large sum of negotiable Maria Theresa thalers. For the next seven years Tesfaye and an older brother and sister were raised under the protection of the generous prince.

Tut abat. My breast father, thought Tesfaye. The soft connotations, so different from the harsh English equivalent of foster-father, had seemed appropriate to the six-year-old Tesfaye after the stern upbringing he had known from his own father.

Much of the time he had actually lived with an uncle back in the Chercher Hills near Asba Tafari. But even when not under Asfa Wossen's roof, the Crown Prince had been his protector. In adolescence, Tesfaye had been enrolled at Kotebe, the boarding school outside Addis Ababa, but his weekend home had been what by then had become the Crown Prince's residence at Sidist Kilo in the capital.

It was a strange atmosphere for the son of a political exile to be growing up in. Key figures among the more liberal members of the government were frequent visitors. Tesfaye was often aware of their whispers about him. He became even more shy and withdrawn. The prevailing atmosphere in the house, however, wasn't political or even intellectual. It was rather a salon of music and the arts. The latest literary trends and ballets in Paris, the newest stage hits in London were often discussed. With little understanding but an avid curiosity, Tesfaye had soaked up the culture of that gentle household.

"His mouth may be small," the Crown Prince used to say of him, "but his ears are big."

It had been to his surprise, and somewhat to his dismay, that as an adult his work as a journalist had led him away from his early interest in the arts to a greater concern with government and social questions. He realized now that he had reverted to a world of hard intelligence, the world of his father, and away from the softer realm of his cultured *tut abat.*

If I am my father's son, he thought, how did it happen? There were times when he felt like one of his father's avocado plants. A seed that had been broadcast on the wind, nurtured by others. That survived. Are all the avocados in Ethiopia my father's? Not even my father would say so.

He had been thinking in Amharic. He forced himself to rethink his questions in English. The language he worked—and wrote—in. Impossible in Amharic to think clearly. Again, I'm like my father in that. His Russian. My English. Not Amharic. How can you find your identity in a language designed for intrigue? How can a man say who he is in words with double meanings? In a country of double-dealing?

As they drove, Harry talked on about their visit to the farm at Mota.

"What a magnificent old man your father is. Really magnificent."

Tesfaye glanced at him. Here was another *tut abat*. A good man, thought Tesfaye, a kinder man than Baria. Yet, his wife would rather ride with Baria. Tesfaye wondered if Harry would ever find his identity. Not in Ethiopia, he thought. Or if the baby sleeping behind them would ever know his. In a world of intrigues.

They had again acquired the infant. He was tucked securely, peacefully in his plastic car bed. With the baby sleeping and Harry repeating himself, Tesfaye was able to pursue his own thoughts, thoughts that drifted back down the gravel road to Mota and the whitewashed mud walls of the room in which they had sat with his father.

He remembered the stub of pencil standing in the spent cartridge. When words fail you can make propaganda with a bullet. He did not want to think about it. He did not really want to think about his father. He did not want to think about the Emperor. About the mosquito and malaria. He tried to focus his thoughts on the Crown Prince, but the image blurred. He saw his father. The strength of the aged arms and shoulders pushing the massive figure up from the skin of the kudu. He saw the heavy staff gripped in the thick, powerful hands. The ancient revolver. He remembered the whip. He did not want to think about death.

Or the Emperor. That other strong old man. How often on public occasions he had watched the Emperor rise so slowly, so painfully from his chair. Like his father rising from the skin of the kudu.

They were climbing now, curving to the right. Trees fell away abruptly. Then, as the road straightened and leveled off, they were suddenly on another, narrow, bridgelike stretch with panoramic views spreading out from either side of the mountaintop causeway. To the south the clouds seemed to be darkening over the lush valley of the Galleti and Ramis rivers. To the north over the distant Danakil the sky was white with reflected desert heat. But Tesfaye was distracted from the chiaroscuro skies as he noted at the far end of the natural bridge a jagged line of buses, cars, and trucks pulled to the edges of the road.

"Slow down, Harry. Something's happened ahead."

They pulled up behind a huge blue passenger bus. The baby woke and at once began to cry.

"I'll find out what happened. You better stay with the baby," said Tesfaye.

"Sure," said Harry. "See if Baria and Julie are up there."

"*Ishi*," said Tesfaye. "I'll look for Baria and your wife." He hoped he wouldn't find them.

He had gone only a few meters up the road when he saw a small knot of people clustered around an old man who was pointing down the southern precipice. Tesfaye walked to the edge of the group and followed the direction of the old man's finger.

About a hundred meters below the road, the sharp drop leveled off to a sloping, heavily overgrown shelf. He could see a circle of men hacking away at the underbrush where something metallic glinted in the sun. As he looked down, trying to determine what they were after, he heard a voice behind him.

"Tesfaye."

He turned. It was Balcha Amara. Years before he and Balcha had worked together as journalists. Since then Balcha had followed a course not unlike Dejazmatch Tessema's, alternating periods of imprisonment and exile in remote provinces with a career as Ethiopia's most popular author.

"I thought that was you," said Balcha. "Come join us. We're just having lunch."

"No, no. I've just eaten. But what's happened here?"

"Terrible," said Balcha. "Nine people. A Land Rover went off the road." As he spoke, he held his wrists together just below the level of his belt. It was a gesture that had become habitual.

"Killed?" said Tesfaye.

Balcha nodded. "Yes. All nine."

Tesfaye knew Balcha to be the most compassionate of men. Yet, at the scene of this mass death, Balcha, who had just invited him to lunch, evidently had stopped for a picnic. How little, he thought, other people's tragedies affect us.

"It must have happened last night," said Balcha. "No one saw it. This old man . . ." He gestured with his joined hands toward the peasant at the center of the crowd. "He's still telling his story.

He's a pilgrim on his way to Kulubi, like all of us here. He's walking the whole way from Asba Tafari. He came along here just after dawn, and down below there was a band of monkeys, screaming and running about with pieces of clothing. He went down to look and found the Land Rover buried in the bush. It hadn't caught fire, but by that time the people were all dead anyway. The monkeys were stripping the bodies.

"The old man says he set up a howl and some people came running from that batch of *tukuls* you see farther down. They drove the monkeys away with stones, and someone was sent to bring the police from Mota. They were taking the last of the bodies into Dire Dawa when we got here."

"God save us," said Tesfaye. He had been scenting death and now here it was. Vultures were still circling in the sky overhead.

"It's a government Land Rover. Probably some chauffeur told his boss the car had to go into the garage and took off for Kulubi with his family."

"I'll check with the police when I get to Dire Dawa," said Tesfaye. "I should do a story."

"Always the newspaperman," said Balcha. "Don't you ever get tired?"

"Yes. I get tired. Who are you with?"

"Frehiwot," said Balcha.

"Really? Frehiwot the *azmari?*"

"The same."

"Ai, you jailbirds," said Tesfaye with a grin. "You stick together."

"We have to," said Balcha. "Our old friends don't like to be seen with us."

"Well," said Tesfaye, looking down at his shoes, "you know how it is. We prefer to have our martyrs stay in jail." He glanced up at Balcha. "It confuses us when they come out and become so successful. Where's Frehiwot?"

"Over there. We were just having lunch. At least you can't accuse Frehiwot of being successful."

"No," said Tesfaye. "That you can't."

They crossed the road to Balcha's car, a blue, secondhand Opel. Balcha's family, a shy young girl he had met during his exile, and their two young children, were in the back seat. The remains of a meatless *injera-wat* lunch were spread over the hood of the car.

"Tesfaye," cried Frehiwot as they approached. "*Tadess?*"

"*Alegn,*" answered Tesfaye. They smacked palms and shook hands.

Frehiwot's eyes were bloodshot; his fair skin was sallow; his teeth were yellow and decayed; his gums, gray. He and Tesfaye went on exchanging greetings for fully five minutes, endlessly asking after each other's health and welfare.

"Come and take some food with us," said Frehiwot. "Not that there's much left."

"Not that there was much to begin with," said Balcha. "These two, Frehiwot and my wife, make my life hard."

"You still follow the fasts?" said Tesfaye.

"Well," said Frehiwot, "you never know. Are you on your way to Gabriel?"

"Aren't we all?" said Tesfaye. He saw Harry approaching, awkwardly cradling the baby in his arms. "I'm taking an American friend. This fellow you see coming. To show him our culture."

"What's that he's carrying?" said Frehiwot.

"Another culture."

"I was wondering what happened to you," said Harry, drawing near.

"Some friends got me found."

The sight of the baby pulled Balcha's wife from the car. Despite Harry's protests, she quickly relieved him of his burden.

"Doesn't it have a mother?" asked Balcha in Amharic.

"Somewhere," answered Tesfaye. With full formalities, he introduced Harry to his two friends. Balcha's wife retreated wordlessly back to the car with the baby.

"What happened?" said Harry. "I mean what's the crowd for?"

"A Land Rover went off the road," said Tesfaye. "Some people got killed."

"How awful."

"Not for our friend, Ato Tesfaye," said Balcha. "For him it's a good story for his newspaper."

"What's done is done," said Frehiwot. "Come, Tesfaye. You must eat with us. Come, Doctor . . . What did Tesfaye tell us your name is?"

"Comfort. Harry Comfort."

"Yes. Doctor Comfort. What a lovely name, isn't it?"

"I guess," said Harry.

Frehiwot took Tesfaye and Harry each by an elbow and ushered them over to the meal spread on the hood of the car.

"Eat. Eat, Doctor Comfort. Forget death and eat."

Tesfaye and Harry politely dipped into some *shuro wat.* "You didn't find Julie and Baria?" said Harry.

"No," said Tesfaye. He hadn't looked. Let them find themselves, he thought. He suspected they already had. Harry, he was sure, did not. It was one respect in which his friend would never be Ethiopianized. No more than he could learn the language could Harry learn to play the game of suspicion, double meaning, double-dealing. He swallowed his mouthful of food and thought, Harry may talk a lot but orally oriented he isn't. Not like us. A nation of gossips. And paranoids.

Though both Balcha and Frehiwot spoke English, they soon lapsed into Amharic as they spoke to Tesfaye. Harry smiled and nodded at the occasional phrase he recognized. But he could sense an edge of hostility in Balcha's words. Tension in Tesfaye's answers. He wondered what it was about.

"Then it's true, Ato Tesfaye," Balcha was saying, "these rumors we've been hearing. That you're still an American agent."

"Ai, Balcha."

"Well, we didn't believe it, of course, but now we see with our own eyes. What Shaleka Shiferaw has been telling people is true."

"Shaleka? The last time I heard about Shaleka's games he was telling people I was a Russian agent."

"What does it matter?" said Balcha. "Because you have foreign friends, Russians, Americans, they can say Ato Tesfaye is a foreign agent."

"You know better."

"Yes," said Balcha, "but they say so. And some people, even your friends, believe. And Ato Balcha, they say, because he now drives this secondhand car, wears suits, and has a nice house and a pretty new wife, and he's been let out of prison, he must be a spy for the Emperor. And some people, even his friends, believe."

"Balcha," said Frehiwot, trying to interrupt, "must you use those ugly words?"

"What words?"

"*Faranj, machina.* Those damn ugly words from outside countries." Frehiwot made it a point of honor never to use words derived from European languages in his Amharic. It was a difficult process.

"You know," said Tesfaye, turning to Balcha, "it doesn't pay to listen to what the gossipmongers say about you. Last year when the students in one of their pamphlets said I was the chief spy for the American embassy, I put a sign over my desk at work, '*Geytoch, yihbakow, sim bal. Y'sallayi aleka yi-serral.*' Gentlemen, please be quiet. Chief spy at work. I don't care what people say about me."

"Your couplet is good advice," said Balcha with a slight bow.

Tesfaye looked uncomfortably at Harry. He could only guess why Balcha was needling him, but he was glad Harry couldn't understand the words. He would surely take them more seriously than Balcha intended. He knew Balcha and Frehiwot weren't being rude in excluding Harry from their conversation. But for both the author and the songwriter the art of playing in Amharic was more than just a professional skill. It was a way of life. They enjoyed it and would have felt crude and limited trying to express themselves in their imperfect English. Yet, there was a certain edge to Balcha's words. He began to suspect what it was. Or am I getting paranoid? he asked himself.

"Eat, eat," Frehiwot said to Harry. "These two want to play with talk. You should eat and enjoy." To Balcha and Tesfaye he said, "You lovers of men and words from outside countries talk too much and eat too little. Eat and stop your outside words." It was one of his contentions that the commonly used Amharic word for foreign—*faranj*—was derived from the French *étranger*. He preferred the purer though more complex *y'woochi ager*, of outside countries.

Tesfaye enjoyed the game though he knew he was no match for Frehiwot. "We were just talking about you," he said. "Your pure Amharic, deriving words from Ge'ez instead of outside languages. With my father. We'd stopped at his place at Mota."

"What?" said Frehiwot. "Is that old lion still alive?"

"He was an hour ago," said Tesfaye.

"You must forgive Frehiwot," said Balcha. "He thinks that while he was in prison all the people who were alive before must have died. *Alem bakagn.*"

Frehiwot had been jailed because of the scandalous political couplets he wove into his songs during performance. He was both a popular composer of modern songs and a traditional *azmari*, a singer of spontaneous, satirical couplets. His friend Balcha had spent a year in prison followed by what was calculated to be a humiliating period in an insane asylum and then two years of exile in a remote western province.

His crime had been getting himself elected to parliament. Political ideas had always been the driving force behind his work. He'd begun his career as a journalist with the Amharic papers, but his reporting and especially his commentaries were far too outspoken for the authorities. He wasn't removed from his job, but cautious editors stopped using his material.

He had taken to writing books only to find another way of reaching people with his social criticism and ideas for political reform. The precensorship of books had led him to adopt a more allusive style. Then, impatient with allegories, he had run for parliament, directly advocating in his campaign talks the political reforms he believed in.

But his direct political oratory had won him election soon after the publication of a powerful satire that had been just subtle enough to elude the censors. His allegorical novel depicted the struggle of unborn twins who studied the world they were to be born into from the womb of their mother. One twin was so shocked by the cruel and backward land they saw that he fought to stay in the womb. The other, equally shocked, struggled to be born so he and his twin could set about changing the world. The struggle ended with one child fighting his way out of the womb while the other clung to its walls unborn. In the wake of Balcha's campaign for parliament, it became clear even to the censors that the poor and unjust country described in his allegory was Ethiopia.

Tesfaye had been among the most ardent admirers of the book, but now, as he talked with Balcha and Frehiwot, he was troubled by his contrasting attitudes to his two friends. It was the shattered Frehiwot rather than the admirable, determined Balcha for whom he felt an instinctive sympathy. Frehiwot's once beautiful tenor voice was gone. He now kept alive by touring the *tej bets* of Addis with his one-stringed *masinko*, singing for his drinks in a harsh, whisky croak. Balcha had managed since his years of jail and exile to publish volumes of poetry, essays, and fables at the rate of one every two months.

Printed in editions of five thousand, they invariably sold out in a matter of days. Second editions did nearly as well. He knew that

Balcha wrote only because of his ideas, and yet the success of his books made Tesfaye uneasy.

In the absence of a publishing industry, Ethiopian authors print their books at their own expense. For most, this means taking substantial losses for the pleasure of seeing their words in print. For the popular Balcha, it meant substantial profits and considerable jealousy from other writers. In a country of twenty-five million with a literacy rate of less than five percent, his sales were astounding.

"Prisons aren't good for people who work with their voices," said Frehiwot. "We need gay crowds to shout and tell us how good we are and buy us drinks. Scribblers are luckier. They need to be shut away every once in a while where their friends can't invite them out and keep them from their work."

"I don't have that problem anymore," said Balcha. "My friends stay away these days. They're afraid they'll get in trouble around Balcha. When was the last time you knocked on my door to invite me out, friend Tesfaye?"

"I don't know your house."

"Of course. But we can fix that. I'll come to your office."

Frehiwot interrupted. "He doesn't mean that. That's a French word." Balcha had used the common Amharic word for office—*bureau*. "He means to say your room of work."

"*Ishi*," said Balcha. "I'll come to your room of work."

"He'll come to your room of work," said Frehiwot, "and leave with you in the box that goes up and down and take you in his box that goes on the road on things that turn and take you to his house so you can invite him out." He had managed to avoid using what he considered the foreign words for elevator, automobile, and wheel.

"Wonderful," said Tesfaye.

"Wonderful if you come," said Balcha. "I want you to know my house."

"I will," said Tesfaye. "Forgive me, friend, Balcha. I only stayed away because I was afraid I would disturb you in your work."

"Truly?"

"No." He again looked down at his shoes. "Falsely. The truth is . . . Well, you remember I published a book of my own once. I had a thousand printed. Eight were sold, and I gave away two hundred. You know how we Ethiopians are. When someone excels us, we get jealous and small. We don't try to equal him by climbing ourselves. Instead we try to bring him to our level. By cutting him down. I may have been guilty of some of that. Forgive me, *gashe* Balcha."

Harry watched them, picking slowly at the food. He was still stuffed from the meal they'd eaten at Dejazmatch Tessema's, but there was little else he could do. Tesfaye noticed how forlorn Harry looked.

"Doctor Comfort and I have eaten," he said to Balcha. "But we must eat with you again." He spoke in English, hoping to be able to bring Harry back into the conversation. He took up some of the meatless *wat* with a ragged piece of the remaining *injera.* The food was Balcha's. Whatever sharp words or past injuries stood between them, accepting the hospitality of Balcha's food was a way of bridging the gap. Food was part of the ritual of weddings, births, holidays, funerals, reconciliations. Eat and enjoy. Forget death and eat. But he knew that Balcha was not religious, and he was sure that his shy, young wife could not influence what he ate. The absence of meat puzzled him. He turned to Frehiwot. "But why this fasting?"

"Don't you remember? It's Wednesday. You've been outside our traditions so long you forget that Ethiopians fast on Wednesdays and Fridays."

"And about a hundred other days each year," said Tesfaye. "At least priests and old women do. But why you?"

"You never know," said Frehiwot, responding in English. "It's like Gabriel. I don't really believe—for sure—in these miracles and vows. But there might be something to it. So why not? Just in case."

"I know how you feel," said Harry.

"Frehiwot wants to be cautious," said Balcha. "But you'll see. He'll fast all his life. Kiss the church every Sunday, and on his deathbed deny God."

"Perhaps you're right," said Frehiwot. "I'm too much like you. Not cautious enough."

"Neither of you is famous for staying out of trouble," said Tesfaye.

"What good man is?" said Frehiwot. "Even though they say our friend Balcha has been tamed by prison. That the books he writes now are tame."

"They say much worse than that about me," said Balcha.

Despite Tesfaye's efforts, their excitement propelled them back into Amharic. Harry watched them, fascinated, frustrated. He'd been intrigued by what Frehiwot had just said about believing in vows and miracles—just in case. He wanted to hear more but hesitated to break in on a conversation he no longer understood.

"Have you read Balcha's new book?" Frehiwot asked Tesfaye.

"I heard," Tesfaye said with apparent embarrassment. "I heard there's one at the printing press now."

"That's the one," said Frehiwot. "He let some of us read it after the writer who strikes with her fingers finished it. My goodness, the correctors of books, God help them, have passed it. But you remember that other book had passed the corrector of books, too. It was on sale for an hour before someone who can read happened to read it and went running to the palace."

"In that hour," said Balcha, "it sold more than eight hundred copies."

"I know," said Tesfaye. "I bought ten myself."

"You must have gotten rich," said Balcha. "After it was confiscated, you could get a hundred dollars for a copy."

"No," said Tesfaye. "I still have one copy. The rest I made the mistake of giving away. I thought people should read it."

"So did I," said Balcha. "And I don't begrudge the ones who sell copies for a hundred dollars. I don't care. I'm not a bookseller. In fact, I was glad they banned that book. You can't kill an idea by banning a book. People have heard of the ideas in that book more than they ever would have if it hadn't been banned. For me, that's good, because books aren't important."

He knew Tesfaye and Frehiwot would never agree with what he was saying. He turned to Harry and asked in English, "Isn't that correct, Doctor Comfort? I was just saying books aren't important. Ideas are important. But books are only like pots. Not even as important, because no matter what you pour into it, a pot has a shape of its own. But a book takes its shape only from the ideas that are in it."

"Gosh, I don't know," said Harry. "Maybe you're right. We write because of our ideas. But I don't think many people read for ideas. They read to learn about things. Information."

"Yes, information. And ideas."

Suddenly being brought into the conversation had taken Harry back. Balcha's words sounded to him like his own ideas about the book he was trying to write. But he didn't want to tell

Balcha that. He was afraid it would sound foolish to say he was writing a book about a country he knew so little, about a culture tied so closely to a language he didn't understand.

"I write about my country and my countrymen," Balcha said to him. "The censors can destroy a book I write. Let them destroy. People will talk more about what's been censored. The book gets destroyed, like a pot gets broken, but the ideas spill out and spread."

"But you must care about your writing," said Tesfaye. "No one writes Amharic better than you do."

"Let it be bad, my Amharic. It doesn't matter. I'm not like you. You care about books and newspapers for their own sake. You think it's important to have newspapers, good professional newspapers. Even if you can't print anything but government lies in them."

"It's true," said Tesfaye. "I do. But only because we need them to be there for those times we manage to print something important–and true. That people can read. Not just hear as rumor."

"The rumors tell more truth than your papers."

"And more lies," said Tesfaye.

"To me anyway your newspapers, books, all such things don't matter. All that matters is how important the ideas in them are to our country, our countrymen."

"For me not just ideas," said Tesfaye. "But facts as well. That's the trouble with too many of our ideas. They aren't based on facts. Our countrymen can't know what's right for our country if they don't know the facts about our country."

"Tell them."

"I try."

"So do I."

"I know you do," said Tesfaye. "That's why I think your books should be read, not just talked about after they're censored."

"Not all my books have been censored."

"No," said Frehiwot. "Sometimes you fool them. But this new book of yours, I'm afraid this time you haven't been cautious enough."

"But the censors passed it."

"Yes, they passed it, but what do they know?"

"What's the book about?" asked Tesfaye.

"This time it's a novel," said Balcha. "About a man in jail."

"A political prisoner?"

"No," said Frehiwot. "A man who shoots another man's wife, thinking it's his own wife being unfaithful to him. That part is a heavy mixture. I won't go into that part of it. But the second half of the book, it's about the man's life in prison, in *Alem Bakagn.* As you read it, you see the way he describes life in *Alem Bakagn,* well, it's just like life you know where."

"That's fascinating," said Harry. "Tesfaye's father was just telling us about *Alem Bakagn* and what it means. He's been there, you know."

"We've all been there," said Balcha. He was growing impatient with Tesfaye's American. He didn't want a foreigner to hear too much of what he had to say. He reverted to Amharic and turned to Tesfaye.

"You see, when I came out of prison, they put me in Amanuel, the mental hospital. It was just another kind of prison. Then I was sent into exile. I had come out of jail, out of the mental hospital, but I was still a prisoner. After exile, I came back to Addis Ababa. They told me I was no more a prisoner. But I looked around. Isn't this Ethiopia? I asked myself. I saw that it was. So I knew I was still in prison."

"And in the book?" asked Tesfaye.

"Well, the book went to the censors and they read it and they said, 'Ah, yes, this is very nice, Ato Balcha, a very nice book, but is it trying to say something about Ethiopia?' "

"So I told them, 'How could it be saying about Ethiopia? It's just about a man who shoots his wife by mistake and goes to jail. What's that to do with Ethiopia?'

"They shook their heads at that and said, 'But what about this part here? Isn't this implying that Ethiopia is a prison?'

"Well, you see, at the time I was meeting with the censors about my book, Our Imperial Majesty had just made a trip to the Ogaden. Our friends in Somalia, of course, say the Ogaden should belong to them. So in his speech there the Emperor used a very nice phrase. He said, 'Ogaden is Ethiopia. Ethiopia is Ogaden.'

"So I quoted that phrase to the censors, and I reminded them that a few years before in Asmara he had used the same phrase about Eritrea because the Arabs claim Eritrea should belong to them.

" 'Gentlemen,' I told our friends the censors, 'His Majesty the Emperor has said that Ogaden is Ethiopia, and Ethiopia is

Ogaden. He has said Eritrea is Ethiopia, and Ethiopia is Eritrea. But he has never said that Ethiopia is *Alem Bakagn*, or that *Alem Bakagn* is Ethiopia. So if our Emperor has never said our prison is Ethiopia and Ethiopia is a prison, how can you gentlemen dare to say it?' "

Tesfaye and Frehiwot couldn't help laughing. But it was worried laughter. They kept looking behind to make sure no one was loitering close enough to hear what Balcha was saying. And Harry kept wondering what they were laughing about.

"They're very foolish, these censorship people. What I said confused them. They were afraid of being accused of believing that Ethiopia could be a prison. So they agreed to accept that part. A few little changes, nothing important. I always put in a few little things that don't really matter for the censors to take out. Because when they're worried about something you have to let them think they've made some changes."

"Tell him about the other part," said Frehiwot.

"Which?"

"You know. The bodyguard fellow."

"Oh, yes," said Balcha. "One of the characters in the prison part. I got the idea partly from a fellow I met there who had been involved in the coup. He had been a prisoner for seven years. Later they put him in the mental hospital, and I met him there again. The way I have him in my book, I make it that when he was in jail they put him to work in the woodworking shop. The way they do most people. Either that or they have you making rugs. Anyway, this fellow turns out to be so hardworking and clever, pretty soon they put him in charge of the whole shop. The warden is so impressed he starts giving the fellow a lot of the administrative work to do for the whole prison. So pretty soon you have this fellow, a prisoner who tried to overthrow the government, running the prison. He was supposed to be included in an amnesty one year on the Emperor's birthday, but the warden didn't want to lose him. He was too efficient, you see. So the warden threw his release papers away.

"But someone figured out he was still there. The security people went to question him. They ask him what in the hell he's still doing in jail. Well, the poor fellow didn't know he was supposed to have been released. So he tells the security people that what he's still doing in jail is running the woodworking shop and he's helping the warden with administration and he's in charge of buying provisions for the kitchen and all the other things he's doing by then.

"The security people decide he must be crazy because they know the warden wouldn't have a prisoner running the jail. Then one of them asks the fellow if he still thinks the government should be overthrown. All he wants, of course, is to be a nice fellow and maybe they'll let him out. So he tells them No, he doesn't think the government should be overthrown. Well, when he says that it convinces them for sure he must be crazy because everyone knows the government should be overthrown.

"I didn't put that in the book, of course. But that's what really happened. In the book I just write that they decide he's crazy because he thinks he's running the jail. So since he's supposed to be released from jail anyway, they release him. From jail, I mean. And then they put him in the mental hospital.

"Well, you know how Amanuel is. They have only that one crazy Yugoslav for a psychiatrist and a half-wit Ethiopian for a director. So pretty soon our friend from the bodyguard starts borrowing psychology books from the crazy Yugoslav. He reads about Freud and starts giving psychiatric care to the madmen and pretty soon he's doing the director's work, too. He starts a handicraft shop that makes a big profit, and he uses the money to order some of these new miracle drugs from Europe. Pretty soon he's curing so many people the Yugoslav and the director figure they better get rid of him or they'll be out of a job."

Tesfaye was bent with laughter. "Ai, Balcha. They'll never let you publish it."

"But they are. Let me finish. So what happens? They can't just release the fellow on their own since the security police put him in. So they call in the security and tell them they have to take the fellow out because he isn't crazy anymore.

"Naturally, the security people question him again. They want to know what he's doing in the crazy house if he isn't crazy. So he tells them he's never been crazy, but since they put him there he's been trying to help out. Giving psychiatric care. Occupational therapy. Ordering new drugs and all the other things he's doing since the director doesn't do anything."

"Well, these security people, naturally they consider themselves pretty clever. They know all crazy people think they aren't crazy and have strange ideas about how they're Napoleon or the Emperor or Jesus Christ or some other big shot in charge of the world. So they decide the fellow must still be crazy only he isn't clever enough to think he's Napoleon, just the director of the crazy house. So they decide he has to stay there."

"Friend Balcha," said Tesfaye, "you're the one who's crazy."

"That's how I fooled them," said Balcha.

"What?"

"I am crazy. That's what I told the censors. Listen. I'll explain. I mean you're right. The censors didn't like this part. They said I was hinting that we put good people in jails and crazy houses and let the dummies and lazy people run the country.

"So I told them, 'Look, I was in the crazy house myself. Everybody knows that. That's why I was put there. So everyone would know Balcha is crazy. And whatever he wrote before and whatever he writes now is the work of a crazy man and nobody will take it seriously. It's just a crazy man's joke for people to laugh at.' "

"Well, all these weeks we were discussing, I was inviting our friends in the censorship to drinks. And if we went out to the ladies, I always paid. So they were thinking this Balcha is a pretty good fellow and anyway a little crazy. Everyone knows he wouldn't have been in the crazy house if he wasn't a little silly. But they said I should write in the introduction that I was in the crazy house when I wrote the book. That way everyone would know it was all just crazy nonsense and laugh. So I wrote. What do I care? Not all people are such dummies as our censors. People will know what's nonsense and what isn't. So I wrote what they wanted and I even flattered them to think they were helping me make my book better. That they liked. So they said, 'That's good. Now you can publish.' "

"No," said Frehiwot. "It will be just like the last time. You fooled the correctors, but they aren't all that dumb. As soon as the book comes out, one of the smart ones will read it. They'll burn the book, put you back in jail, and give the correctors jobs on the street corners selling letters of events."

"He means newspapers," said Balcha.

"That's a word from an outside country," said Frehiwot. "But don't try to run away from what we were talking about. As soon as one of the smart ones reads your book, you'll be back in jail."

"Nonsense. As my book proves, the smart ones are all in jail or the crazy house. You don't appreciate our country. We have spies and security police and censors, it's true. But they are all so silly and foolish and lazy that Ethiopia is the freest country in the world. What we would have to worry about is if they took someone like the bodyguard fellow out of the crazy house and put him in charge of the security or the censorship. But they won't. Our Imperial Majesty only lets dummies run things because he's afraid if he had smart ones running things they might get together and kick him out."

"Don't underestimate that old man," said Tesfaye.

"I don't," said Balcha. "He's clever. And a great man. If he read my book himself, I would be in trouble. But he has too many important things to do than to read silly novels by crazy fellows like me. And the people who do his dirty work, reading what we scribblers produce, are all dummies."

"No," said Tesfaye. "Frehiwot is right. There are some smart ones. And . . . I hate to tell you this, Balcha. But one of the smart ones may have read it already."

"How . . .?"

"I was in the printing press, two or three nights ago, checking the paper. One of the printers told me. Negash Mengistu had ordered a copy of the page proofs of your novel sent to him."

"Those bastards," said Balcha. "They took my whisky then squealed to Negash."

"No. Not the censors," said Tesfaye. "Negash has people of his own. Shaleka Shiferaw is one."

"That soldier."

"Yes. What this printer told me was that Shaleka, who snoops into everything he can, took a look at your book in the press and told Negash about it."

Balcha had again pressed his wrists together at the level of his belt. He stood as though bound in invisible chains.

"They have an order," said Tesfaye, "not to release any copies without written permission from Negash himself."

"From what I hear," said Frehiwot, "this Negash isn't one of your dummies."

"No," said Tesfaye. "He's one of the smart ones."

"I wonder what happened to them?" said Harry.

"Who?"

"Julie and Baria."

"Oh."

They were walking back to Harry's car. Harry carried the

sleeping baby on his shoulder. Tesfaye walked with his hands plunged deep in his pockets.

"I mean you'd think with a crowd like this they would have stopped to ask what happened."

"Maybe they were in a hurry," said Tesfaye.

Harry gently lowered the baby into his car bed. "Why don't you drive?" he said to Tesfaye. "I'm tired."

"If you insist." He climbed in behind the wheel and adjusted the seat for his long legs.

"You'll have to tell me later what you were talking about back there. It must have been awfully funny."

"Not so funny," said Tesfaye. Harry handed him the car keys and he started up the car.

"You sure were laughing a lot."

"Well, yes. We were talking about a book. Part of it was very funny. But the ending is sad."

"It's terrible to think about," said Harry. He was looking out the window at the crowd still strung out along the edge of the road.

"What?"

"That accident. Those people killed."

"You're right," said Tesfaye.

Nine people killed, he thought. Nine people. And one book.

"Gosh, I'm tired," said Harry. "Tired and worried about Julie."

You have the ethics of a bitch. Her mother's words. In a letter. After Julie had made the mistake of writing to tell her she was marrying Harry. And why. If I'm a bitch, what does that make you? Her own words had been no answer. Despite the half-absorbed lessons of biology classes and paperback Freud, she knew she'd made her own life. Knowing it was no comfort.

Harry was a comfort. She'd told him that once. That she loved him because of his name. He hadn't like it. He wanted to be more than a comfort. That was what frightened her. There was a time when she'd had ambition. Like Harry. It was hard to remember. So many things she'd wanted to do. So many things she'd tried. None jelled. Even when she was good at them. None ever jelled. She couldn't remember when ambition had begun to fade. When the search for the right career, the right man, turned into drifting.

When she knew she'd be willing to live in the shadow of some man. If she could find a man capable of casting a shadow.

A man who could excite her. A man like Baria. A man who would love her. A man like Harry. A man whose work, whose importance she could share in. A man she could love. A man like no one she'd ever found. A complete man. Not Harry. Not Baria.

She never knew what he was thinking. He'd barely spoken to her since Miesso. Since she'd told him, as directly as she could, that he was the father of her child. She never knew what he was thinking, and he never asked her what she thought.

Harry's miracle. Baria's child. Harry was always asking her what she thought. She rarely told him. She never had any need to ask Harry what was on his mind. Harry, she was convinced, couldn't think without talking. Like people who can't read without moving their lips. She'd said something like that to him once. The comments of a bitch.

Her mother, she knew, hadn't made her that way. I'm pregnant, she'd written. Someone has to marry me. She'd been deceived. She hadn't been pregnant. And all their life together, since before their life together began, she'd been deceiving Harry. She hated herself for it. And worse. She hated him. Harry wanted more than being a comfort. She wanted more than being his wife. Mrs. Comfort. She couldn't laugh. She felt stifled, but she knew no one had stifled her. The world hadn't put her in chains. No one had killed her ambition, or forced her to be useless, dependent. No one had shotgunned her to the altar with Harry. She was saddled now with a child because she'd let happen what she wanted to happen. She'd been Daddy's little girl because she'd wanted to be Daddy's little girl. No one forced her to go on playing the role—or trying to. Wanting the approval, the applause she'd known then. Daddy's little girl with a mother who hated her for it. Daddy's little girl. At my age. With no daddy.

She knew she'd put herself in these chains. Like that madwoman at Awash Station. Like all the women she'd known. The straps of a delivery room table. She remembered being strapped to that table. Her legs forced into those braces. Straps on her wrists. The weight of a man. Casting no shadow. Hands on your wrists, your shoulders. Fingers on your throat. All her life she'd let herself be strapped to that table. A table like a coffin.

And yet, when she'd seen a woman, another woman, in chains,

she had done what she could to free her. Christina. A good Christian name. She put herself in chains. Because of a man who had died. Today she put herself in chains, the police major had said. All his life she kept him chained up. Poor Harry. Sometimes he scares me and what would I do? Christina described him as tall, strong, handsome. Then they had told her he was slight, meek, stooped. How would she describe Baria? And people would say he was a leper. She wanted a man—like a man she imagined. Weak. Strong. Hers. From paperback Freud she remembered, What does a woman want? Chains? Not chains, Christina had said. Christina, who had put herself in chains. Like me.

The world, the changing times tried to free her. She resisted and clung to the ethics of a bitch. Her mother's words. She clung to them. She'd picked out the leash and the collar. Then blamed Harry for buying them—and not being able to handle the chain. A pampered bitch, her mother had said. You gave me the name *bitch*. Then that's what I'll be. But I won't blame you. I can't.

She knew her mother's words hadn't shaped her. Nor her father's love for a little girl. She'd shaped herself. A bitch who wanted to be happy. Who used to look good in a bikini but wouldn't anymore. Who wanted to be loved, not useless. Loving, not dependent. Not saintly ever but decent. Vulgar even, but not faithless. Who wanted to live something better than the ethics of a bitch. Who tried, who searched, but in such strange places. Places where she was sure to find chains, contempt, abuse. Not Baria's contempt. Her own. She knew it when they'd made that trip. She knew it when she decided she wanted Baria for herself. She wondered how much it mattered to her that others might know. She hoped it didn't matter very much. She suspected it did. Will you tell him? Some day I swear he'll drive me too far and I'm scared. I want to be happy. Haven't I got a hell of a nerve? She remembered when she decided.

She'd grown tired of hearing Harry talk about Baria. She'd met him only casually at a few of the endless chain of diplomatic and academic cocktail parties they attended in Addis. She'd been repulsed by his skin. Drawn by his quiet force. By the way other women were drawn to him. They'd rarely spoken, but when their eyes met, glanced away and met again, she knew that with Baria she could find trouble, the kind of trouble she'd so often sought before she secured her safety with Harry.

Since her marriage, she'd tried to avoid that trouble. Sometimes trouble found her out, recognizing her need. But with Baria she went looking. She'd never felt as trapped as she had in Ethiopia. It was a man's country. Women, especially foreign women, were expected to bear their cross. She felt pale, shabby, old in comparison to the young, exotic, and so easily available women of the country. She supposed that even Harry, with a little luck, could find a mistress among them. She was sure he must have at least taken an occasional girl from one of the *buna bets*. The other wives said all the men did. Not my Harry, she thought at first, but then began to wonder if even Harry, so often off on his trips with the fellows, Baria, Tesfaye, and the others . . . She began to wonder if she could hold him. Even Harry. She began to doubt herself more than ever before.

Baria's such a wonderful friend. So loyal, Harry had said. There isn't anything he wouldn't do for a friend. Even sleep with his wife. He enjoys life but he's so disciplined in his work. For their anniversary he'd bought her a painting of Baria's. Madonna and child abstracted in cool, cruel circles of blue. It hung in their bedroom. Harry, in his mystical way, now linked it to his miracle—the birth of the child he'd wanted to name Menelik. She'd first heard of Menelik during the trip they'd taken together.

Baria had been commissioned to do a series of paintings for Ethiopian Airlines along the tourist circuit called "The Historic Route." Each stopover, Gondar, Lalibela, Axum, took them further back into the past, back, it was claimed, to the time of Solomon and Sheba. Baria had invited Harry along. Julie invited herself. She had decided she wanted to get to know Baria better. But she'd never gotten any closer to Baria. Not then. Not later. Not even in bed. She'd only discovered herself. Again.

The castles of Gondar were pretty enough. She'd enjoyed watching Baria sketching them. They were what—three centuries old—and reminded her of castles she'd seen in Spain. It was disappointing to find that Portuguese masons had built them.

They rented a Land Rover in the afternoon and drove out to a distant Falasha village. Like proper tourists, they visited the synagogue and bought some pottery.

For the first time she felt her mind jogged by a sense of the past deeper than any she'd ever felt in Europe. No one knew how long the tribe, practicing a primitive form of Judaism, had been isolated in this remote corner of Africa. To Julie the people looked no different from other highland Ethiopians, and even their synagogue looked like a smaller, shabbier version of some of the poorer mud and thatch churches she'd seen.

The rabbi told them he'd been to study in Jerusalem on an Israeli foundation grant. The revelation was too much for Baria.

"You see, you don't have to be a great artist to get a foundation grant. You can live as isolated and primitive as this fellow, and still some foundation will find you. And what do they send him all the way to Israel to study for? His religion. The one thing he's good at and that the people don't need more of, mumbo jumbo, they teach him to be better at. So he can come back to the poverty of his village and be a better Jew."

He led them out of the tiny synagogue and across the village to the area where pottery was sold. He bought Julie a souvenir, a miniature in clay of Solomon and Sheba in a bed topped by a Star of David.

"I can guarantee you," he said, "before you are back in Addis Ababa this will be broken." What happens in bed, she'd thought, is never permanent. But still we try. "Their pottery is poor," Baria said, "and they are poor farmers. They are Jews, and among us, just as Jews in Germany, they are outcasts. Here not because they are Jews, mind you, but because they are potters. We consider it a taboo trade, like metalwork or almost any useful skill."

She had found it hard to believe that a country so in need of manual skills could consider them taboo.

"We believe they have the evil eye," Baria said. "After all, they work with fire, isn't it? Do you know what Ethiopians say when red spots appear on a pot while it is being fired? They say the *tayb*, the *budda*, the evil eyes are fighting." He grinned. "Some people, you know, say it about me. When they aren't saying I'm a leper. They say that my spots, my mottled skin, is because the *tayb* are fighting inside me. And so the spotted slave Baria is an outcast, too."

Julie and Harry hastened to assure him, as foreigners always did when he called attention to his skin. But in the exchange Julie had lost that sense of the distant past unveiling that she had felt in the synagogue. The next day, among the rock-hewn churches of Lalibela, it was Harry who stole her awakening awareness from her. Harry made Lalibela his own. His enthusiasm allowed no one else a share in appreciating the monolithic churches. Wow. This can't mean as much to you as it does to me but wow just look at those arches. She had been looking at those arches, great vaulting curves that made the space of the last of the eleven churches they visited seem infinite with density and time. But Harry had stolen the arches from her, just as Baria had stolen the Falasha village. Men always cheated you, even of yourself. A woman was never allowed to enjoy what she could know. For man's will, man's need, always intruded, shattering the silence.

They spent several days at Lalibela, giving Baria a chance to sketch each of the churches in detail. At night, in the handsome new hotel, she lay in her monklike bed next to Harry's, aware that Baria slept just beyond the whitewashed stone wall between the rooms. His bed was as close to hers as Harry's. Only the wall made a difference, but it was a barrier that only heightened her awareness of the man beyond it. She tried to ignore Harry, chattering again how admirable Baria was. Men always cheated you. Harry could even steal a lover that then she had only dreamed about. While a whitewashed stone wall stood between them.

When they finally flew on to Axum, she was cheated again, excluded by custom from the old church of Mary of Zion. The new church, a hollow, echoing dome, had all the charm of a barren airport terminal. To this she was admitted, but the old church, with its treasury of the crowns, jewels, vestments, and ceremonial crosses of the kings of Ethiopia, was a male sanctuary. It galled her that women should be refused entry to a church named for a woman.

One of the priests brought a few of the crowns and gold crosses out into a small courtyard behind the church so she could stare at them through the bars of the black iron fence. Baria wanted to do extensive sketching of the ornate, jeweled crowns. Harry, enthralled, insisted on staying with him.

Julie was left to wander among the ruins of Axum with the skeptical tour guide they'd hired. He led her among the tall, narrow granite obelisks that towered like giant sentinels over the site. Some had fallen long ago. Shattered slabs littered the ground, tombstones of a history that had died so long ago no one remembered its name.

"No one knows who built these," the guide told her. "Or how long ago. Some of the priests they say God built them, or Menelik. But no one knows who built."

The tallest of those still standing soared perhaps a hundred and fifty feet high. The face of a door was carved into the base with seven blind stone windows ascending above.

"Some say a house going to heaven, but no one knows who built these or why."

He was tall, prematurely stooped, with a voice bent as low as his back. She had to strain to hear his words.

"Don't you want to take pictures?"

"No," said Julie. "I'm no good with cameras." She had a taste for travel, for seeing and doing, but no desire to record what she saw. And less to remember what she did.

"I can take the picture of you standing so."

"No. I have no camera." She especially hated having her own photograph taken, another obsession of Harry's. He'd photographed her, a piece of cardboard set among the facade of every tourist attraction in Europe, the Middle East, and Asia. She'd gone into a violent tantrum when he tried to pose her in front of his parents' home in California. "You can't own me," she'd screamed, "by locking me into that goddam camera." Hysterics alone could convince Harry. He hadn't tried to take a photograph of her since.

The guide led her to the rock steps which tiered down to a vast stone pool with a shallow covering of water at the bottom. Peasant women hauled jugs of water up the steps.

"They say this was the bath of Sheba."

"Tell me more about Sheba."

"No one knows much about that. They say she slept with King Solomon."

She tried to imagine Elizabeth Taylor shedding royal robes to bathe here. Then remembered that had been Cleopatra. But surely there must have been a movie about the Queen of Sheba. Something she had seen on television. With Victor Mature? No, that was Samson, not Solomon. But what movie was it? Who had played Sheba?

"To us she was Makeda," said the guide, as though reading her thoughts. "Saba means these Red Sea places where she ruled. But no one knows much, or why foreigners say Sheba."

She smiled. The guide didn't notice. He didn't see the movie, thought Julie. She wondered if she had. On television late at night? Escaping Harry's parents. Or her mother. The ethics of the bitch. What kind of ethics did Sheba have? It remained a mystery. A movie she couldn't remember.

She followed the guide up a slope to ruins he said were the tomb of Emperor Kaleb and his son. They had seen the stone mummies of other kings and queens at Lalibela. She couldn't remember the names. She stooped to follow the guide through other cool rock tombs. The fables he told her rolled away. He shrugged. He wasn't impressing her. He wasn't himself impressed. They climbed back into the sunlight.

"Isn't there a palace of Sheba's?"

"They say so." He shrugged with one shoulder.

"I want to see that."

"It's part of what you paid for. But it is far. We will have to get your friends and take the car."

"But I want to go by myself."

"Your friends have paid, too."

"Please. It's important to me. I have extra money . . ."

She reached into her handbag. The guide shrugged.

"You have already paid."

He took her back to the zebra-striped Volkswagen combi that had been fitted out as a small bus for tourists. He swung the combi slowly around, hunched so low over the wheel that his chin seemed to rest on the rim. They drove out of the park site and past the long line of souvenir shops. They cut through the back end of the town and out a dirt road that paralleled the open field where cows grazed and, twice a day, a plane landed.

About a mile beyond the edge of the town, the guide stopped the small bus in the middle of the road.

"It is very hot," he said. "From here we must walk. Are you sure you want?"

"Yes," said Julie. "Please." She wasn't sure why. It wasn't just to see the ruins of a palace that the Queen of Sheba might have lived in. She knew she wanted to see it without Baria or Harry. Their words. Their opinions. She didn't want to be cheated again. She wanted to find this woman, this queen for herself.

She climbed down from the bus and followed the bent, slow-moving guide who picked his way among the rocks that littered the landscape. They hadn't come far when the guide stopped.

"It's just here," he said. "We have to climb down. The French dug it up. All this was buried till a few years ago."

She hadn't realized they were standing directly above what looked like a shallow foundation of crudely piled stones.

"How did they know it was here?"

"From the rains. Each year in the heavy rains coins and pots were found around this place by the people when the earth washed away. A big Frenchman with a small beard came and said, 'Dig here. Dig there.' They digged three or four places before they found this. Come. We have to go down to see all."

They scrambled down into a ditch which flanked walls that looked as though they might have been piled up by children building a fort. Julie, afraid of knocking the walls over, picked her way carefully over loose stones into what might once have been a small room.

"See? Here are steps. And here, another room."

"This is all?"

"Over there, more rooms." He shrugged. "Three or four rooms only. Perhaps more still buried. They made them stop digging."

"But why?"

"The government in Ethiopia." Another shrug with one stooped shoulder. "They said the French didn't protect the ruins."

She was beginning to find the shrugs irritating. They seemed more a habit than an expression.

"A bad rain, the government said, washed some of the ruins away because the French didn't dig properly. The government said. Some say the French found the ruins were not old enough to be a palace of Makeda. A thousand years before Christ they say for Solomon and Makeda. And Emperor Kaleb, you saw his tomb up there, he was six hundred years after Christ. This"—his hand, palm down, described a sad arc over the stones—"is perhaps not so old. But they want us to say it was the palace of the Queen of Sheba. For foreigners we say Sheba. We need a place of tourist attraction."

She wanted to weep. The sun beat down on them. The walls were just high enough to block any breeze. The heat, the slight exertion of the walk, drenched her with sweat.

"All this way," she said. She tried not to cry. "I wanted to find her." She climbed two stone steps and looked into another room. Flies buzzed around her head. "She isn't . . ." She leaned against the wall, her back to the guide, and wept. Loose stones fell clattering from the wall to the steps. She had come by herself with only a bent, soft-spoken guide. No Harry. No Baria. And still she'd been cheated. She wondered if they were to dig up her own past would they find anything more than these walls around nothing; empty rooms; sad, unimpressive ruins. There was no queen. No ancient woman of legend and romance.

"Perhaps it is true as they say."

She shook her head. She wouldn't turn. She didn't want him to see her crying.

"It is the story they tell," said the guide. "No one knows surely."

"Another of our fables," Baria declared at dinner that night in Axum's Tourist Hotel. Dinner was pasta, fried meat, and salad as it had been at the hotels in Gondar and Lalibela. "But foreigners like these paintings very much."

"So do Ethiopians," said Harry. "I've seen these paintings in lots of Ethiopian homes."

"Many Ethiopians have become foreigners," said Baria. "Since so much that is foreign started coming to us."

One of the traditional panel paintings of the legend of Solomon and Sheba hung on the dining room wall near their table. Four horizontal rows each with eleven, cartoonlike panels. With each panel there were brief captions in Amharic script. The panels were highly stylized, the colors, bright.

Wordlessly, she sat, listening to them argue, watching Baria coolly mocking the fable Harry was so fond of.

"You shouldn't make fun of it. It's such a beautiful legend."

"To our people, dear Harry, it's no legend. To us it's history. Makeda, the Queen of Sheba, was an Ethiopian. She lived here in Axum, not in Saba, across the Red Sea. She journeyed to Jerusalem to visit the wise King Solomon.

"On the last night of her visit, Solomon prepared a great feast with many highly spiced, thirst-provoking dishes. He wanted, perhaps, to provoke her, for she was very beautiful. But he served very little to quench her thirst. At dinner.

"He saw to it that the banquet lasted far into the morning. Then suggested that the beautiful Ethiopian queen sleep that night in his palace rather than return to her own quarters. She accepted, but only after making him agree that he would not force himself on her, because, she told him, she was a virgin. That, too, perhaps, was provoking.

"Solomon promised to take nothing so precious as her queenly virginity without her consent—provided she would take nothing precious of his. Without his consent.

"And so to bed. Separate beds. A wall, perhaps, between them. I don't mean to be provoking, but sometimes a wall . . .

Yes. Well, Makeda awoke. Thirsty, of course. Thirsty, perhaps for a king. Wise Solomon had left a jug of water in the room. Makeda saw it, and, without seeking consent, drank from the jug.

"Solomon, as you see here, sleeping with one eye open, was on her in an instant. He accused her of breaking her pledge because, as he insisted, there is nothing more precious on earth than water.

"Makeda, perhaps, was not too hard to convince. And so she surrendered her most precious possession. And slept that night with Solomon.

"The son she gave birth to, for of course she gave birth to a son, she named Menelik. And all our kings, all our legitimate Solomonic kings to this day are directly descended from that same illegitimate Menelik. So they say."

Thinking about it now, as she drove beside Baria, Julie remembered that Harry had wanted to name her baby Menelik. Perhaps he conceived the notion that night that the name would be "so appropriate" for a child born in Ethiopia. She glanced at Baria. They'd named the child Jonathan, her father's name. But Menelik would have been appropriate. More appropriate than Harry knew. Bitch, she said to herself. She turned away from Baria.

That night she had hated him for the smug way he mocked the story. The way he told it, he mocked all women. She'd agreed so quickly when Harry had said:

"You tell it like some kind of joke. Some kind of dirty joke or something."

"No joke," Baria had said. "We take it all very seriously indeed. It's even very Solomonly written into our constitution that Haile Selassie is a direct descendant of the Jew and his Ethiopian whore."

"Don't say it like that."

"I should tell it, I'm sure, nicely as it's told in the official chronicles. But in these paintings you admire, for all their Byzantine style, the story is told more honestly. Has anyone ever translated the writing for you?"

"No," said Harry.

"Allow me." He left their table and went to the painting. He began explaining it, panel by panel, jabbing at each with a blunt finger. And Harry, she remembered, poor Harry kept asking for more.

"No one has translated it for you. And of course you can't read it yourself."

"I'm trying to learn Amharic."

"You should try harder. Perhaps if you had an Ethiopian mistress. Like Solomon did."

Bastard, she had thought then. Harry calls him his friend. What does he see in this cold, nasty bastard? He is a leper. Not his skin. Him. And yet, she'd listened so closely to every word. The first part of the story had blurred for her. "He is taking the goat to the python." She remembered that strange phrase. "That's how it begins," Baria had said. "Abrupt, isn't it? Direct."

There had been something about—she could never remember the name Ethiopians called her by—there had been something about Sheba's father killing a serpent who ruled the people. She'd forgotten it now. Like so much else she'd heard and read about the country. Ethiopia's history, she knew, would remain a closed book to her. Like Baria. There was always something missing in what she read. In what he said. And did. Something held back. Something perhaps not mysterious. Or only mysterious because concealed. Provoking. Spices and thirst.

"Here it says simply 'Makeda and Solomon.' They've met. And here, where they're looking at each other, it says again simply 'Makeda and Solomon.' And here, 'Preparing a dinner for Makeda.' And this one, 'Dinner for Makeda.' And here . . ." The blunt finger jabbed, " 'Let us spend the night together.' "

"No nonsense here about spices and water and mutual pledges to take nothing without the other's consent. Here no nonsense, no romance. And here . . ." He pivoted and poked his finger against the first panel in the third row.

"Do you know what it says here? Here it says simply, 'He grabs a servant.' And here, 'He sleeps with the servant.' Though you can see they aren't sleeping. And then, under this one, it says, 'He grabs Makeda.' And then, 'He sleeps with Makeda.' A bit less romance here than in the fanciful chronicles. The painters are perhaps, for all their style, more realistic. He grabs a servant. Perhaps to show the virginal queen how it's done. He grabs Makeda."

The ethics of a bastard, thought Julie.

"Much more like it is," said Baria. "He sleeps with the servant. He sleeps with Makeda."

What you need is a bitch. Like poor Harry has.

"And here he gives her a ring. After all, she is a queen. The servant gets no ring. 'Makeda goes to her country. Menelik is born.' Later, down here, Menelik is given the ring by his mother and returns to Jerusalem. Solomon acknowledges Menelik as his son. Though who knows. Perhaps on the way home, Makeda grabs a servant. Makeda sleeps with a slave."

"That isn't in the picture," said Harry.

"Who knows? Perhaps the painter left it out. But who knows? Perhaps one day in another painting. And here we have Menelik—as you can see we're getting near the end—this is Menelik being instructed in the laws of Israel.

"And now here we have a strange episode. After all this kind treatment, what does Menelik do? He steals the Ark of the Covenant from Jerusalem. That, perhaps, proves the legend really is true. Who but an Ethiopian, I should say who but a member of the ruling clique, would do such a thing?"

"That's not how the official version goes."

"There are many versions. As in all gospels. I'm giving you the traditional, unexpurgated text. From the Red Sea scrolls. And here you see Menelik returns. 'He gives the *tabot* to his mother. She makes him king. She gives him a seal. Makeda's last testament. He sets up an obelisk.' The legend, written as gospels always are, long after the fact, has Menelik build one of these obelisks you see still here at Axum. And from here, for many centuries we believe, our kings ruled."

"You can't say the obelisks aren't here."

"I can't. I've seen them just today."

"And you can't say they aren't very ancient."

"I don't. And yet, isn't it odd? We boast that all our kings are descended from a woman who sold her virtue for a glass of water. And her son, the first of our kings descended from this lady, was not only a bastard but a thief.

"Our kings base their legitimacy on being descended from an illegitimate thief. Our religion claims to be ancient and Christian and we worship a *tabot* stolen from the Jews. No wonder our poor country is such a sad mess."

"You'd destroy everything," said Harry. "It's a beautiful legend. You sound like some old American puritan telling it. So disapproving."

"Please," said Baria. He had glanced at her then. "I'm an Ethiopian. We aren't puritans. We only know how to enjoy."

"It's a lovely old legend."

"History, dear Harry. The history of our country. Chapter one. The birth of Menelik."

Chapter one, she thought. Perhaps one day. Yes. One day when Harry's away. She'd taken herself back two, three thousand years. And found nothing but empty, improbable ruins. Back before history. Back to the time of legend. Looking for a woman who was queen. And finding herself. Provoking. Much more like it is. He sleeps with a servant. He sleeps with–Sheba. And Sheba. Sleeps with a slave.

She hated him then. She hated him now. And that night she had known she wanted him. She wanted him still. When Harry was away, away at Kulubi, she'd been flattered, sadly flattered, by the attention he showed her. How badly she still needed attention. Harry called him his friend. Poor Harry. At least she knew herself better than that. It should have been a man like Solomon. A man of force. And wisdom. Any woman would thirst for such a man. If such a man lived. He wouldn't need spices to seduce.

But there was no Solomon. Nor Sheba. Only us. And the lies we live by.

"So you see, dear Harry," Baria had said that night, "if you want to get at the truth of Ethiopia, you'll have to write fiction. That's all we have. Three thousand years of legends, of lies. Lies, perhaps, that we need. But not yet any history."

"I'll get to the truth," said Harry.

Dear fool.

She wondered if she could ever live without Harry. She wondered if she would always need someone like Baria.

Wandimu limped into Erer Gota just as the imperial train was arriving. It had been fifty-eight days since he had set out from his village north of Gondar with the small ox he had pledged to Gabriel. Now, his own neck was bent under the yoke by which he had led the dumb beast. The ox was dead.

The shrill ululations of the women in the crowd surrounding the train cut through the trance he'd enveloped himself in. The cries of the women pierced him like a keening echo of the screams he'd known in the desert night. The sudden apparition of the crowd frightened him. He backed away.

For days his mind had been empty of thought. Now the events of that savage night whirled like a dust devil behind his eyes, frightening as the shapes of the excited crowd around him. He had planned to kill the young Danakil that night. He remembered it now. It had seemed as though the murder in his heart had taken shape in the form of the leopard. He was still alive. The ox was dead. The leopard was dead. The boy had been killed. And Wandimu was still alive. His own survival frightened him.

They had crossed deserts of scrub, deserts of wind-whipped sand that stung their skin like needles and deserts of harsh stone that tore through their sandals. They had crossed the Awash at a place the boy called Barakala where they had luckily met a group of Danakil cattle herders. Once the boy put their suspicions to rest, they put Wandimu's ox among their own cattle. The men formed two lines as far out into the river as they could stand and beat the cattle out into the deeper waters, forcing them to swim.

They had seen crocodile and a hippopotamus along the banks of the river, but the commotion of the cattle drive frightened them downstream. The river was just shallow enough that camels were able to walk across. The men, Wandimu and the boy among them, hung from ropes tied around the camels' backs and were hauled through the deeper water. The land around the river was comparatively lush, fringed with delicate mimosas and fed by many streams. Game abounded, but an eight-hour march brought them back to semiarid bush.

They stopped that fatal night by a clump of withered desert acacias. The young Danakil had indicated there was water to be found in the dry riverbed below them. He motioned Wandimu to wait with the ox while he scrambled down the banks of the *wadi*. The moon, half-full above them, bathed the desert in its cool white light. Wandimu, ashamed not to have struck sooner, resolved that this was the time to kill the boy. He was sure the boy was feeling a similar shame for not having already earned his feather by killing him. There had been times when he wondered whether the boy might not be sincerely trying to help him reach Dire Dawa. But he had heard too much of Danakil treachery. He knew he must strike now to save his own life.

He tethered the ox to an acacia. He let the Danakil's camel wander. The boy had propped his rifle against the spindly trunk of a tree. Wandimu picked up the rifle and started cautiously forward to the edge of the riverbed. He looked down. The boy was already digging in the sandy bottom. His bare back glistened in the moonlight.

How easy it will be, thought Wandimu.

He heard a rustling behind him. Before Wandimu could move, the boy, in a single, catlike motion, spun around and leaped from the shallow wadi to its bank. He grabbed the rifle from Wandimu's hands.

A succession of screams tore the night air. The first was the strangely high-pitched bellow of his ox. Then a low, savage growl and the distant cries of hyenas.

The boy had rushed past Wandimu without stopping. A single crack of the rifle deadened the peasant's ears to all other sounds. For a moment he thought he'd been killed. Then a human cry slashed through his fear.

He fumbled for his knife as he turned.

He saw the boy go down under the force of what at first seemed only a blur of motion. Wandimu saw it was a leopard. He fell to his knees wet with fear.

The boy braced the rifle above him, trying to keep the jaws of the leopard from his face. But the jaws snapped down.

As Wandimu lost consciousness, certain he would be eaten alive, he wished the boy had put a bullet in his back.

He looked up into the sinking sun beyond the crowd that swirled around him. Where had they been, all these people, when he had been in the desert alone? He stared into the sun and saw the sinking half-moon that had been on his face when he had come to his senses by the banks of the wadi.

The stunted acacias cast long shadows across the blood-soaked sand. His small ox still stood, but great strips of flesh had been torn from his back and side. The boy was dead. His face was gone. The flesh of his shoulders and chest were ripped to the bone.

Wandimu crept on hands and knees, first to the boy, then toward his ox. Hyenas screamed, hysteric laughter, frenzied cries. He was afraid to stand.

The leopard. He could see it again, leaping from the back of his ox into the face of the Danakil. The rifle. He crept back to the boy. The rifle was still in his hands. Summoning the last shreds of his strength, Wandimu pried it loose.

He pushed himself up. He was covered with blood. The ground was still wet with it. He knew he couldn't have been unconscious for long.

The hyenas howled in what seemed to be a tightening circle. And the leopard? He looked around him across the moonstruck desert. There was no sign of the leopard. And the camel? The young Danakil's camel had fled.

A short distance from where the boy lay, there was another broad pool of blood. From this spot Wandimu saw a trail of blood leading off toward another grove of acacia along the banks of the wadi. He made no attempt to follow. He was sure the single bullet fired by the Danakil must have torn into the leopard just as it had sprung.

He noticed a second trail along with the blood spoor. Apparently the leopard was dragging one paw. Wandimu suspected this limp was not a result of the bullet fired by the Danakil. The leopard was bleeding too heavily for a leg wound. He must have been already crippled when he attacked.

Why else, thought Wandimu, would a leopard attack an ox protected by two men in this region where antelope, baboon, and other smaller game were plentiful. He shivered. Wounded, dying, the leopard would be more dangerous than ever. The scent of blood on himself and his ox would excite the hyenas to the point where even those cowards might attack living flesh. *Nebr. Jib.* Gabriel had saved him from the Danakil by sending the leopard. But what would save him from the leopard? And the hyena? Or the desert itself?

The Danakil had indicated by signs that they had been only a few hours from the village called Gewani. The track must be heavily traveled here, but he was not sure he could follow it by fading moonlight without the boy's help. Yet, he could not wait here by the wadi, hoping other travelers might find him by dawn. The leopard might return. Or the hyenas would surely tighten their circle and attack before first light.

If they moved on, the dead body of the boy, and of the leopard if he, too, died of his wound, would give the hyenas an easier meal than himself and his ox.

He searched through the garments of the dead Danakil for bullets for the rifle. Finally, in the leather pouches of his knife sheath, he found two. But Wandimu had no idea how to reload the gun. Many of his neighbors owned rifles, but he had never been able to buy one. He knew there were rifles that held more than one bullet, but he didn't want to waste a shot by testing the rifle now. He secured the two bullets in the folds of his cloak and went to examine his ox.

The wounds on the animal's back weren't deep. Wandimu's

gabbi and the other provisions tied to his back had given the ox some protection there. But a large hunk of flesh had been torn from his side. Wandimu thought the leopard, desperate with hunger, must have done that after he had killed the boy.

He went down into the wadi where the Danakil had been digging for water. The boy had reached mud, which was just what Wandimu wanted. He filled the gourd and stumbled back up the bank to his ox. He carefully folded the torn flesh on the back over the slashes made by the claws of the leopard. He applied a paste of mud over the wounds. The drying mud would seal the gashes on the back easily enough, but Wandimu saw there was little he could do for the gaping wound in the side.

Here there was no flap of flesh to paste back over the wound. Hide as well as meat had been torn away. He decided to smear the rest of the contents of the gourd over the wound anyway in hopes that the drying mud might stop some of the bleeding. The ox quivered at the touch of his hand on the raw flesh but made no sound.

Wandimu didn't want to take the time to unpack the ox. He worked around and under the pack ropes. He then stuffed the gourd in among the other equipment. He untied the ox's tether and set off.

He carried his own walking stick in one hand and the Danakil's rifle in the other. The ox plodded faithfully behind him.

His mouth was parched, but as he crossed the wadi he didn't pause by the half-dug water hole. He had to beat and drag the ox up the far bank and then search for what he could only hope was the right track. He knew he had to move essentially south. He checked his path as best he could with the stars.

As he went, he prayed, not to Christ nor even to Gabriel. He prayed to Mariam. Like most Christian Ethiopians, his greatest idolatry was reserved for Mary. He prayed to the mother of Christ for guidance in the desert for himself and his ox. As you and your donkey found your way through the desert by the light of Bethlehem, show us our way. He piously prayed to Mariam for help, but, hours later, when he saw the white ball of the barely risen sun glinting off the tin roofs of Gewani, it was to Gabriel that Wandimu gave thanks.

Shrill hyenas had trailed him through the night but had not attacked. Hooded vultures now circled above him but did not swoop down. He staggered into the village with his bleeding ox, and, when he had told his story to the villagers, he was greeted as a man who had himself worked a miracle.

On the advice of an Amharic-speaking Arab shopkeeper, he surrendered the rifle to a group of Danakils who, later that morning, came into the village to trade skins. They had come across what the hyenas had left of the body of the boy. And, a short distance away, the remains of the leopard.

"Give them the rifle," said the shopkeeper. "It will show your good faith. Otherwise, they may think you killed the boy to steal his gun. Then they will follow you when you leave this village and kill you."

Sure the Arab was making some money on the deal, Wandimu at first resisted. But he was too weak to struggle. He gave the Danakils the rifle, the two bullets he had taken from the boy, and half the handful of empty cartridge shells the young man from Tendaho had given him to distribute as gifts to the Danakil. He had forgotten the shells till now.

He rested for two days in the village. It was a comfortable region of unexpected lakes and surprising desert mountains, one of which, though it bore the Amharic name Ayelu, was worshipped as sacred by the Danakils.

Midway through his second day in Gewani, the ox died. Wandimu prayed to Gabriel, insisting that although he had not made it to Kulubi, the ox had been given in death as a sacrifice to the saint. To complete his *silet*, he vowed to walk the rest of the way with the yoke around his own neck and to offer himself to the priests of Kulubi as a slave.

That night he set out, guided by a withered old Afar. Two nights' march brought them to within sight of a collection of huts called Osboli. The Afar left him, and he made his own way into the village. From here an Issa shepherd boy, not yet in his teens, took him to within twenty kilometers of Erer Gota. He covered half the remaining distance along a well-marked track in the cool of the morning. He rested through the heat of the day under the shade of an umbrellalike acacia. He walked the last ten kilometers in the waning afternoon.

He stood now, dazed and uncertain, nearly as frightened by the crowd gathering around the Emperor's train as he had been by the leopard that killed his ox. He had done his best to wash the blood from his clothes in Gewani. But they were now stained and shredded rags. He had given all but one of his cartridge shells to the old Danakil who had guided him as far as Osboli. Somehow, he had lost his water bottles. The last of his money was spent. His *agalgil*, now draped by its leather thong across his back, was empty.

His shoes, repaired a dozen times with strips of rubber he'd cut from the remnants of a tire he'd found at Tendaho, were in such shreds he'd thrown them away that morning. His bare feet were bruised, swollen, and bleeding. Strips of flesh hung from his burning lips. His hands hung weakly from the yoke around his neck. His blankly staring eyes were bloodshot. He had every mark of one of God's own madmen. But no one in the crowd gathering to welcome the Emperor did more than glance at him.

He stood unmoving in the roadway till the bleating Klaxon of a Land Rover startled him. For a moment he thought he was back in the scrub desert with hyenas on his trail. He half turned around, then backed out of the roadway.

"*Tadess?*" said Hagos, at the wheel of the Land Rover. "Don't let Eleni see that one. She'll be off on another errand of mercy."

Eleni looked out at the mad peasant with the yoke around his neck.

"No," she said. "I've had enough of the good Samaritan business for one day."

"The quality of mercy is strained," said Makonnen in English. Since Claude was traveling with them, he made an effort to keep the others from speaking among themselves exclusively in Amharic. "In fact, not merely strained, but ruptured. The times we live in. Anyway, why help this lunatic. He's only an Ethiopian. It's not as though he were something important. Like an American lady who needs her hair combed."

"And her baby's diapers changed," said Zenebetch.

"Very funny," said Eleni.

"Very apt," said Hagos.

"I think I better leave," said Claude.

"No, man," said Makonnen. "Stay with us, man. We're all brothers here."

"Yeah. 'Cept for us foreigners."

"That old man might just as well have stayed where he was in the road," said Hagos. "We aren't going much farther with this crowd."

As they edged round a final curve into the heart of the village, they saw that their way was blocked, not only by the crowd, but also by the train which had come to a halt at the station and now was stretched across the road before them. The train had passed them as they covered the last few kilometers into the village. Hagos had tried to race it, but a particularly deep riverbed had slowed them down.

"Never mind the crowd," said Makonnen. "As usual our Emperor presents himself in the form of a roadblock in the path of the young."

"I don't even see him," said Zenebetch.

"Nevertheless, we all know the Imperial presence is tucked up in that iron maiden somewhere," said Makonnen. "We'd best get out and bow."

"Yeah," said Claude. "You guys get out and bow. And I can get me some pictures."

"You never rest, do you?" said Hagos.

"I don't make no livin' by restin', Jim. I gotta keep movin'."

Claude Jackson had run his way from the streets of Harlem through the Haaren High School track team to a scholarship at Princeton. But once having escaped the streets of New York, he could see no reason to keep running. He weathered his first year with good grades and good trial times in the 440. But coming back to school after the summer vacation, he found he had lost not only his interest in track, but his interest in Princeton as well.

Claude had begun to discover that he was black. And this always visible fact suddenly began to interest him more than anything else in his life. Growing up in the all-black world of Harlem, he had been barely aware of whites. And blackness was then something taken for granted.

"The colonialists they stayed downtown," he tried to explain to his new African friends. " 'Cept for the Man, and I could always run faster than cops."

But times were changing, and Claude was changing with them. At Princeton, what had long been visible was suddenly conspicuous. When he went back to the streets of Harlem after his first year at college, he began to see the world he'd grown up in with new eyes. He started to let his hair grow. When he returned to school, this led to his first trouble with the track coach.

"Crazy fool told me it would add weight, catch wind, slow me down." He bought a relaxer so he could soften his hair and pull it out even longer. He stopped trying to talk white as his mother had always advised him to do and slipped comfortably back into the language of the streets where he'd first learned to run.

Midway through the second year of their uneasy marriage, Claude and his track coach agreed to a friendly separation. With Claude no longer interested in track, Princeton was no longer interested in Claude. He went back to New York.

Cameras had been a passion since high school days at Haaren where the track coach also conducted the photography club. With his new eyes seeing black, he went back to New York and photography. He took a job on the staid *Amsterdam News* and, in time, landed his first magazine assignments.

He let his Afro grow fuller, began wearing *dashikis*, and started taking lessons in Swahili. He was active in a black arts group that took its African heritage seriously, and he appeared in a play by Wolye Soyinka.

Then, with an irony that seemed to Claude quite natural, he found—through a white man—an opportunity to go to Africa. He had kept in contact with only one friend from Princeton, another 440 specialist, the only one on the team who could match Claude's time.

Fred Barrow was a Philadelphia Main Liner. At Princeton, Claude had discovered the term meant something quite different from what it did in Harlem. Fred was the only white Claude had ever met who seemed totally free of prejudice, even of the reverse prejudice of the uneasy liberals who convince themselves that black, and only black, is beautiful. In its place. Claude decided Fred's traits must run in the Barrow family, for Fred's sister had married a delegate to the Ethiopian mission at the United Nations.

She had since returned to Ethiopia with her husband who had become a key official in the government. At Fred's urging, she invited Claude to visit her husband and herself at their home in Addis Ababa. Fred also had friends in Nigeria, Ghana, and Kenya who extended similar invitations. Armed with these credentials, Claude had obtained a series of assignments from *Ebony* magazine. He was to do a photo spread on Afro hairstyles in Africa and on various black Americans living on the continent.

Since arriving in Africa, he found his interests changing and expanding. His cameras were seldom at rest. In Addis, through Fred's sister he had met her husband, Negash Mengistu. Through

Negash he had met Zenebetch. And, through Zenebetch, Makonnen, Hagos, and Eleni. In Ethiopia his camera was busier than ever.

"You know how it is," he said to Hagos. "I may of quit the track team. I don't run no more, but I gotta keep movin'."

Hagos pulled the Land Rover to the edge of the road and parked it under the branches of a fig tree. A road marker tilting dangerously toward the ground told them Addis Ababa was an unspecified distance behind them; Dire Dawa, sixty kilometers ahead, and a place called Gewani one hundred and sixty to their left. They climbed down from the Land Rover, locked it, and walked slowly toward the railroad tracks.

His Imperial Majesty Haile Selassie I stood in the doorway of his car on the opposite side of the train. The crowd here was even thicker than the mob among which Wandimu, Claude, and the four young Ethiopians wandered on the far side of the tracks. Baskets of fruit were offered up to the Emperor. With a smile, he accepted a single orange from the trembling hands of a small girl who was allowed to pass between two of the soldiers with automatic weapons who ringed the train.

We are loved, thought the Emperor as he accepted the orange. He looked down on the steel helmets of the soldiers. We are loved, and we must fear for our life.

This farm had once been his. Before the occupation, an Italian engineer had devised the simple irrigation system that, from a single shallow river, had turned hundreds of hectares of scrub desert into a tropical paradise producing citrus fruits, bananas, tomatoes, avocados, and papayas.

The river had also been tapped to turn the turbines of a primitive power plant that served both the farm and the nearby resort hotel with its thermal baths. A decade ago, the Emperor had turned the farm over to the prize trust that bore his name. Like several hotels in what were now resort areas, the hotel here had once been a private rainy season retreat for himself and his family.

We have given our people so much, he reflected as he looked out from his train. We have given so much, and still there are those who would plot against us.

Negash stood behind him, cradling the Papillon in his arms. If all went well, he would be driving back here this evening in a car to be supplied by the governor in Dire Dawa. If all went well, Zenebetch would be here waiting for him at the hotel. He looked out over the Emperor's shoulder, wondering if she were out there somewhere in that crowd.

From the doorway of the second-class compartment, the Honorable Ato Getachew Tessema was negotiating with an old Somali hag for a wicker basket of oranges. He drove a hard bargain. The woman had begun by asking for a dollar. Getachew knew the oranges could be had for twenty-five cents. He offered ten. The woman said fifty. Getachew called out to another woman. In less than thirty seconds he had his oranges for twenty-five cents.

He knew the stop would be short. As a former minister of agriculture, he also knew the high quality of Erer-Gota fruits. In quick succession he bought a much larger basket of bananas for fifty cents; two plates of tangerines and a basket of papayas in a tandem purchase for sixty cents. He dumped the fruit into a large duffel bag he had brought empty from Addis Ababa for the purpose. He tossed the empty baskets and earthenware plates back out to the Somali women. One of the plates hit a young girl in the face.

The plate fell to the ground and shattered. From the open doorway in which he stood, the Emperor watched the girl as she stooped to pick up the pieces. He knew precisely who the occupants of the rear compartment were. Among them he could guess it was Getachew Tessema who most likely had made the rapid, greedy purchases and thrown the containers back into the faces of the Somali women.

And we wonder why so many of our people hate our government, he said to himself. Our officials in action.

He remembered the famous day when the elderly Blatta Sirak, elegantly dressed in his customary flowing cape, dark European suit, and soft felt hat, had driven a dozen donkeys through the streets of Addis Ababa. At the time there were twelve ministers in the cabinet. Old Sirak told all who asked what he was doing that, since the Emperor had a dozen asses in his cabinet to herd around, he had decided to do the same. When the story was related to him by his chief of police who wanted to arrest the old man, the

Emperor had smiled and said, "Leave him. In truth, he's right. We shouldn't appoint donkeys to our cabinet, but we have so little to choose from."

He sighed the memory away. He waved once more to the crowd, then turned back into the car as cheers and shrill, joyous ululations rose behind him.

Baria had parked the station wagon off the shoulder of the road near the stone cross. A sign pointed the way to the church two kilometers above the little roadside village of Kulubi. It had rained in the mountains, and the clay surface of the road up to the church was slick and treacherous. Cars slithered, stalled. Drivers cursed. Horns wailed. Traffic was backed up from the final steep rise leading to the church to within a hundred meters of the stone cross.

The rain had stopped but the air was chill and damp. During the last thirty minutes of their approach to Kulubi, they had driven through rain clouds that swirled up from the rich river valleys to the south to break themselves on the mountain chain.

To Julie the rain clouds had been an echo of the clouds of dust mingled with early mist they had climbed through after crossing the Awash River that morning. Then, the feeling of flying through clouds had been an illusion. Now, high in the mountains, real clouds swirled around them.

The rain had not been heavy, but nagging, persistent, cold. The clouds at last were lifting, and, behind them in the west, the red globe of the setting sun broke through. It struck the blue and gold dome of the church with fire and, off in the direction of Dire Dawa, the arc of a rainbow appeared in the sky.

Julie sat shivering behind the rolled-up windows of the station wagon. Baria, arms folded across his chest, leaned against the fender, quietly trying to explain to two excited policemen why he would contribute less to the traffic congestion by parking off the road than by continuing up the muddy path to the church and adding another vehicle to the long tangle of cars. He listened patiently to the nervous, wildly gesturing policemen.

His own words were few.

Slowly uttered.

Calm.

Polite.

Deliberate.

The way he makes love, thought Julie as she watched him. She knew beyond doubt that Baria had been the father of her child. And yet, the child was so much more like Harry. Chalk up one for nurture, she thought, over nature. She wished she could share her thought with Baria. But she knew he wouldn't want to talk of the child. She wondered if he believed her when she'd told him the baby was his.

He went on with his patient wearing down of the policemen. Gradually he won, if not agreement, at least a truce. First one policeman, then the other, walked off to join their comrades directing traffic in confused patterns around the stone cross.

Just then, Harry pulled up in his Volkswagen. He had again taken over the driving from Tesfaye. He drew up parallel to the station wagon and stopped square in the middle of the road. Slanging policemen swarmed around him like furies.

"All right. All right, already," said Harry. "I wasn't going to park."

Baria quickly urged him to drive, not up to the church, but further along the road to Dire Dawa.

"But we're supposed to go to the church," said Harry. "And pitch the tent and all that."

"I think we need a change in plan," said Baria. "Drive up the highway a mile or so to where we can park in peace, and I'll explain. Go ahead, quick. Before these madmen throw us in jail."

Harry drove off in a rush, spinning the Volkswagen around the stone cross, narrowly missing a stalled bus as he went. Frightened policemen leaped out of his way.

"Those policemen are crazy," said Harry.

"You're right," said Tesfaye, who now held the wailing infant on his lap. "Madmen all."

Despite the rain, the rock-strewn but hard-packed surface of the main road was firm. Harry drove less than a kilometer before Baria's rhythmic thumping of the station wagon's horn signaled him to stop. He found a stretch with a reasonable expanse of shoulder and pulled over. Far below them they could see the pink glint cast by the sun on the rooftops of Dire Dawa. All four climbed from their cars, warmed by the view from the edge of the mountain but chilled by the damp air.

"My God," said Harry, "what's wrong with those policemen back there? Hello, Julie."

Julie didn't answer. She had wrapped herself head to toe in

Baria's *gabbi.* Tesfaye quickly made her a present of the baby. She cradled it awkwardly in her shrouded arms. A group of pilgrims walking to Kulubi stared at her fixedly as they passed.

Baria explained the effect of the rain on the road leading up to the church, the hopeless tie-up of traffic. The four, according to an arrangement carefully finessed by Julie, had planned to drive up to the camping area near the church and pitch the expensive, partitioned tent Harry had bought. Harry and Tesfaye were then to drive down to join the pilgrims who would walk overnight from Dire Dawa to Kulubi. But now, cold and peevish, Julie found no appeal in the thought of spending a night in a tent in these chill, damp mountains.

"I'm afraid it would take us an hour or more just to drive up to the church," said Baria. "We would have to put the tent up in the dark on muddy ground. And in all that mess up there you and Tesfaye might never be able to get back out."

"But I've got to," said Harry. "I've got to get down to Dire Dawa and walk. It's . . . it's a vow."

"You and your damn vows," said Julie. "You should have been a priest if you want to take vows."

Another scene of domestic bliss, thought Tesfaye. If all bachelors had married friends like Harry and Julie, marriage would cease to exist.

"Well," said Baria, "Tesfaye and Harry could go on now to Dire Dawa. The two of us could go back up to Kulubi, pitch the tent for the night and meet you there tomorrow."

"But if we don't know where the tent is . . ." Harry began.

"You can yak all you want," snapped Julie. "But I'm not spending a night up here. It's freezing."

Most of her makeup had worn off or been layered over with dust. Under the white folds of the *gabbi,* even with the whimpering infant in her arms, she looked like a harsh-tempered nun.

"But there's no place to stay in Dire Dawa," said Harry.

"There must be a hotel room somewhere," said Julie.

"There won't be any hotel rooms," said Tesfaye. "By now they'll have people from Addis sleeping in the closets."

"But there is that camping area in the compound of the Ras," said Baria. "I think they charge you two dollars or something. We could set up our tent there."

"That's true," said Tesfaye. "And not many people use it."

"At least," said Baria, "it will be warm in Dire Dawa. And dry."

"That settles it," said Julie. "We're going."

The others agreed. Harry shrugged.

"I just don't like all these changes," he said. "All this switching around."

"I'm freezing," said Julie. "Let's go."

As they started back to their cars, Harry for the first time noticed the arc of red, yellow, and green in the sky to the east.

"Look," he called out to the others. "A rainbow."

"God bless," muttered Julie.

From the balcony of her room at the Ras Hotel in Dire Dawa, One Thousand Eighty saw the rainbow soaring above the hills over the city. Natural phenomena held no interest for her. She looked away from the rainbow and out over the teeming town, now coming to life after the long, somnolent afternoon.

In the intervals between the roar of buses and lorries on the main road, the bells of horse-drawn *garis* tinkled on the warm breeze. No rain had fallen in the lowlands. Dire Dawa was its usual dry, dusty self.

There was a muted scattering of bathers at the hotel pool below her window. Among them was the hostess who had served them on the plane. At least she thought it was the hostess. Pretty girls all looked alike to her. With so many around willing to give it away, One Thousand Eighty often wondered how her own profession managed to prosper so widely. But these foolish creatures knew neither how to hold a man or how to profit from him. A whore needs a mouth of gold and a heart of steel. One Thousand Eighty prided herself on having both.

Behind her, Fat Margaret was hanging up clothes, chattering meaningless comments which One Thousand Eighty filtered out till her friend's words became a familiar, reassuring drone. One Thousand Eighty liked familiar things. She had rented this same room on the top floor of the Ras for seven consecutive years at Kulubi time, ever since the hotel first opened. The first few years she had always arrived early to make sure her reservation would be honored. But now her status as a regular, coupled with the manager's awareness of the importance of her circle of friends, assured her the room would be hers whenever she arrived.

In the distance off to her left, she heard the soft hooting whistle of the train. The Emperor would be arriving. She smiled to herself, wondering how many guests would be routed out of their rooms to make way for the ministers and court officials who would soon arrive demanding accommodations. She knew she would not be among the dispossessed.

She looked out over the hotel's camp area with its scattering of tents. She looked beyond the now quiet yard of the adjacent school, over the brightly painted facade of the church of Medhane Alem to the bougainvillaea-covered sandstone walls of the Emperor's Selam Aderash palace.

Built on a low knoll, the multitiered palace with its outside stairways towered over the city. Usually dark, tonight it would sparkle like a candled cake. The king of kings would be in residence in his favorite retreat. She glanced again at the rainbow. Its colors were like the color of the flag. She didn't care about flags either. Or kings. Only generals and ministers.

The reflection of the rainbow shimmered in the green waters of the pool. Fallen leaves floated through it. A diver broke its patterns. Zewditu watched them reform. She wasn't thinking about rainbows or leaves or swimming. She was thinking about the bathing suit she was wearing. She wondered how much longer she could risk it. Airsick, she said to herself. A stewardess shouldn't be airsick. Or pregnant. She wondered if Negussie was staying at the hotel. Or had gone off somewhere with Captain Hilary. She wondered if she would ever tell him. Or, on her next flight to Frankfurt, do what the other girls did. Would she ask Gabriel? She wished she believed. Would she tell Negussie? She hoped he would believe.

The hotel Tiruwork and Alganesh were staying at was close by the Ras, but not nearly so elegant. Its motellike rooms were on an enclosed, dusty courtyard. When the gate was closed, the only access to the rooms was through the bar. The one window of the room they shared looked out on a barren back street.

Yet, the hotel was as respectful of its regular customers as its more regal sister up the street. Alganesh had been staying there at Kulubi time for as long as the current owners could remember. She was always assured of a room. But the three other women with whom they had flown from Addis Ababa hadn't been as lucky. They were now off hunting for a place to sleep.

Alganesh had already inherited one of the beds and was softly snoring. Tiruwork stood by the window but studied her sleeping friend. Alganesh was stretched out on top of the sheets. She wore only a slip. Even as she lay flat on her back, with each breath her enormous breasts swelled like inflated pillows. Her throat was so heavily tattooed that she seemed to be wearing an intricate, multi-stringed blue necklace that descended to the cleavage of her breasts.

Swathed in her national costume and with the *netela* she wore draped over her head and wrapped across her shoulders and neck, the tattoo was hidden. But now its countless crosses and jagged, abstract lines were on full display. If the tattoo were a necklace of gold, thought Tiruwork, its weight would make Alganesh a wealthy woman. But she knew her friend did not reckon her wealth by gold or cattle or land or the cars her husband owned or by the income he enjoyed from farms in distant provinces. Alganesh calculated her wealth in terms of the succession of lovers she took and discarded. It was a game with her, and Tiruwork couldn't keep herself from admiring the skill and gaiety with which Alganesh played.

"Oh, I'm poor this month," she would lament. "Only one small fellow no bigger than a flea to warm the bed." Or she would boast, "We are rich these days. A colonel from the bodyguard, a charming old landowner from Bahr Dar, a nice young police captain—he's so clean—the new director of the school my son goes to, and a retired army major."

Tiruwork considered herself a poor scrawny thing compared to her full-fleshed friend. She turned from Alganesh and looked out at the rock-littered street, as desolate as her own life. She had produced children for Shaleka as regularly as the annual summer rains. She knew her husband was right when he told her that her life was blessed. They had their home, their servants. Her husband held an important position, and she herself had a job of her own with the generous maternity leaves granted women in government employ. Her life was blessed, but she found it as empty as the dusty streets outside her hotel room window.

Alganesh's snores sounded behind her. Tiruwork looked up over the dwarfed acacias across the road and saw the rainbow. A brief, startled laugh escaped her lips. She turned quickly to see if she'd woken Alganesh. Her friend snored on. Tiruwork looked again at the rainbow. *Kasta Damana.* Rainbow. It was the name of the restaurant in Addis Ababa where she had first met the man.

She and Alganesh had driven in one afternoon to enjoy some raw *kitfo*. They had planned to eat their meal in Alganesh's car, but then the man came up to them. He was a friend of Alganesh, though Alganesh later swore they had never been lovers. They had joined him in one of the curtained *tukuls* in the restaurant's compound. As they ate and talked it seemed to Tiruwork that not once did he take his haunted, dissipated eyes from her face.

She blushed now at the memory and turned away from the window. She sat on the edge of her bed, looking down at her clasped hands. He said he would be coming. They would meet at Kulubi. She was sure. She hoped Alganesh hadn't told him the name of the hotel where they were staying. She wanted to meet him at Kulubi. That was how it should be.

But now she had seen the rainbow. She was afraid to look for it through the window again. It was at the Rainbow in Addis that they had met. Surely, she said to herself, the rainbow is a sign. She glanced at the snoring Alganesh. Surely, she thought, he'll be at Kulubi.

Shaleka's chauffeur guided the Land Rover down the twisting road toward Dire Dawa. Just then, a taxi coming up the mountain road swung out around one of the blind curves. The two vehicles were within meters of a head-on collision. Shaleka's driver blared his horn and pulled as far to his right as he dared. The steep drop into the canyon where the rainbow hung yawned beneath them. The taxi snapped in toward the rock face of the cliff and swept past.

Shaleka swore inwardly but said nothing. His driver was a good one and had done well. He knew the local taxi drivers loved to take reckless chances on this dangerous road. They only rarely killed themselves but often sent others less familiar with the road spinning to their deaths. Fortunately, at the spot where the vehicles had nearly collided, the road had been free of people making the long climb to Kulubi. Otherwise, it might have been impossible to avoid an accident.

Shaleka thought again of how close at hand death always

seemed in Ethiopia. We all have our guns which many use so wildly. And now we have our cars which many drive so recklessly. He shook the thought off.

Till this moment the trip had been a smooth one. Even with its load of pirated copies of the Kulubi pamphlet, the ministry vehicle had made relatively good time. Shaleka was glad to be arriving before dark. The air around them was still damp and cold. But, as they continued their descent, he could feel the warm air rising. It was good. He liked Dire Dawa and was already tasting the pleasures his stay would bring.

Tiruwork, he knew, would be staying at the Senait Hotel, but he wanted to delay until tomorrow the pleasure of surprising his wife. It would be better, he had decided, to meet her, as though casually, at Kulubi itself. He had arranged to stay at the home of the National Lottery representative who was lining up peddlers to handle the sale of the pamphlets among the crowds at the festival. Tonight and early tomorrow were to be for business. Then there would be time enough for finding Tiruwork. And time enough to do what he could to spin new strands in the web of intrigue in which he hoped to catch Tesfaye.

He glanced at the rainbow, wondering if his wife could see it from her hotel in the city below. He wondered if she, too, might be looking at it this moment, never dreaming that her husband, whom she thought was in Addis, was doing the same.

The taxi that nearly smashed into Shaleka's Land Rover had been hired by Hilary Blankenship ten minutes before. Like most of the taxis in Dire Dawa and Harar, it was a four-door Peugeot sedan. The driver had swung wide on one of the hairpin curves. The Land Rover's Klaxon bellowed, and the tires of both vehicles bit the narrow shoulders on opposite sides of the road. The taxi driver laughed.

"Man, I bet I scared that Addis Ababa monkey in the Land Rover," he said in English.

"You scared this American monkey in the Peugeot," said Hilary.

"Oh, don't you worry. I look he was coming. See, I always watch the road ahead around the curves and I figure how fast. I go over this road very much. Listen, you see that bus coming down now? In another four minutes exact we meet him. I know just the spot. But I like to play with them. It makes more exciting."

"On my twenty dollars," said Hilary, "let's leave the excitement."

"Okay, chief. No more tricks."

Hilary had agreed to pay the inflated rate because he knew the driver could make as much loading the big car with pilgrims for breakneck races to Kulubi and back. Thousands were already making their way to the village in the mountains though the main service of the festival was still thirty-six hours away.

He noticed many foreigners among the clusters of pilgrims the taxi passed. The main trek, he knew, would not start till after dark and would cut through the countryside rather than following the more gradual but longer climb of the road. But many were now taking advantage of the cool clouds to get an early start from the warm lowlands. A carnival spirit prevailed among them. Hawkers in Dire Dawa had been selling enormous, gaily colored hats of loose straw. He now saw several of the younger pilgrims wearing them. Many of the people they passed waved as his taxi bore him by. One pretty young girl called out for a lift. He was tempted to stop but forced himself to look away.

After his second shuttle flight to Addis Ababa that day, he had checked into Antonakos'. The hotel now styled itself the Continental but Hilary, like the people of the town, still called it by the name of the Greek family that had run it for generations. Before the Ras had been built, it had been the best hotel in town. Hilary remained faithful. The rooms faced a palm-shaded courtyard. The breeze-swept concrete verandah was a popular spot for drinking and haggling with street vendors over the price of contraband goods.

The railway had created Dire Dawa, but smuggling kept it in business. Which, Hilary knew, partly explained the Peugeot-sized taxis. In Addis the smaller model Fiats served as taxis which took their name, *siecento,* from the smallest of all, the Fiat 600. But the bigger taxis were needed here mainly for their role in the smuggling trade. At least half of the smuggled goods came in from Djibouti and Somalia on camel trains. The railroad hauled most of the rest. Before the train reached the customs sheds of Dire Dawa, the contraband was tossed from doors and windows to be picked up at prearranged spots by taxi drivers. It was said, with only some exaggeration, that anything that was for sale anywhere in the world could be bought illegally on the verandah of Antonakos'.

Hilary loved this relaxed bazaar. He had one drink on the porch and was tempted to spend the evening sitting there. But the lure of Harar beckoned.

There would be too many people he knew in Dire Dawa to be able to prowl its elegant brothels in peace. The drinking places in Harar were shabbier. But the girls were just as pretty. You're not a dirty old man yet, he said to himself. But you are getting sneakier.

Fikr, at the wheel of the descending blue bus the taxi driver had pointed out to Hilary, also kept a wary eye on oncoming traffic. It was difficult with the old peasant standing beside him whispering excitedly in his ear. But with so many blind spots on the tight curves, he had to have a good idea of what was approaching.

The peasant was again running on about Colonel Wilson. Fikr had managed to calm him down at Mota, at Deder, at Chelenko, and at Kulubi itself where they had left off half the passengers by the stone cross which marked the road leading up to the church. Now the old man, who had again left his seat at the back of the bus, was insisting that they take the colonel straight to the police when they got to Dire Dawa.

Fikr had been torn between trying to convince the peasant that Colonel Wilson wasn't an Arab agent plotting to assassinate the Emperor and trying to convince the pretty young mother not to get off with her baby at Kulubi as she planned. He had finally succeeded with both.

He had told the girl he would bring her back up to Kulubi that evening. He told the peasant that only the police in a big city like Dire Dawa could handle an important case like an assassination plot against the Emperor.

He edged the bus past a group of Somali men in their ankle-length skirts who were leading a pack of balky camels down to Dire Dawa with firewood. It was the first time they had seen camels since climbing into the hills above Miesso.

In a moment they would be meeting the Peugeot coming up from the town which he had spotted earlier. Probably this curve. Yes, there it was. A taxi as he'd suspected. The driver carefully hugged the inside shoulder, giving the bus plenty of room. Fikr noticed a foreigner sitting in the back.

Another taxi had been impatiently trailing him downhill. Now it swung by, its horn wailing. It ducked back into its own lane just in time to avoid smashing into an ascending truck.

Fikr nodded to the peasant's whispers. How in the hell, he wondered, will I put this old man off when we get to Dire Dawa? And how will I handle the girl? He had no intention of hauling her back up to Kulubi that night.

They passed the truck.

Oh, well, he said to himself, we'll see. When we get there we'll see.

In his seat at the back of the bus, Colonel Wilson was asleep. The only European on board, he alone had paid much attention to the rainbow. He had watched it vanish and reappear with the vagaries of the road ever since they left Kulubi. In the end its beauty had hypnotized him. He'd fallen asleep.

He slept peacefully, untroubled by any awareness of what the old peasant who'd been sitting beside him was up to.

Balcha watched the Peugeot swing past the slow-moving bus below. The Volkswagen in which Tesfaye was riding with his American friend and the station wagon in which they'd seen the painter Baria Medhane Alem with some foreign lady, were still between them and the bus. A nervous, supremely cautious driver, Balcha had no intention of trying to pass.

"No," he said to Frehiwot, "I don't believe in taking chances."

"When you drive, you don't take chances," said Frehiwot. "Only when you write."

"That I have to do. It's my work. You should be the same, and only take chances when you sing. Not this other business."

In the seat behind them Balcha's wife and two young children were respectfully quiet. Balcha slowed almost to a crawl as they approached a curve. He crept around it in low gear.

"People shouldn't take such chances," he said. "You know who her husband is."

"I know," said Frehiwot.

"He can be a very difficult fellow."

"Ai, Balcha, look how pretty the rainbow is."

"I don't take my eyes off the road when I'm driving."

"Something so pretty . . . There's so few things in life can make you feel so good."

"I know this husband well," said Balcha. "A former soldier. He always goes armed. Such men are dangerous."

"Such men are dangerous. Driving is dangerous. Making songs, writing books, making love, looking at rainbows. In Ethiopia everything is dangerous. Anyway, the husband is in Addis Ababa."

"Do you know where the lady is staying?"

"I know," said Frehiwot, still watching the rainbow. "But I won't go there. No. Tomorrow up at Kulubi I'll set myself up with my *masinko* someplace and sing. People will gather and listen. Let her find me like that at Kulubi. Let my *masinko* call her. It will be better like that."

Zenebetch stood on the back porch of the bungalow they had rented at the resort in Erer Gota. Eleni and Hagos were in the hot mineral bath. Makonnen and Claude had gone up to the hotel for a game of table tennis. She was glad to be alone after the long trip.

She had already bathed and changed clothes and now was content to stand on the porch and watch the rainbow. She imagined it must be hanging directly over Dire Dawa. Negash's train would have arrived there by now. She pictured him walking under the rainbow. With the Emperor, of course. She hoped the old man would be tired from his journey and would sleep early that night and leave her handsome Negash in peace.

In peace to come to her. Under the stars. When the rainbow had vanished, and the stars mounted the sky in its place.

Wandimu, bent under his yoke, climbed up the steep, stony bank after wading across the shallow Erer River and set out on the road to Dire Dawa. It was sixty kilometers. The walk would take him the whole night. He would rest on the edge of the town during the day. Then, when the sun began to set, he would begin his final climb to Kulubi.

His ox was dead and he would get to Kulubi later than he hoped. He wanted to be there for the eve, but the *dabtara* who had fashioned his scroll had predicted sixty days. That he would arrive on the day of the feast. And the *dabtara* was right.

But enough of that. He would be there in time for Gabriel's day. Let others dance the dance of David in the church on the eve. Let others drink in the *tej bets*. He had no money for *tej*. And no strength in his legs even for the dance of David. Enough. He would be there for Gabriel's day, in time to present himself, yoked, to the priests.

He took no notice of the rainbow.

The Emperor had decided to walk from the train station to the palace. The evening was pleasant, and the distance wasn't great. He waved aside his son and the governor and the other officials who insisted he should ride in the waiting Mercedes.

Seeing him walk at his usual brisk pace always made a good impression on the people, especially on those who thought he must be too old to last much longer. It irritated him that sitting down and getting up were such difficult processes for him now. But he took pride in the fact that once in motion there were few who could match his pace.

He would walk and let his walking convey the message to his overweight son and others who would have to puff to keep up with him.

As they crossed the open square before the station, Negash, whose lungs were bad from too many cigarettes, had to catch his breath as he haltingly spoke, calling the Emperor's attention to the now vivid rainbow that hung over the hills beyond the city. The Emperor frowned. To his eyes the rainbow was only a dim curve of light. But he immediately realized that a rainbow in the hills meant there must have been rain up at Kulubi.

Rain at Kulubi meant mud. He remembered one other year when an unseasonal rain had made Kulubi a sea of mud. His car had barely made the last slope up to the church. The steps were caked with mud. Footing was treacherous. He had nearly stumbled.

An Emperor stumbling in front of tens of thousands of his people. He hoped the sun would shine all the next day and dry the place out.

He waved politely to the applauding crowds that lined the sidewalks as he made his way with his entourage up the middle of the street to his palace. He glanced again at the patch of light in the sky.

A rainbow. And mud. He was not pleased.

The Crown Prince trailed in his father's wake. They passed the ice cream parlor facing the station that was named for his dead brother, Makonnen. It was Makonnen who had been given the title and governorship once held by his father, Duke of Harar. Asfa Wossen, though the eldest, had always been slighted. But now Makonnen was dead. Let ice cream parlors be named in his honor.

It was only two blocks to the palace. He wished they had taken the cars, but he had known his father would insist on walking. The crowd along the sidewalks, fattened as usual by flag-waving school children, was well dressed and respectful. There was applause as the Emperor passed, but no unseemly cheers or shrill ululations.

They went by the cinema, two more open air cafés. The prince looked ahead at the handsome Selam Aderash palace. Above its filigreed roof, he saw the rainbow.

Oh, God, he thought, what the parasites will make of that.

A rainbow appeared in the sky above Dire Dawa as His Imperial Majesty stepped from his train. The day had been overcast, they would write in the Amharic papers, and there had been rain in the hills. But the sun miraculously broke through to shine as it always does when His Imperial Majesty arrives. . . .

Why can't they do the same for me? thought the prince. No, not that. I don't want that. No sentimental miracles. Justice and progress for our people. I want to be an honest ruler.

It was a relatively straight stretch of road, but Harry refrained from trying to pass the big blue bus. This mountain road crowded with people climbing to Kulubi terrified him.

The view was spectacular. The rainbow hanging there over the great chasm that the road leaned toward. And lush green hills rolling away. The brown ribbon of dry riverbeds leading down toward the desert. Terraced growths of coffee and *chat*. The sky aflame in the west, purpling in the east. Occasional glimpses of the beckoning town. But the beauty terrified him.

He remembered to check his rearview mirror. Baria's station wagon followed at a respectful distance. Beside him Tesfaye sat tensely quiet. The baby was with Julie. He was glad of that. One mistake and the drop was a thousand, two thousand, three thousand feet.

He drove as carefully as he could. He knew he was tired, and he knew he and Tesfaye would have only a few hours' rest before they must begin their long overnight climb to Kulubi. It was his vow.

He watched the road carefully. He wished the rainbow weren't there. Its beauty distracted.

He knew he must walk. He felt in his bones something dreadful would happen to the son that had been born if he didn't fulfill this half-joke of a vow.

As he studied the hills they were driving down now, he thought of the hills they must climb that night. He had been preparing for this pilgrimage by walking up Entoto, the peak above Addis Ababa, each Sunday. He was sure he could make it to Kulubi. He glanced at a group of pilgrims struggling up the steep incline. If all these fat old women can do it, he told himself, so can I.

But he was frightened. He was frightened now, driving down. And he was frightened at the thought of walking back up. A climb of more than two thousand meters over a distance of fifty kilometers. Something was going to happen. He knew he had to do it, but something was wrong. He could feel it in his bones.

PART TWO

LET US CRUCIFY OUR MINDS

HIS LEGS ACHED FROM THE LONG HIKE THROUGH THE SAND OF THE dry riverbed. Now their climb took a sharper angle over an ill-defined, rocky path. Tesfaye and the Dire Dawa street boy who had agreed to guide them were well ahead. Harry paused, breathing hard, sweating. He knew he had to keep up. He knew it, and at the same time he wondered why he was here at all.

He'd taped the results of dozens of interviews with pilgrims who had walked in other years. He knew he had more than enough facts about the ordeal to write that section of his book. But still he insisted on undergoing the test himself. He wasn't sure the passion for research or even his uncertain vow justified the pain and fatigue he already felt. And he knew they'd barely begun.

They'd kept to their original plan, taking the shortcut through the bush. Harry had been afraid that the rain that had fallen in the mountains would make the going slippery through the last leg of their journey.

The highway would have been surer and easier. But Tesfaye had insisted they take the old way.

"If we're going to do this fool thing, let's do it right. We'll take the way of the people." He turned now to call back to Harry, "Are you all right, pilgrim?"

At first the idea of their trek had struck Tesfaye as only mildly absurd. Now it was beginning to embarrass him. He tried to cover his feeling of foolishness by pretending to a bluff joviality.

He heard Harry's voice answering through the night, "I'll make it."

Tesfaye waved the beam of his flashlight in the direction of the voice. Harry swung his own flash high.

"Long as I . . ." The voice paused. "Can pick one foot up . . . lay the other one down. I'll get there."

"Brave words."

With the help of a half-dozen hotel porters, they had pitched Harry's multiroomed tent in the camping grounds of the Ras. They ate a light supper, napped briefly, and set out at midnight, leaving Baria, Julie, and the child behind. Baria had steadfastly refused to join them.

"I hate unnecessary effort. I won't even read your book," he said to Harry. "I'll wait for the movie."

The street boy Tesfaye had recruited to guide them was an amiable, undersized teen-ager. He told them he was fifteen. He looked ten. His name was Demsie.

Shoeless, in shorts and a clean but raggedy polo shirt, Demsie took his role as guide seriously, naming for their benefit the hotel they had just left, the Italian restaurant nearby where they had eaten, the abandoned residence of the late Duke of Harar, the ramshackle YMCA, the soccer stadium, the orthodox Christian cathedral being built on the edge of the old Muslim section and, the last outpost of the city, its handsome new high school with a dozen broken windows.

Demsie had led them up the paved highway into the sudden hills on the edge of the town. Often along this road at night, drivers would encounter packs of hyenas and even catch the quick shadow of a leopard or caracal. But this night with the heavy flow of pilgrims passing, the wildlife had abandoned the road.

A large, low-branched fig tree marked the spot where Demsie led them off the highway and into the bush. A stolid, humpbacked bull stood by the tree like a sentinel.

"Another Kulubi pilgrim," said Tesfaye. "Shall we interview him for your book?"

"Very funny," said Harry.

"Stupid cow," said Demsie, picking up a stone. "What are you doing here anyway?" He flung the stone. It bounced off the bull's shoulder. The bull didn't move.

"Stupid cow."

What are you doing here? thought Harry, remembering the bull as he continued his climb in the wake of Demsie and Tesfaye. One foot after the other. Pick them up. Lay them down. One foot after the other and sooner or later you'll get there. He was no Abebe Bikila, no marathon runner. But one foot after the other and sooner or later.

His calves already ached as he had known they would. But as they climbed he became aware of unexpected strain in the backs of his thighs. Each step it took an effort to shove the path behind him. He leaned sharply forward as he climbed, like a man walking into a sharp wind. The warm lowland air was still, but he walked as if the mountain itself were blowing down against him.

He had loaded Demsie down like a gun bearer on safari. Straps around his thin neck supported binoculars, camera, and the portable tape recorder. One hand swung the handle of a large thermos of coffee; the other balanced two blankets, a *gabbi*, and two heavy jackets on his head.

Demsie and Tesfaye waited for Harry to catch up to them.

"Are you all right?" Tesfaye asked.

"I'm okay. I'm coming," answered Harry. "If all these fat old ladies can do it, I can do it."

"Some of these fat old ladies are the toughest," said Tesfaye.

They had covered nearly ten kilometers when scrub began to give way to rock, and the grade of their climb became still sharper. Under low-lying clouds, the air was warm around them. Off to their left, a late-rising moon brought a gray glow to the heavy clouds that shrouded it.

Behind them and ahead they could see the occasional flashlights of small clusters of pilgrims. They already had passed a few groups of heavy, slow-moving women. A few briskly pacing young men swept by them. But for the most part they were locked in place along an unevenly moving chain of people.

Harry didn't know why, but he had expected there would be singing. Songs were such an important part of every feast, and at Kulubi itself last year there had been singing. But the ascending pilgrims were strangely quiet. The only music he heard was occasional hard-rock phrases echoing among the hills from hand-held transistor radios tuned to the American armed forces station a thousand kilometers away in Asmara: Jimi Hendrix skip-hopping across the Danakil desert with an acid version of the "Star Spangled Banner," and, again and again, some faintly heard lament or loud challenge by James Brown. The only other music he heard was the hallooing of a group that had wandered astray and the answering yodels of strangers who helped them find their way back. He had expected singing and maybe even torches, but there were transistors and flashlights. He resisted saying anything to Tesfaye, because he knew what Tesfaye would answer.

The flashlights are progress, better than torches.

They came to what Harry first took for a sheer rock wall. Demsie and Tesfaye waited for him at its base. He played his flashlight over it and saw it was a broken scarp, perhaps fifty feet high.

"From this begins bad hill," said Demsie. "The Kotu call it Busa. From this up, then long climb over the hilltop they call Busa."

"We climb *that?*"

"If fat old ladies do it . . ." said Tesfaye.

"I know . . . I know."

Demsie went up first, fully loaded, swift. He parked the blankets, thermos, and jackets somewhere out of sight and scrambled most of the way back down.

Tesfaye began to climb. Demsie reached a frail hand down to help him over the rougher spots. Tesfaye did the same for Harry who wished there were a stronger hand—Baria's perhaps—to haul him up. He slipped once, skinning the palm of one hand and banging his knee. He shook his head. Said nothing. And went on climbing.

At the top they found two policemen, bundled in long brown overcoats, perched on tree stumps, peering like vultures over the lowland below.

"Do you think they're enjoying the view?" said Tesfaye softly.

"I doubt," said Harry.

"Look what they're missing."

Harry turned. Behind them, below, they could see the flickering flashlights of thousands of pilgrims strung out for miles in broken patterns. With the sudden elevation, they could see as far back as the sandy riverbed. A radio wailed. A chill breeze rustled through the branches of cedars. They were beyond the scrub and thornbush, and the air around them was cold with mountain dampness. The moon, as though on cue, broke through the clouds, milkily strobing the ghostly rockscape around them.

"We better put our jackets on," said Tesfaye.

Harry nodded. He reached for the London-bought tweed that Demsie held out for him and dropped his arms into the sleeves.

The moon was nearly full, one wedge clipped from the top. Harry looked down at the snaking river of flashlights below, then up at the bruised globe of the moon. It's less than perfect, thought Harry, and better.

Harry flicked his flashlight back on. "We're part of that chain of light," he said. Tesfaye nodded.

The presence of the policemen made Harry uneasy. Each cradled a rifle between his thighs. One of them was watching Demsie, who edged closer to Tesfaye. The other went on staring at the scene below. As the moon grew brighter, a few of the flash-lighted pinpoints below disappeared. The policeman watching them shifted his position on the stump.

Harry wished they weren't there. Along the way they had encountered several police patrols, some on foot, some or horse-back. One team had stopped them, and Tesfaye was politely asked if they had seen any trouble along the way. Tesfaye politely answered they had not.

"I hate cops," Harry had said as the patrol moved on.

"They're here to protect us," said Tesfaye.

"I know."

"There might be bandits."

"Sure."

"You know, at Kulubi time they round up all the known pickpockets and bandits in Harar and Dire Dawa. And put them in jail till the festival's over. Just like they round up all the beggars in Addis whenever there's an OAU summit or a big international conference."

"Window dressing," said Harry.

"Well," said Tesfaye, "when the store is empty, the least you can do is dress up the window."

"It's pretty by moonlight," said Harry.

"True," said Tesfaye. He stared out at the scene below and sadly shook his head. "By moonlight and Technicolor. By day-light, in black and white, it isn't always so pretty. You know . . ." His pause was so long Harry thought Tesfaye had forgotten what he wanted to say. But at last Tesfaye went on.

"One night, when I'd first come back from America, I was coming out of the printing press. Late one night with another journalist. There was a moon like that. Even more full. I stopped on the steps and said to my friend, 'Look at that. What a beautiful moon.' The other fellow laughed. 'Ai, Tesfaye. You're crazy,' he told me. 'Is that what they teach you in America? To look at the moon and say it's beautiful.'

"He thought I was loony because I looked at the moon and said it was beautiful. He said I would never have acted that way before I went to America and learned such silly notions. And he was right. Ethiopians live in Ethiopia all their lives and never think it's beautiful till some foreigners come and show it to them, or they go to America and learn such silly notions for themselves. Like thinking the moon is beautiful."

"It's not such a silly notion," said Harry. He nodded below. "The flashlights are beautiful, too."

He noticed that both the vulturing policemen had turned their eyes toward him. He shivered and buttoned the three buttons of his jacket. He turned his back on them.

"They give me the creeps," he said to Tesfaye.

"In a police state, dear Harry, you have to expect police."

They shared some warm coffee with Demsie, watching the procession of lights below them. Then loaded the young guide down with their gear and went on.

Another two hours of steep climbing brought them to a level spot where there was a village of Kotu woodcutters. The Kotus were selling tea. Half a hundred pilgrims were gathered around low-banked fires, some sipping tea, some talking softly, some stretched out asleep wrapped head to toe in *gabbis* or blankets.

They had been walking six hours and were well into the mountains. The waning moon had already begun the first stage of its descent to their right. Stars were fading and on their left the gray shadow of dawn filtered through the black.

Tesfaye suggested they sit close to one of the fires and take tea.

"We still have our coffee," said Harry.

"It would be more sociable to take tea," said Tesfaye. "We haven't been very sociable this night."

It was true. Tesfaye had exchanged brief greetings with some of the old women they had passed. The young men who had outdistanced them had been grimly silent.

Harry had planned to put his tape recorder to use interviewing pilgrims along the way, but now he had no desire to intrude his questions. The long walk had tired him. Yet, he felt not fatigue but only a quiet easing of the nervous quivers that so often distracted him.

He agreed to tea but sat quietly on a log while Tesfaye squatted near the fire, chatting with a simianlike woodcutter. It was now Tesfaye who needed a translator to talk to the Kotu Galla. Demsie played the role with solemn pride. Occasional mentions of Kulubi caught Harry's interest, but he was strangely content not to know what was being said. Their words washed over him, meaningless and soothing as the chanting of a priest in Latin. Kulubi, again. When the woodcutter said it, the explosive *k* was even harsher, more guttural than Tesfaye's. He knew it was a Galligna word. For the moment, he had forgotten its meaning. He would check, but he suddenly wondered how much he could learn by learning all there was to know about Kulubi. Kulubi: Key to Ethiopia. He wondered how much he could learn by learning all there was to know about Ethiopia.

A sudden pang. He missed Julie. Yet, he realized he was glad she wasn't there. If she were, he would try to tell her the things that were on his mind. And if he tried to say them, he would lose them.

The flashlights had something to do with it. A chain of light marking out the way he had walked. Even the police. Something outside himself. Something he resented. There to protect him. One foot after the other. That had something to do with it, too. Pick them up and lay them down. Sooner or later you get there.

He realized he was breathing deeply. Slowly. Each breath so deep it was nearly a sigh. Slowing him down. Giving him time to think before he rushed into words. He didn't usually breathe like this. Shallow. Too quick. Tripping over himself. Julie had said it so often. Not just about sex. About so many things. He usually tried to hide from such thoughts. He took another deep breath. Slowly exhaled. Tesfaye turned to glance at him. Harry went on staring into the fire. Tesfaye turned back to Demsie, talking about what the woodcutter was saying in an Ethiopian language Tesfaye didn't understand.

Once at a cocktail party in Addis, he had overheard Julie saying to someone, "Poor Harry, he's such a poorly wrapped bundle of nerves."

What a terrible thing to say. He had never let her know he had heard her, but at the time he'd thought what a terrible thing it had been for her to say. He didn't think so now. She had been right. He was a poorly wrapped bundle of nerves. Not much comfort in that. And yet, long before, she had told him it was his name, his comfort, she'd wanted. And even his name had turned out to be a lie.

He loved the poetry of Ethiopian names—Tesfaye, my hope; Workanesh, you are gold; Tegegne, he is found; Desta, happiness. Every name had a meaning, and he found it beautiful. But the same quality in his own name only embarrassed him.

Julie had told him his name had been the first thing that attracted her to him. "I need a man who's a comfort," she'd said. He hadn't wanted to be only a comfort. He was hurt, but he tried not to show it. He didn't want to lose her.

Now, for the first time in his life, staring into the embers of the woodcutter's fire, he didn't hate his name. It was an invented name, but now he saw there was nothing wrong in that. Ethiopian names were invented, too. New names invented for each generation, and no name lasting beyond the next generation. Tesfaye had been given his name because his father had seen his new son as his new hope. The new son that had been born when his best wife died. Perhaps the grandfather who had made his name Comfort had found new comfort in America after fleeing the pogroms of the Ukraine. There was poetry in that. And there could be meaning. He could be a comfort. To Julie. To himself. If he stopped being a bundle of poorly wrapped nerves.

His breath was deep as a sigh.

"Are you all right?"

"Fine. Just thinking."

"This man is telling us why he doesn't go to Kulubi."

Harry looked up at the apelike woodcutter. His forehead ended in a sparse, graying hairline not more than an inch above thick brows. As he squatted by the fire, his knees looked like twins of the thickly muscled shoulders they were level with. Arms so long his forearms rested on the ground. Flat, blunt toes.

"He says he doesn't go to Kulubi because he can make more money here selling tea than he can there selling wood. He says Arabs from Harar come in and corner the market on wood. He doesn't speak any Amharic. He only speaks Kotuigna so he can't bargain with most of the pilgrims. But he says the Arabs speak every language there's money in. He's a very clever fellow. Comic."

Instinctively, Harry reached for the tape recorder Demsie had put on the ground behind them. He withdrew his hand.

"No. Tell me about it later. Later we can put it on the tape."

"Shall we show him your guessing game cards?"

"It doesn't matter. Later you can tell me, and we can put it on tape."

"You're tired."

"A good tired. I've just been thinking." He took another sip of the cooling, heavily sweetened tea and turned back to the fire.

Comfort. The fire was a comfort. Burke. Another name. His mother's. Another grandfather. No, great-grandfather. He didn't know. Who had changed his name. In an age when so many people had become conscious of their past, Harry and his parents had moved so far from their Jewishness that there wasn't even a memory to recall. So many people finding identity in—what? Being black. Being Mexican. Being Jewish or pan-Arab or African. And now even just being a woman. It was an age of consciousness. But Harry's past had been so long unconscious he wondered if it could ever be stirred.

He looked again at the simian woodcutter. He has his village, thought Harry. His trade. His tribe. He knows who—no—more than that. He knows what he is. And why he won't go to Kulubi. He won't go, and I do. Do I know why? Because I'm a Catholic? If I am. Because of Jonathan? Do I really believe? Or because I'm a Jew. He didn't believe he was a Jew.

He'd never had a desire to visit Israel. Africa, the Arab world, all the rest of the Middle East interested him more. Yet, he remembered one of the things that had first fascinated him about Ethiopia. It had been Eisler's contagious excitement when the old Semiticist began telling him of the Jewish elements in Ethiopia's Christian Church. Not just the Falashas, the black Jews of the north, but the Orthodox Church itself.

The dietary laws, pork and shellfish taboo; the ritual cleanliness; circumcision; the menstrual prohibition; women and men separate in the temple. The temple. He remembered his visit to the rock-hewn churches of Lalibela. He'd been overwhelmed. "They're not churches," he'd said to Baria, "they're temples." What had he meant? Those great stone monoliths carved centuries ago out of mountains by Ethiopian Christians. He'd read about them. He'd seen photographs and movies. But nothing had prepared him for the shock of walking through those massive vaults. He had seen them and his response had been—Temple.

He remembered Eisler had told him all Ethiopian churches had their holy of holies, the innermost circle where the Ark of the

Covenant lay. The circle only priests and kings could enter. Ethiopian Christians descended from Solomon or Moses; still observing the Saturday sabbath as well as Sunday. The importance of the psalms; a religious calendar based on the moons; customs set to time periods of eight days, forty days and seven years; new year observances in September so much like Rosh Hashana; an Easter called Fasika observed like an echo of Pesach.

Harry responded to Eisler's excitement. But with what? Was there some memory buried under his flesh, in his bones? He remembered Eisler's joke. "In Ethiopia, inside every fat Christian, there's a thin man, a Jew, trying to get out." At the time, he'd appreciated only the humor. Not the meaning.

He looked at his hands. He felt the fat of his stomach pressing against his belt. He had come to Ethiopia. Something in him had responded. He still wasn't sure what. He wanted to be moving. He wanted to get on to Kulubi and see it again. Perhaps there would be—what?

Revelation. He was afraid of the word. But he wanted to go. He took another sip of his tea and said in Amharic, "*Inn hid.*" Let's move. It's a Semitic language, he remembered. Back in California with old Eisler it had all begun with that.

Tesfaye stood, paid for their tea, and spoke to Demsie in Amharic, telling him to gather up their gear. Harry struggled to his feet. His legs were stiff. He handed his cup to the woodcutter. He'd drunk only half the tea.

"Thank you," he said to the man.

The man nodded. Harry returned the gesture. He didn't repeat himself and say thank you very much. He took another deep breath, slowly exhaled, turned, and set off behind Demsie and Tesfaye.

Frehiwot and Balcha were just coming into the woodcutters' clearing.

"Look,"said Balcha. "There's Tesfaye."

"I see him," said Frehiwot. Then, in his pure Amharic, he added, "Never mind. He's with one of his friends from outside countries. We don't need that kind. Let them go."

"As it happens," said Makonnen, "I'm an Amhara."

He sliced the ball just over the net. It caught the edge of the table. Claude lunged far to his left and with a backhand flick managed to return it. Makonnen was waiting. He smashed it to an undefended far corner.

"You little bastard," said Claude.

He walked the length of the room to retrieve the ball. The hotel at Erer Gota was asleep. The game room, bare except for an unconnected sink, a few chairs, and the Ping-Pong table, was behind the bar where one last waiter dozed.

"How many times that you beat me?"

"You won a few games before dinner."

"Yeah, that's when we weren't playin' for money. How many times you beat me since we ate?"

"Seven," said Makonnen.

"Six, motherfucker."

"As I said, I'm an Amhara. You have to watch us. We're tricky."

"Amen to that."

"Another set?"

"One more time. This time I'm gonna whip your ass."

Claude didn't consider himself a particularly good Ping-Pong player, but it embarrassed him to be beaten by the unathletic Makonnen. Makonnen played as though table tennis were a chess match, planning and setting up his point shots well in advance. He kept a conversation going as a distracting tactic.

"Volley for serve," said Claude. He fed Makonnen an easy backhand serve. They volleyed.

"So as I was saying, I grew up in Asmara but only because my father worked there. But we're Amharas from Gondar."

"I have trouble gettin' all this tribalism business straight."

"But there is no tribalism in Ethiopia. Some regional differences, perhaps. But no tribalism."

"Tell that to whitey. You know it, and I know it. You got tribalism. Shit. You serve."

"You see," said Makonnen. "You made your point, but I won the serve."

"Yeah. You tricky all right."

"I have many friends who say they're Ethiopian. Not any one tribe. But Ethiopian."

"Yeah. Like I could tell you I'm an American. But I know what I am."

"An African?"

"Hell, no. That's what I thought I was. Till I got here. Come on, serve."

"What are you then?"

"Claude Jackson, nigger."

"What harsh language."

"I quit talkin' Princeton when I quit Princeton. Serve, mother."

Makonnen's best serve was a half-speed low skip over the net to a near edge of the table. He let Claude's slamming return hit his paddle. The ball floated back over the net, dead center. Claude had to lunge the length of the table to return it. Makonnen's backhand wasn't strong enough to force Claude out of position. Claude's overhand slice spun away from Makonnen's paddle.

"Your point," he said drily.

"I'm gonna whip your ass."

"So, as I was saying, having grown up in Asmara, I can understand Hagos's point of view. You Americans are simply fantastic. There are thousands of you at Kagnew Station, right in the heart of Asmara, but you live a life apart."

"God's chosen people," said Claude. "Shit. One-one. You talk too much."

"We have perfectly good Coca-Cola plants in Ethiopia. Built by Americans. Including one in Asmara. But your Americans at Kagnew fly in Coca-Cola all the way from America."

"Tastes better," said Claude.

"They fly in fresh tomatoes, oranges, bananas, carrots. From Eritrea we export those things to Europe because the ones we grow are so good. We export most of our coffee to America. Tons of it. People say our coffee is the best in the world, but at Kagnew they fly in planeloads of instant Maxwell House."

"It's quicker."

"One year for the Fourth of July they flew in a cotton-candy machine. One enormous plane with nothing in it but a machine to make cotton candy for their Fourth of July picnic."

"Yeah. That's how we celebrate our revolution. Shit. Two-one."

"It's no wonder you can't win the war in Vietnam. Your planes are probably all filled with Coca-Cola. Your tanks probably have popcorn machines instead of cannons."

"We are exporting the American way of life. And people eat it up."

"You occupy half the world and still think nothing but America exists. Like your football. You call it football, but you carry the ball around in your arms and throw it and catch it with your hands and hardly ever kick it with the foot and you call that football. The whole rest of the world plays football with the foot. All of Europe, Asia, Africa, and even your own South America, people play football with their feet. No one else in the world plays football like you do, but then two American teams get together and play what they call the world championship—of football. Two of your baseball teams play each other—no one else is invited—and you call that a world series."

"Yeah. Well, we think the world of America."

"I'm surprised to hear you say that. To hear a black man say that. I've read about your Watts, Detroit, Harlem. What it's like in the South. The prisons. The schools."

"What are you bitchin' about? You just gotta read about it. I gotta live with it."

"You aren't living with it now."

"Soon enough. I'll be there."

"Why not come back to Africa?"

"Don't you start jivin' me with that stuff. I been jivin' myself with that shit long enough."

Makonnen placed shots from the near right to the far left corners. Then the left forecourt, the back right corner, the near left edge. Claude lunged from one side of the table to the other. Makonnen barely moved.

"I thought black Americans were beginning to identify with Africa."

"Tryin'," said Claude. "But back there we mostly get it all fucked up. Guys get all strung out on this Islam bit. Become Muslims. Start learnin' Arabic. Come to Africa find out most black Africans hate Arabs. Shit. Arabs was the slave traders sent my people off to America in the first place. In chains. Right now you come to go to Chad, Sudan, like Nigeria a couple years ago. You find Muslims and A-rab types killin' black Africans every chance they get."

"Liberation movements," said Makonnen. "We have one in Eritrea as well."

"Yeah. Liberatin' black men from they life."

Makonnen's gentle backhand return kissed the top of the net.

"Shee-it. Now you got me talkin' too much. Six-one."

"Seven."

"Okay, seven. Hell, no. What am I sayin'? That's six. Come on, serve."

Claude served. Makonnen returned.

"Other bag lot of guys get into, me for one, is this Swahili gig. Speak a African language, you know. Make us all brothers. English is a slave language. Well, shit. Come to Kenya find out Swahili's no real African language nohow. Come from Zanzibar back when Zanzibar was all Arab slave traders. Find out that's how Swahili got up into East Africa, Congo. Arab traders set up posts for takin' white ivory and black slaves outta Africa. Take the black man sell him into slavery in Arabia. And leave their language behind. Swa-fuckin-hili."

"They sold Ethiopians as slaves as far away as Persia and India," said Makonnen.

"Well, then, you know it. But my brothers back home don't know it. East Africans use Swahili 'cause it's the only language they got in common. But it ain't *their* language. Damn slave traders' language is what it is. Back home guys sayin' Christianity's a slave religion. So they gonna be Muslims. What's that? Slave trader's religion. Guy says Joe Jones is his slave name. Gonna call hisself Mohammed Shabaz Shabang. Slave trader's name. English a slave tongue. Gonna talk Swahili. Like a slave trader."

"What's wrong with that?" said Makonnen. "From slave to slave trader. It's a step up."

"You hit it, Jim. Most times the way a black man gets a leg up is by stickin' his foot in another black man's face. Lots of that back home. And I've seen a whole lotta that in Africa. . . . Like you Amhara pricks."

Makonnen looked up at him. Claude slammed a shot by.

"Six-two, mother."

"Touché."

"But don't matter nohow," said Claude on a sharp, backhand return. " 'Cause we ain't African, nohow. Like we let our hair grow out and say we got a Afro. Come to Africa you find Africans wear their hair all kinds of ways. I been all over Africa takin' pictures African hairstyles. 'Specially chicks. You can find the most down tribe in the bush, you find chicks got their hair plaited, straighted, pigtailed, rolled, cartwheeled, beehived and, yeah, you even find a Afro here and there. Like those Arussi Gallas. They got a beautiful Afro. Looks like a helmet. But round here you see these Kotu Galla chicks got their hair piled in big black buns on their ears look like headsets and maybe bangs in front. Must take a pound of grease and years of old Mama pullin' on it to get it long and straight enough to style it like that."

"They use butter," said Makonnen.

"Smell like it," said Claude. "But it's the same all over. There is no Afro hairstyle for Africa. You got a thousand hairstyles in Africa. And not many of 'em is Afro. You got more hairstyles than you got tribes, and you got too many of them. And don't tell me it's white brainwashin' that did it. I been places they hardly know what white skin is, much less white fashions. And they doin' all kind of things with their hair. 'Cause they don't do their hair for no African identity. They do it for tribal identity. It's tribe that counts. But maybe go to a place like Lagos you find the chicks got them Afro *wigs*. Wigs. Got their own hair straight but when they wanna do the bit like they see in the magazines they get from the States, they put a wig on. Most times in the city you see a guy wivva boss Afro, it ain't 'cause he thinks he's a African. He think he's James Brown.

"But he ain't. 'Cause I found out one thing. Africans ain't niggers. We may look alike. We all black, brown, or somethin' like. But we been over there our own side of the water for three hundred motherin' years. We've changed. Hell, I maybe got more in common with some peckerwood white boy from Atlanta than I got with some cat out there in the bush. Oh, there *some*, some Africans, mostly guys been to the States or live in the big cities, they see the movies, get the tapes, the magazines. They know the songs and they know the handshake and they can say 'brother' and 'gimme the dark side, man.' They can all say 'man.' But 'cause you meet some guys here like that don't mean *we're* African. Just means *they* ain't much African either."

"Or at least," said Makonnen, "trying not to be African."

"Yeah. Maybe everybody doin' something like that. Lookin' to find yourself, you maybe try bein' somethin' different from all that *same* scene you got around you. But with us it's sad. I got brothers with a dream about Africa that's nothin' but a nowhere dream. They think Africa's home. Shit. Home is Lenox Avenue.

"Some guys come over here, head of this committee, chairman of that, they get the VIP treatment and some minister went to Lincoln or Howard slaps 'em on the back and says, 'Welcome, brother.' Guy says, 'Yes, I was right. Africans are my brothers.' Like that made a difference anyway. Hell, I know *families*, families where one brother kill another. What good's a man bein' my brother do me if he got his foot in my face."

"At least it's a black foot," said Makonnen.

"It still hurts. Anyway, black VIP he got his *dashiki*, got his picture shakin' hands with the minister of ministries, so he goes home and he preaches it, 'Africans are my brothers.' He preaches it and some more guys like me we get the dream, too. He goes back to the States and preaches 'Africa is our home,' but he don't stick around and scuffle with the African that *didn't* go to Lincoln or Howard or Oxford or Paris. The African that didn't go to school nohow. Which is most Africans.

"I been poor before, and I got no eyes to be poor again. But I'd for damn sure rather be a poor black man in New York than a poor black man in Addis Ababa."

"I might agree with you about Addis Ababa," said Makonnen. "But what about the rest of Africa?"

"The same. Hell, Addis Ababa one of the nicest towns *in* Africa. Nairobi is cleaner if you hung up on clean, but hell, that's still a British or a Indian city. That's no African city. Lagos, Accra, they filthy, 'specially Lagos, and too damn hot. You on your ass in Lagos, you really on your ass. They swing, I give 'em that. In their own way those West Africans swing, 'specially some of the chicks. But Hi-Life ain't my life. No."

"You haven't been keeping count," said Makonnen. "That's eight-two. My serve."

"Yeah, well Ping-Pong ain't that important." Makonnen served. Claude returned. "You take Dar. That's a African city. Not as nice, not as lively as Addis. And it's hot. But I could maybe live in Dar es Salaam. They got somethin' goin' in Tanzania. But they ain't too hip on Americans down there. White or black. We all the same to them. They got their *own* thing goin'."

"With a few thousand Chinese around."

"Yeah, well that's okay. Them Chinamen just workin' on the railroad. Still a black man's country. And they makin' it work *for* the black man. No. I take that back. They makin' it work for the Tanzanian."

Makonnen continued slowly building points. Claude now played like a sparring partner, willing to provide a workout but no longer determined to punch back.

"They're friendly enough in Dar. But cool. Like one guy said to me, 'We have our problems. And we're workin' on them.' That's all he said. He didn't say go home and solve *your* problem where it's at. He didn't have to."

"You only talk about the cities," said Makonnen. "Addis, Dar, Nairobi, Lagos. What about the countryside?"

"The *real* Africa, huh? Don't talk to me about the countryside, Jim. I'm a city boy. Just about all of us are. We been tryin' to get off the man's plantation ever since when. Stop breakin' my back and start usin' my mind. Oh, we got guys talkin' back to nature jive same breath they talkin' back to Africa. Let 'em try it. It's hard, Jim. Your African farmer, he's got it very hard. But see, we don't dig that back home.

"We think freedom. Black man in Africa is free. Well, maybe he is free. But nothin' else is free. You gotta scuffle for the rest. And it's hard. Very hard over here. 'Cause you're scufflin' in a poor country that doesn't have enough for its own. That's a lot different from scufflin' in a rich country where you know where it's at.

"But we got guys maybe know a little bit about a place like Ethiopia or Guinea where you got black men puttin' black men up against the wall. Or some idea what it's like to be a Luo or a Masai in Kenya where the Kikuyu run things. Or a Ibo in Nigeria or any black man in the Sudan. But they say anyway it's better to be down in a black country, shoved around by other black men than to get your ass kicked by the white man in a white man's country."

"And they're right," said Makonnen.

"No," said Claude. "It don't matter. If a man has got his boot on your neck or his bullet in your ass, it don't feel no better if he's black than if he's white."

"You're letting me beat you," said Makonnen.

"No I'm not. You aren't just tricky. You're good."

"But you aren't even keeping count. If you let me keep score, I'll cheat you."

"You don't need to cheat. You're gonna win anyhow."

"It doesn't matter. If you let me, I can't help cheating. It's twelve–three. You serve."

Claude fell silent. He played without his usual energy and speed, but with skill and concentration. Despite the disadvantage of Makonnen's having the serve, Claude took the set, 3–2.

"A comeback," said Makonnen.

"Maybe."

"That's sixteen–four."

"That's fourteen–six, Jim."

"I was afraid you might be paying attention."

"I don't mind losin'. Sometimes. But I don't like gettin' shafted."

"Then you have to watch me very closely."

"I'm learnin'."

He stopped talking and took the next serve, 4–1.

"And that's fifteen–ten. Your serve."

"A rally. But yours is a hopeless cause."

"No," said Claude. "I'll be goin' home. That's where it's at."

"And what will you do?"

"Work. I'm a photographer, Jim."

"Is taking pictures enough?"

"No. I'll be into some other things."

"What about Africa?"

"Well, for Africa, for me, maybe takin' pictures is enough. I used to have a idea of Africa, me and a lotta other guys, that was way outta line. When I get back, I'll have a whole lotta pictures to look at and keep me straight."

"But what about other people?"

"Whatchu mean?"

The question came as sharp as one of his better serves.

"Straighten out other people. You should write a book. Use your pictures."

"Like *How a Black American Discovered the Truth About Africa?* Some jive like that?"

"Something," said Makonnen. He shrugged one shoulder.

"Noooo-oh," said Claude. "None of that for me. I may tell *you* I found out Africans ain't niggers. And that my brothers, my black brothers back in the States, aren't Africans. I may tell you that, 'cause even if you ain't no kind of my kinda nigger, at least you're black. But too much of what I got to say is the kinda thing whitey wants to hear. A lot of what I've been sayin' to you would make whitey feel—like comfortable, 'specially comin' from a black man. I don't mind makin' my brothers feel *un*-comfortable. They could use some of that. But I don't want to make whitey feel good. We got the white man pretty shook up these days. Pretty scared. And he's a whole lot better to get along with when he's scared. I mean to let him go on thinkin' black Americans and black Africans and all the other brown, yellow, and red people are brothers in the big world revolution that's gonna come. 'Cause we *are* brothers in that. And that shakes whitey up. Let him stay shook up. But *our* part of the revolution, if it comes, we're gonna have to fight in New York, not Nairobi.

"What bugs me is the idea my African heritage is some big thing means more to me than my American heritage. My African heritage was long ago and far away. I get my American heritage shoved in my face every fuckin' day."

Makonnen took the serve 3–2.

"That's eighteen–twelve," he said. "You don't have a chance."

"I have a chance," said Claude. "But whitey's got the guns. I gotta face that, too. Whitey's got the guns. And the money. It comes to war, that's what counts. I gotta chance. But not at Ping-Pong."

His service whizzed past Makonnen.

"Maybe you do."

Four more serves, each smashed with devastating speed, each spinning off an edge of the table, gave Claude a sweep.

"That's just to give you a idea of what I'm like on my home turf. I make that eighteen–seventeen, my favor."

"My favor," said Makonnen.

"Mine," said Claude.

"We both know it's mine. That last service was eighteen–twelve."

"Yeah," said Claude. He smiled. "But I thought maybe you weren't payin' attention."

"You are learning," said Makonnen.

"Better believe it."

"All right, then. Leave alone the white people." He served, deceptively slow, with a heavy backspin. Claude's lunging return left him off balance. "What about the other black Americans who still think Africa's their home? Can't you tell them what you found."

"Oh no. Uh-uh."

"Why not?"

"It's their dream."

"But it isn't true. You know it isn't true. They *aren't* Africans."

"Maybe. I could try, but they wouldn't believe me. We need that dream. No. I couldn't do that." He sent a shot flush into the net. "Maybe they would believe me." He watched the ball skim off the table.

"Maybe they would believe me. And it would break they heart."

Hagos was asleep. One arm was thrown across Eleni's breasts. She stared into the dark, not wanting his arm but unwilling to move it. She didn't want to wake him. She didn't want to talk. She didn't want the frustration of making love again.

They had made love that afternoon in the poollike sunken bath of the bungalow. In the days when the resort had been the private retreat of the imperial family, the gray, red-shuttered, wood frame bungalow they'd rented had been the duke of Harar's.

"He must have liked his pleasures royal," said Eleni when she saw the bath.

Four steps led down into its tiled depths. Hagos filled it with steaming mineral water tapped from Erer Gota's hot springs. He noticed that many of the tiles were broken. The pipes were rusty and paint peeled from the walls. But the air of casual luxury was still there.

"You see how they live, our imperialist princes. On money they suck from the people. Then, when it gets too shabby for them, they build some new palaces and turn these places into hotels."

"Ai, Hagos. Don't preach," said Eleni. "We're paying five dollars for it. Let's enjoy."

They did. They splashed in the steaming waters like children. Hagos even tried to swim a few, aborted strokes. They lathered each other's bodies till cleanliness and excitement stung in every pore.

Though of different tribes, they shared the common beauty of young highland Ethiopians of their class. They were light-boned and in clothes seemed slender. But the body Eleni washed was hard and muscular. Hers was heavy-breasted, narrow at the waist and hips, but her buttocks were high and full. Soft hair, long lashes, full mouths, and skin of the same light brown made them like brother and sister.

They splashed and swam. They laughed. They kissed and soaped each other's tingling flesh again. When Hagos leaned back against the steaming tiles and drew her to him, she was ready for him. The water swirled around their hips, embracing, caressing. They shivered, crushed against each other, kissed again. Hagos bent his knees, fitted himself neatly into her. The slow eddying of the water gave Eleni the rhythm she wanted. She moved gently as the water, closer, surrounding. Their mouths met. Eleni knew she was ready but not for the almost instant quivering and abrupt sliding away as Hagos moaned and wasted away inside her.

"That was beautiful," said Hagos.

"It was?"

"I think I could fall in love with you."

"So quickly?"

"Yes."

"Myself. I don't think I could fall in love so fast."

"This trip could be only a beginning."

"Really?" She smiled, a smile that showed nothing but her teeth. "When could we have our next one?"

"Maybe in a few weeks."

She laughed, touched his cheek.

"A weekend at Langano," he said.

"Hagos, talk sense." She withdrew her fingers. "Do you always get it over with that fast?"

"Uh? What?"

"Happen. Come. Orgasm. Finish. Is it always so fast?"

"I was excited."

"So was I."

"I mean I'm not used to these Roman bath orgies."

"It wasn't much of an orgy."

"I thought it was pretty nice myself."

"Yourself, maybe it was nice."

"What do you expect?"

"I expected . . . I guess I thought you'd be different from most of our boys. You seem more grown-up. You've traveled, been to Europe, America. I thought you knew more about a woman."

"I know a lot of women."

"Do you know any well?"

"Well enough."

"I wonder." She turned from him, waded to the far corner of the bath, and climbed the steps. At the top she looked back down at him. Her body still steamed and droplets of water clung to her like jewels. Hagos felt himself excited again.

"We could make love again."

"For two minutes this time?"

"It will be better this time. You'll see. I'll have more control."

She took an oversize towel from the rack and wrapped it around her.

"Pull the plug out, Hagos. The bath is finished."

"No. We aren't finished. I'll show you."

"You've already shown me. You're a child. Like the others. I thought this time maybe I'd found someone different. You're no different. You think every woman is like one of your Nefas Silk whores. So anxious for your ten dollars she makes you think you're king of the bed."

"I never pay more than five."

"Ai, Hagos."

"When I go. I'm not one of your brothel boys. I don't have to. There are other girls."

"But I'm not one of them, Hagos." She stared down at him. Alone in the huge bath, he looked like a little boy lost. She was less angry at him than disappointed in herself for having thought he would be different.

"I'm not looking for dates or weekends," she said. "I'm not looking for someone to buy me clothes. And I'm not a simple countryside girl content with simple country pleasures."

"What are you then?"

He was angry now, one fist clenched as he started across the bath to the steps. An involuntary shiver of possible excitement went through her. She pulled the white towel more tightly around her.

"I'm a woman," she said. "With a mind and body of my own. I've had an education, a good job. I've traveled. I've . . ."

"I know." His voice was tight. "You've traveled. You've had many lovers." He was at the steps.

"No," said Eleni. "Not many. But one or two who knew something about a woman. One or two who weren't selfish, who weren't children or cruel. If only you . . ." Her words trailed off.

"What do you expect me to do?" snapped Hagos. "Lick you like some foreigner? Like some dog?"

His voice was like a whip. His words, a slap.

"I don't go to foreigners," said Eleni.

He started up the steps. She saw that he was aroused again.

"I'll show you what a real man is like."

"I know what a real man is like."

He pulled the towel roughly from her. She stumbled away, but he caught her wrists, forced her hands to her sides, and kissed her harshly. He half carried, half dragged her to the bedroom. Full evening had fallen. The room was dark except for the light that spilled through the bathroom door. She made no sound but tried to dig in her heels as he dragged her, tried to make herself heavy, tried to keep her fists clenched before her breasts. He threw her to the bed and forced his thigh between hers.

"It will be good, Eleni." He burrowed inside her. "This time you'll see."

Anger drove him as much as desire. But then, as her flesh went soft and cleaved to his, he controlled his rage; he controlled his body. Slowly and still more slowly he ground himself into her. He shifted and rode her high. He swung her from side to side and her moans were real. One hand went to her breast and the nipple hardened to his fingers.

Excitement began to tense within her as he went on and on. Then, as he went on and on, the tension of excitement began to fade. If left a tight irritability in its wake. Eleni knew she was being fucked. She knew they weren't making love. He went on and on and her right thigh began to cramp. When orgasm shook him at last, her eyes were shut tight. Her arms held him close. She didn't want to look at his proud, handsome face.

He stayed inside her, lying heavily on her. When her hands finally eased his shoulders away, he pressed himself up, out. He looked down at her and said:

"You see?"

She nodded.

He rolled away.

"It was better, wasn't it?"

"Yes." She stared up at the ceiling. "It was better."

"You see? I told you it would be better. It was just, I was too excited before. This was good."

"Are you satisfied now?"

He nodded in the dark and his hand reached out to her leg.

"Yes," he said.

"I'm not," said Eleni. Her voice was flat. "Not at all. Not even a little."

He swung around. In the half-dark she could see his teeth, the whites of his eyes.

"You're lying." The outline of his head took shape. "You enjoyed it. I could tell."

"It was better," said Eleni.

He fell silent. They hadn't argued further. They'd eaten dinner up at the hotel with Makonnen and Claude. They'd come back to the cottage and roughly, uselessly he'd made dry love to her again. And then he had fallen asleep. Now, with his arm flung across her, she stared into the dark, sleepless, not even tired.

In the next cottage, a newer, smaller handsome stone *tukul* with a decorative thatch roof over practical tin, Negash Mengistu looked down into the smiling, sleep-filled face of the most beautiful woman he'd ever known.

"You know how to make a man happy," he said.

"Only you," said Zenebetch. "I only want to make you happy."

There was a purity to the lilt of her Amharic that gave Negash almost as much pleasure as the purity of her flawless skin. With her, he always wanted to make love with the lights on so he could enjoy his awareness of her beauty. With his pale, bony American wife, he made love in the dark and tried to think of Zenebetch. Once he made love to his wife while the radio was still on, a program of music introduced by Zenebetch. Her voice made his fantasy real.

Apart from her beauty, apart from the special quality of purity he found in her, he enjoyed the way she could make conversation a step in the long, continuous process of making love. She never asked him about politics and inquired after his family only in the line of formal, conventional greeting. But even in these conventional greetings, Zenebetch had the knack of conveying loving gestures.

When he'd arrived that evening, driving in less than an hour the sixty kilometers over the rough road from Dire Dawa to Erer Gota, she'd greeted him at the door of the stone *tukul* she'd taken. She took his hand and led him inside.

"May God give you health, my lord."

In Amharic the phrase had only two words: *Tenastelign Getoch*." But to Negash's ears, Zenebetch infused them with meanings all her own.

It was evening and so, conventionally, she asked him how he had passed the afternoon.

"Well," said Negash. "Thanks to God."

The greeting was a formula, but Zenebetch managed to make him feel she'd expressed concern over the quality of his particular afternoon.

When he echoed the greeting to her, she answered. "Well." And then with a shy smile, added, "But I shall pass the evening much better now that my lord is here."

She cast her eyes down, then reached up to take his shoulders while she kissed him, first on one cheek, then the other. He bent to kiss her cheeks before taking her in his arms.

He kissed her lips warmly, then leaned back to whisper a line from a popular song. "*Fikr le bichaie*—you are my only love." She sang a few lines from the song, then took his hand to lead him to a chair by a *messob*, a basket of gaily dyed straws woven in an intricate Harari design in which she'd had his supper brought from the hotel.

She washed his hands and face with a warm cloth. Her fingers fed him fiery *wat* in delicately wrapped morsels of *injera*. With each mouthful Negash savored the act of love.

When he'd first met Zenebetch soon after his return from the long years in America, Negash was struck not only by her classic beauty, but also by that unique aura of innocence he never failed to see in her.

"She's so innocent," he'd said to a colleague at the time. "Her innocence makes me want to attack."

The attack had been swift, thorough, successful. Negash knew people spoke of him as "one of the great hunters." He felt such a reputation could do him no harm, but considered that in his case it was exaggerated. Compared to others he knew, he thought himself reasonably faithful to Zenebetch and his wife. Even when with other women, some of whom were nearly as beautiful as Zenebetch herself, it was often Zenebetch he imagined himself with.

She nearly always wore a traditional white *tibeb* with expensive embroidered borders. He bought her many gifts, earrings and bracelets and crosses of gold, perfumes and costly handbags and shoes. He had seen to it that the ministry where she worked put a car at her disposal and had arranged for a royal grant of land. But most often when he brought her a gift it was a dazzling national dress, each more elegant than the last. He considered them gifts to himself as much as to her. It was the way he liked to see a woman clothed.

There were also times when Zenebetch herself asked favors. She asked one tonight as she fed him.

"I wish you would do something for Makonnen," she said.

"Makonnen? Makonnen who?"

"Makonnen Seyoum. He works in your ministry."

He was tempted to ask her which ministry. The Emperor involved him in the affairs of so many. But Zenebetch, happily, wouldn't understand that.

"Seyoum? Is he a Tigre?"

"No. An Amhara."

"Good. What does he do?"

"He's my friend."

"Oh." He laughed. "Then we must do something for him."

"Please. He's with us on this trip. He speaks so highly of you. He's very clever, and so helpful to me."

As a cover, thought Negash. That makes him helpful to me, too.

"Can he be trusted?"

"Oh, yes. He's very discreet."

Negash registered: parasite, hypocrite. He often found men with such traits useful.

"A university graduate?"

"Oh, yes. He's also a writer though they say what he writes is too clever to be published. They say he's very clever. Hagos respects him."

That means he believes us old men are robbing the people. He'll be full of silly Marxist ideas, in favor of tribal separatism. Nothing helpful in that, but often such types needed only a chance to share in the riches.

"Married?"

"Oh, no. He's very young."

"Attractive?"

"Oh, Negash. He's a boy."

"Perhaps," said Negash. "Perhaps I'll have a chance to talk to him in the morning. Is he here?"

"He has a room up at the hotel. With your wife's black American friend."

"What number?"

"How would I know? But you can find him. Makonnen Seyoum."

"Remind me to write his name down in my notebook. In case I don't have a chance to see him in the morning."

Negash believed deeply in the importance of small favors for relatives, for friends. Zenebetch was more than either. It wouldn't hurt to find her young man a better job.

"Don't worry," he said. "We'll do something for this Makonnen."

"Thank you."

She leaned over the *messob* and kissed him.

In bed he took his pleasure with her easily and felt the pleasure she had in making him happy. If she ever yearned for any other fulfillment, Negash never knew it. She was the perfect mistress, and it only occasionally occurred to him how boring she would be as a wife.

His own wife was a challenge, stimulated by politics, gifted with an abrasive intellect against which he sharpened his own. She was demanding in love, expensive in her tastes, caustic in judgment, and petulant about his frequent absences. She was often irritating, never dull. To Zenebetch he came for pleasure at his ease. He never stayed long enough to be bored.

He had recently decided that if his ambassadorship came through, he would arrange a marriage for her in his absence. He already had the man in mind, a retired general, a great hero of the resistance, now a member of the prestigious Crown Council. He was an aging widower, but still handsome, vigorous, wealthy, and universally respected.

Zenebetch was already twenty-five. He had decided it wouldn't do for her to stay single, particularly if he were to be out of the country for three or four years. After marriage, she would stay on her job and later, when he returned, discreet afternoons could always be arranged.

But today the Emperor had crushed his dream of an ambassadorship. Things would have to go on as they were. It could be worse, thought Negash as he looked again into her lovely face. She slept, gently, conveying love. The sweet fatigue of satisfied desire filled him.

He kissed his woman lightly on the forehead. He had much to do in the days ahead. He kissed her eyes. They would make love again, he decided, in the morning. He turned out the light. Tomorrow would be hard. How pleasant now to rest in love. Here in the lowlands in the warm night air. He pulled the sheet over them. Her body nestled into his. They slept.

One Thousand Eighty drifted into sleep. Memories of her evening floated through her mind. Except for Kalamawork crowing about her new car, the hours in the park had been best. But the scene at the hotel had also been all that she expected. She preferred the food at the nearby Omedla Restaurant, but she and Fat Margaret dined at the hotel because that's where the people she wanted to be seen by would be.

Fat Margaret had been hoping for Omedla. "Well," she said with a heavy sigh, "at least the hotel has gin."

"Yes, dear, they have plenty of gin."

They each took three gin tonics before dinner at white wrought-iron tables in the hotel's busy patio. It was early and there were few men of real importance among the serious drinkers and casual strollers with hunting eyes. But One Thousand Eighty greeted all who *selammed* to her. Why be snobbish? she believed. One could never tell which of today's eager young men might quickly ascend to be tomorrow's vice minister.

Dinner was routine: hotel chicken and hotel peas, both soaked in the same pale hotel sauce. The bread was hard; the salad, limp. Only the ice cream pleased them.

"You can always get such good ice cream in Dire Dawa," said One Thousand Eighty.

"Yes," said Fat Margaret. "And the gin is good, too."

After dinner it took the two women forty-five minutes to cross the hotel's elegant, compact marbled and mirrored lobby. They moved like a single stately ship, creating waves of attention as they passed. Ministers of public works, communications, justice, finance, and education greeted them. Even the illustrious Negash Mengistu had stopped to speak with her briefly. He called her Itegue Million-esh, an old joke of theirs from the days when he had been a regular visitor to her house. He would tell her that One Thousand Eighty was a poor name for her and call her instead Itegue Million-esh, You Are Empress of One Million. Negash was pleasant, courtly but clearly in a hurry. His nod to Fat Margaret was curt.

"Give my regards to His Majesty," teased One Thousand Eighty, for she was sure he was rushing to the palace.

Several lesser government officials and military men paid their respects. The dashing young bachelor recently named chief justice stopped for a word. The Emperor's aide-de-camp nodded in his crisp, military way. Even the prime minister, his handsome French wife on his arm, glanced at her knowingly.

At moments like this she thought Negash's joke might not be far off. Itegue Million. Why not? She wouldn't have made a bad empress. Others from Makeda to Zewditu to Menen had known how to make use of the bed as a weapon of rule. Were they so different? As she made her regal way through the lobby, Fat Margaret by her side, she was convinced she was sister to them all. Perhaps not as beautiful as Makeda and Mintuab. Not as ample as Menen nor as cunning as Zewditu, but beautiful and ample and cunning enough to be the match of any. She even imagined that perhaps her day—or night—might come. Many who later wore the crown had been courtesans or the wives of several lesser men before they climbed the imperial bed. And people said the old man was still active. An old man, a widower, could do worse, she thought. She'd be more than a comfort, more than a bed. She was sure she could tell him much about his cabinet that his security chief would never know.

"After all," she said to Fat Margaret as they walked through the gates of the hotel compound, "I don't tell him everything, do I?"

"Who?" said Fat Margaret. "Negash, that spy from the Emperor?"

"*Indet?* Why, Margaret. Sometimes you scare me, the way you read my mind."

"Well, I can't read books, and I don't like magazines. So I have to read something."

"Impossible. Enough. If you read me that well, I'm going to have to start censoring what I think."

"It isn't a bad idea," said Margaret. "Men should do the same."

"Precisely. Isn't it a fine evening?"

"Too hot. We should have taken a taxi."

"The walk will do us good. It isn't far to Kalamawork's.

What would you do if I were walking to Kulubi this year and asked you to come with me?"

"Ha. I'd call a taxi."

One Thousand Eighty laughed that special laugh that made tired men relax.

"You're precious," she said.

"Sure. If I was worth my weight in gold, I wouldn't have to do the things I have to do."

"Goodness. What terrible things do you have to do?"

"Same things you do," said Margaret sourly. "Only for less money." She glanced at One Thousand Eighty, hoping she had noticed nothing odd about the behavior of Negash in the lobby. She hoped he would not give her away. At least not till it was over.

They walked past the Omedla, crowded with noisy diners on the verandah. Margaret sighed, wishing they'd eaten there.

"I know how you love pasta," said One Thousand Eighty. "Maybe tomorrow we can eat here."

"That's what you told me last year, too," said Fat Margaret. "We ate that hotel garbage every night except for the night Kalamawork fed us." She snorted. What did she care? With the bonus Negash had promised her, she could buy all the pasta she wanted. And all because she had slept late one morning when One Thousand Eighty thought she was out. All because she had slept late one morning when the general had come to relax. And talk about his schemes.

They walked along the darkened street where the fat green pods of the now flowerless flamboyants hung from motionless branches. Margaret hated walking. But she always did what One Thousand Eighty wanted to do. One Thousand Eighty, she thought. It could be the number of humiliations she'd suffered at the hands of the woman who had so ungenerously given her a home. Betraying the general to Negash—it wasn't just the money. It was the chance to betray One Thousand Eighty as well.

They walked past the somnolent Greek Church. At the corner they could hear the music from the sound track of the film at the open air theatre off to their right and, coming from their left, music from the tape recorder playing at the bar in the park. A movie would be fun, thought Margaret. A chance to sit in peace and watch somebody else's life go by. But no. They'd be going to the park so everyone could watch One Thousand Eighty play queen.

One Thousand Eighty noticed the brand-new Peugeot parked by the hedges which fenced in Kalamawork's bar. The plates were local, nongovernment. Some big merchant, she thought. Or an important Frenchman from the railway. She was impressed and did her best to make her entrance regal.

Heads turned as she walked among the round stone tables in the faintly lit garden. Some were vaguely familiar, but she recognized only one—the girl who had been their hostess on the plane. One Thousand Eighty smiled, nodded. The girl stared through her. She sat with a handsome young man. Out of uniform she couldn't be sure—but, yes, it was the one. He'd been one of the pilots on their plane.

She put them behind her. They mattered no more than the others scattered at benches and tables through the garden. What mattered, her people, chattered on the porch of the bar and crowded its loud, brightly lit interior.

As she moved into the rectangle of light spilling from the bar, it was Kalamawork herself who first recognized her and called out:

"Itegue . . ."

One Thousand Eighty laughed. Empress. Was everyone reading her mind tonight?

Kalamawork, the color of gold, was fair, fat, girdled and uplifted, sheathed in black, sleekly powdered and heavily perfumed. She curtsied as deeply as her upholstery would allow.

"Haile Selassie is the First," she said. "Emperor Menelik was called the Second. Yohannis, I think was the Fourth. But you are our Empress One Thousand Eightieth."

"It's a long line," said One Thousand Eighty.

"All the way from Saba."

"All the way from Asmara, you mean."

"All the way from Queen Saba," said Kalamawork.

"From Saba to *tej*," said One Thousand Eighty. "Can't you offer us anything but words for welcome?"

"I know Margaret would prefer gin to *tej*. How are you both?"

They kissed cheeks and exchanged an endless volley of how are yous and how have you been since I saw you last and how did you pass the afternoon and how are relatives, friends, the house, the land, the cattle, the servants—all anointed with thanks be to Gods and thanks be to Gabriels. It was Kulubi time, and Gabriel could not be forgotten.

One Thousand Eighty was soon surrounded by a score of old friends. Some she had seen no more than a few days before in Addis Ababa, but here all greeted her like a sister unseen for a year. All the great madams, many of the famous singers and actresses were there. They ranged from the well-known Abebetch whose Lumumba Club was vast and loud to Workanesh whose "private" house was a minor imitation of One Thousand Eighty's. The beautiful Bizunesh was there from the Bodyguard Band and Aselefetch from the theatre of the National Patriotic Association; "Tcherai Karesh" of the Haile Selassie Theatre, and Hirut Bekele, the Police Band's famed singer. Great ladies all, expensive, well known, bold on the stage and in bed, shy and quiet in social settings and now, among themselves, coarse, vulgar, and loud.

One Thousand Eighty—their queen—was given a throne of red plastic and chrome on the porch. Fat Margaret was left to stand. Gin was brought, tonic and ice, chunks of raw meat and pepper sauce and *injera*. The queen's coronation feast had begun. At Kulubi time, Dire Dawa's usual midnight curfew was waived. The feast could continue all night.

It all went well until One Thousand Eighty asked who owned the new Peugeot she'd seen parked by the hedge.

"It's mine, dear," said Kalamawork.

"Oh. Who is he?"

"Who's who?"

"Exactly. Who is the who who gave it to you?"

There was laughter but subdued. Everyone sensed a challenge in the air. Kalamawork gestured grandly at her bar, the garden crowded with customers.

"Business has been good."

"Nonsense," said One Thousand Eighty. "You don't get that kind of car from selling whisky. You get that kind of car from a man."

"Well, I suppose you're right," said Kalamawork. "There is a man. I asked Kulubi Gabriel for it."

Now the appreciative laughter was for Kalamawork. She tried to follow up her advantage by insisting that One Thousand Eighty and Fat Margaret come with her for a ride.

"Not tonight, dear. It's a lovely car, but tonight I just want to sit with all my dear friends and enjoy. But we'll let you take us to Kulubi."

"Oh, but I was going to walk," said Kalamawork. "It's my *silet*. But never mind. For you, my sister, I'm sure Gabriel won't mind. I can walk another time. You can ride in my Peugeot to Kulubi."

"How sweet of you, dear," said One Thousand Eighty. To herself she added, and beware. Gabriel takes his revenge on those who abuse his vows.

Baria rolled away from her. She unfolded herself slowly, stretching out the coiled spring of flesh she'd become under him. She had wanted him to undress, and he had extinguished the lamp in the tent before he would. Light spilled in from the lights of the hotel, from the fluorescent glow above the pool, from a streetlamp arcing above the wall enclosing their campsite. Her eyes had grown used to the half-dark and to him.

She watched the dark silhouette of his body cross the tent. Even in the pale, filtered light, she could see the discolored patches on his flesh. He squatted by an open, half-unpacked suitcase and came back with a towel. He stretched out on another sleeping bag beside her and handed her the towel.

She turned toward him. When her hand reached out, it touched a diseased circle of pink on his chest. It felt no different from the brown flesh around it. But she knew it was there. Discolored. Not leprous, but discolored and catching more of the filtered light in the tent than the dark flesh around it. He didn't flinch. She guessed that in the dark he thought she wouldn't know. How often? perhaps a dozen times he'd penetrated her, but this was as close as she'd ever been able to be to him. She touched him where she knew the diseased patch was.

She guessed. He thought. She wouldn't know. To know what he thought she always had to guess.

"You know, you're the only man . . ."

"I know. You told me that before."

"That's not what I meant."

"What did you mean?"

She took her hand from his chest.

"Forget it."

"What does Harry do?"

"Harry? Poor Harry doesn't do anything."

"Nothing?"

"Oh, he dribbles. Then goes to sleep."

"But he's a father now."

"You shouldn't make fun of Harry," said Julie. "He's very fond of you."

"Yes. I know."

"Is that why you took him off on that trip last year?"

"At Timket?"

"Is that the baptism thing?"

"Yes."

"That's when it was. He'd just come back from his silly Kulubi. The week you and I had. Then you ran off with my husband."

"Not exactly."

"Harry said you had a wonderful time. Poor Harry. He always becomes so fond of my lovers. He usually likes them much better than I do."

"Have there been so many?"

"Not so many. One would be too many, I guess."

"You should be kinder to your husband," said Baria. "He's a very nice chap. And you have a family to think of now."

"I have a son," said Julie. "Harry doesn't."

"I think he does," said Baria. "But I know nothing. My charm . . ."

"Your charm?"

"Mmm." He sat up, wrapping his arms around his knees, and stared at the canvas wall of the tent.

She wondered what he'd meant to say. That his charm misled her? That it was his charm to know nothing? The urge to probe, like the urge to touch the diseased patches of his flesh, twitched at her nerves. She resisted, but not for long.

"Is that why you deserted me?"

"Deserted you?"

"When the baby was coming, you just deserted me."

"Silly girl. You're a married lady. You have a husband. You were having a baby. Nothing could be more normal."

"Your baby. I was having your baby. Don't you care about that?"

"Perfectly normal. When true. All my children seem to belong to other people."

"Are there so many?"

"Hundreds. Perfectly normal. Wind scatters the seed. One of my poems. Something . . . if I can say it in English. Something like, I have spilled my seed in hallways—under stairs—on makeshift beds and cars—something like that, something—the ominous slopes of forests. Each child I sired—died—in jells, in rubber traps—and cunning withdrawals from women—well, the poem said something like—from women I did not love."

He stretched out again on the sleeping bag. His hands, clasped, pillowed his head.

"And yet—this juice still flows, desire—irrelevant—as camel's thirst. In the desert land of Onan—a dying man is king."

"It's sad."

"Yes."

"What are your poems about? Your other poems."

"Oh, about love. Mostly about love."

"They don't sound it. When you read them. In Amharic. Tesfaye took us once when you were reading your poems. I didn't know what the words meant, but when you read them, you sound so dramatic. I thought they were about war."

He laughed softly.

"Yes, war. Suffering, loss, defeat. They're about love."

"Is that what love is?"

"Isn't it? You're the one who should tell me. Love is a Western idea, foreign to us."

"But your poems are about love."

"My poems . . . are also foreign to me. I even write in a foreign language."

"You write them in Amharic."

"You forget. My people were Galla. To me Amharic is a foreign language. Not as foreign as English or German. But not my own."

"But I've heard you say you're an Ethiopian. Not a Galla. Not an African."

"Yes. Have you heard me say that? Desire, my love, is the only father of many children. Perhaps that's a proverb. But they don't let me forget what I am. Like my poems. An Ethiopian, a real Ethiopian, will tell you my poetry isn't poetry at all. In Amharic their word for poem is *gitem*. It means joined—or fit together. It also means rhyme. If it doesn't rhyme, if it doesn't join, it isn't a poem. The poem I was telling you ends with a couplet, a rhyme, a joint. To an Ethiopian those two lines may be a poem. But not the rest."

"But people like your poetry."

"Young people. Modern people. Westernized people. A real Ethiopian wouldn't like my poems."

"And your paintings?"

"The same. Only foreigners like my paintings. Only foreigners buy them. So my paintings become foreign to me, too. Like my children."

"Don't you ever want any of your own?"

"Children? Perhaps. And even a woman of my own. All my women seem to belong to other people."

"You wouldn't want a woman of your own."

"No?"

"You'd be afraid."

"Afraid?" He glanced at her briefly, turned, and went back to staring at the walls of canvas. "Silly girl. Afraid of what?"

"She might love you. You might have to love her."

"Love, like poems that don't rhyme, it's a Western idea."

"Since when are you afraid of Western ideas?"

"I'm not afraid. I'm an Ethiopian."

"Ha. Sometimes. Sometimes you're an Ethiopian."

"Ha. And what are you?"

"Me? A silly little girl."

"Really? You look like a nice grown-up lady."

She shook her head.

"A little girl. That's what I've been. Ever since my father died."

"Oh. When was that?"

"When I was a little girl."

"You're going in circles."

"You taught me that. Everything goes in circles. Churches, *tukuls*, time, crowds, dances."

"And my paintings."

"But they're foreign to you."

"Not the circles."

"I used to have dreams like that."

"Like what?"

"Circles."

"Ah, then you, too, are an Ethiopian."

"No. A little girl. When I was twelve I used to have these dreams. My mother'd bought some records, why I don't know, of African music, African drums. Every night she used to play her old Victrola. She must've got it from her grandmother. God—you had to wind it up by hand. And play her records. Especially that one. Over and over she used to play that one. It was after my father died. One of those old seventy-eights, you know, and it used to scare me. I'd pull the covers over my head like I did when I was a little girl and afraid of the dark. Somehow with the covers over my head the dark didn't seem to matter. Like I was in someplace safe and snug but I'd feel silly because now I was twelve and, you know, I thought I was such a big grown-up lady but anyway I'd pull the covers up over my head and finally I'd go to sleep.

"But then I'd have these dreams. Night after night the same dreams. Or almost the same."

"Ya, so," said Baria, "you say you were twelf vhen you start to haf t'ese dre-hims. Tell zee doktor . . ."

"Shut up."

"Ya, so."

"They'd start with tom-toms. Drums. Just like on the record."

"Quiet. The natives are getting restless." He ran his finger up her thigh.

"Stop it." She pushed his hand away. "You couldn't do anything now anyway."

"You know me too well."

"I don't know you at all."

"Ya gut. Tell zee doktor your dream."

She wrapped her arms around her knees, glad to feel the warm desert air around her.

"It would always be dark. In the dream, I mean. Like when I went to sleep. But I could hear the tom-toms. I mean drums. At first I'd think I hadn't fallen asleep and it was just my mother playing her records downstairs. But then I'd wake up. I mean in the dream I'd know I was waking up and then I'd be in this clearing, then I could see the drums at the edge of the woods and there would be these Africans, not playing the tom-toms but dancing. Usually nobody played the drums. They just played themselves, I guess, or sometimes one of the dancers would go and play on this one big drum and they'd all be motioning to me while they danced, motioning me to come and dance . . ."

"Did you?"

"God no. I was scared to death. I just stood there shivering."

"Naked?"

"No. I always had on some kind of white dress."

"That's nice."

"Not like a wedding dress but like some kind of graduation dress or maybe communion dress, I don't know, but then the worst part was when the one that sometimes played the drum would get up and just walk toward me and then the others would be around us except it wouldn't be the dancers it was like the jungle closed around us and closed up the clearing but then the trees and vines and spider webs would start swaying to the drums like dancers and the other one that sometimes played the big tom-tom by himself would be trying to make me dance and I'd close my eyes shivering and trying to scream and I never could."

Her eyes were closed now. Baria was silent. She could smell the flowers in the garden by the pool and hear the soft sound of music coming from the hotel and laughter in the street beyond the wall. She went on with her dream.

"They were all around me, a black circle around me, dancing. And sometimes I guess I would scream and my mother would be there asking me what was wrong. I used to tell her a black man was chasing me and she'd say I shouldn't be silly because after dark there wasn't a black man in all of New Canaan."

"Really?"

"There wasn't a Jew either. Not then. That's where we lived then. To get away from all that in New York."

Baria propped himself up on an elbow.

"Is it still like that?"

"Probably. I think there may be a few Jews now. But I'll bet there's no Negroes."

"What would your mother say if she saw you now?"

"She'd die."

"That's nice."

He flopped back down on the sleeping bag.

"She's not so bad. My mother, I mean."

"So that's how your dream ended."

"At first. But then they kept going on and started changing."

"Tell zee doktor how."

"These circles started coming into it. Big white circles. I don't know what they were made of They looked kind of like Life Savers."

"Lifesavers?"

"Only bigger."

"What are lifesavers?"

"Oh, you know. Candy."

"Really?"

"Please shut up. They were big white circles, some of the circles in your paintings remind me of them."

"Ah, so. Now zee doktor unzerstands."

"And when the Africans started coming—I mean the dreams would start the same with the tom-toms in the dark and all, but then when it got to the part where the dancers or I don't know maybe the jungle would start coming at me, the circles would come over me. One would be on the ground and one, sometimes two would be around me, and one over my head and then they couldn't get at me."

"The dancers or the jungle?"

"It didn't matter. They were all the same."

"Then what happened?"

"Nothing. I was safe, surrounded by my white rings." She giggled. "I think once I sang a hymn."

"And lived happily ever after."

"No."

"Why not?"

"Well, the dream started changing again. I mean I must've dreamed this way for I don't know how long. But then, I don't know, maybe my mother got tired of the damn tom-tom record or something. Anyway, all that part of it, the tom-toms and the natives, started going out of it, not all at once, but more and more of it was just the circles and the more the other parts went out of it the smaller and smaller the circles got except there were more of them. I don't know, at first just a few and then all of the beautiful dancers and the drums were gone and then the dream would be just the circles coming around me getting smaller and smaller, hard and white. I don't know. Maybe they were made out of plastic; they held me in all over and I couldn't do anything."

"Where were you?"

"Same place. A clearing in the woods."

"Still in your white dress?"

"No."

"Naked?"

"Yes."

"That's nice."

"It was awful. Make love to me."

"I don't think I can."

"Why?"

"Do you still have these dreams?"

"I need you."

He made no move. She tightened the circle of her arms around her knees and dug her nails into her palms.

"They went on. Please . . ." She looked up, staring straight ahead. "They went on for a long while. Then they stopped. Sometime, I don't know, maybe after I went to Europe. Maybe after I got married. They started coming back. Only not the same. It was just the circles but they weren't white anymore, kind of gray and gummy. I could push against them and they'd give but never enough and then they'd clam back around me again so tight I can't move."

"Then you still have them."

"Sometimes. Please . . ."

He touched her back. She shivered, uncoiled. She fell against him, pulling at his shoulders with her hands. His shoulders were hard as smooth, round stones. Her hands slipped away. She touched his chest with the tips of her fingers. His stomach. There. He was hard and swelled to her touch. She was afraid to look at his face.

He placed his hands on the ground by her shoulders and propped himself over her, touching her, sliding in, impaling her only there with slow, deep, indifferent strokes. She clung to his arms. Sweat fell from his chest onto hers. She clung to his arms and tried to pull him to her. His arms were rigid. He thumped on and on, swollen enormous now, tunneling inside her. She clasped her hands behind his back and took the punishment of his slow, rhythmic strokes.

Then, as pain twisted her toward pleasure, one hand slipped from his arm to still the nervous twitching where he would never caress her. Her own fingers accompanied his cock till she came. He plowed on through her sobbing. Finally, he stopped. He withdrew, still swollen.

She clung to him, pulling herself up to him as he drew back.

She kissed his shoulders, his chest, her lips instinctively finding the bright, discolored patches of his flesh.

"Why won't you ever let me love you?"

He stood. She knelt before him.

"You can."

"No. You won't let me. Because of these."

She reached out and touched his thigh. He pulled his leg away as though stung.

"Your damned spots. You won't even tell me what they are."

"Leprosy."

"It's not."

He turned away from her. He searched the rubber floor of the tent for his clothes. He found his pants and slipped them quickly on. Then plunged into his shirt.

"I told you once what it is."

"I know. But I couldn't remember the word."

"Then call it leprosy. It will make you happier."

"I wanted to look up the word. To find how to cure . . ."

"There is no cure. You know the saying. The leper can't change his spots."

"You're not a leper."

"Socially. In the best of circles, I am."

"I don't mind your spots. I only wish you didn't mind them."

"You are a very silly girl."

"You make me feel naked."

"You are naked."

"I didn't feel naked before."

"Get dressed."

She shook her head.

"I'd do anything to make you forget. To make you know it doesn't matter. Or find a cure. Then maybe you'd know I could love you. Maybe you'd let yourself be loved."

Baria crossed the tent and sat on the cot where the diapers were piled. He peered through the half-open canvas flap into the next partitioned compartment of the tent.

"Don't you think you ought to go look after your child?"

"He's asleep."

"He may be dead."

"He's not dead," said Julie.

"I think you forgot he was here."

"I can't forget him."

"There is one cure," said Baria. She thought he meant one cure for the baby. But he was talking about himself.

"One girl in America. I read somewhere in a magazine. They said they'd cured her. She was a Negro. Brown like me with these circles of pink. They said she was the only one who'd ever been cured. With drugs and lotions and skin grafts. They cured her in their way. By making her white. I'm a black man. An Ethiopian. I don't want to be white."

"Not quite Ethiopian. Not anymore. Your paintings. Your poems, you're as much European."

"Perhaps," said Baria. "Another disease I have. But that, too, doesn't matter. It's only a disease of the skin. Like these damn spots. Superficial. They don't matter."

"They matter to you. It makes you afraid, withdrawn . . ."

"My charm."

"It hurts."

"Also, my charm."

"I'd do anything. Walk to Kulubi. I'd be as silly as Harry. Sillier. For a miracle for you. I'd walk all the way from Addis with one of your paintings as a gift for the saint if Kulubi could take away your disease."

"Get dressed, silly girl."

A shiver went through her. She did feel naked and suddenly cold in the warm night air. She thought of Harry. Always when she didn't want him he came. She wondered if he would be at Kulubi by now where it would really be cold. She had said the words without thinking. Like Harry. Asking for a miracle. And then his stupid vow had been born inside her. Baria's baby that Harry had prayed for, sleeping now beyond the canvas on the far side of the tent. The cold that pimpled her flesh was the cold of fear. Her hand reached numbly for her dress.

"Don't ask for miracles," said Baria. "You only get trouble."

Harry went slithering through the mud. His right hand caught at an exposed root. His left clawed at the ground.

He yelled.

Tesfaye and Demsie, walking ahead, turned and hurried to him, digging their heels into the treacherous surface.

"Hang on," called Tesfaye.

"Uh."

Harry had already pulled himself up to his knees. He looked

up to his left at Tesfaye. He was afraid to look to his right. The curving, ill-defined path poured over the edge of the cliff they were circling like a brown waterfall tumbling over slippery rocks toward the deep, narrow defile below.

Harry clung to the root he had grabbed and reached up to Tesfaye with his other hand.

"Wow."

Harry looked down at the mud on his hands, on the sleeves of his jacket, the legs of his trousers. The mud caked his boots. Demsie handed him his glasses, still tinted with a fine brown film.

"At least they aren't broke."

"And no broken bones?"

Harry tapped his knees, his thighs. He tried a few cautious steps. He swiveled his neck from right to left.

"Okay. I guess."

"Good. We should be moving. But this time, watch your feet."

Demsie had somehow gotten around behind him. Demsie shoved. Tesfaye pulled. Harry stumbled to his feet. He was covered with mud.

"Wow. That was close."

"Any closer," said Tesfaye, "and it wouldn't have been close."

"Wow. Thank God for that root."

"For all roots we give thanks. Did you trip?"

"No. I just slipped. I was looking up."

"Always a mistake."

"My glasses . . ."

"Demsie has them. They need a cleaning."

"Oh. Sure. Wow."

In the hills, high above the warm desert town they had left at midnight, a light rain had fallen at dawn. They had shivered through it in the shelter of a cedar oak, sharing the last of the warm coffee in their thermos.

The rain hadn't lasted long, but it had been enough to make the path slippery and treacherous in several places.

"Don't worry," said young Demsie. "No hurry now."

"Really?"

"Sure. It's almost here. Soon the highway comes."

"Let's move," said Tesfaye. "It won't come if we just stand here."

"Just a little time, it comes."

"Move," said Tesfaye.

Demsie gathered up the gear he'd dropped to help Harry. And they moved.

The path climbed more steeply now, and Harry followed it more carefully. He watched his feet, ignoring the play of the sun in the trees above. Over the most treacherous spots, he moved sideways digging his feet laterally into the mud, like an ascending skier seeking purchase in the snow.

One foot after the other, he repeated to himself. Sooner or later.

Another quarter of an hour brought them to the police camp sprawled out along the edge of the highway.

"Why are there so many guns?" asked Harry.

"To protect us," said Tesfaye.

"From what?"

"Each other. Ourselves. *Shiftas.* Who knows? I don't like guns either."

"But you carry a gun."

"That, too, is a sign of the times. And the place."

"But you don't need a gun here."

"*Minalbat.*"

Harry didn't know what the word meant. But he didn't want to ask. *Minalbat,* he repeated to himself. He vowed to look it up later.

There were a dozen police tents, as many trucks, and perhaps a hundred haggard policemen in long khaki coats, most with rifles slung over their shoulders. There were also first-aid tents, a tent where mothers could warm cereal and milk for their children, and a score or more tents and temporary grass or wood pole shelters where vendors sold sodas and mineral water, hot coffee and tea, fresh fruit, long, tapering beeswax candles, and crude paintings of Gabriel on thin paper or handsome, expensive skins.

They spread their blankets on the ground and sat while Demsie, financed by Tesfaye, went off to buy mineral water. Tesfaye said get three bottles. Demsie came back with four. He proved right. Harry used one to wash the mud from his hands and face. He then spent five minutes scouring his glasses before thinking of his thirst.

There were perhaps a thousand people clustered around the

camp in small groups. More arrived every minute, both from the trail they had followed through the bush and along the highway.

"I didn't know so many people walked the highway," said Harry.

"Most probably come from Harar," said Tesfaye. "Some from Dire Dawa who don't like mud, but most from Harar."

"That's where Julie and Baria were going this morning. Julie wanted to go to the market. She loves Harar."

"Foreigners do," said Tesfaye. "Picturesque, they call it."

"And you prefer Dire Dawa."

"I do."

"Because it's *cleaner*." He said the word as though it meant "dirty."

"That, too," said Tesfaye. "Cleaner. More modern. More jobs for more people. Wide streets. Flies not so many. Fewer people drugged on *chat*. It was the same in New York. I didn't like Harlem. The addicts on the streets. The flies, the roaches, the rats. The filth. The crime. The poverty. In New York I preferred the upper East Side."

"Wow. You are conservative."

"It doesn't matter. They wouldn't let me live there anyway. Excuse me. I see someone I know."

He stood abruptly and walked to one of the vendor's tents. On a bench outside he had seen Shaleka's wife. He hadn't thought to speak, but the urge to escape Harry for a moment had overcome his reluctance.

His relations with Shaleka, the soldier who tried to rule his work, were always outwardly friendly, correct. It didn't seem proper to approach a superior's wife when the man himself was not present. Especially when he couldn't remember her name.

They exchanged formal greetings. And Shaleka's wife introduced him to her companion.

"Ato Tesfaye, this is my friend, Woizero Alganesh."

"Really?" The name startled him.

"Of course it's real," said Alganesh, hefting her bosom. "Don't the bed's pillows look real?"

He felt the blood rush to his face. He liked to think that Ethiopian women, apart from the new breed of city girls, were shy in manner, chaste in speech. Kulubi fever, he thought. At Kulubi, it was said, everything is allowed.

"We saw you sitting there with your foreign friend. Tiruwork was telling me all about you."

Tiruwork, at least that was something. At least now he knew her name. But he could think of nothing to say.

"Sit down." Alganesh patted the bench beside her. "Sit down and have a Coca-Cola with us."

"Thank you," said Tesfaye, bowing. "I just finished a Babile."

"Tell us about your foreign friend. What's he doing at Kulubi?"

"He wants . . ." He scratched at the back of his neck. "I think he wants to see the real Ethiopia."

"That's good," said Alganesh. "Bring him over and introduce me to him."

"Alganesh. Please."

Tesfaye appreciated her. The embarrassment in her voice sounded real.

"What's wrong? Bring him over. He wants to meet the real Ethiopia. That's me."

Tesfaye smiled. "I don't think he's ready."

"Ai. What's he waiting for?"

"That's a good question. May I sit down?"

Alganesh moved to one end of the bench. Tesfaye sat between the two women. He hunched his shoulders. He drew his knees together. His hands were pressed between his legs.

"Have a Coca-Cola with us," said Alganesh, "and tell us about your friend. Is he rich?"

"He's American," said Tesfaye.

"Oh, that's very good."

What could he tell her about Harry? Alganesh went on asking. He answered in monosyllables and shrugs while Alganesh created a portrait of her own. What was the real Harry? Harry in the mud. Harry in the dark. Harry wanting the real Ethiopia. How could he tell Alganesh? Or Harry? That they were building portraits of their own. Harry, wanting to see the real Ethiopia. And Alganesh, wanting to meet a rich foreigner. Neither could speak the other's language. They would never meet each other, only themselves.

"Yes," said Tesfaye. "You're right. All Americans are very rich."

And Harry. His lust for seeing the real Ethiopia. Harry might in his way be better than most. The foreigners all said they wanted to see the "real" Ethiopia. Tesfaye saw it as their way of trying to rule Ethiopia. They would come not to see what was real but to tell you what was best, what you should develop and what you should preserve. They would tell you that Harar with its poverty and its filth and its flies was more "colorful," more "real" than Dire Dawa with its clean, shaded streets. They would tell you that a peasant wrestling with a single-bladed wooden plow was the real Ethiopia and what a shame it was to "contaminate" the pure land with tractors and, in the same breath, they would chide you because the highways they drove on from one resort to the other were not better maintained. They would gush over Kulubi and its superstitious pilgrims—"how real"—and mock you for being so slow in building a modern hospital for the rich in Addis Ababa.

"He doesn't know Amharic," said Tesfaye.

"I could teach him," said Alganesh.

"I think he's too old to be a student." He turned to Tiruwork. "Where are you and Shaleka staying?"

"Shaleka? No. My husband didn't come."

"Ai. But he's coming."

"No. Alganesh and I came together. With some other lady friends."

"I see." But Shaleka, he knew, was coming. In fact, was here. He'd seen the ministry Land Rover on the road yesterday going down into Dire Dawa. Strange, thought Tesfaye. First my father, thinking the Emperor was coming today through Mota by car. When actually the Emperor came through the lowlands yesterday by train. And now Tiruwork thinking Shaleka isn't coming when Shaleka is already here. My father. He suddenly felt an impulse to get up and walk—or run—to Mota.

"I must be going," he said. "The *faranj* has a *silet* to walk to Kulubi."

"Which way are you walking?" asked Alganesh.

"The shortcut. Over the hill," said Tesfaye.

"Ai. Leave the hill. Go by the road with us."

"Too long," said Tesfaye. "And besides, highways aren't the real Ethiopia. We go through the bush."

They watched him return to Harry.

"Ai," said Alganesh. "He wants to keep his rich foreigner to himself."

Harry, Demsie, and Tesfaye set out again. It would be the last hour of their trek. The sky was rapidly clearing. Even in the crisp mountain air the sun was warm on their backs. They shed jackets, adding to the pile hauled by Demsie. He was loaded down with their blankets, jackets, thermos, tape recorder, camera. The only cross that burdened Harry was himself. By now they had been climbing for more than ten hours. Each new step he took was a calvary of effort. The fatigue that had put his nerves to rest along the way was now a dead weight nailed to each of his limbs.

His right calf had begun to cramp. There was a nagging pain in his left ankle. He suspected he must have turned it when he'd gone sliding through the mud. Even with two pairs of heavy socks cushioning his feet in their felt-lined boots, he was aware of blistering on his heels and the ball of his right foot. He tried to forget the pains. He tried to ignore the sweat that clung now to his back and his neck.

It was only another hour. He looked at the hill they had just begun to climb. It swelled above them, rounded, rocky. He knew scaling it rather than following the road would save several kilometers. He wondered if it were worth it. But this was the path most of the pilgrims would take. This was the way he wanted to go. He stopped for one deep breath. And went on.

Each step became more of a struggle. The thinner air of the mountains left him winded. Once he had to call Tesfaye and Demsie back to him while he sat on the ground, stretching his right leg out to ease the cramp in his calf. As he climbed on, sweat poured from every part of his body. The sun was now high and merciless. It seemed to fall like an avenging angel straight to the top of his head. He wished he had a hat. Flies swarmed before his eyes, buzzed into his ears. He knew it was useless, exhausting to swat them away with his hand. But he couldn't refrain. He wished he had a fly whisk. He wished he were somewhere, anywhere, else.

One thought sustained him. In the pocket of the heavy, muddy jacket Demsie now carried on his head, there was a copy of the pamphlet he'd written on Kulubi. They were nearly there. Soon he would present the pamphlet to one of the priests—his gift to Gabriel, his vow fulfilled. And soon—in earnest—he would ask Gabriel's help in completing the great book he would write on Ethiopia.

He looked up. The crest seemed still far away. He gulped for air. Each breath stung. And each step forced another gasp. He stopped. He tried to force himself to breathe through his nose.

Slowly. Slowly. The flies buzzed around him, persistent as the sun. He went on.

The stream of pilgrims was now thick around him, swollen by thousands coming from Harar, Alemaya, and hundreds of towns, villages, and farms nearby. Many swept by him, swiveling their heads to stare for a passing moment at the panting, slow-moving foreigner. None spoke. None stopped. Harry pressed on, trying not to lose sight of Tesfaye and their guide.

I'll make it, he told himself. One foot after the other. Pick them up. Keep going. Lay them down. If all the fat old ladies . . .

He collapsed.

A crowd gathered around him like a knot. He was still conscious, crouched on his hands and knees. The world was black, airless, heavy with smells of other sweating, exhausted people. Heavy with the smells of Harry Comfort. He couldn't speak.

Where was Tesfaye?

When he came to, he was sitting against a rock. There was a wet cloth on his forehead. He looked up. The sun struck his eyes. He thought he had seen Tesfaye's face, but now he saw only pinwheeling stars. When he looked again he saw the backs of three rifle-bearing policemen forming a semicircle just beyond his stretched-out legs, keeping away the curious, drifting crowd. He closed his eyes. Tesfaye's voice echoed. Here to protect us. From what? Ourselves. Each other. A breathing space, he thought. A space—he inhaled as deeply as he could—a space to breathe. Slowly exhaled. Like a sigh.

"Are you all right?"

Tesfaye was there.

"Yes."

"Don't try to talk. Rest. You'll be all right in a minute."

"Sure. Look how big he is. He's strong, this American."

It was Demsie.

"How did you find me?"

"Don't talk. We looked back. We saw the crowd gathering. We couldn't see you. So we came back."

"And the police?"

"They saw the crowd, too."

"I'll have to thank them."

"Rest. You can talk later."

He rested. Breath came easier. He didn't try to look up. He was aware that Demsie was leaning on the rock next to him, waving away flies.

"Stupid flies. Go home."

He tried to sit up. His body felt chained to the rock. He sank back against it. Soon, he thought. Soon it will pass. Soon I'll get up.

In another few minutes he was back on his feet. The policemen were thanked, tipped.

No. He wouldn't have to be carried.

No. No need for a stretcher.

They went on. Tesfaye and Demsie stayed close by him.

They had gone only a few hundred meters when they again came to a sheer rock face. Hand over hand scrambling. Tesfaye pulled. Demsie shoved. He made it.

And went on.

The last steep hundred meters to the crest of the hill were the longest hundred meters he'd ever walked. They paused to rest at the top still some distance from their goal. Harry turned and looked back the way they had come.

"My God," he said. "How did I ever make it up that?"

"You did well," said Tesfaye. "How do you feel?"

"I feel fine."

"Good."

"It's like a river," said Harry. "A white river."

The long line of pilgrims climbing toward them stretched unbroken to the police camp at the edge of the highway. Others could be seen bunched along the road as far as the distant, sparkling lake at Kersa. Most wore the traditional white cottons of the national costume. Brightly colored umbrellas danced among them like flowers floating on the white water.

"A white river that flows uphill," said Tesfaye.

"Beautiful," said Harry. "Just beautiful."

"The real Ethiopia."

Harry turned. Tesfaye was smiling. But gently.

They moved along a narrow, descending path through a gantlet of peddlers and chanting beggars. A turn, a slight rise, and then, there it was.

The church below them shone in the sun. Light leapt back toward the sky from the blue and gold dome with its eight-pointed cross. He could see other crosses on each of the bell towers. He wondered how many crosses there were. One at the back. Were there others obscured? He wondered why it should suddenly matter how many crosses there were. Somehow it did.

He could hear drums. Distant. Muffled. And the people. Here not a river but a sea. Tens of thousands pressing on tens of thousands in the great bowl below them. A sea of people being fed by rivers flowing down the hills from a dozen directions.

"It was worth it," he said. "Every step."

He looked at his watch. It was nearly noon. By the time they reached the gates of the church, Julie and Baria should already be there.

"Let's hurry," he said. "Julie will be waiting."

A troop of street boys bearing parcels followed in their wake as they moved leisurely through the market in Harar.

Their morning had been long, casual, relaxed. With the help of a hotel clerk, Baria had found a *mamitay* to sit with the baby at the campsite. They'd driven up from Dire Dawa in the station wagon and stopped at Alemaya to visit the American-run agricultural college and its zoo. Harry had told her so much about it, said Julie, that they really must see it. She was glad they had. She'd made a discovery about Kulubi.

They were shown around by an eager but disheartened animal husbandry expert from Montana who had made the development of the zoo his personal mission. They were allowed to scratch the back of a friendly hyena, to hand-feed lettuce leaves to an oryx whose spearlike horns were over three feet long. Sommering's gazelle and Gréby's zebra looked on, envious, but shy. They bent low to peer into the box of hissing, spitting, big-eared caracals.

They were entertained by a cageful of clownish, acrobatic baboons and watched a half-dozen lions enjoying a hose bath.

"That one must really like it," said Julie. "The way her tongue's hanging out."

"No, ma'am," said the zoologist. "That's not why her tongue hangs out. It's a sad story. Like, begging your pardon, sir, the story of most animals in Ethiopia."

"Most of the people have sad stories, too," said Baria.

"Yes, I suspect that's true, but animals are more in my line." He puffed slowly on a pipe that never seemed to need relighting or refilling.

"Tell us about the lion," said Julie. "The one with her tongue hanging out."

"Poor old girl. She can't get it back in her head. It's a story like, well, everything that's wrong with this country. Begging your pardon, sir."

"Surely not everything that's wrong," said Baria.

"Well, a lot. You've heard of this place called Kulubi?"

"Of course," said Julie. "We're going there today."

"Give it my regards. Well, this old girl was brought there when she was just a cub. Some woman brought her as a gift to the saint."

"Why that must be the one," said Julie. "It's in that pamphlet Harry wrote. There was a woman with a uterus problem. She couldn't have children. Then, you know, these silly vows. She said the saint whatever his name is cured her and she had a baby."

"Seems there was something like that to the story. Anyway, if it is the same one, the priests didn't know what to do with a lion. They wound up giving it to the Third Army Battalion over to Dire Dawa as a mascot. Put a chain round her neck and chained her up to a tree. Took good enough care of her, food and water. But after a while she started to get on poorly. Makin' a sound all the time like a cough. Stopped eatin'. Tongue hangin' out like you see."

He put his hand through the bars of the cage and stroked the head of the tawny lioness.

"Happened I was called over. They asked if the zoo would take her. One look and I knew what was wrong. Never occurred to them that a cub's goin' to grow. Same chain was still around her neck, slowly chokin' her to death as her neck grew bigger. I took the damn chain off and got her back to pretty fair health. But some of the damage was too far gone. That tongue she'll never get back in her head is only what you can see. There was brain damage, too."

"Do lions have brains?" said Baria.

"Yeah. They do. More than some people."

"I doubt."

"I must tell Harry," said Julie. "He'll be fascinated."

"Well, if Harry, whoever Harry may be, has as much brains as a lion, he won't be fascinated. What he'll be is mad." He sucked on his pipe and turned to Baria. "I've been here seven years. Land and animals are the only wealth this poor country's got. And all you give either is abuse."

"I'm sure your college here will teach us to change all that."

"No." He shook his head sadly. "It won't. I've preached it to a thousand and one Ethiopians. Yourself makes a thousand and two. I've been here seven years and this is my last. I've had maybe half-a-dozen students who went through here that actually went out and did somethin' on the land. The rest are mostly in Addis Ababa, sittin' around in that damn ministry of agriculture. Drinkin' coffee. Shufflin' papers. It's all they seem to want to learn how to do."

"Seven years isn't long," said Baria. "Perhaps you expected too much, too fast. Maybe in seventy years, or seven hundred, enough of our people will have learned."

"Maybe. Maybe I'm too damned American. Or somethin'. Too damned impatient or somethin'. But I disbelieve that if man can't learn in seven years to take care of the only thing he's got, I disbelieve he's goin' to learn in seventy. Take a good look at this poor old girl, with her neck half-broke and her tongue hangin' out. She's about two years old now, but she won't live to be three. I call her Sheba 'cause she could be a queen, but they kept her in chains too long. And what she is is crippled. That's what it means in Amharic, doesn't it? *Sheba*. It means lame, crippled. And that's what she is. She's two years old now, but she won't live to be three. When I'm gone, with no one who cares to look after her, she's goin' die. Like a country you abuse too long, animals and land. She could've been a beautiful lion, but you kept her in chains, abused her too long."

Like Christina, thought Julie. In chains. And her brain damaged. She thought of the zoologist, freeing the lioness. Too late.

"It's only one lion," said Baria.

"It's only one country. You abuse her too long, she's goin' to be crippled. She's goin' to die."

"Harry will be fascinated," said Julie, staring at the lioness. "I've got to tell Harry."

By the time they reached Harar, Julie had forced the lioness out of her mind. She recited to Baria a list of all the things she wanted to buy as they sat sipping coffee in the busy square where Medhane Alem Church challenged the old Arab city. It was after eleven when they finally made their way down the rocky path to the market with the white mosque brooding above it.

"I love this place," said Julie. "I really love it. It's like the Middle East. Like an Arab bazaar."

"There's so much to buy," said Baria.

"I love the Middle East."

"But not Ethiopia." It was a statement, not a question.

"I love Harar. I love you."

"I'm not the Middle East."

"It's such a wonderful market."

"*Magala*," said Baria.

"What?"

"*Magala*. It's the Arabic or maybe just the Somali word for it. They call it *magala*."

"I like it," said Julie. "It's romantic. Like Casbah. Magdalene."

Baria grimaced.

"Not Magdalene. *Magala*."

"Yes. It sounds so romantic."

Julie shopped for an hour. One of the bearers trailing them now carried a spectacular *messob*, bright straw woven into bold geometric patterns with a domed top. It looked like a treasure chest. The other boys were burdened with half-a-dozen smaller baskets, a black-and-white monkey rug, a serval skin which Julie thought was leopard, two leather shields, a spear, a curved sword, a Danakil knife in its leather sheath, and a collection of cheap colored beads. More expensive items, bracelets and crosses and earpicks of silver, a necklace, and a costly stone of questionable value, were stuffed into the pockets of the light jacket Baria was wearing.

Julie next wanted to visit the house in which the French poet Rimbaud had once lived. Baria refused. They were more than an hour's drive from Kulubi, and it was already past the time they were due to meet Harry and Tesfaye by the gates of the church. They had just started up the shop-lined alley leading out of the market when they met Hilary Blankenship heading down.

"Julie. What the hell's an awful girl like you doing in a nice place like this."

"Shopping."

Julie had once found the graying pilot attractive. She had done all she could to make her interest clear. Hilary had not responded.

"I'll say you've been shopping." He glanced at the bearers behind them. "This can't all be for Harry's *bar mitzvah*. You must have a new boy friend."

"This is Baria. Ato Baria Medhane Alem, the painter."

Hilary put out a welcoming paw. Baria, hesitant, accepted it.

"This is Hilary Blankenship," said Hilary. "The pilot."

"Still breaking little girls' hearts?" said Julie.

"They get littler and littler."

"How's Madge?"

"Bitterer and bitterer. How's Harry?"

"You are a bastard, you know that?"

He turned to Baria. "Excuse me. I misintroduced myself. This is Hilary Blankenship, the bastard."

"It's always a pleasure to meet a, uh, pilot. We should be going, Mrs. Comfort. Harry will be waiting."

"Where is the old sod?"

He asked the question of Julie. Baria responded.

"Kulubi."

"Good God. Everyone's a pilgrim."

"We must be going."

"And I must be shopping. Though I don't think I'll need quite so big a safari to bear the burden."

"That's one advantage of chasing such very young girls," said Julie. "The little gifties you buy them can be so small."

"Touché. I must be more on my guard. Well, ta-ta. Remember ol' Hill to poor ol' Harry. Pleasure to meet you, sir."

He went hurtling down the alley beyond them.

"Who was that?" asked Baria.

"I told you. Hilary Blankenship, the bastard. He works for EAL."

"Flying their airplanes?"

"And seducing hostesses and their baby sisters."

"Oh, *that* Hilary Blankenship. They say he's the greatest flying swordsman in Christendom. I've heard much about him."

"Everyone has."

"An old lover?"

"You can see what kind of dirty old man he is. Lover I wouldn't know."

"He looked fairly clean."

"I wouldn't know."

"Hell hath—my, my—no fury."

"Forget it. I wouldn't know. He reminded me of my father, that's all."

"He doesn't look old enough to be your father."

"Thanks. You're getting to be almost as considerate as Harry."

"Does Harry remind you of your father?"

"Good God, no."

"I see."

"You don't. But that's all right. Look. Look at the fabrics in that shop. Let's go in. I need some new fabrics."

Hilary wasn't shopping for gifts for little girls. He wanted to buy something for Madge. He did every trip. It used to help. It didn't anymore, but the habit was there.

He was no sooner in the market area, however, than he forgot about Madge. The girl was incredible. One of the Harari thoroughbreds. Perhaps sixteen, costumed like the dreams of a thousand and one nights. Brocades that sparkled like diamonds. Silks that made the air seem heavy. Beneath the voluminous skirts, tight trousers and golden slippers. A coquettish awareness that made the clothes seem invisible. And yet, he knew, unapproachable. Untouchable.

He remembered stories he'd heard about Harari girls. So beautiful. So jealously guarded. At puberty the clitoris was removed. Not an unusual custom in Ethiopia. But the Harari girls were also sewn up. The stitches would remain till her wedding night. As a guarantee of virginity. Stitches and trousers under long skirts. They don't take chances. With dirty old men like me around, I don't blame them.

"Don't stare so hard, Hilary. Your poor eyeballs may jump out."

He turned.

"Abebetch. Good God."

"Sometimes God is good. Hello."

"The most amazing female animals in the world can be found in this market. What in hell are you doing here?"

A faint sense of embarrassment warmed the back of his neck. He'd just asked that question of the god-awful Julie Comfort. What are you doing here? To repeat it to Abebetch seemed like blasphemy.

"I'm sorry," he said.

"Pourquoi?"

"Show-off. Parce que—my French stinks. Because it's been six months since I've seen you. And that's made me very sorry indeed. How's Assab."

"Dead."

"I warned you. It's always been a dead end of a hellhole."

"Not always," said Abebetch. "But he's dead now."

"Whaaaa—at?"

"At least I think he's dead."

"You mean . . . your Russkie?"

"Yes."

"How?"

"I'll tell you later. Come on. Buy me something lovely. And I'll tell you about it later. What were you shopping for?"

"I was shopping for you," said Hilary.

"Liar."

"Honest. How do you say it? *Ewnetegna?*"

"*Wushata.* That means he possesses lies. Our way of saying liar. But never mind. Buy me something lovely. And then you can take me to Kulubi."

"Kulubi?"

"Yes. I have to go to Kulubi."

"What for?"

"You."

"Me?"

"Yes," said Abebetch. "You're my *silet.*"

"*Wushata.*"

"No. You're here. My *silet* has been given me. And I have to keep my promise to Gabriel. Buy me something lovely."

"Let's find a silversmith. I'll buy you a bracelet. And a ring. And maybe even a necklace."

"No. Not something for me. Something for Gabriel. Will you buy me a cross?"

"I'll even buy you a cross. Assab may be a hellhole, but it hasn't hurt you."

"It has. Come on. I'll tell you about it later."

"Okay," he said to Abebetch. And to himself he said, I'll buy you a cross and nail myself to it. Good-bye little girls. Good-bye, stitched-up Harari beauty.

"I was even going to buy a scissors," he said aloud.

"I don't want scissors," said Abebetch.

"Okay. Come on. You can tell me about it later."

They went and found a silversmith.

It was three o'clock. Tesfaye, rolled up in a blanket, was asleep on the ground. Demsie, well paid, had left them. Harry sat on the low stone wall near the gates of the church. Watching the steps. Waiting. Worrying.

The good feeling that had swept through him completing the walk now ebbed. In its place came the mingling currents of fear and suspicion. They had entered the church, only half-full this day before the eve. The doors of the inner sanctuary where the gold altar stood were open. A gold relief of Virgin and Child presided above the shimmering, intricately worked gold of the altar. Behind it, forbidden to the eyes, was the holy of holies where the Ark of the Covenant—the *tabot*—was kept. Paintings on the wall of Michael, the Virgin and Child, Gabriel. A triptych of Christ crucified, Joseph and Mary with blood dripping from the feet of the dying Jesus onto a gray skull. Velvet drapes and across the tile floor a narrow velvet carpet from the door to the four carpeted steps leading to the altar.

Candles in crystal chandeliers and candles on stands on the bare, unbenched floor. To the right of the altar, a tall wooden pulpit. To the left a kiosk with painted gold trim and a painting of Christ as a child within. In the far left corner, a grandfather clock with a slowly swinging pendulum.

A pretty, costly, unimpressive church. When Harry compared it to the old Tsion Mariam church and the towering stele he had seen at Axum, or to the even more impressive monolithic churches carved out of the stone mountains of Lalibela, he could see no reason why Ethiopians by the tens of thousands should flock here while Axum and Lalibela were visited by foreign tourists, but by Ethiopians were largely ignored. He and Tesfaye had looked into the old church of Kulubi. It was even less impressive, moldering, neglected.

But the miracles associated with Axum and Lalibela were ancient legends. The miracles of Kulubi were still being recorded.

Outside they went to the corner above the old church where gifts to the saint were received in fulfillment of vows. There were three concrete wells with signs above labeling one for donations of cash, the other for jewels and gold, and the third for other precious gifts. A deacon at the gate of a fenced-in corral accepted the miscellaneous: thousands of decorated umbrellas, long beeswax candles, rugs, ostrich eggs, doves, chickens, paintings.

Harry reached into the pocket of the heavy tweed jacket draped over his arm and took out the pamphlet he had written. He handed it to the deacon. Across the top, the letters—KULUBI—were emblazoned in red against a yellow background. Below it, a four-color photo of the church. The deacon recognized the church, smiled, and accepted the pamphlet. He propped it up among several religious paintings on top of a stack of candles.

"There," said Harry. "That's done."

"Amen," said Tesfaye.

Among the other gifts in the corral were crutches of the lame and the white canes of the blind. There was even a wheelchair. Harry pointed to them.

"Look," he said. "The lame were made to walk and the blind to see."

"I think I've seen those same crutches and canes propped up in the same place every year. Propped up," Tesfaye repeated. "Like props."

"Cynic," said Harry.

"Skeptic," said Tesfaye. "There's a difference. I do think the wheelchair is new."

"And what about all these other gifts people bring? You can't say these people don't believe."

"Oh, they believe all right."

A peasant in bloodstained rags with a yoke around his neck pushed his way past them. He spoke to the deacon. The deacon nodded and reached for the yoke. The man pulled back and spoke again. The deacon shook his head.

"*Aichallim.*"

"What's he saying?" asked Harry.

"Wait," said Tesfaye.

Wandimu told the deacon he was offering both the yoke and himself to Gabriel. The deacon said it was impossible. Years ago slaves could be accepted, but no more.

"But my ox is dead," said Wandimu. "My *silet* was to bring my ox to Gabriel but the leopard and the desert have killed him. I must give myself instead."

"Impossible," said the deacon.

"Or Gabriel will punish me for breaking my vow."

"Old man," said Tesfaye. "Gabriel will understand."

"My ox is dead," said Wandimu.

He told them his story. Tesfaye spoke to the deacon.

"Let me talk to him," he said. "I'll try to make him understand."

"He's crazy," said the deacon. "Tell him to go home."

"I'll talk to him," said Tesfaye.

"What's it all about?" asked Harry.

"Later," said Tesfaye. "You can put it on your tape."

He took the old man aside. Harry followed.

With the elaborate logic of the mad, Wandimu detailed his story step by careful step. The long years of semi-idleness, content to play the clown, content to scratch out an existence on a seventh share of his father's land. The sudden productive years when he worked with Gabriel's hands. His vow, his pilgrimage through the desert, the ox, the Danakils, the leopard.

Tesfaye retold it to Harry, letting him spool it out on his tape recorder. A curious crowd gathered around them.

"It's beautiful," said Harry.

"Are such things beautiful?"

"A beautiful story. What faith he must have. But we have to do something for him."

"What can we do? He's mad."

He spoke to the peasant for several minutes, then turned to Harry who again started up his tape.

"He says he's given everything away. He left a few dollars at home with his wife. His ox has been killed. His money is gone. He's lost his mind, and now he wants to give what's left of himself to the priests as a slave. All for the glory of your Kulubi Gabriel."

"I wish I had faith like that," said Harry.

"Do you know what you're saying?" snapped Tesfaye. "You're saying you want the faith of an ignorant, half-crazy peasant."

"It wouldn't be bad," said Harry. "It's better than nothing."

"You have everything," said Tesfaye. "It's this poor fool who has nothing."

"Please don't get mad at me," said Harry. He shook his head. "You don't understand." He closed up the tape recorder. "Can't we at least give him money to get back home?"

"I offered," said Tesfaye. "He would just give it to the priests. To bribe them to take him as a slave. So Gabriel won't be offended because he didn't bring him the ox he promised."

"There must be something somone can do."

Tesfaye thought of Balcha and the political prisoner in his novel who took over the jail and then the mental hospital, curing the mad with therapy and miracle drugs. But he knew it would take more than weaving and woodworking and hallucinogenic miracles to cure this peasant. He thought of the millions like him, only slightly less mad, who were slaves to a system and a land that chained them like animals.

"Leave him," said Tesfaye. "There's nothing we can do."

The peasant spoke to him again and from the folds of his cloak took out the one empty cartridge shell he still carried. He told Tesfaye how he'd been given the shells to pass out to the Danakils he traveled among. This was his last, the only possession he had left except for the yoke around his neck.

Tesfaye looked at the empty shell and remembered the stub of a sharpened pencil stuck in the empty cartridge on his father's bookshelf. A shiver went through him. Mota. He died. He took the remnant of the bullet from the peasant and stared at it. Its message was death. Mota. Who died? He realized he should have stayed with his father, but wondered what he could have done. If the old man was hatching another of his plots, he would not allow Tesfaye, or anyone, to stop him. Except death.

"There must be something we can do," said Harry.

"There isn't," said Tesfaye. "It's too late." He handed the empty cartridge back to the peasant. There must be something I can do. What had his father said? You can make propaganda with a bullet. He asked Harry to take a photograph of the old man.

"Just as he is. In his yoke. I'm going to write his story. Let them hang me for it. We'll make propaganda with a yoke."

Harry took the photograph and looked around the circle of faces that surrounded them, listening to the peasant's story.

"They understand," he said. "Don't they?"

"Yes. They understand."

"Ask them what they think."

Tesfaye did and relayed a series of answers.

"This one agrees with you. He says it's a great faith. He calls your friend in the yoke a holy man. This one says it's Gabriel's power. The lady says the holy spirit has moved into his mind. And this fellow says your friend here is crazy as hell."

Wandimu pushed his way through the crowd and walked away from them.

"Where's he going?" said Harry.

"Nowhere," said Tesfaye. "Let him go. There's nothing we can do."

Harry watched him go.

"Such faith," he said. "Such beautiful, simple faith. That man's not crazy. He has faith."

"I'm beginning to think it isn't that peasant who's crazy," said Tesfaye, "it's you. Let's move. Your wife and Baria may be waiting by the gate by now."

They turned back toward the front of the church. As they went, Harry peered through his thick-lensed glasses at the faces of the pilgrims they passed.

"Maybe for someone like you," he said, "someone educated in the States, you're too much like the rest of us. But look at these people around us. God may be dead in Europe, America. But I have news for the West. God is alive and well in Ethiopia."

Tesfaye leaned toward him, fishing a notebook and ball-point from his pocket.

"Can I quote you on that, sir?"

"You can laugh if you want to," said Harry. "But just look around. That peasant, these people. They believe. Okay. Maybe you and I can't see it. God hides from us most of the time. But he isn't dead. We have to find him."

"Where?"

"Here."

"I don't see the old chap."

"You can laugh if you want to. But I can identify with these people."

"Perhaps," said Tesfaye. "But I doubt that they identify with you."

They went back to the black gate at the head of the flight of broad stone steps leading up to the church compound. There was no sign of Baria and Julie.

"I hope we didn't miss them," said Harry. "I hope they didn't come while we were in the church or down below and think we weren't here yet and go off."

"I doubt," said Tesfaye.

"You doubt everything."

"It's my nature."

"The skeptical journalist," said Harry.

"A mere witness to events."

"You don't even want to have faith. That's your problem."

They waited an hour, watching the slow but steady gathering of the pilgrims, before Tesfaye opted for sleep, wrapped himself in the blanket, and stretched out on the ground.

Harry sat on the low stone wall. Not thoughts but images filtered through his fatigue. Images of his son being born; of their long walk through the night. The river of flashlights behind them. Images of Kulubi on the eve of Gabriel's feast the year before. The fantastic scene at dawn when shapes of waking pilgrims emerged through the gray light of mingled smoke and mist like ghosts framed by the spidery branches of overhanging trees. An image of himself at work on his book, *Kulubi: Microcosm of Ethiopia*, acclaimed by scholars and critics.

Fatigue and the images he saw entranced him. Kulubi in all its aspects swirled before him, a phantasmagoria of memory and dreams. He nodded, almost asleep, when a slowly growing spot of warmth on the back of his neck made him turn. He saw them. Holding hands. He stood. They were coming up the path flanked by begging lepers. He removed his glasses and found a handkerchief and wiped them. He put the glasses back on. They were holding hands as they walked the path up to the church.

"My God," he mumbled. What are you doing? My God, what have you done? He crossed himself. He wasn't aware that he'd done it. And where is our son?

Julie glanced up. She stumbled. Baria caught her by the elbow. She hadn't fallen, but she made the motions of brushing herself off. She said something to Baria. He didn't look up. A beggar touched him on the knee with a handless stump. Baria reached into his pocket. He held out some coins. The beggar swept the coins up with his stump. They didn't fall.

Julie and Baria started up the path. They watched their feet as they walked.

Harry locked the index finger of his right hand into his left fist. He watched them coming up the path. He freed the locked finger and turned.

Ten feet away a policeman with a rifle slung over his shoulder was staring at him.

Negash put down the phone. The palace room was crowded. He looked around. He knew everyone in the room, but that instant he could recognize none. The call had been from Getachew Tessema. In Mota.

He turned and stared at the open double doors that led to the room where the Emperor was receiving local officials. He would have to tell him. But how? How could it have happened? It wasn't supposed to have happened like this. He looked down at the phone. It was black. Silent as death.

How can I tell him?

He turned and walked toward the open double doors.

Harry, sleepless, was stretched out on one of the sleeping bags in their tent at Dire Dawa. The girl Baria and Julie had hired to watch the baby now sat outside the wide-open flaps of the tent. He could hear the click of her knitting needles.

Tesfaye was asleep on one of the cots. Julie had taken the baby to sit by the side of the pool. Baria had gone into town to see friends. He wasn't holding my hand, Julie had said. He was just helping me walk. My legs were so tired. All that walking we'd done. First the zoo. Then the market. Shopping is so tiring. There was something I wanted to tell you. Something we saw. I forget. Shopping is so tiring. Wait till you see what I bought. When you're not there to support me I need someone to lean on. Harry, don't be silly. Jonathan's all right. Wait till you see what I bought you. In whispers. Tense whispers by the gates of the church while Baria woke Tesfaye from his blanket on the ground. Tense whispers. Tense quiet all the ride back as Baria drove them back down to Dire Dawa. The tent on the camping grounds of the hotel. And the effort to sleep.

His voice echoed hers. "Don't be silly." Both hands clutched the silver, twelve-pointed Lalibela cross she'd given him. It was heavy on his chest and he wondered what it cost. Don't be silly. He'd always wanted a Lalibela cross. Silly . . .

His eyes flickered. He was dimly aware of voices outside the tent. All the flaps of the tent were open. A light breeze danced through but still the heat stifled under the sun-baked canvas. The heat called him to sleep. Don't be silly. His eyes shut.

"Excuse me."

Don't be silly. Sleep. Don't dream. He felt the weight of the cross on his chest.

"I'm terribly sorry. Excuse me."

The cool breeze stirred.

"I really am sorry to disturb . . ."

His eyes opened. Don't be . . . The voice rode on the breeze. Still clutching the cross in one hand, he propped himself up on an elbow.

"Please excuse me. It is Mr. Comfort, isn't it?"

Harry recognized the handsome, graying head peering through the open double flaps of the tent.

"Yes, why, yes. Why, Ato Negash. I mean Your Excellency." He sat up. "Ato Negash."

"We've met before, haven't we?"

"Yes. Why, yes, we have. I was just asleep. Excuse me. Sleeping a little."

"I'm sorry. I'm terribly sorry to disturb you." Still stooping, he glanced at the cot. "Ato Tesfaye . . ."

"Yes. Yes," said Harry. "I'm afraid he's . . . We walked to Kulubi last night. All the way. I'm afraid he must be asleep."

"I am sorry. May I come in?"

"Oh. Yes. Yes, of course. Please come in."

He struggled to his feet, holding the cross before him. Negash stepped into the tent. His eyes fell on the cross.

"Oh. This. Ha ha. This. It's a cross. Ah, I'm not a priest or anything. Ha . . . I mean it's a gift. It's a Lalibela cross, you see."

"Yes," said Negash. "Lalibela."

"My wife just bought it for me. She's here now. She's at the pool."

Negash nodded. He looked back at the cot.

"He's . . . I guess poor Tesfaye is asleep."

"Would you mind waking him for me, Mister . . ."

"Comfort," said Harry. "Harry Comfort."

"Yes. Comfort. Of course. We have met before. Please. I really must speak to Tesfaye. It's urgent. The Emperor in fact . . . I've just come from His Majesty."

"Has . . . has something happened?"

Negash's eyes were on the cot. "Do you mind if I wake him. It concerns his father."

"His father? Not something's happened. . . . We were . . . were there just yesterday."

"I'd heard." He put a hand on Tesfaye's shoulder. "I really must speak to Tesfaye. His Majesty . . . the Emperor wants to see him."

One of the double doors opened. Tesfaye came into the room where Negash was waiting. Tears streamed down his face. He didn't try to stop them. The door closed behind him.

"I'm sorry, Tesfaye."

"His Majesty also is sorry." There was no sound of crying in his voice, but tears continued to stream down his face.

"He and your father . . ."

"Always were close. He told me so. Even from boyhood."

He didn't look at Negash. He stared straight ahead. There was no one else in the room.

"They won't even allow me to go to his funeral."

"Tesfaye, there can't be a public funeral in a case like this."

"Is his son public?"

"There couldn't be a funeral. There might be . . ."

Tesfaye glanced at him. Then away. He spoke to the hollow room.

"Trouble? Demonstrations. Weeping. Gnashing of . . . Perhaps a riot. Someone might get hurt."

"You know what he planned."

"To kill the mosquito."

"What?"

"He told us yesterday. He wanted to kill a mosquito."

"He had bazookas. Land mines. The road was mined. He had mortars. Machine guns."

"He didn't want to miss," said Tesfaye. "He thought he could eliminate malaria."

"Tesfaye . . ."

"You know the proverb."

"Tesfaye."

"Can I go?"

"Where?"

"To pray."

"The Emperor told me to make his car available for you."

"Yes," he said. "A touching gesture. With his own chauffeur. The driver he made a general."

"Tesfaye, don't be bitter."

"Sweet . . ." He gulped. "Should I be sweet, Your Excellency?"

"I'm sorry."

"Who but a general could be fit to drive a king. Excuse me. A king of kings. And so you make the driver—a general. And murder my father."

"He shot himself, Tesfaye."

"Did he? While you poured tear gas and bullets into his mud house and told him to come out with his life in the air."

"Your brother was sent to talk to him."

"My brother?"

"Getachew."

"Hardly my brother. One of my father's children in another century. I don't know Getachew."

"He was sent this morning to tell your father his plot had been discovered. To urge your father to give himself up. He even fired a shot at your brother."

"He missed?"

"He missed. But that started the firing. Your father had men stationed in the fields. We never thought he'd attack. Just your brother and a small detachment only went to his farm to bring him here."

"He killed the small detachment, I'm told."

"And many more," said Negash. "Before . . ."

"Before he was killed."

"He shot himself. Rather than . . ."

"Did he? I hope so. I hope he kept that from you. And Getachew escaped?"

"Yes. Your brother was lucky."

"Yes," said Tesfaye. "He was lucky. Luckier than our father."

"It was a battle, Tesfaye. A war. He had a score of men, weapons . . ."

"All trained on the road. Just to kill the mosquito."

"Mosquito? You keep coming back to that."

Tesfaye nodded. "That's what I told my father. He kept coming back to it. You know the proverb. I thought he was talking in riddles."

He saw his father. It was in the field where with his staff and his great strength he had pushed himself up from the skin of the kudu where he'd lain. Only now his father wasn't rising to his feet. With his failing strength, slowly, so slowly, he sank back to the skin of the kudu where he lay. Over and over again, the scene ran in reverse. Slowly, the reel running backward. He'd witnessed this falling, failing dream before. How? He was silent and tears still streaked his face.

"Who killed the kudu?" he said aloud. "Can you tell me, my father, who killed the kudu?"

Negash touched his arm. Tesfaye stared straight ahead. He saw the kudu, falling, its throat slit, falling to the side of the road.

"Perhaps you, Your Excellency, can tell me who killed . . ."

"Come with me, please, Tesfaye. This has upset you."

"Not upset, Your Excellency. It's just that somehow my father has died."

"I understand. I'm sorry."

"And his son can not bury him."

"They've already buried him, Tesfaye."

"Ask the general to drive me there. Let me put my hand in the wounds. Let me count the bullet holes."

"No one can go."

"No. I'll walk. Let the general drive himself."

"Come, Tesfaye. Come with me."

"Where?"

"To my room. We can talk."

"Take me to his room. And my father and I . . ."

"Come with me. You're upset. We can talk."

"You can talk. I can hear. Here."

"At least sit down."

Tesfaye nodded. His legs were trembling. Negash took his hand and led him to a sofa. Tesfaye pulled away his hand and sat stiffly in a straight-backed chair.

Negash couldn't bear to look any longer at his face. He moved behind the chair. He wanted to put his hands on Tesfaye's shoulders. He hesitated. He put his hands on the back of the chair.

"Try to understand, Tesfaye. Not just what happened. Not just . . . His Majesty."

"His Majesty," said Tesfaye. "Not just."

"Try to understand. Not His Majesty. Your father. Try to understand your father."

For the first time, Tesfaye sobbed aloud. Negash took his shoulders. The sobbing stopped. The tears went on.

"Try . . . For years, try to understand, for years, decades, your father fought the Emperor. Today, this morning, it happened early this morning."

"They came too soon," said Tesfaye.

He remembered the lunch his father had prepared. The lunch they had partaken of. His father had even prepared *tella* and *tej*. His father didn't drink. The Emperor didn't drink. But the followers. The ministers. The aides. The soldiers. They would want their *tej*. And their blood.

"What happened today," said Negash, "was history. History that had been happening for years. History that's been being written since long ago. What happened today . . ."

"Written long ago . . ."

people talking about the woman killed that morning when her car backed over the edge of the cliff. They said she had vowed to walk to Kulubi but had broken her vow because of vanity over her new car. When a vow was broken, people were saying, Gabriel takes his revenge.

But there was nothing more he could do. He knew he would have to go back. And he would. He would have to beg. He had no money for the bus, nor strength to walk. He would beg. He would have to pray to Gabriel for forgiveness. He would pray. When he returned to his land, he would have to begin all over again. With no ox to help him. With no son to work by his side. Only his wife and daughters. And someday, like his ox, in the desert his life had been, he would die. Till then, his neck would always be bent in another man's yoke.

That poor old man, thought Harry. He must have given his yoke to the church. To fulfill some silly vow. Like mine. But he still walks like his neck was in it, going around the church like he was plowing his field. He felt as alone, as desolate as the half-mad peasant must be.

During the night the infant he'd carried had become a stone, dead weight in his arms. But now he missed it. He thought again of the peasant who had surrendered his yoke. He looked for him but the man had vanished in the crowd. The yoke had been only a crude working of sapling sticks bent to form a bow joined together by leather thongs to a heavy, round base. As poor as the man had been, he could no doubt replace the yoke without trouble.

But, a moment before, when Harry had seen the peasant walking without the yoke, the man had a bewildered look. Like a man cut loose from his home, his family, his faith. Slightly mad, thought Harry. But he must have needed that yoke.

Negussie found it hard to believe he was going to be a father. Yet, when Zewditu told him it could be no one else, he'd believed her at once.

"I've been afraid to tell you," she said. "I decided to have an abortion rather than tell you."

"No," he said. "There'll be no abortion."

He had tried to keep their affair casual. Another pilot; another hostess. But he had sensed from the first it wasn't going to be that way. When they'd met early that morning in the lobby of the Ras and decided to go up to Kulubi together, he had the feeling something he'd never planned was about to unfold. The car they'd hired brought them to the village just before the road was completely closed.

They had walked from the village to the church, stumbling in the ruts of the rough track. Where the grade became steep, she took his arm, and the secret she had meant to keep poured from her.

Now, as they walked among the pilgrims circling the church, Negussie, with each turning, feeling the weight of her arm on his, slowly made up his mind.

Zewditu looked up at the mosaic of the saint over the door.

"Shall I ask Gabriel to give me a miscarriage?"

He shook his head. "Gabriel doesn't listen to evil."

"Do you think it would be evil?"

"Yes."

"What should I do then?"

"Maybe you could ask Gabriel to find you a husband?"

"Where?"

"He won't have to look far."

"Negussie, don't play with me. You don't want marriage."

"I hadn't been planning on it. But make your *silet*. It's hard enough to resist you. I don't think I could resist you and Gabriel."

"Do you mean that?"

"Make your *silet*. And I'll make mine."

"I don't want to cry."

He reached out and brushed a tear from her cheek.

"I hope you don't mind if I ask Gabriel that our first child be a son."

"Oh, Negussie. I thought I was going to grow up to be a bitch. A real first class EAL hostess bitch. Maybe there's hope for me."

"There's hope," said Negussie.

Shaleka saw Tesfaye standing by the gates. The scheme he'd been searching for was suddenly there. A gift of the *azmari* who'd taken his wife. The idea that Frehiwot could be linked with Dejazmatch Tessema's plot was absurd. But the police major had swallowed it quickly enough.

How much easier it would be for them to believe Tesfaye was

in it. His father's son. He had admitted that he'd been there the day before the planned assassination. He must have known. He could have been involved. Tesfaye, the thorn in his side, could be plucked.

He turned and his eye caught the huge mosaic of Gabriel over the church. Golden wings outspread. The sword raised over the halo. Let me eliminate these people, degenerate *azmaris*, defiant editors. Let me destroy them, he vowed, and I will return next year, walking from Dire Dawa, bearing you a golden sword. Let me be rid of them, and I will bring you a sword of gold. Gabriel, his head cocked like a bird, looked down. And Shaleka begged his vengeance.

"Tesfaye. What happened to you?" Tesfaye turned. Balcha, in his sad, handcuffed attitude, stood behind him. "I've been looking for you the whole morning."

"I got myself lost," said Tesfaye. "Have you seen the others?"

"No. I left them at the Melotti place after you disappeared. After that, I went back to my tent. I couldn't leave my wife for long."

"And Frehiwot?"

"No word. I thought it best not to inquire too soon. That's why I wanted to find you. I thought if we went together. You know, our leading journalist asking after a famous *azmari*. They might be afraid of trouble."

"Let's wait," said Tesfaye. "Negash Mengistu will be coming with the Emperor. Let me enter a word in his ear about it. He owes me some favors."

"Good. You might mention my book to him, too."

"Friend Balcha, that would only keep Frehiwot in jail longer. One favor at a time. It's the best we can do."

"Very well. Singers are more important than books. It's a well-known economic fact." Tesfaye did not respond. "By the way," said Balcha, "I saw your friend. The nervous American."

"Where?"

"On the other side." Balcha nodded across the divide marked by parallel lines of facing bodyguard troops. "Maybe ten minutes ago. He looked tired. Not so much nervous."

"He's probably been up the whole night," said Tesfaye. "Making his research."

"What kind of research?"

"For a book he wants to write. He's another foolish fellow who doesn't know singing is more important than books."

Eleni and Zenebetch, Hagos and Makonnen stood in the shade of a tree by the far wall overlooking the cemetery. They still had not found their friend Claude, but now Baria had joined them.

"My American friends have disappeared with the keys to my car," he told them. "And I suspect the car as well."

"That's what you get for trying to be nice to Americans," said Hagos. But he was quick to suggest that Baria stay with them and ride back to Dire Dawa in their Land Rover. Baria accepted. They commented cynically on the scene around them, which they watched with inward fascination.

"Are you inspired by all this," Hagos asked Baria, "to a painting or a poem?"

"It's too busy for a painting," said Baria. "Perhaps a poem."

"An ode to Gabriel?"

"No," said Baria. "An epic on Kulubi. To be entitled 'The Onion.' "

" 'The onion'?" said Eleni. "Why onion?"

"That's what Kulubi means," said Baria. "In Galligna. Kulubi is our word for onion. That's what my poem will be about. A modest proposal for putting a stop to all this fashionable nonsense of everyone running off to Kulubi every year."

Each time he said the word, he cracked the initial explosive *K* with particular vehemence.

"*K*ulubi, people forget, is in Galla country. Kotu Galla country occupied by you Amhara imperialists." He bowed mockingly to Eleni and Zenebetch. "Like Eritrea," he added with a nod to Hagos. "So what we have is a great Amhara feast at a place with a Galla name that you Amharas don't know the meaning of. And because His Holy Majesty comes each year, everyone else figures he must come, too. It isn't even a national holiday, but in Addis Ababa nearly everything comes to a halt because everyone comes to Kulubi. The government stops functioning, farmers leave their fields, even the brothels are empty because so many fine ladies come here."

"Then we should have more Kulubis," said Hagos. "If it stops this government and other forms of prostitution from functioning."

"No, no. Don't be cynical," said Baria. "Government and prostitution must go on. Excuse me, ladies. Like the stars. But a way has to be found to stop all this . . ." He gestured grandly over the crowd-filled fields. "All this excessiveness."

"Truly spoken," said Makonnen, who had been listening intently, like someone taking mental notes. "And what is your solution, sir?"

"We Amharaize it. Like you do with other occupied Galla places. You've changed the name of our Bishoftu to Debre Zeit. Wolliso is renamed Ghion. Adama was turned into Nazaret. Ambo to Hagere Hiwot. Everything to make us forget they were Galla. So what we do with Kulubi, we simply translate our Galligna onion into Amharic. *Shinkwurt*. Then you Amharas will know it for what it is. Just a place where Gallas grow onions. No one will want to go to an onion field. Nothing fashionable in that, you see. Who will want to boast that he has a vow to go to the onions this year?"

"It won't work," said Makonnen. "Kulubi Gabriel is already too engrained in our culture. Making it *Shinkwurt* Gabriel will just make onions more fashionable."

"My sympathies are with Baria," said Hagos. "But I'm afraid Makonnen is right. A people that can believe their Solomon and Sheba nonsense can swallow onions as well."

Eleni joined them in a round of punning, often rhyming jokes, wasting wit to kill time while they waited for their Emperor to arrive.

Baria participated sadly. He knew he had run away again, as so often in the past. He boasted of being a Galla, but he knew, like so many of his people, he had become an Amhara. Too clever by far, too shallow by half. He glanced at Zenebetch. He thought her beautiful, but he fled the attraction he felt by clowning. He had fled his friendship with Harry by accepting the easy availability of his wife. He had fled the involvement he had allowed with Julie by hiding.

"And now," he said, smiling, "our Emperor is walking through the onion fields. But he won't acknowledge the onions. Only the crowds."

"There are no more onions," said Makonnen. "The crowds have squashed them into sauce."

"An Amhara sauce," said Hagos.

We never tire of our jokes, thought Baria. He remembered

what Dejazmatch Tessema had said to them. The day before he died. What can you do in a sad country, but tell funny stories?

The valley filled with the trilling *illill-ing* cries of thousands of women. The ululating wave began on the edges of the village, quickly swelled to the church, and billowed up the hillsides over which new arrivals still hurried to Kulubi Gabriel.

Harry turned, standing on tiptoe, trying to see over the heads of the soldiers ranged from the gates to the doors of the church. Baria, twenty meters away, climbed up on the low stone wall and looked toward the village. Julie stirred sleepily in the station wagon. The baby woke up.

"He must be coming," Tesfaye said to Balcha.

Shaleka looked at his watch and asked one of the passing vendors how many copies he still had to sell. Tiruwork stood up from her bench in the corridor of the jail and made her resolve.

Zewditu squeezed Negussie's arm.

Wandimu cringed closer to the walls of the church.

"The last act of the circus," said Hagos. Zenebetch glanced at Makonnen. Eleni thought of Tesfaye.

The Abuna, waiting in the doorway of the church, deepened his scowl and glared over the heads of the crowd toward the gaping black gates.

Klaxon wailing, Major Abebe raced down the road in his jeep. Police began clearing the church, driving reluctant pilgrims out the side doors.

The crowd was electric. The signal begun in the village carried on taut wires. Women who had no idea where the Emperor was yodeled the traditional *illill* in praise of his arrival, knowing the cries raised by others could mean nothing else.

Harry witnessed the casual harshness with which police drove people from the church. He stood close to the line of bodyguard soldiers who cradled automatic weapons in their arms. He remembered the armed police on the trail they had followed through the bush. The wrecked Land Rover with its cargo of dead. The animal they had found with its throat slit in the game park. The violence that had broken over Mota the day after they'd been there. The beating of the singer last night. It had been brutal, terrible. And yet, that bitter young radical with his slogans had been right. How did it compare to the burning of hundreds in a mosque? Or riots he had read of in New York. Los Angeles. Chicago, Detroit. We say they're savage. He remembered Dallas. Houston, Birmingham. He knew he wasn't a savage. He knew how swiftly violence had come, and, in the tense excitement around him, he sensed how swiftly it could come again. It would take but one quick spark to turn this waiting, expectant mass into a force no army could hold, no guns could stop. For the first time in his life he welcomed all the paraphernalia of control. He only hoped it would be enough. Emperor and church. Soldiers and police. People of punishment. Here to protect us, Tesfaye had said. From ourselves. Each other. Who knows? He hated his fear. And he feared the hatred he felt. He had never been savage. He could never be part of what he felt could happen here.

Then, for a quick, terrible moment, he felt he wasn't savage only because he was afraid. Of other people's savagery. Of what he might be himself. If he wasn't afraid.

The soldiers scanned the crowd nervously. The waiting went on. The ululations rose and fell. Distant intensities marked the slow passage of the Emperor along the track from the village. Twenty minutes had passed since the first cries shrilled from the village before people by the gates could see him, waving as he came up the thronged, curved path. The noise pierced through Harry like a high, deafening keen, not joyful but fierce in its exultation.

Harry could see him now, and he knew why they cheered. He looked down at the slight, smiling figure ascending the steps in topi and military cape. He remembered that this was the man Dejazmatch Tessema had wanted to kill. And this was the man who had caused the death of that tough old warrior. Another battle won over death. And the people, even though the man he'd vanquished had been respected among them, hailed the victor. Not just because he had won, thought Harry, but because of the boldness he showed as he marched before them.

People were dancing, leaping, shouting, and above it all rose that sound like no other, the piercing *illills* of the women, wave after wave rising and falling and endlessly rising, a wail that could cut through mountains of stone.

Let the hills know it and the valleys and the towns and the skies. The Emperor has come to Kulubi.

Long live Haile Selassie. Someone standing near him had shouted it first. Others took it up. Long live Haile Selassie. Die, my father, thought Tesfaye, and long live Haile Selassie. The Dejazmatch is dead. Long live his killer, my king. The mosquito my father took a swat at still buzzes. Long live Haile Selassie. How easy to mock those words. If he lives long, others might say, Ethiopia dies soon. Tesfaye knew better. I am not Hamlet, he told himself. We need this man. Oh look how we need him. Our sadness is this. That we need him so much. Without him, we're nothing.

"Long live," he said softly, "Haile Selassie."

Harry saw the handsome graying Ethiopian who was walking with the Emperor fall deliberately behind and speak to the tall bodyguard major with the swagger stick. It was Negash. The major nodded, stepped briskly toward the opposite line of soldiers, and pointed commandingly with his stick.

Two of the stony-faced troops moved aside and Harry saw Tesfaye step between them. Harry called out, but there was no chance of Tesfaye's hearing him. The wall of noise around them was as solid as the lines formed by the backs of the soldiers. He watched the pantomime of the elegant major pointing to Negash; Tesfaye nodding, moving hesitantly forward. Negash smiled, took Tesfaye by the arm, gestured toward the Emperor who had paused at the doors of the church.

He saw the Emperor greet the Abuna and turn again to the crowd. A new wave of ululations rose on cue. Others in the entourage moved slowly by. Harry recognized the Crown Prince, Princess Tenangne, the Prime Minister, Ras Imru.

The Abuna and the Emperor entered the church. The others followed, including Tesfaye and Negash, who still held him firmly by the elbow. Harry called out again in vain. For the moment he had forgotten his quest for Baria. He wanted only to join Tesfaye in the church, to witness the services. He again felt the book he wanted to write slipping away from him as he watched Tesfaye's back moving out of the sunlight into the cool, dark interior of the church.

Tesfaye blinked, momentarily sightless after the harsh glare of the sun. Clouds of incense softened the light that filtered through the abstract panels of the stained glass windows and fell faintly from the gold chandeliers. The hand at his elbow urged him forward.

Negash had already quickly briefed him on his new assignment. He was to write a story on the Emperor's walk to Kulubi, the cheering crowds, the strong sun, the steep grade of the road.

"Did he have a *silet?*" Tesfaye asked.

"Nothing overdone," cautioned Negash. "Just a straightforward story." Now, as they moved slowly forward in the church, he added, "Stay close to me. His Majesty may want to speak to you himself."

"Again," said Tesfaye.

"Leave that," said Negash.

They stood together through the ceremony. Tesfaye was torn by his anger, his loss, and the resolve he had been forcing himself to. He was determined to go on being what he had been, what he wanted to be, a newspaperman doing all that he could for both his profession and his country. He knew that meant accepting the rules men like Negash worked within, doing his best to bend them, unwilling to break them. He looked around the church. The Emperor, his ministers, military officials, courtiers, the royal family, the sycophants and hangers-on. Their rules. Their deceptions and failures. Corruption and incompetence. Even their murders and their denials of the truth.

He knew there were others: men like his father; the radical students; intellectuals among the military and militant intellectuals who would not accept the way he had chosen. Men who would want to destroy—what? The mosquito? But who themselves had nothing to replace the malaria.

The Emperor and members of the royal family moved behind silver screens which had been set up on either side of the altar. They would worship—or sleep—in private. Tesfaye tried to envision the scene. The old man, an unblinking stone effigy, sitting in a tight circle of relatives; men with prayer sticks in hand to the left; women to the right; weak attendants to power who fidgeted, coughed, whispered. He could not see them now, but he had seen them all on other public occasions. The Crown Prince, he was sure, would soon fall asleep. Tesfaye tried to picture the old man among them, wondering again if that spare, strong will had ordered his father's death. But the Emperor was screened by silver. Tesfaye could only guess, and his journalist's blindness refused to let him imagine what he could not see.

He could wonder if his father had willed that death himself, a final act of rebellion against the king who might have forgiven him, and, by forgiving, have humbled him again. He knew what he wanted to believe. He wanted to believe that the official truth, this time at least, was the real truth. It made better men of them both if only his father had voted for death. He knew what he wanted to believe, and he knew he would always be condemned to wonder.

He lost the ritual services of Gabriel's feast in a haze of incense and chanting and doubt till the commanding voice of the Abuna broke through. He had mounted the pulpit for the sermon. Raven eyes set above a hawk nose; black beard streaked with gray. He could be a king himself, thought Tesfaye. The words of the sermon, quoting the synaxarium text for the day, cut through his thoughts:

> . . . *and let us put away hatred, and make peace among ourselves, and agree with our neighbor, and love each other, and let us crucify our minds with God the merciful* . . .

Yes, prayed Tesfaye. Let us crucify . . . and put away hatred. If we can.

> . . . *and with all our hearts, let us make supplication to this glorious angel, Gabriel, and his companion, Michael, who are glorious and exalted in their offices, to pray to God on our behalf that he may deliver us and protect us from the nets of Satan, for without the help of God and the intercession of His chosen ones we can in no use be saved* . . .

Tesfaye glanced from the stern Abuna to Negash, standing by his side. The intercession of his chosen ones, thought Tesfaye. Let us crucify our minds. There was Shaleka to be dealt with. Frehiwot in jail. Balcha's book, perhaps, to be saved. He vowed, not to Gabriel but to himself, to do all that he could.

Let us crucify our minds, he prayed.

Let us crucify, he vowed.

With God the merciful. And put away hatred.

If we can.

The Crown Prince had a pain at his chest. He put a hand over his heart. The fluttering was still there. He had managed to control his breathing, but his sweat-soaked shirt clung damply to his flesh. He looked down at his father, the Almighty Tyrant. Twelve kilometers of walking was well enough for him. He has a heart of cold steel. But why torture the rest of us? Twelve kilometers. It had taken two hours. At this altitude. Under this sun. Old tyrant.

He had seen Tesfaye standing with Negash. Impossible to talk to him now. But he decided he would send Tesfaye a note of condolence on the death of his father. Ask him to call at his palace in Addis Ababa. There they could talk. He had once helped Tesfaye's father escape the steel clutches of the monument that sat there now, immortal as stone. Tesfaye had been raised in his house. He needed allies, now. Tesfaye could help, if he would. But Tesfaye stood now with Negash. He put a hand to his fluttering heart. When would this end? He needed so much. The church, the press, the military, the young, the peasants. There was so much to be done. It was time to be moving.

One of the priests, surrounded by chanting, censer-swaying *dabtaras*, emerged from the holy of holies. On his turbaned head he bore the *tabot*, the Ark of the Covenant, a flat, inscribed stone veiled in velvet brocade fringed with golden tassels that hung to his shoulders like an ornate, miniature tent. The Emperor followed the *tabot*. The others followed the Emperor.

As they were leaving the church, Tesfaye encountered his elder half brother Getachew. He stopped, greeting him formally.

"*Tenastelign getie*."

"How are you, Tesfaye?"

"Well, and how are you, Your Excellency?"

"Well, thanks to God."

"I hear you've been to our father."

"Yes," said Getachew. "Yesterday."

"Was he well?" said Tesfaye.

"You mean . . ." Getachew registered real surprise. "You mean they haven't told you?"

"Oh, yes. I've been told of his untimely death."

"Oh. Then you know. He told me . . . the old man told me you had been to see him, too."

"Not yesterday," said Tesfaye. "The day before. What else did he tell you?"

"That he wouldn't . . . come out."

"And then?"

"He started shooting at us."

"He started shooting at you. But he's dead. And you live."

"He took his own life, Tesfaye. I was just outside. All shooting had stopped. I called to him again, begging him to surrender. There was one shot. I'm sure from inside. The big pistol he had."

Tesfaye nodded. "I'm glad," he said.

"Glad?"

"Not that he was killed. But that he wasn't killed by them."

"I understand," said Getachew. "I must follow the *tabot.*" He moved off.

Tesfaye rejoined Negash and followed the procession which was to circle the church three times.

"Here we go again," said Negash. "Another hike."

"Did you walk the whole twelve kilometers?"

"All."

"You must be tired."

"Very." He smiled, sadly. "I don't have time to keep fit."

"Nor I," said Tesfaye. He didn't want to embarrass Negash by telling him he'd walked from Dire Dawa.

"Tesfaye."

"Yes."

"This Shaleka of yours. He fell in beside me just before we reached the church. He said he had something urgent to tell. About your being involved in your father's plot."

"Really?"

He had been wondering what to do about Shaleka. Now he knew.

"He informed me you'd been there the day before."

"You knew that."

They had fallen well behind the Emperor. Both walked with heads bowed and hands clasped behind their backs. They spoke softly.

"I knew the fellow was lying. But why would he invent such a story?"

"Shaleka doesn't need a motive for evil. Or a reason to do harm. Scheming is as natural to him as breathing."

"Like others we know," said Negash.

"Like too many others we know. Intrigue is one of our national sports. There are some who cook schemes and invent stories even against their own interests. Just for love of the game. But Shaleka's fantastic. In a class by himself. No matter what troubles or ventures he has of his own, he'll always find time for cutting at others."

"Does he have troubles of his own?" asked Negash.

"Oh, yes. His wife, for one."

"What's she done?"

"You know of this singer, Frehiwot?"

"I do. In fact, your friend Shaleka also told me he was involved in the plot. With you."

"Fantastic Shaleka. I can tell you why he tossed Frehiwot in. But I don't understand why he picked me. I've always tried to get along with Shaleka."

"I can guess why he attacks you. He's always been jealous of your ability on the job. The way people regard you. Compared to the way they regard him. But what of this Frehiwot?"

"Tiruwork, the wife, had a rendezvous with him here. She didn't know Shaleka was coming."

"I see."

"Not quite. There's more. Frehiwot was singing last night by his tent. She was there, of course, Shaleka's wife. I came by with some friends. A crowd gathered. He sang some verses about my father. About what had happened. There were police. Then some chaps from security. You know how they are. Like characters out of some movie. He began improvising couplets about them."

"It's never wise to play with the police."

"I know," said Tesfaye. "I'm sure by now Frehiwot knows it, too. They beat him. Dragged him off. Shaleka's wife was hysterical. She ran off after them. No one could stop her."

"Does Shaleka know?"

"By now he must. It explains why he's trying to accuse Frehiwot. The police must have told him. I saw him before with one police major who seems to be involved with him in peddling these pamphlets."

"Pamphlets?"

"The Kulubi pamphlet this American chap wrote for us. Shaleka took all the Amharic copies the ministry had published. He's selling them here."

"For himself?"

"For himself."

"How can he do such a thing?"

"In our ministry anything's possible."

"Are you sure of this?"

"Very sure," said Tesfaye. "It's a journalist's habit to keep well informed. Even if he can't write everything he knows."

"I wish you would keep me better informed."

"It's I who depend on you to be well informed."

"I'll have this Shaleka brought to me as soon as we're back in Addis. I've always thought it foolish to have a trained journalist like you working under a semi-illiterate monkey like him."

"He doesn't do much to help the work."

"I'm sure. This should be enough to have him removed. And I'm sure His Majesty will approve my recommendation to put you in his place."

Tesfaye stopped.

"Me?"

"Let's walk," said Negash.

Tesfaye fell back into step beside him.

"Don't you believe the man we have in charge of our newspapers should be a journalist?"

"Please," said Tesfaye. "Don't turn me into a bureaucrat. I would be no more a journalist."

"You would. But instead of just one paper you would control all the papers."

"I don't want to control. I want to contribute."

"You could always contribute."

"I'm good where I am now," said Tesfaye. "I don't want to become Shaleka."

"You? I don't think you could ever become a Shaleka."

"I've seen it happen too often," said Tesfaye. "Men who become their jobs. The job calls for an intriguer, a spy, even a thug. And the decent, progressive fellow becomes intriguer, spy, thug, censor, reactionary. All that the job requires, he becomes."

Negash unclasped his hands from behind his back and looked at them. "It's happened to me," he said.

"I didn't mean that."

"No, but it's true. It happens. I told you last night history is harsh. It works its own ways. Even His Majesty. He was the man of change. But the country needed holding together even more than it needed change. He became what the times demanded. The man to conserve as much as was necessary and change as much as he could. And there are those who call him conservative. Students, radicals who call him much worse."

Tesfaye hadn't expected this frankness from Negash. But he didn't want it to trap him.

"Don't put me where I'll be useless," he said.

"I won't. I need you too much for that."

The answer left Tesfaye worried. He might become useless as a journalist, but he could still be useful to Negash if he were to become another Shaleka, a Shaleka that Negash could depend on as his own.

"In any event," said Negash, "this Shaleka must go."

"To that I'll agree," said Tesfaye.

He felt that for the moment he'd done what he could to protect himself. He decided to see what he could accomplish for others.

"And Excellency," he said, "this chap Frehiwot. He's as innocent of any plot as I am. He's just an *azmari* who drinks more than perhaps he should. With a fondness for women."

"Human failings," said Negash. "I'll contact the security people. He'll be free in a few days."

"If they haven't beaten him to death by then."

"I know what you mean. I'll have him transferred today to Addis Ababa. Under my personal protection. For his release I'll have to discuss with security, but you can be sure he won't be touched."

"Thank you."

They had completed two circles around the church. He had only a few more minutes. He knew asking another favor might push his luck too far. But he had vowed.

"Friend Negash."

"Yes."

"You asked me to keep you better informed."

Negash nodded.

"There's one other thing you should know. This book that's being held up. The book by Balcha Amara."

"Yes. I know the case. I intend to read it, but I haven't had time."

"It was brought to you, I believe, by Shaleka."

"Yes. Another of his schemes?"

"Balcha is one of our great writers."

"He's been in trouble before."

"I know. But he's wiser because of it. I've discussed this book with him, though like yourself I haven't had the chance to read it."

"What does he say, this Balcha?"

"He's convinced it's harmless. It's been through the censors. He made the changes they wanted."

"Our censors aren't always as capable as they should be."

"True. But I hate to see you overrule them on Shaleka's word."

"I won't. But the way he described it . . ."

"He's gifted at that. Though I suspect from my discussion with Balcha there may still be parts that should be changed. But it would be a shame to see such a great writer silenced. Such things hurt us in the world's eyes."

"The world need never know."

"Somehow the world always seems to find out. Look how the Russians have been hurt by what they've done to their writers."

Negash glanced at him, grinned. "You won't let me forget what I said about the Russians, will you?"

"Should I?"

"No. But do this for me. Handle this business of the book. Read it. See what you think should be done. Talk to Balcha. Then let me know."

"I'm not sure I'll be able to persuade him to make all the right changes."

"Do what you can. Be my eyes in this, Tesfaye."

"I'll do all I can."

"And Tesfaye. There's this fellow Makonnen. I can't remember his father's name. A friend of Zenebetch."

"I know him."

"He's been to see me. We discussed Balcha. And you. Beware of him, Tesfaye."

"I will." He considered this a real mark of friendship. Negash was evidently warning him against his own spy. "I'll do all that I can, Excellency."

"Good," said Negash.

Harry watched them circling the church. He could join Tesfaye now. Security, so tight when the Emperor was entering the church, was now visibly relaxed. No lines of soldiers separated the dignitaries from the people. All were free to march round the church in the wake of the *tabot*.

He had stood outside the church throughout the long service. Loudspeakers carried the incomprehensible Ge'ez of the ritual and the equally unknown Amharic of the sermon. Now, the devout circled the church, but he still stood apart. He was a stranger, *faranj*.

The Emperor took his place on the canopied throne by the doors of the church. The *tabot* was carried inside. Local officials and clergy approached the throne to bow to their king. Harry knew it was over. There would be no book. No microcosm revealing the whole. No key to Ethiopia from the hand of Harriston Comfort. He could look from outside. But he could never see from within.

He had given up hope of finding Baria now. And of joining Tesfaye. He turned sadly from the church. He would return to the station wagon. To Julie and the baby. And wait. For Baria. For Tesfaye. If they didn't return, no matter. He had the keys. He could drive his wife and child back to Dire Dawa where his own car was parked. This was done. A new life, with Julie and Jonathan, waited to begin.

"There's Claude with his camera," said Eleni.

"How close he is to the Emperor," said Makonnen.

"If Claude's camera were a gun, the Emperor would be dead by now," said Hagos. "All the preparations Dejazmatch Tessema made. And failed. When one small man with one small gun could do it so easily."

"Men have been hung for thinking such things," said Makonnen.

"Never mind hangings and guns," said Baria. "Did you watch how they march. How they went round the church."

"They go round and round," said Makonnen. "In circles."

"Round and round, yes," said Baria. "But in which direction? They go counterclockwise."

"Like everything else in Ethiopia," said Makonnen.

All five had climbed on the low stone wall, watching from a distance over the heads of the crowd.

"You boys are so cynical," said Eleni.

"Three times they went around the church," said Baria. "Going opposite the way the clock goes. You see how we are? How our church—and others—lead us? Against the clock. Always turning back time."

"Not always," said Hagos. "Not all of us."

"Baria," said Eleni. "You sound like Tesfaye. Last night we were watching the people dancing the *iskista*. He said much the same about the way we dance."

"Tesfaye watches closely," said Baria.

"No," said Hagos. "The wheel is a circle. But it doesn't just turn. It moves."

"Wheels can be turned," said Baria. "Isn't it? Anything we turn in this country turns in a circle. Back where we started. We drove from Addis to Kulubi. Soon we'll be turning around. Full circle. Driving back to Addis. Back where we started."

"Let us pray," said Makonnen, "that we'll all be lucky enough to get there."

PART THREE

TURNING FULL CIRCLE

HARRY EASED THE VOLKSWAGEN'S SYNCHROMESHED GEARS INTO LOW to execute the tight, ascending hairpin curve where the roads from Dire Dawa and Harar merged to become the road to Addis Ababa. It frightened him that he could remember so little of the previous afternoon and night. Even the drive back from Kulubi to their tent in the camping grounds of the hotel was a blur in his mind. The good tired feeling he had known after their long walk had given way to total exhaustion. He had driven Baria's station wagon from the church in a bumper-to-bumper procession of buses, trucks, and cars. He knew he had nodded over the wheel but instinct preserved them.

Had he slept the whole afternoon? Had he swum at some point in the pool? Or was that only a cooling dream under the sunbaked canvas of the tent? And the bird he had seen. It had flashed orange and black and white through the green leaves of the trees. Surely that had been by the pool. He remembered that later he had tried to find the bird in the wildlife books he'd brought. The tips of the wings were striped black and white. He hadn't been able to find it in any of his books. He'd watched its flight through the trees, over the wall and away and then a few minutes later again flashing brilliant orange and white and black through the green of the trees. Surely a bird so lovely must have been part of a dream.

The music he'd heard from the hotel might just as easily have been part of another dream. Had he slept all day and night? He was sure he'd eaten no dinner. A whole day like so much of the rest of his life he'd done nothing with. It was midmorning now as he turned off the paved road snaking up into the mountains and onto the dirt highway across the chain of the Chercher Hills. They'd been later in getting away then he'd hoped. They'd agreed to drive straight through but now it would be nightfall before they could reach home. Julie and the baby in her lap both slept. He was glad his small family was again together. But he had already decided that before this trip was over, he would drive alone with Baria. He and Baria had things to say to each other from which neither could hide. But that would have to wait till Baria was sober. And awake.

Despite the dust, Tesfaye drove with both windows open. Baria, snoring fitfully, reeked with the whisky smells of his long night through the streets and bars of Dire Dawa. After returning from Kulubi in the Land Rover driven by Hagos, Baria had done his best to avoid Harry and Julie. Tesfaye had finally found him late in the evening deep in the old quarter of town.

In the afternoon, Tesfaye had phoned in his stories on the festival, the Emperor's walk, the death of the woman in the Peugeot. He returned to the hotel, cleared off a cot, and carried it from the tent to the shade of the trees in the garden by the pool. He hadn't wanted to disturb the Comforts. The phrase had become a litany on which he lulled himself to sleep: do not disturb the Comforts the comforts the comforts of sleep *zinkwulf matsenannat* do not disturb, comfort, sleep.

When he awoke at sunset and there was still no sign of Baria, he had begun his search. He'd begun in the lobby of the hotel. The first person he'd found that he knew was Negash. After the estrangement of their talk in the palace, their meeting at the church had drawn them closer together again. At the hotel their banter was light, warm. As though the distance of death had never been between them.

"Are you coming to the dance?" Negash had asked.

"Not if I can help it."

"You're not a dancer then?"

"Not a-tall," he'd answered in a self-mocking clipped British accent.

"In any event," said Negash, "I'm sure you prefer dancing in the villas."

Dire Dawa was famed for the luxury of the villas left by departing French railroad officials that had been converted into brothels.

"Quite possibly," said Tesfaye. "You haven't seen my friend, Baria Medhane Alem have you?"

"The painter? I haven't. I didn't know he was a friend of yours, too. You intellectuals all stick together, don't you?"

"Don't flatter me. A newspaperman is no intellectual."

"Oh, but I thought you all were. Perhaps the French term, *clerques*, would be more exact."

"Exactly exact," said Tesfaye. "In our system the reporter is a clerk all right. Though our officials all think we're spies. Or conspirators. And what we should be is workers." Punning, thought Tesfaye, always punning. *Sera* for conspirator, *sera* for worker. It shows what we think of work.

Negash laughed. "Well, spy (*sallay*), I haven't seen your painter (*sayi*)." Not punning but still playing.

Tesfaye wondered if foreigners could ever appreciate how much pleasure Ethiopians took from hearing their language spoken playfully and well.

"We have Baria's car," he said, "but he disappeared at Kulubi. I'm afraid the priests may have made him a slave."

"To his name (*simu*) they listened (*semu*)."

"We could play on forever," said Tesfaye, "but I really must find him."

"Good luck."

"That I need."

He made a circuit of the terrace, the gardens, the pool, greeting dozens of people he knew, asking for Baria. Twice he was told Baria had been seen earlier in the town with Zenebetch Desta and some others. That would mean Eleni, thought Tesfaye. Eleni.

He checked the roof where preparations for that evening's post-Kulubi dance were underway. No sign of "the slave." He lingered to watch the sun settling into the desert, a red hole in the sky descending into dun. Dun. Dawn. Dune. Down. Done. It can be done in English, he thought, but we don't do it. At the opposite end of the roof, he watched the effects of the fading light on the white and weathered pastel houses of Magala, the old town beyond the sandy riverbed of the seldom flowing Dakatu River. To his left the pale ochre stone of the palace was tinted rose.

A whistle signaled the end of the work day in the railroad yards. Its cry soon faded, replaced by the amplified muezzin cutting across the wadi. The church bells were silent. The Christians have had their day, thought Tesfaye. Now it's time for the

Muslims and soon, with the coming of night, time for the pagans we all are. Below him, tall trees sheltering the paved streets of the new town shrouded most of its buildings in a green now dusky with evening.

He had always loved this gentle city that took its ease on the edge of the desert under mountains now just beginning to purple in the last, swiftly failing light of day. Purple for a moment, then black till the waning moon would rise above them. He looked again across the dry riverbed. Dear, dusty Dire Dawa. He wasn't sure why he felt he should search for Baria. But if he must, he knew there was no place else he would rather hunt.

He again checked the pool, the gardens, the terrace, the lobby, briefly the camping area, and then into the streets already dark. He looked in at Omedla and chatted briefly with the Ethiopian woman at the cash drawer and with her Italian husband, sweaty from his work in the kitchen. He stopped at the bar in the park where he was caught up in the drunken mourning for its late proprietor, Woizero Kalamawork of the broken vow and the wrecked Peugeot.

The notorious One Thousand Eighty, reigning on the verandah in a chair of plastic and chrome, sent one of the prettier bar maids to ask him to join her.

"I consider it a royal summons," he said and followed the swaying hips of the girl.

"You're Tesfaye, the editor, aren't you?" said One Thousand Eighty.

"At your service."

"Don't tease me. I know you're a very important man and a good friend of my friend Ato Negash. But I have a story you must write for your paper."

"Concerning the late . . ."

"My dear friend, Kalamawork."

"The story is done. I was at the scene this morning while you were talking to Major Abebe. I phoned the story to my paper this afternoon."

"But you must make it very sad. How all her friends mourn her."

"It is a sad story."

"Take some whisky with me."

"Gladly." He took a chair beside her, knowing he was being honored.

"And bring Ato Tesfaye some *kitfo*," she ordered one of the girls. He wondered if she'd inherited the bar. She proceeded to tell him the story in great detail. He dutifully took out his notebook and pen but put them down when his food and whisky arrived.

It was an hour before he was able to escape. Before he left he promised to visit her house by the marker on the Asmara Road. He meant to keep his promise. It was a house he'd never had access to before. And not a bad one for a journalist to know.

He strolled from the park to the sports field by the railroad tracks where, under soft amber lights games of tennis and basketball were being played and, in a barnlike hall, the bodyguard band was warming up for a dance of its own.

He visited each of the handsome brothels on the wide street bordering the tracks. Finally, at Mamitay Zulu's, he was told Baria had preceded him by an hour.

"He said he was mourning your father's death," Mamitay told him. "He was drinking too much."

At a much shabbier bar with an open-air courtyard where a band was already in full blare, Tesfaye found another friend, a painter who had studied under Baria and now sedulously imitated him. He was holding a blood-soaked handkerchief to his nose.

"Baria hit me," he wailed. "For no reason. I was telling him about this American lady I've been fucking and all of a sudden, for no reason, he hit me."

"Perhaps for a reason," said Tesfaye. And left.

He circled the edge of the square before the railroad station, now crowded with passengers from the train that had arrived late from Djibouti. Nearly all were Somalis, and most were involved in smuggling. He knew that many of the incredibly fat women he saw were not nearly as fat as they looked. Under their flowing robes they carried everything from Swiss watches to sugar produced in Ethiopia. The sugar was shipped legally to the French colony of Djibouti, bought there at the favorable export price, and smuggled back for resale at a cost still below that of the protected domestic price that prevailed in the empire that produced it. Only in Ethiopia, thought Tesfaye.

As he made his way down the new quarter's main street, he was approached by peddlers of contraband goods ranging from Hong Kong sandals to French perfume, from British cigarettes to Dutch radios and German cameras. One hustler summed it all up:

"You want good Scotch whisky?"

Tesfaye shook his head no.

"Rothmans?"

Another negative nod.

"Shirts? French leather?"

Still no.

"Beautiful ladies? Arab boy? Ah, I know. Hashish."

He checked the verandahs and bars of the Leul Makonnen, the Continental, the Sports Bar. Finally at the National Hotel he was told Baria had been seen twenty minutes before. Switching from Scotch to gin tonic, then heading across the riverbed to Magala.

A film of sand covered his shoes as he started his quest through the cheaper, dirtier, noisier, and nastier bars of the old quarter. Shops were still open. The streets were crowded. He noticed that here, as across the river, nearly all the cars bore, not local license plates, but those with the double Amharic *A* of Addis Ababa.

He was amused to find that the Chereka Hotel, which had housed a popular bar called Vers d'lune, had changed its name to Apollo 13. The crescent moon, which had once been its emblem, had been replaced by a rocket phallic as a mosque.

"What are you looking for Baria for?" asked a friend he encountered in the hotel's Astronaut bar.

"I wonder myself," said Tesfaye. And went on looking.

He made a circuit of the two paved streets that radiated from the main crossing of the riverbed. Then began a tiresome trek through the dusty back streets. He crossed the riverbed again to the new produce market where the city's worst slums had been torn down and open-air grain sheds had been built. Behind them, the Orthodox cathedral, under construction for years, loomed like a hopeful Christian spirit in a Muslim ghetto. There were only a few bars in this out-of-the-way section, but in one of them Tesfaye found a Somali girl of incredible beauty and, sitting at a table with her, Baria.

"*Tenastelign, getie*," said Tesfaye.

"*Tenastelign, geytoch*." Baria half stood, half bowed, lurching against the table, spilling his gin tonic and the girl's orange soda. "Join us," he said. "Then I can spill your beer, too."

"I'm drinking whisky, thank you."

"A whisky for my lord," Baria called out to a short, pimpled half-caste girl behind the bar. "And more of the same for us."

Tesfaye sat. For the moment he had all but forgotten that he'd been searching for Baria. He couldn't take his eyes from the Somali girl. Her pert, pretty face and shy, dimpled smile set off dancing, maroon-tinted eyes that dazzled him. She wore a sheer blouse that veiled in light mist breasts impressively full and remarkably high and firm. Tesfaye guessed she couldn't be more than fifteen.

"What's a beauty like that doing in a hovel like this?"

"I don't know," said Baria. "But I know what I'm doing here."

"Fantastic."

"Indeed. You will notice, perhaps, the nipples. They point not merely out, but up."

"Fantastic."

"And the nose. That tiny nose. It, too, points up. And those eyes. You may also notice what a good Muslim she is. Takes tea or soda only. She drinks no alcohol. Takes no tobacco. But she does, I assume, fuck."

The half-caste laughed nastily. She brought their drinks, sat next to Tesfaye, and put an active hand in his crotch.

"It's forbidden," said Tesfaye, placing her hand firmly on the table.

It developed that the beauty spoke no language but Somali. Baria had been communicating through the half-caste who seemed to speak a smattering of every language known to man. Including Japanese.

Baria had learned that the girls had been working in the huge, Japanese-run cotton-fabric plant on the edge of town. Several of the expatriate managers had pooled resources to buy the girls the house and provide for their marginal upkeep. At times when the girls were reasonably sure their benefactors were unlikely to appear, they hung strings of colored beads in their doorway, rearranged the furniture, which included a bamboo bar, and turned up their lights and tape recorder full volume.

"And presto," said Baria, "a brothel, a bar. They've been caught at it by the Japs a few times. But they don't seem to mind."

Tesfaye took a nervous gulp of his whisky.

"I see that you, too, are avoiding the Comforts of home."

"This is no time for puns." For the first time since he'd sat down opposite the girl, he turned to Baria. "I came out looking for you. We were all worried."

"Good. I'm glad to cause some anxiety among friends."

"And anger?"

"Is there anger?"

"Something in the air," said Tesfaye. "The mild Mr. Comfort is issuing commands. The wife is to take better care of the child. Tesfaye is to find you. We're all to leave for Addis at first light of dawn."

"Bad omens," said Baria. "But never mind. At first light of dawn I intend to be pillowed in the honey of those breasts."

He reached out a hand and squeezed. The girl smiled and pushed away his hand.

"Fantastic," said Tesfaye.

"Why don't you take this other one?" said Baria. "She isn't a beauty, but I'm sure she'll amuse you."

Tesfaye shook his head.

"We can't go back to that tent," said Baria. "The atmosphere will be unhealthy. And where else will we find a bed this night but on top of a girl in one of these places."

The half-caste nestled her hand back in Tesfaye's crotch. He was drained of all feeling. He let it lie.

"Insane," he said to Baria. "We can't stay here. The kamikaze squad will descend on us in our sleep. The yellow pygmies will hack us to death with samurai swords."

"Fear not, master. Your slave is well armed."

"Myself," said Tesfaye, glancing down, "I seem to be disarmed."

"Very well. I'll take the half-caste. You can have this one."

"You discuss them as though they were different brands of whisky. You take the Red Label. I'll settle for the Black and White."

"Well said. But what else are they? You may want this girl because she's beautiful. I want her because she's available. Like a bottle of whisky on the shelf. And I need a bed. Like our dear friend's wife. She has no breasts. Her behind is broad but flat. She is often vulgar and crude. But Mrs. Comfort has one very comforting quality. She's available. Even to lepers and slaves. And the husband doesn't seem to notice. It makes her very attractive."

"You've had hundreds of women," said Tesfaye. "There are thousands more you could have."

"It takes all the available ones there are, and more, to make up for the ones . . . you can't have." He spoke very slowly. And, for once, Tesfaye felt sure he could believe that Baria meant what he was saying. "The ones who shudder at the sight of you. The ones who politely keep distant and cold. And even worse. The sick ones who want you because of this. There are times I wish I were dead. He was my friend, you know. Till she offered her comforts."

"Let's leave."

"Why? Is the topic forbidden?"

"Not here."

"Forget them. They're part of the furniture. Two beds. Though I admit this one is better pillowed than most."

"Let's move."

"I must stay."

"You're too drunk."

"Another reason to stay. I may well be too drunk to walk. Or even stand. But this other damn thing, no matter how drunk or dead the rest of me is, he's always ready to stand."

Tesfaye turned to the half-caste.

"We must go. How much do we owe you?"

Her hand tried again but found no response. She shrugged.

"Thirty-four dollars."

Baria laughed. "Four dollars, perhaps."

Tesfaye stood. He took several bills from his pocket. He counted out exactly thirty-four dollars, three tens and four ones, and gave them to the girl.

"Keep the change," he said.

"It's too much," Baria shouted.

"Do you want trouble?" said the half-caste. "This is our place. Not yours. I have only to call."

"We've paid," said Tesfaye. He glared at Baria. "Let's move. The girl is right. We're foreigners here. Imperialist devils."

"We're all Ethiopians."

"Tell that to the knives of the Somalis you'll be meeting."

"I'm armed."

"With whisky," said Tesfaye. "Let's move."

At a nod from the half-caste the full-breasted Somali girl scurried from the table and disappeared into the back room.

"You see?"

Baria nodded. He reached into his pocket.

"Here. Take my pistol. I'm not capable."

Tesfaye took the gun. It was a .38 revolver. He checked the cylinder. It was fully loaded. The half-caste watched him impassively.

"Let's move."

Baria stood. Tesfaye took his arm. The muscles were tense, hard as steel. But Tesfaye knew it was now useless steel. He kept the gun in his hand and guided Baria to the door. He glanced over his shoulder. The half-caste hadn't moved.

"Good night," he said. "Say good night to your beautiful friend. May the blessings of Gabriel be upon you."

Now, on the highway home, they were just approaching Kulubi. It seemed no more than another sleepy mountain village. He glanced down at the snoring, limp bulk of Baria. He looked no more impressive than the village which gave no sign that a day before it had been packed with tens of thousands of pilgrims. They drove through in less than a minute.

They hadn't been followed from the bar. But Tesfaye, wanting to avoid the dark, narrow streets of Magala, steered Baria to the riverbed. They followed its course toward the lights of the palace and the new quarter beyond. They could hear music from the dance on the roof of the hotel, and, from the other side of the river, the competing blare of music from the bars that lined its right bank.

It was the same riverbed he had trudged through farther up on his walk to Kulubi with Harry. He had once seen a *gari* caught halfway across by a flash flood racing down from a storm in the mountains. A wall of water sent it tumbling. Driver, passengers, and horse were drowned. By the next day there was only mud where the river had suddenly been. But three people were dead. Their bodies were found several kilometers downstream. Horse and *gari* had washed up against a sandbank on the edge of town. The memory now made him shudder. He didn't want to be driving. But there was no hope of waking Baria.

Getting him away from the bar had done little good. He still refused to return to the tent.

"I'll never be able to sleep there," he said. "Do you know, I went back there this afternoon. The wife and baby were asleep in the tent. I don't know where Harry was. I didn't see you. I sat for a while on a stool by the tent, watching the most beautiful bird I've ever seen darting through the trees by the pool beyond the wall.

"I'd never seen a bird like it. The breast was orange. A crested head and a long, curving orange bill. The wings and tail feathers were striped like a zebra. I wondered what in hell it could be."

"You should have asked Harry," said Tesfaye. "He could have shown you his bird book."

"That's what I did. Not Harry, but the book. I remembered seeing it in the tent. I crept inside. The baby was asleep. The wife was snoring. I found the book. It was lying on top of a suitcase. I took it outside and sat on the stool, trying to find that damn bird. The bird, the real bird, kept disappearing, coming back through the trees. But I looked all through the book and I couldn't find it there. I went back in the tent. The baby, still nice and quiet. The wife, snoring not so much. That baby . . . she thinks, at least she told me, I'm the father."

"Oh."

"And by now, from the way he's been acting, I suspect she must have told him."

"I suspect," said Tesfaye.

"So I stood there, you see, with his book in my hands. I leafed through it again. Still trying to find that fantastic damn bird. I couldn't. And then, how strange, I'd never felt guilty with the wife. But I stood there fingering through another man's book. Looking for a bird I couldn't find. You know how hot it gets in a tent under the sun. I was sweating like anything. He didn't know I had his book in my hands. I put the book down and crept out of that damn place, feeling ashamed. I'd had a few drinks before, but then I started really to drink. Like I do too often.

"No, Tesfaye. I'll never be able to go back there to sleep. Let's find someplace more safe. Two other girls with beds to pillow us."

Tesfaye looked away. He could see the colored lights strung out on the roof of the hotel. He could hear the music from the dance.

"I'd been wondering about you and your business with the wife."

"Even you wondered," said Baria. "But it seems it never occurred before now to Harry."

"No. It wouldn't have occurred to Harry. He's not like us. Suspicious. Intriguing. He has an innocent mind."

"I wonder how innocent now. Dear Lady Comfort was never so much innocent. She seems to seek out trouble. Not just for herself. She wants to punish us all. And most of all him."

"Poor Harry."

"Maybe he won't be so poor anymore," said Baria. "She may make him tough."

"Perhaps," said Tesfaye.

A dust devil swept through the riverbed a few meters from them. It seemed to stop, hovering in one spot.

"Look," said Baria. "The devil himself."

"Dust," said Tesfaye. "A whirlwind."

"You know, if a good man like yourself threw a stone into the heart of that thing, it would fall."

"Nonsense," said Tesfaye.

"But if I did it, the best stone, the truest aim, nothing would happen," said Baria. "I'm a dust devil myself. If some righteous man like yourself threw a stone in me, I'd collapse."

"Ask Harry," said Tesfaye. "He may be in the mood to accommodate you."

"Try it," said Baria. "Not at me. At that one." The dust devil still swirled near them. "One stone in his heart thrown by a righteous man. That's what they say. I'd pick up a stone for you except I don't right now trust my head to bend over."

Tesfaye looked at the ground around his feet. He spotted a stone. He still had Baria's gun in one hand. He bent and picked up the stone with the other. Anything to shut Baria up. Then he might be able to get him back to the hotel.

"Now throw it. Right in his heart."

"It's all nonsense," said Tesfaye. "Let's go home." He tested the weight of the stone in his hand. It was flat; edges, jagged.

"It's a perfect stone," said Baria. "If that doesn't work, you can try the .38."

"No, it's absurd," said Tesfaye. He tossed the stone to the ground.

As they watched, they saw the dust devil rise, then abruptly collapse.

"You see?" said Baria. "If you had thrown the stone just then . . ."

"You could have said I'm a righteous man."

"You have to give up this role of always the journalist, the impartial observer," said Baria. "And become a man of action. Think of the reputation you could develop."

"I'm afraid my reputation concerns me very little. Let's move."

Walking through the sand was tiring, but he kept Baria moving. Despite the fate of the *gari,* he felt the wide expanse of the riverbed gave them a margin of safety. He looked once more over his shoulder, saw no one, and put Baria's gun in his pocket. It was there still. With his own .22. He hated guns. But he carried one always. Like a good Ethiopian, he said to himself.

He reached into his pocket and took out the .38. He dropped it into the left-hand pocket of Baria's jacket. At least that's one less, he thought. Baria didn't stir.

When they'd reached the main crossing place between the old and new towns, he and Baria had stood in the riverbed, arguing again. Baria insisted on going on, drinking till dawn or finding two beds of flesh.

"You'll end up getting yourself killed," said Tesfaye.

"That's what I'm hoping."

"No need to rush. It will happen soon enough. You don't have to sleep in the tent. I can bring cots or sleeping bags outside and set them up somewhere by the pool."

"I might fall in and drown."

"Isn't that what you want?"

"No, I'd rather burn. In a warm bed of flesh."

"That too. Soon enough we'll all burn. But now let's go get some sleep."

Baria shook his head and took Tesfaye's thin arms in his strong hands.

"He was my friend, Tesfaye. Till that other Comfort presented itself. He was my friend. Till I abdicated that honor to you. And became instead *her* Ethiopian."

"Let's get some sleep," said Tesfaye.

"I can't," said Baria. "Listen. There's a book I once read about a painter, not so very famous, named Arshile Gorky. It said that this fellow had learned from Picasso that if an artist was depressed, he should draw. If he got drunk, he should go home and draw. If there was a shooting outside his window, he should go on drawing. Because for the artist, it said, there is only one solution. And only one salvation—ART. In capital letters. I took that passage, translated it into Amharic, and painted a very beautiful sign, red letters in your beautiful Amharic script, and nailed it up in my studio. To inspire me. The way I should live. Very fine words. Picasso, he's a famous and very great painter. Poor Gorky, he killed himself later, not so famous but also very great.

"But Baria, the slave, he'll never be great. He's a slave to himself. If there's a shooting outside my window, I grab my gun and run out. If I get depressed, I drink. If I get drunk, I go on drinking. And when I'm ashamed, I drink even more. For me, there's no solution. Above all, no salvation."

"You are a great painter," said Tesfaye. "Or so people tell me. I don't know about painting myself."

"Perhaps I'm not bad. The foreigners think so. They buy my paintings. And sometimes their wives take me to bed. But it's no solution. Not my own people. Not our own girls unless they're whores and even then . . . sometimes even them. So instead of like Picasso I'm like Gorky. I drink, drank, drunk. Dying, dead, death. That's salvation."

"When you're dead," said Tesfaye, "you can't drink anymore."

"But I'm not dead yet," said Baria.

"You'll feel better tomorrow."

Baria let go of his arms. He again shook his head and looked back toward Magala.

"The leper can't change his spots."

Finally, Tesfaye had left him. Standing in the middle of a riverbed of sand.

Julie woke. Harry had slowed to edge his way past a bus stopped in another village.

"Wow," said Julie. "I must have really gone out. Where are we?"

"Not far," said Harry. "A place called Chelenko. Back there, maybe ten minutes, we went through Kulubi."

"I'm glad I slept through that." She looked down at the infant still sleeping in her lap. "I never want to see that place again."

"We won't."

"What about your book?"

"No book."

"I ruined that for you, too, didn't I?"

"No. Not you."

"Are you angry at me?"

"Yes."

At the far edge of the village, he accelerated. "Let's not talk about it," he said. "I need to keep my mind on the road."

She watched him. His eyes were on the road, but she knew his mind was not. She waited for him to speak, sure he could not keep silent. He said nothing. She tried to guess what he was thinking. About her. His book. Baria. She usually didn't have to guess what he was thinking, and now she was afraid to ask.

Since they'd come down from Kulubi, he'd been quiet, withdrawn. Chains. She'd been dreaming. The baby on her lap. Harry by her side. She remembered now she'd been dreaming about chains. While they drove. Harry and the baby and her past, chains all tangled with the story she'd told Eleni about the mad Greek woman in chains.

Eleni had stopped by their tent that morning. Still no sign of the missing Baria. Harry and Tesfaye packing their equipment into the station wagon. At Harry's command.

"Changing diapers again," Eleni had said. She was with Claude, the black American Julie had thought was Ethiopian. No Hagos.

"You keep losing your friends here," said Eleni, "and meeting other people. Can I help?"

She helped with the diapers. Claude joined Harry and Tesfaye stuffing the station wagon.

"Women's work," said Eleni.

"Women's shit," Julie muttered. "Pardon my language."

"No apologies needed. I lived in a girl's dorm for four years at college in the States. I've heard it all."

She must have mentioned something about chains to Eleni. Said something about a woman's chains. And told her the story of the Greek woman who had chained herself to a flagpole.

Harry and Tesfaye had stopped their work to join the conversation. Both were taken with the girl. Julie saw it. She couldn't blame them. Eleni was everything a man, a real man, would want in a woman. Attractive, intelligent, articulate. Everything a real man would want. And everything most men would fear. Thank God, thought Julie, or there'll be no chance at all for the rest of us.

While they talked, Julie noticed Claude uncase his camera and begin clicking them all into his black memory box. She felt she was on stage. She tried to ignore the camera and wondered how she was performing.

"I felt sorry for her," she said. "I knew we had to help her. But by the end, I didn't really want to see her come down. She had a right to those chains. They were all she had to hold her to the past."

"A woman's right," said Eleni. "To chains?"

"No. A right to her past. Him. The husband that died. That place." Click. Into the camera.

"Maybe the past is always a chain," said Eleni. "But you're right. If there's nothing else, it's hard to break. Sad to lose."

"In America, from what I read," said Julie, "women are beginning to break their chains."

"You mean you want to break yours," said Eleni.

"It's a movement," said Julie.

"Yes," said Eleni. "A movement for white, educated, well-off American women. Chained to their washing machines. And here, it's your servants who need liberation. Not you. Even at that, your servants are much better off than most African women.

"If you told me your women's movement is for women who really need it, like our peasants or your servants, I would join. Or if it would liberate our women who break their backs hauling wood for your fireplace. But it isn't for them. It's for women like you. Maybe even me. But our wood haulers need liberation far more than I do."

"I want to write an editorial about those women," said Tesfaye. "I was telling Harry. 'The Human Being as a Beast of Burden.' "

"Good," said Eleni. "Write it just that way. The human being who needs liberation. Not just women."

Julie listened. She remembered now how she had dug her nails into her palms. Who's going to liberate me? she thought. But she had been afraid to say what she thought to Eleni.

"It's funny," said Harry. "We think we have problems. But our problems are so small. Selfish. Personal. It's funny being an American in a country like this. It makes you realize. We have to grow up."

"You will," said Tesfaye. "You've already started."

She listened. She felt alone. She watched the men watching Eleni. Especially Tesfaye. And Claude's camera, watching them all. Click. He was like Baria. You could never tell what he was thinking. Behind his camera. And then he put his camera down and said to Harry:

"Don't sweat it, Jim. You're gonna grow up all right. Back home. We gonna see to that."

She glanced at Harry now. Grow up. We should. But our own problems go on.

The men had gone back to work, striking the tent to pack it away for the long trip home. She and Eleni took the baby and sat on packing crates in the shade of a tree.

"You see," said Eleni. "The men liberate us from work. An occasional diaper. A bottle. They'll build homes for us. Buy clothes. Hire servants. You can say the homes are prisons, the clothes, a convict's uniform, the servants, our guards. But if we let them liberate us from work, from ourselves, we can't accuse them of making us prisoners."

"It's easy for you to talk," said Julie. "You have a job."

"It isn't easy for me to have a job." She told Julie about the OAU. How strongly African men resented her. The intrigues against her. The constant sexual advances.

"Now you sound like a candidate for women's lib."

"No," said Eleni. "That's just another way to divide. Putting people who are oppressed at each others' throats always helps those who do the oppressing. Set tribe against tribe. White against black. And this, maybe best of all, women against men."

She went on attacking the movement that had fired Julie's imagination when she'd read about it, at a distance, in the weekly newsmagazines. But Julie's attention wavered. "Your women's lib," Eleni was saying, "for all the things it says about others, the movement itself is sexist, racist. Narrow. Selfish. Divisive." But Eleni, though her argument never faltered, was no longer focusing on Julie. She was looking toward the tent. Julie realized it was Tesfaye that Eleni concentrated on.

"What do you think of him?" asked Julie.

"Of who?"

"Tesfaye."

"I like him," said Eleni. "I admire him."

Julie was relieved. She couldn't sustain talk about anything as abstract as a movement. Even a movement for women. They talked about men. Tesfaye, Harry, Hagos, Claude. And again about Tesfaye.

"You're right," said Julie. "He's basically good. Like Harry." Girl talk. She enjoyed it, and in Ethiopia she'd found few women she could talk to. But she wondered how frank she dared be. She was sure Eleni was involved with Hagos. He was handsome, arrogant, exciting. Tesfaye was decent, like Harry. But if Eleni marries Tesfaye, she'll have affairs with men like Hagos.

Just like me.

She knew she envied Eleni: her looks; her assured ideas; the career she'd carved out for herself. But she didn't imagine being like Eleni. She thought of Eleni being—just like me. Married. Having affairs. She told her about Baria.

"You needn't tell me all that."

"But a woman needs to talk to someone."

She'd no sooner spoken the words than Baria appeared. Bloodshot. Stumbling. Muttering apologies to Harry, Tesfaye. She remembered the vow she had made. Her vow for Baria. It seemed absurd to her now.

Maybe Eleni was right. Tesfaye. Harry. Or maybe none of them. What had Eleni said when they'd first met at Miesso? Not for marriage. But she knew herself better. She would always define herself in terms of some man.

She was watching Harry, silent at the wheel as he drove. Harry, she thought. Poor Harry. Not Hagos. Not Baria. But Harry. Poor Harry.

Dire Dawa was three hours behind them. The road's sudden change to white gravel told him they were descending to Mota. Beside him, Baria stirred. He sat up. He blinked his eyes open and looked down into the valley below them.

"Your father's place," said Baria.

"*Mota*," answered Tesfaye. He died.

"Why did they give the village that name?"

"That's why," said Tesfaye.

He put the car in second, kept his foot off the gas, and crept slowly down, tapping the brakes only on the sharpest curves.

"I'm glad it's you who's with me," he said. "Not Harry. I wouldn't want a foreigner's sympathy walking on my father's grave."

"They buried him here?"

"*Mota*," said Tesfaye.

The village seemed normal. Like Kulubi, it gave no sign of what it had witnessed a few days before. No police in sight. No visible soldiers. If the road to his father's farm was blocked, it was at some discreet point that couldn't be seen from the highway. Possibly, thought Tesfaye, at the bridge that got broken. The bridge to the farm of the man who somehow got killed.

He drove through without stopping. Beyond the village, he knew that if he looked to his right he could see the farmhouse nestled at the edge of the trees above. He kept his eyes on the road. As they climbed the twisting white road back up out of the valley, Baria fell back to sleep. *Tegna,* thought Tesfaye. *Mota.* He slept. He died.

They were turning back. Another sweep of the hands of the clock. The next day, he remembered, would be the Western new year. Some new beginning, perhaps, for the foreigners. But not for us. For us the cycle goes endlessly on. In another week it would be Genna, the nativity. Already in fields by the side of the road, boys and young men were practicing the holiday game. A rough ball knocked back and forth between two teams armed with curved, knob-ended hockeylike sticks of *kitkita.* The playing field had no boundaries and the game only one real rule: batter your opponents. The hardwood sticks were weapons; the ball, an excuse. To celebrate the birth of the prince of peace, we bloody each other with sticks. And slaughter another lamb. Blood of the lamb. Blood of the lion. His father had been one of the lions. *Mota.* But the Lion of Judah survived. *Haile Selassie aimuwt.*

His father was dead; the Emperor lives, and the cycle would go on. He'd been told that the students in Addis Ababa were rioting, and he knew that when that had been repressed there would be new rebellions, followed by new repressions and another upheaval.

The first he'd heard of the latest student troubles had been the night before when he'd finally returned to the hotel. He was exhausted by his long search through the city and depressed by his encounter with Baria. The gate to the camping area had been locked. Rather than trying to raise the *zabagna,* he decided to go through the lobby. He entered just in time to see Negash at the front desk slamming down the telephone. Music drifted down from the dance still in progress on the roof. For a moment there was no other sound in the nearly deserted lobby. Negash turned, saw Tesfaye, and said in English:

"Blunderers. Idiots. Fools. They've let him be killed."

"Again?" said Tesfaye.

The reference was lost on Negash.

"Walk with me," he commanded Tesfaye. "The Emperor has to be told."

Now what? Tesfaye had wondered. He was tired, but he walked with Negash. They walked a block in silence before Negash said, "It's young Tekle Gugsa. They've killed him."

"The student president?"

"Yes."

"Who did it?"

"Some thugs pulled the trigger. But the man behind it . . . Well, you may as well know. It's General Tadesse."

"The hyena?"

"You know him."

He remembered his father's words about the hyena. He said nothing of this to Negash. He was sure Negash knew. He suspected the hyena himself had betrayed his father's plot to the Emperor. The pieces of the puzzle shaped by his father's words were beginning to fit together. What was the Latin phrase? Post mortem. Latin was another language his father thought little of. After death was far too late.

"The students flatter themselves," said Negash, "that one day they'll topple the government. But it's these old bastards . . ."

"Like my father."

"No," said Negash, "not like your father. Your father had the heart of a lion. This one is well named. He has the soul of a hyena. We knew of his scheme. Men were assigned to watch the boy. Young Tekle. To protect him. He realized, I'm sure, he was being watched. These security idiots are never very subtle."

"I know."

"Their story now is that tonight Tekle wanted to be with his girl. He managed to lose his guardian angels. Later, he was walking with the girl in back of the university. The girl says three men walked by them, going the opposite way. Then she heard two shots. They'd shot him in the back."

They passed a dance house. Its soft red lights and loud rock music spilled into the street.

"Our informant in this business . . . our information came from a prostitute."

"One Thousand Eighty?" said Tesfaye.

Negash glanced at him sharply.

"No," he said. "It was another. Someone who works for her. But how did you know about that?"

"The gossip of the town," said Tesfaye.

"We're a people of secrets," said Negash. "Except we can't keep secrets."

"We're also a people of gossip," said Tesfaye. "It makes keeping secrets difficult. You can control the press. But you can't censor gossip."

"You're always working," said Negash.

"It's my profession," said Tesfaye.

"I wonder if after tonight I'll have a profession," said Negash. "This is the second time in two days His Excellency Ato Negash will have had to tell the Emperor news he doesn't want to hear."

"Cheer up," said Tesfaye. "He may exile you to Washington."

"You're a difficult sort of a friend," said Negash.

"It's my heritage showing. I had a difficult father."

"I know. So did this Tekle. The boy's of a noble family, Tesfaye. His sister's a princess."

"Half sister," said Tesfaye. "I know the family. Tekle wasn't close to the rest."

"The Emperor's fond of him."

"Fond of a rebel?"

"He's fond, sentimentally fond, of many rebels. Including your father."

"You seem more human," said Tesfaye, "than when you lectured me last night."

"I'm sorry," said Negash. "But you weren't easy to talk to last night."

"Do I seem easy now?"

"Hardly. You're a difficult friend."

"Good. I don't intend to be easy."

They went by a back gate to the palace. Negash looked up a the tier of lights.

"It's for me to tell him. He isn't an easy friend either."

"Why did this General Hyena want to kill Tekle?"

"Insane. An insane scheme. He plotted it so he could uncover the plot. Save the nation. And hope the Emperor would forget what else he's been up to."

"The embezzling rumor is true?"

"Embezzling and selling army equipment. Guns, trucks, ammunition, bazookas. Even overcoats. He planned to come up with Tekle's killers himself. Two would be dead. The third, who's dying of cancer, would confess. Implicate others. The hyena promised he'd take care of the man's family."

Tesfaye had been guessing before. Now he was sure the hyena had worked a similar betrayal of his father.

"What will happen to him?"

"The hyena? He'll be arrested," said Negash. "He'll be tried for embezzlement. We can't acknowledge this other business. He'll be convicted of embezzling. But we'll hang him for treason."

"Thank you," said Tesfaye.

He left Negash at the main gate of the palace. He hadn't seen him again. No news was released on the killing of Tekle, but in the morning he heard on the radio that the Emperor had cut short his visit to Dire Dawa and was flying back to the capital.

In the absence of news, rumors spread like toadstools after rain. In Dire Dawa it was being said that Addis was in flames. Workers from the Mercato had joined the students in bloodly riots that swept the city. He met Hagos, who told him confidently that several ministers had been killed. The bodyguard had been called out, and troops were being recalled from Eritrea.

Before they'd left the city, Tesfaye managed to get a phone call through to his office. His assistant editor told him there were no flames and the rioting, real enough, was confined to the campus. Students had forced their way into Haile Selassie I hospital next to the university and had taken Tekle's body to the campus from where they planned a protest burial march. Tekle's half sister the widow of the prince who had been the Emperor's favorite son, insisted the body be turned over to the family.

Bodyguard troops had moved in. An unknown number of students had been killed. Many were wounded, including one expatriate professor who had locked himself in his office. A stray high velocity bullet had pierced the wall and shattered his knee. The body of Tekle had been recovered and turned over to the family. The campus was surrounded. The shooting had stopped. The rest of the city was calm.

It sounded to Tesfaye like a *Genna* match. Tekle's sad young corpse, like the ball, was used by all factions as an excuse for their own viciousness. He told Harry and Julie what he'd found out, and, at that point, Baria, still drunk and apparently sleepless, had finally returned. Now, Tesfaye listened to his peaceful snores.

He had been useless in striking the tent, in loading up the cars. As they'd started out, Baria, his eyes already shut, had said, "I think I'm coming to the end."

"No," said Tesfaye, turning left onto the highway. "Only the beginning of the end. We still have a long way to go back to Addis."

"Full circle," said Baria. "That will be the end."

A few moments later he was asleep. The final circle, thought Tesfaye. That shuts everything out. Till you wake and the circle starts turning again. Sleep. A cycle that opens. Not like death. A circle that's closed. Gabriel's feast was done, but soon it would be Mikael's day, a feast for another archangel. Genna, Christ's birth in a week. Timket, Christ's baptism and Mikael's day in three. Birth. Baptism. And archangels of death. Timket in three weeks and perhaps, he feared, more violence. He drove Baria's car across the hills beyond Mota and thought of more violence.

Harry hadn't recognized Mota as they'd driven through it. He'd been expecting troops guarding the road, perhaps a roadblock and a search of cars. It was only when he checked his watch and saw they were nearly four hours out of Dire Dawa that he realized they must have driven through. He wondered how he could have missed it. Mota. Tesfaye had told them what it meant. Death? Same stem as *muwt. Haile Selassie y'muwt.* But no one in the village knew whose death it was. Who it was that had died. The old *dejazmatch* had told them that.

Mota. How could they have gone through it and not known? Surely the scars of what had happened there must be visible. Or was death, *mota,* that casual, that quick? Even the death of so great a man? Not death, he remembered. He died. That's what it meant. He died. And no one in the village knew who it was who had died.

He remembered the fear of violence that had gripped him at Kulubi. And his fear of the savagery that might be part of himself. He had seen and felt the palpable reality of violence so often in Ethiopia. Its stink was on him. He hated violence, all wars, needless death. But he knew his hatred did no good. Violence still was there. From birth. In violence the child had come screaming into the world. The child that was theirs. Not his, but theirs. From birth, from baptism. The pit of the old church. And Timket. Las year, first Tesfaye, then Baria had warned him against the violence of Timket, baptism.

Fired by his first trip to Kulubi, he had been anxious to see the Timket services at Janhoy Meda in Addis. Crowds from all the churches of the capital marched to the vast "Emperor's Field" and the baptismal pool which, the devout believed, was fed by underground streams from the River Jordan where Christ had been baptized. Tesfaye had told him how colorful the services were but also warned him that toward evening fights often broke out. Baria had been more specific.

For two successive years, he told Harry, the festivities around the baptismal pool at Janhoy Meda had exploded into bloody fights between Gallas and Tigres. It was rumored that security agents circulating among the crowds deliberately provoked the tribal brawls. At the second of these battles, Baria admitted, the Gallas had shown no signs of needing to be provoked. They had come prepared, carrying hardwood clubs under their cloaks.

The Tigres, who fought like goats, using their heads as battering rams, had usually gotten the better of such fights in the past. But this time when a Tigre bent his head and came charging, his Galla adversaries dodged aside, whipped out their clubs, and struck at the exposed base of the skull. Of the four deaths claimed on the rumor circuit, three were supposedly Tigres.

"It's all arranged," said Baria. "These Amhara tyrants send Galla and Tigre provocateurs to stir up the trouble. They let the other tribes battle each other. Then their police come in and pick up the pieces, and they go on ruling the victims."

"Divide and rule?" said Harry.

"Exactly. A very clever people. They divide the rest of us so well, they deserve to rule."

"I can't believe that," said Harry. "I can't believe anyone would stir up trouble like that on purpose."

But he had been worried enough to let himself be convinced to travel instead to a small village near Debra Sina where Baria had friends.

He thought of it now, heading home, as another revelation unlocked by this sad trip to Kulubi. A trip they'd made when he still thought Baria was his friend.

At a cutoff near Debra Sina, they had left the main road. They arrived in midafternoon, Timket eve, at the home of Baria's friend, a man named Rufael.

Rufael, a subdistrict governor and landowner, insisted they have coffee. Coffee proved to be a full meal which was interrupted by the strident wailing of a trumpet drawing closer.

"What a shame," said Rufael. "We must be late. We should have been at the church before now."

They hurried outside. A procession bearing the *tabot* from the nearby church of St. Giorgis was just coming over a rise opposite Rufael's house.

Baria and Harry blinked against the dazzling white of freshly laundered, sunstruck national costumes worn by the scores of worshippers following the *tabot*. Many of the men carried prayer sticks, leaned on for support by the old, shouldered like spears by the young. It was the one day of the year when the tablet bearing the Ten Commandments was taken outside the church compound. Through all the Christian sections of the empire, Harry knew, similar processions would be underway. At Janhoy Meda, where violence was feared, the services would he held by a concrete pool. But the feast fell in the midst of the dry season and in many places the *tabot* had to be carried great distances to a stream or river that flowed the year round. Rufael's village was fortunate. A spring-fed rock pool was nearby.

After an hour's hard walk they scrambled down a final sharp slope to a woodland that bordered the pool where the congregations of several other churches in the area had gathered.

The sun was setting as they arrived. Darkness fell quickly and with it sudden cold. The light of an early moon turned to silver the golden tassels of the brocade covering the *tabot* before it was placed in its own special tent by the pool. There were several other tents around it where priests and acolytes would spend the night.

Many of the worshippers settled down for the long vigil, eating light meals carried in metal bowls or woven baskets. Harry and Baria trekked back with Rufael and his family to the farm and another heavy meal. Near midnight, the family set out again for the pool where mass would be said in the early morning hours. Tired from their trip and stupefied by *tella*, Harry and Baria slept on mats in the front room.

"It's perfect," said Harry, "except I hoped your friend would live in a *tukul*. I've never slept in a *tukul*."

"Rufael's very proud of his tin roof," said Baria, settling down on his mat. "It's a sign of status and wealth."

"I guess so. Where do you know him from?"

"Don't tell his neighbors, but he's actually a Galla. One of my people. He was an old friend of my father's. He's become the complete Amhara, as you can see. I suspect I embarrass him, but he's always kind."

"What a wonderful life it is out here. I wish I could live like this."

"Go to sleep, dear Harry. Tomorrow will be a full day."

It embarrassed him now to remember. He had even told Julie how he had lain awake enjoying the warm feeling of sleeping in an Ethiopian house with Baria—his Ethiopian friend.

They woke near dawn, shivering with cold, and were led by one of Rufael's servants back to the sacred pool. Hundreds had now gathered by its banks to be blessed by the priests. Baria, to please Rufael, knelt at the edge of the pool to have his head sprinkled with water. Harry, standing under leaves still dripping with moisture, watched as naked children, and men and women with the hems of their cloaks held high, waded into the pool, splashing, laughing, scraping slime from the bottom to rub on their faces and arms. Above him, wagtails, black feathers edged with white, whipped through the trees crying sharply as they went, then soaring to the rocks above where their song became a soft, low warble. He'd been pleased later to be able to identify them in his book of Ethiopian birds.

Remembering it now, he realized he'd never managed to have Jonathan baptized at Kulubi. He looked down at the sleeping infant. What did it matter? He glanced at Julie, her head thrown back, again deep in sleep like the child. None of it mattered now.

Baria had rejoined him under the trees.

"I feel baptized myself," said Harry.

"Perhaps you are."

It was midmorning when the last of the priests climbed up from the pool, leaving it to the children. They followed the *tabot* back to the modest, *tukul*like church which its presence made holy. Their return to Rufael's house had been a slow, weary winding down of the excitement of the day. They washed and consumed another vast meal. Early that evening, they had headed back for Addis, overriding Rufael's insistence that they stay over for the next day's celebration of the feast of St. Mikael.

"Two feasts in as many days I'm afraid would be too much for my *faranj* friend," said Baria.

"You may be right," said Rufael seriously. "He looks stout enough, but these foreigners are never too strong."

Baria happily translated for Harry. Through all of their long drive back to Addis, Baria, revealing far more of himself than he ever had before, filled Harry with stories of his growing up in the countryside.

"Before the missionaries got me and made me a foreigner."

Harry had come back to Julie nearly as excited as he had been after his trip to Kulubi with Tesfaye. It had been Baria, even more than Timket, that he'd talked about.

"He's a wonderful, wonderful friend," Harry had said. "He told me so much about himself."

What had Julie answered?

"Not everything, I'm sure."

The memory of her words stung him like the lash of a whip.

"No one gets to know Baria," Julie had told him, "no matter how close you think you get, he keeps himself locked in."

"After this trip," Harry had said, "I understand Baria."

"Far better than I do, I'm sure."

Of all the stories Baria had told Harry that night, the one burning most clearly in his mind was the story of Buhei. It had far more meaning for him now than it had then.

Baria had told him that the vitiligo that still marred his features had settled on his flesh early in childhood. Coupled with his name, it had made him doubly an outcast.

"You know how cruel children can be. 'Slave. Leper,' they called me. They even used to throw stones. But I was always strong and not afraid to fight. But there was one boy, older than I was, I could never beat. He used to lead the others in throwing stones at me.

"At all the things we did as kids, *genna*, fighting, throwing stones, I was good. But this other boy, he was four years older than I was and much bigger, he was better. Except at one thing. The *giraf*. I was better with the whip.

"I've read about it," said Harry.

He knew of the legend based on the dating in Ethiopian fable of the night on Mount Tabor when the transfigured Christ appeared to the apostles Peter, James, and John. A mist descended on the mountain. Shepherd boys lost with their flocks cracked the whips to signal each other till dawn came and burned away the mist. But the legend of the shepherds and their whips had given birth to a violent game.

Practice for Buhei began with the advent of the rains. Each year boys fashioned whips of braided tree bark. Their elders repaired old whips or made new ones from oxhide. By early July hills and villages and even the back streets of the cities would crackle with the explosive sound of whips being snapped in the moist air.

On the feast of the Transfiguration in August teams would gather in an open field and boys, young men, and even elders would lash out at each other till one was forced to surrender. It was not only a sport but a chance to settle old grudges.

"I was twelve that year," Baria had said. "It was just before the missionaries got me and started civilizing me. I was still no match for this other boy, who must have been sixteen or so. I was no match for him. Except with a whip in my hand.

"When Buhei came, I was ready. I had made my whip with bark, oiled it well, plaited it tight as I could. I called that whip 'the snake,' and the way it hissed through the air before I cracked it, the snake earned his name well. We'd been practicing for weeks, that snake and I. I could crack it fifty times in a row without missing a beat, coiling it three times over my head, hissing, then crack. Like a gun. My father used to say it wasn't a whip. It had become part of my arm.

" 'Leper. Slave,' they still called me, and it's what this boy called me that day when I faced him. I'd felt the sting of the whip myself other years. I knew it could cut like a sword, scarring, even blinding. Only a fool would face it without fear, but Buhei was the day for the brave to show they could act like fools. I found my bully was a fool, more frightened of the scorn of his elders than he was of my whip.

"I told you I was good. In a few minutes his shirt was in shreds. His shoulders and arms bled. He was barely able to lift his own whip. But he wouldn't give up. Other people stopped their own contests to watch us. He had backed away from me, but he wouldn't give up. I kept at him, trying not to do more than raise welts and burns on his arms and shoulders. But the muscles of my arm ached. My hand was beginning to cramp.

"But still he wouldn't surrender and I knew I had to go for his face. That first lash, I had to close my eyes against the blood. But then he caught me on the shoulder. The people around were cheering for him. He was so determined to fight despite all his wounds. 'Whip that dirty slave, that *shankila.* Kill the filthy leper.' You can't imagine. I knew I had to end it. And quickly. I cracked my whip twice. Once right, then left. The first caught him on the shoulder. The second cut open his neck. He ducked, he dodged, he lost his balance. I came in closer and smashed his right arm so hard he couldn't lift it. I snapped my whip back, coiled it twice, three times over my head, moving closer each time the whip hissed. My 'snake' screamed like a woman, then, BAM, like a gun, and almost the whole length of it snapped around his head. When I jerked it back, it spun him completely around. He dropped his whip and his hands went to his face. But my whip was there first. My snake bit him from the top of the head to his mouth. He fell to his knees and I slashed at his back again and again till some men got behind me and pulled me away.

"They held me and asked the other boy if he wanted to go on with the fight. He shook his head and backed away from me on his hands and knees. No one loved me for it. But they never called me a leper in that place again. Or a slave.

"And I never took a whip in my hand again. Soon after that the missionaries got me. And started their civilizing process."

Harry had trembled as he listened to the story. He felt then that he could understand why Baria had lashed out. But now he realized that Baria hadn't stopped. The whip was part of him still.

That night, it was well after midnight when they finally got back to Addis. Despite the hour, Baria insisted on taking Harry on a tour of his favorite brothels. In the last bar they visited, the fat madam sat on Baria's lap and another girl fondled Harry. He squirmed with embarrassment.

"The ladies are so nice," said Baria. "I can always come to the ladies. They accept me. Except for some. And when I can't afford the ladies, there are always your Peace Corps and others.

"Yes. How good of you to send us all these lovely girls with a passion for black men and lepers. You share your wealth so kindly."

He thought then Baria had been spilling out the bitterness, the sadness of his life. He knew now Baria had been gloating. And Julie. He'd told Julie all about it. Even the bars.

"Well, I hope you got yourself a nice little piece out of it anyway."

"No, Julie."

"Just get yourself checked out for clap. You and your Baria."

I understand Baria now. I'm sure you do. Far better than I. A wonderful, wonderful friend. But his life has been sad. No wonder he's bitter. A leper. A slave. And people throwing stones.

Soon it would be Timket and a new season of weddings would begin. Let me find you a *Lominat*. He thought of Eleni. She hadn't understood. And he was afraid to say more. The season of weddings would end with the coming of the small rains and the start of the long lenten fasts. And Tesfaye knew he would still be alone.

He had counted out the forty days and knew that this year a week before Lent began, a *tazkar* should be held by his family in memory of his father's death. He wondered if the government would allow them to hold it. He hated the costly orgy of eating and drinking and ritual crying such memorials involved, but he did want to honor that sad death. And, even more, to know where his father's body had been buried. In time, perhaps.

But better not to feast for the dead, he thought. He almost welcomed the thought of the harsh eight-week regimen of Lent. Like most young men in the cities, he normally did not fast. This year, he decided, he would. Not for God or the church. But to honor his father. Through the grim weeks of the nagging rains it would mean no meat, eggs, butter, or milk. No food or beverage of any kind till afternoon. Then, before Easter, a final forty-eight hours of absolute fasting.

He remembered one year as a child, the first he was required to fast like an adult for fifty-six days. When Easter finally came, though starved for meat, he was unwilling to eat the lamb that had been slaughtered. Afraid to confess the real reason, he pretended to be sick. He knew his relatives would think him a fool. But his full initiation into the church had taken a serious hold. He saw the white-faced lamb whose throat he watched being slit by a male servant as the Paschal Lamb, as Christ, the Lamb of God the priests had so graven on his mind. He felt that to eat the flesh of the lamb would be to share in Christ's murder. Sacrificial lamb. Sacrificial old lion. The memory seemed so distant, but he could still feel the shame of the child. Now, that shame made him face, for the first time, something other than anger, other than sorrow or rage at the death of his father. It was the shame of a man whose father had been killed, and who knows he will not avenge that death. He drove through the hills he'd been born in and knew that he was not brave and strong like his father or even cunning as Shaleka.

He would never know for certain, despite his half brother's words, if his father had taken his own life or been murdered. He had not even been able to bury him. His father, his family, himself had been dishonored. He did not believe in feudal vengeance. He did not believe in the concepts of honor and bravery he'd grown up with. He did not want to beget new violence. He believed in the work he did and in the government he worked for. Not because it was good. But because it was the only government he could imagine that could work for his country. He did not believe, as his father had, in assassinations. And yet, though he no longer believed in the Paschal Lamb, he still could feel shame he'd known one Easter as a child.

There would be no fasts after Easter. No chance to shame the body to cleanse the soul. For eight weeks, not even Wednesdays and Fridays would be days of fasting. Butcher shops, closed for two months, would reopen. Harvests of wheat, barley, and chickpeas would be stored. The young would again be free to marry, and new crops of pulses would appear in the fields.

It was considered a joyous time of the year, but Tesfaye never found it so. By *Ginbot*, the month of the flies, the long dry season would have begun to take its toll in withered fields and festering, unwashed towns. Walls in the city and ditches bordering the road would reek with the stench of urine and offal. He would long for the rains and the cold they brought. For they came like a cleansing bath, renewing the earth, making possible the crisp beauty of *Maskaram*. He knew his view was eccentric. Most people thought of the rains as bringing mud, colds, arthritis, depression, and anxiety. Highway fatalities would mount, malaria would break out in the lowlands, and typhus on the upper plateau.

The rains came in the summer months, but Ethiopians called the rainy season winter. Tesfaye wished it would be truly winter, not just rain but months of purifying snow. The rains were good but not enough. In the countryside pools and riverbeds would be swollen. Even in the city steep roads and steps could become sudden cascades. It would begin in early June with storms that would whip thunder and lightning across the surrounding hills but which only occasionally brought rain to the city. But soon there would be daily torrents that would last through mid-September, making a joke of the tourist organization's boast of thirteen months of sunshine.

Flocks of lilies would cluster the hillsides and scores of other bulbs would flower. Plowing and replowing went on, often with ox and farmer shin-deep in mud. Barley and wheat were sown. *Teff* and other grains flourished in the rain. But bridges and dirt roads would wash away, and potholes would erupt on paved roads and city streets. It would only be in *Pagume*, the five-day, thirteenth month of the calendar, that the rains would begin to break.

For Tesfaye the rains were another kind of fast, a way of earning the feast of Maskal, the new beginning that would start another timeless turning of the cycle. Midway through the rains there would be another fast, shorter and less demanding than the fasts of Christmas and Easter. For sixteen days before the mid-August feast of the Assumption of Mary, a meatless hunger would again growl in the stomachs of the devout. But it was the rains themselves that were the real penance, and, just before the Assumption, it was the whips of Buhei which gave the period its crackling symbol. It was a sound he hated, but a sound that went on despite the new laws against it. By Buhei the rains would be starting to ease. The thunder of the whips would fade and, like a vanishing echo, the thunder of the skies would grow distant, less frequent.

A sudden explosive snore from Baria startled him. He looked down. His sleeping friend stirred. But only for a moment. He settled his head back against the seat, and the muted pattern of the snoring resumed.

Tesfaye slowed to avoid a series of rocks. Someone had placed them carefully in the road, apparently in hopes of damaging or wrecking passing cars. It was a common postholiday sport. Another part of the cycle, thought Tesfaye. The cycle of holidays, of violence. Of seasons from drought to rain to drought to rain. Of years from famine to war to plenty to peace to famine.

The rains baptize the new year and give birth to fields of Maskal daisies and the cycle of hope begins again. Endlessly. Hopelessly. Our sleep of a thousand years, endlessly repeated. The circle that shuts everything out.

"Except dreams," said Julie. "Even if I do block it all out, never think about it again, I'll still have dreams. I hate your Kulubi. I hate the filth of it, the beggars, the stink. The smoke, the vomit. I hate myself."

"It's over," said Harry. "Forget it."

"I will," said Julie. She pressed the waking baby to her flat, dry breast. "Except in dreams."

Her words echoed in his ears. And merged with his own. His Kulubi. The poverty. The filth, the beggars. The lepers. The smoke. Is Addis in flames? The stink. The violence. The vomit. The cripples. His Ethiopia. For the moment he'd forgotten the faith, the nobility, the traditions, the beauty, the cleverness, the culture, the history. He'd forgotten all Tesfaye had tried to tell him about progress and growth. His mind was on Baria. He remembered the betrayals he'd seen. He'd forgotten the friendship he'd known.

"We'll soon be in Addis," he said. "No more Kulubi."

"I don't see any flames," said Hilary.

"No visible flames," answered Negussie.

The plane circled low over the sprawling city.

"That's one city I hope never burns," said Hilary. "There's a couple I helped burn in that last great world war of ours. Saw flames so high they blistered our plane. But I hope I never see that one burn."

"I've got a nephew," said Negussie. "A student. He thinks it will all have to burn before it gets better."

The city had slid by under them. Hilary banked steeply to his left, bringing it back.

"For twenty-five years now I've been watching that old who-er down there. She hasn't burned yet, but Addis just gets better all the time. Bigger and better and better lookin'. Fuck your nephew. I hope I never see that town burn.

"If your nephew wants to see Addis in flames, I hope he's one of the ones they shot."

"Thanks. I appreciate your good wishes for my family."

"Welcome, Uncle Negus. Don't mind me. It's just that I love that town. I've seen most of 'em around this world. But there's none I'd swap for her."

"Not London? Rome? San Francisco?"

"Fuck 'em. A city's like a woman. Some like 'em old. Me, I like 'em young. Those other old places have had their day. Addis, she's like the new girl in town. Her day's comin', and that's how I like 'em."

"Like Abebetch?"

"Addis Abebetch. She is my new flower."

"Your Amharic is improving."

"Damn near time, too."

They eased the big plane into its landing run.

"Let's get this crate down," said Hilary. "I got a date tonight."

It wasn't till they were neatly down and taxiing toward the terminal that Negussie resumed the conversation.

"And you're really going to get her a house?"

"I am. And you? You and beauty really gonna get married?"

"We are."

"Be good to her," said Hilary. "Be better to her than I've been to ol' Madge."

"I will," said Negussie. "I've learned a lot from watching old Hill."

"Ouch."

"You're welcome, Uncle Hill."

Abebetch had recognized the woman sitting next to her on the plane as the famous One Thousand Eighty. It seemed odd to see the famous madam alone and showing none of the charm she was famous for. She'd sat rigidly silent throughout the flight, her eyes shut, yet clearly too tense to be sleeping. Abebetch assumed she was frightened of flying and, after one thwarted effort, left her alone. But even when they'd landed, the woman sat as unmoving as the sphinx.

"We're here," said Abebetch.

"Yes," said One Thousand Eighty. "I know."

"Were you frightened?"

"No. It's over."

She didn't move. Her eyes were still shut.

Abebetch shrugged and left her. She had other things on her mind than the problems of an aging whore. Hilary had bought her a ticket and managed to get her on board despite the angry mob in the terminal howling for seats on the oversold flight.

Now there was a bungalow at the Ghion Hotel reserved in her name. A bath, a nap, and then Hilary would come. Dinner, the casino, the nightclub, and bed. God only knew what he had told his wife. She made her way slowly up the crowded aisle of the plane. Perhaps one day she would find out. When he began telling the same lies to her.

There would be time enough to worry about it then. The problems of an aging woman. She wondered if the problems were the same for all women. Most of the passengers on the plane were women. Ahead of her she noticed one of them, weeping, supported by a heavy-bosomed friend. Had she lost a husband, a child, a lover? She thought of Assab. Of her Russian. Again, she shrugged. She was beginning a new life. Not the life she had wanted. But, she told herself, it had to be a better life than the old.

Tiruwork had held back tears throughout the flight. Now, with the realization that the plane had landed in Addis Ababa, tears, not of sorrow, but of terror, began to flow. She had no idea of what to expect. Shaleka had seen her. She was certain of that.

"Don't worry," said her friend Alganesh, who shepherded her down the aisle. "I'll go home with you. I won't let him beat you."

He had seen her and walked away. He knew. And had said nothing. Done nothing.

"Don't worry, don't worry." Alganesh kept whispering her simpleminded litany. "Don't worry. I won't let him beat you."

Tiruwork tried to stop the trembling that threatened to shake terrifying sobs from her. She had told Alganesh everything, but Alganesh didn't understand. A beating held no terror for her. But if he were going to beat her, he would have beaten her then. When he found her crying for Frehiwot in the police station. What might happen at home today or tomorrow didn't frighten her. It was the rest of her life. She had resolved at Kulubi that no matter what Shaleka did to her, she would stay alive. She could take a beating, but what she feared was what else he might do. Would he put her out? Take her children from her? What kind of life would he make her live?

She shook with a sudden realization. She saw what was coming. A lifelong effort to humble her. The tears stopped. Her shoulders convulsively twitched. She straightened. The trembling stopped.

"You see?" said Alganesh. "It's better not to worry."

She wasn't worried. For now she was certain she knew what it would be like. She'd been a child. A silly girl with a crush on a singer. That was done. By the time she reached the door of the plane, her spine had steeled. She was a woman. A twitch of her arm shook off Alganesh's hand. She looked out across the Tarmac. She was a woman. And from this day on she knew she would have to fight for her life.

One Thousand Eighty forced her eyes open. She unbuckled her seat belt and pushed herself up. She wanted no one else to ask what was wrong.

Negash had stopped her that morning in the lobby of the hotel in Dire Dawa. He didn't greet her but said abruptly, "I've been meaning to ask you. Why didn't you tell me of the plot your friend was cooking?"

"My friend?"

He turned on his heel and walked away. She knew what friend. She knew what plot. Fat Margaret had disappeared from the hotel. And now she knew why. Somehow Margaret had heard the general boasting of the scheme that amused him so much. To have the boy killed. Then present his murderers to the Emperor on a platter.

She wondered how long Negash had been paying Fat Margaret. And why her friend would betray her like this. But she didn't have to wonder what would happen next. Her house would be deserted. The word would be spread. It wasn't a safe place to relax. Or talk. That life was done.

Poor Kalamawork, she thought, remembering how she had watched her old friend and the Peugeot she was so proud of go over the cliff at Kulubi. You're finished, Kalamawork dear. And so am I.

Wandimu had managed to beg only enough money to cover his bus fare as far as Addis. When he counted it out for the driver, he said, "Gabriel help me. It's all I have."

"Where are you from?" Fikr asked him. "I can tell you're not a Shoan."

"Begemdir," said Wandimu.

"How will you get from Addis to Begemdir?"

"I begged this. Perhaps I can beg more. Or walk." In clipped disjointed phrases he told Fikr how he had walked from his home to Kulubi, leading his ox that had been killed in the desert.

"Fantastic," said Fikr. He glanced at the mother of Ho Chi Minh who had already taken her seat with her child on the aisle. Nothing else had moved her. Perhaps charity would impress her.

"Here. Keep this," he said to Wandimu. "With us you won't need a ticket. Don't worry. We'll see that you get to Begemdir."

When he had finally maneuvered his bus into the Mercato's crowded open-air terminal, he helped the girl off first. Her infant was already tied to her back in the folds of her *netela.*

"Wait for me," he said. "I want to give this old man a few coins and make sure he knows what to do."

"I must be gone," said the girl in her most formal way.

"You can't," he said. "Even when you're gone, you won't be gone. From today, whenever I drive this bus and look in my inside mirror, I'll see you in that seat behind me."

"Good-bye," said the girl.

"Wait. I mean what I said."

"I, too, mean what I said. Thank you. Good-bye."

She turned and walked away. She didn't hurry. He didn't try to follow. He knew no words, no force or kindness, could stop her. She had given him nothing of herself. Not even her name. And yet, he hadn't lied, she would be with him always. She would always be in that seat behind him. Whenever he glanced in his mirror.

Other passengers climbed down from the bus. He watched them and thought of the girl. Perhaps, he thought, it's better this way. The breasts that had suckled the infant would never sag or wither. The tattoos would remain a necklace on a throat that would be forever firm. It was as though she had given him not love of her flesh, but a portrait. Flesh aged. Love died. The portrait would live.

Wandimu stumbled at last from the bus. Fikr took him by the arm.

"Old man, take this," he said. "With what you have, it will be enough. Go to that office there. Buy your ticket now for Gondar. Keep out one dollar. Wrap your ticket and the rest of your coins tight in your rags. Go to that hotel across the street. Get a bed for the night. It will cost you fifty cents. Pay no more. Another fifty cents will buy you a good supper. Your bus will leave at seven in the morning. Don't miss it. Don't stay in Addis."

Wandimu took the tightly folded two dollars Fikr handed him.

"Go back to your farm," said Fikr. "I don't know how you'll plow your fields without an ox, but you'll have to find a way."

"Gabriel is good," said Wandimu.

"Yes," said Fikr. "Gabriel is good."

Wandimu left him and circled round the crowd of screaming porters and confused passengers. He would do as the driver had said. Buy his ticket. Sleep that night at the hotel. Ride the bus to Gondar. Walk back to his farm. And begin again. He had failed. But Gabriel's strength was still in him. He vowed to be as he'd been. Sober. Hardworking. Saving. He would save for another ox. Beg. Borrow. Work. And when—with Gabriel's help—the farm was again secure, he would fulfill his vow. Debts paid. A surplus stored. He would return to Kulubi. Walking. With a new ox for Gabriel to replace the beast killed in the desert. He vowed it as he squeezed his way through the crowd outside the ticket office. If it took him the rest of his life. He would fulfill his pledge to Gabriel.

They drove by the student hostel. Bodyguard troops stood at the gate. On their right the new engineering college building was guarded by police. Hagos circled the Land Rover once around Sidist Kilo. Troops with automatic weapons eyed them suspiciously.

"Hey, do that one more time," said Claude. "I wanna get some pictures."

"Leave your camera in its case," said Hagos, "or we'll all be in jail."

He drove farther along the street that bordered the main campus.

"You see that monument back there we just drove around?" said Makonnen.

"Yeah," said Claude, peering through the back window.

"It marks the spot where the Italians murdered hundreds of students after an attempt was made to assassinate Graziani."

"Oh yeah. I read about that."

"They call it the martyrs' monument," said Hagos. "But you won't read that this is the same place where yesterday Ethiopian soldiers made martyrs of more Ethiopian students. Because they oppose our own fascist government."

"That's a good quote," said Claude. "But I wish I'd got a picture there yesterday instead."

"It looks quiet now," said Eleni.

"Very quiet," said Zenebetch.

"Like a cemetery," said Hagos.

On the back seat, the baby slept. In the passenger's seat beside Harry, Julie sat, filing her nails. Traffic along the highway was heavy. The empire, which had converged on Kulubi, was heading back home. Home was Addis Ababa. The modern city. The center of growth and progress. Of relative sanity. Kulubi was only a throwback to an earlier, savage time. Harry was convinced he'd been wrong to look for a key to Ethiopia. Anywhere. But especially at Kulubi. Kulubi was the past. And the past was madness.

Everyone said the villages, the countryside, was the real Ethiopia. Even Tesfaye. But they were wrong. They had to be. Or Ethiopia had no future. Only a past. He wanted no more of the past.

"The Dudleys' party is tonight," said Julie.

He ignored her.

"Harry, you didn't forget the Dudleys' party, did you?"

"Hon, I don't think a party . . ."

She dropped the emery board into her purse and took out a nameless implement she used to torture her cuticles.

"Julie, at a time like this, do you have to do that?"

"It's better than tearing my hair. Why can't we go to the Dudleys'?"

"What in God's name . . . I mean what is it going to take to make you realize . . ."

"Realize what? Ouch. God damn it." He glanced down. There was blood on her finger at the base of the nail. Like the blood red polish she sometimes used. The road was too rough for her to apply polish. The acrid smell of the remover she'd been using a few minutes before still lingered.

"This damn trip has ruined my nails." She dabbed at the blood with a ball of pink cotton. "I'll polish them when we get home."

"We aren't going to any party."

"It's New Year's Eve. We should celebrate the New Year."

"It isn't just the New Year," said Harry. "We've got a whole new kind of life to begin. But we're going to be awfully tired. The two of us can just celebrate New Year at home."

"I'm not tired now. Why don't you stay home and get a good night's sleep? I can go by myself."

"Oh God . . ." He took his foot off the accelerator. The car slowed. He put his foot back down. The motor pinged. He shifted to a lower gear.

"Why don't you ask Baria to take you?"

"Don't be silly."

"That's good advice. Don't be silly."

"Baria wouldn't fit in at the Dudleys' at all. They never invite Ethiopians."

"Put that damn cuticle thing away."

"It keeps me occupied."

"I'm the one who should tear your hair out. Maybe then you'll realize."

"I wish you would. Maybe that would make you realize."

Back to normal, thought Harry. Madness is normal.

"No," he said. "Things are going to be different. Forget the party."

His last visitors left. The aide-de-camp ushered them out, pulling the door shut behind him. The Emperor sat rigidly erect in the ornately carved straight-back chair. His small hands, clenched into fists, rested on the long marble table before him.

"This is a sad business," he said.

"Yes."

"I want these security people who were supposed to watch the boy punished."

"Very well," said Negash.

"They may have done it deliberately. They may have been part of the plot to have that poor child murdered."

"Perhaps," said Negash. He doubted it. He was too aware of the incompetence that surrounded them to attribute every disaster to conspiracy. He considered incompetence a crime that did more damage to his country than all the conspiracies combined.

"In any event," he said, "they'll be punished."

He sensed the fatigue that had overcome the Emperor. The old man fought it with his steely posture, but Negash knew it was there.

"That's the last for today," he said.

"No," said the Emperor. "This is a sad business. It's never the last. It always goes on. We fear always. We suspect all." He glanced up at Negash. "Don't tell me. I know. I should rest now. But how can we rest? They murder our children. And then our children riot against us, and more of our children are killed."

He looked down at his fists, opened them, and stared at the palms.

"No. So many deaths. How can we say which is the last? Or which was the first?"

Negash knew at least part of the list the Emperor was reviewing in his mind.

"We must have rest to go on," he said.

"Perhaps," said the Emperor. "But must we go on?"

"Yes."

"If we were to live forever, it would not be time enough. Help me stand."

Negash went to his side. The old man took his hands from the table and placed them on the arms of the chair. Slowly, feebly, he pushed himself up. Negash supported him under the arms.

It was only when they were alone that the Emperor allowed himself to be helped this way. In public, no matter how slow and painful the process, he always forced himself to stand unaided. He looked down at his table.

"They use marble for tombstones, don't they? An idea we took from the Italians. I wonder how many we could make from our table."

Not enough, thought Negash. Not nearly enough. He said nothing.

"How many were killed this morning?"

He'd been told several times. Negash knew he hadn't forgotten. The number was seventeen.

"Three," he said.

"Good. That's better. That's the number we should announce."

"Yes, Your Majesty."

"Would to God we could make all our numbers come true. Three would be more than enough."

Asba Tafari. Tesfaye repeated the name to himself as he drove Baria's station wagon into the village. Asba Tafari. The region he'd been born in. Suddenly, he hated the name. Asba Tafari. Mota. What Tafari has wrought. He died. But it wasn't Tafari who died. It was Tessema.

He remembered that Balcha had once done an historical essay for one of the Amharic papers in which he'd written, "In 1930, when Ras Tafari Makonnen changed his name to Haile Selassie and became Emperor . . ." It had caused an uproar. The editor had been fined and Balcha was reprimanded. But in Ejersa Goro where the old man had been born, they still called him Tafari.

It had been his father who had given this village its name, for its development had been one of their earliest projects when Tafari was still regent—before he changed his name. The thought was Tafari's. His father had turned it to reality. And his father was dead.

He pulled the station wagon into the Agip station where he'd agreed to meet Harry. The station was crowded with cars heading back to Addis. It was a moment before he spotted the Volkswagen. He was surprised to see Balcha leaning against it. He could see Julie in the passenger's seat. Her head was bowed. She didn't look up. There was no sign of Harry.

Baria woke as Tesfaye was parking.

"Where are we?"

"Nowhere," said Tesfaye.

"There's Balcha."

Balcha crossed to him, walking with small steps, like a prisoner in chains.

"Hello, Balcha," said Baria from inside the car.

"Ah, you're here, too," said Balcha. He turned back to Tesfaye. "And I met your American friend. He said you would just be coming. I was just ready to leave—my car was fixed here—when I met your friend and decided to wait for you."

"What happened to your car?"

"A stone."

"Left in the road?"

"Not just one. Three. Usually I drive very slow and watch very close. But today my mind was on too many other things. Frehiwot. My book. What they did to your father. The students and their riot. I didn't see the rocks in time. Strung across the road. To kill someone, they wouldn't care. You know our people."

"I know," said Tesfaye. "They don't like all these cars running through their country. A lamb gets killed. Or a child. The driver doesn't stop. So they take their revenge another way."

"No, Tesfaye. Just spite. They don't need a reason. Sure, sometimes a lamb or a donkey gets killed on the highway. But they don't need a reason. For them it's a game. They put out stones and they hide. A car gets wrecked, and they laugh. I know them."

"Some, perhaps," said Tesfaye. "But not all our people are like that." He realized his own thoughts when he'd seen the three rocks in the road had been much like Balcha's. He was often critical of his country and its people. But he wondered at the strange quirk in himself that made him always defend Ethiopia against the criticism of others.

"Your car's all right now?" he asked Balcha.

"Maybe. A real mechanic they don't have. They wired the fuel line back where it goes. Maybe some patches. You know. Maybe it will last till I get back home with my family."

"I'll say a prayer to Gabriel."

"Thank you very much," said Balcha. His tone was mocking. He stood as though his invisible handcuffs were firmly in place.

Tesfaye looked beyond Balcha to the Volkswagen.

"I see my friend's car," he said. "But I don't see my friend."

"He's inside the station," said Balcha. "Paying for his benzine. I forgot how poor Frehiwot would try to say benzine. 'The food you feed your donkey that has things that turn instead of feet.' Something like that. If I tried like Frehiwot to use only pure Amharic I could never finish a book. Maybe with songs it's easier."

"Frehiwot doesn't seem to have an easy time with his songs," said Tesfaye.

"No," said Balcha. "His songs give him trouble. I went there this morning. To the police at Kulubi. They said he'd been taken to Addis."

Negash had been as good as his word, thought Tesfaye.

"I didn't know whether to believe them," said Balcha. "But I noticed that his lady friend, the wife of your Shaleka, was no more there."

"A good sign," said Tesfaye.

"Perhaps."

Baria dragged himself from the car and went silently to a water spigot at the side of the station to wash.

"Friend Balcha, listen. I've been asked to be your censor. On this book of yours."

"My book?"

Tesfaye hoped to see Balcha's hands lose their handcuffed look. They didn't.

"You'll have to trust me," he said.

"You won't be harsh?"

"I mean to be gentle. I love your books. I don't want to see another one burned."

"I prefer censors who aren't so clever as you."

"If I'm not clever, and if you don't trust me to work with you, the book will end up being burned. And maybe us with it."

"Negash asked you to do this?"

"Yes."

Balcha shook his head.

"No. If Negash trusts you, then how can I?"

"Only by trusting me. I mean to test limits. But I may have a better idea what the limits are. We may both end in trouble. But I hope you'll help me do what I can to save your book."

"Why are you doing this?"

"Because I have the chance. Because it's maybe something I

can do. People like my father cook plots. People like you write books. Like everyone else, I do what I can."

"Well, we can try. Shall I come to your office?"

"Remember, I don't know where you live now. So come to my office. Then we can go together to your house."

"*Ishi, getie.*"

It won't be easy, thought Tesfaye. Balcha still stood as though handcuffed.

Baria joined them.

"We're all faces of stubble and dirt," he said. "It will be good to get back to Addis. Is there coffee?"

"Not here," said Balcha. "But there's a small restaurant there. They have."

"What they have, I need," said Baria.

He started off in the direction of the restaurant Balcha had pointed to.

"Just a minute."

It was Harry, calling from behind them. They turned.

"You'll be coming with me the rest of the trip," he said to Baria. "I've had a long talk with Julie. And now you and I are going to talk."

"You think I'm a bitch, don't you?" said Julie.

"Not a'tall," said Tesfaye.

"I know Harry's your friend, and you think I'm no good to Harry. And I don't take enough care of the baby."

They must have had a long talk, thought Tesfaye. He drove Baria's station wagon but now his passengers were Julie and the baby. Why did Harry do this to me? The Volkswagen had been just in front of them as they pulled out of the station. But Harry was driving much too fast. Tesfaye soon lost sight of the car.

They'd agreed to drive through to Nazaret where they could be sure of finding something to eat. That would be nearly four hours, but Tesfaye didn't mind hunger. What bothered him was the thought of spending four hours in the company of this shrewish woman and her whimpering child.

She had stuck one of the endless supply of plastic bottles in the small creature's mouth, but the child still managed to whimper around it. He knew there must be some core of humanity in Julie. Beyond the nails she was filing there must be fingers, hands, even arms—a woman. Harry and Baria had both found the woman that must be there. He knew he never would and wondered how much the failure was his. A failure not just with Julie. With Eleni. With others. Himself.

"So does Harry."

"I beg your pardon?"

"Don't be so damn polite. Harry thinks I'm a bitch, too. And he's right."

I wouldn't contradict a friend, thought Tesfaye. He wished she'd be quiet. But I shouldn't complain, he said to himself. Baria's probably even more uncomfortable than I am right now.

"But isn't there anyone," said Julie, "anyone who can . . ." She let the thought die.

He didn't want to read her mind. But he had.

"Harry can," he said.

"You're right. Harry can. He's a better man . . ."

Tesfaye said nothing. Let her say it herself. Or be quiet. He thought she'd decide to be quiet. Several minutes passed before she spoke again.

"I made a vow there. At your silly Kulubi. Something for Baria. A joke. I should have made a vow for Harry. The book he wanted to write. Or be happy. Something. Instead of . . . his skin. That disease he has. Whatever it is. It makes him afraid to . . . Maybe if he didn't have that . . ."

Tesfaye shook his head slowly. He said nothing.

"Baria could never love anyone. Harry can. Even a bitch like me. He's more of a man . . . than any of you. I wanted to go to a party tonight. He wouldn't let me. I would have been ashamed of myself if I went to a party. At a time like this."

"Well, I'll tell you something." His arms were rigid, locked to the top of the wheel. He leaned far back in the seat, staring dead ahead as he drove. His knuckles were white. "I'll tell you something you wouldn't understand."

After the winding rough mountain roads, the relatively smooth downhill run from Asba Tafari to Miesso tricked him into speed. The speed made him reckless. The words, the anger so long bottled up broke loose.

"You won't understand this, but Julie and I have something. We have something you wouldn't understand."

"I'm sure you're right."

Baria sat, watching the road race toward them. His hands were carefully folded in his lap.

"But aren't you trying to make too much out of it, dear Harry? It isn't high drama after all. Our little—what would you call it? Our little domestic comedy."

"I could kill you. Do you know that? I really could kill you."

"You would please me," said Baria.

"Don't be too sure. After everything I've seen. At Kulubi. And Tesfaye's father. All of it."

"We didn't really see much," said Baria. "You should have listened more closely to Hagos. Those people burned to death in a mosque. All he told us about Eritrea. That's perhaps not so small. You heard about some violence. But we saw not so much. And none of it happened to you. We've been privileged. For most of us, most of the time, the violence is always offstage."

"Most of the time," said Harry.

"Our little drama, it's not quite the same scale. It isn't quite like a plot against an Emperor. Against a country. Like riots or murders. Some of the things you've seen. Some of the things you've been hearing about."

Harry was silent for a moment. For a moment his foot on the accelerator was a fraction less heavy. He relaxed the tension of his grip on the wheel.

"Maybe I did learn that here. Being an American living in a country like this. I realized that today. You start to see how small your own problems are. Compared to what's here. It makes you start to grow up."

"You're exaggerating again," said Baria. "You've seen a few things. But you're still an American. You never grow up."

"Don't be too sure," said Harry. "Just don't be too sure."

"Careful, Harry."

He snapped the car back from the far left to the center of the road.

"You're driving too fast."

"Never mind that. You just listen. I can handle the car."

Baria locked his arms on the rubber hand mount on the dashboard. Harry's knuckles whitened again on the wheel.

"We don't have to talk about Ethiopia anymore. And I've heard enough lectures about America. We're talking about you and me. And Julie."

"It's your car," said Baria. "But I wish you would drive more careful."

"I can handle the car. . . ."

He knew he was driving too fast. But he wouldn't slow down. Baria was silent, staring straight ahead.

"And I'll tell you something else. You aren't going to see her again. Not that it matters. Not that those things matter all that much. You aren't the first. You aren't all that important. And don't think you'll be the last. She needs . . . she has needs. But she needs love more. And you aren't capable. I know I'm not saying it well. I'm not gifted . . . with talk. But respect . . . don't get me wrong. I don't mean me. I don't give a crap about all that. But Julie needs it. She needs respect for herself to be able to love. She can't hate herself and love me. And I need . . . I have my needs."

He fell silent. The car raced on, heading down the sharp decline. They could now catch occasional glimpses of the distant mosque and the tin roofs of the lowland railroad town below them.

"You forgive her, isn't it?"

"I love her."

"But you can't forgive me."

"I . . . I don't know."

"You shouldn't."

"You know why? You know why I can't?"

Baria didn't answer.

"Because you didn't love her. You had no respect. You just . . . you can't. You aren't capable. And you know something else?" He glanced at him. "I'll tell you." He snapped the rearview mirror around so that it faced Baria. "Take a look at that. Your face. Your skin. You think because of that no one can care for you. And you think that gives you the right . . . to go around . . . and hurt other people. Not even friendship. Not even a friend. You aren't . . . you aren't even capable of a friend."

Baria reached up with his left hand and twisted the mirror back toward Harry.

"That's a very dangerous thing to do," he said. He put his hand back on the rubber mount on the dashboard, gripping it tightly. "Your wife has that habit, too. Twisting the mirror. To look at her face."

"You know all about my wife, don't you?"

"Very little. But I remember she does that. Straighten the mirror, Harry. Make sure you can see what's behind you."

"I know what's behind me."

"Do you?"

"What's behind me is you. I used to think you were my friend."

"I used to be your friend."

"That's behind me. For one thing."

"A pity. Julie . . . your wife once told me you always became such good friends of her lovers. That you usually like them much better than she did. I don't think she liked me very much."

"I guess you know all about me, don't you? All about both of us."

"I know nothing. I try to know nothing. Even about myself I wish I knew nothing."

"I could tell you some things about you. I should have known a long time ago. Way back when we made that trip at Timket last year. I thought you'd become a good friend of mine then. I even—how stupid—told Julie. I should have known . . . when you told me that story, how you beat that boy with a whip. I thought then I could understand. Why you'd been cruel with that whip. But that's still how you are. You haven't changed. We never called you a slave. We never called you a leper. But you lashed at us. Anything, to hurt, destroy. Like you whipped that boy."

"How strange you should talk about that," said Baria. "I never whipped that boy. I made that story up. Like so much of my life. It's something I used to dream about. About using a whip on that bastard. I never did. I still wish I had."

"I can never believe . . . anything you say."

"You're beginning to learn."

"I used to think you had to hide. The things you'd say. It was hard to know when you were serious. When you were playing games. I used to think you needed that. Like a mask to hide what you really felt. Because I thought you were sensitive, I even told Julie I understood how you really were. After we made that trip together at Timket. But I was wrong. Masks, games . . . that's what you really are. That's all you are."

"Enough," said Baria. "You know how to hurt. When you've been hurt."

"I don't give a damn about hurting you. I wish I knew how to use a whip. Because you don't give a damn about anyone."

They sped rapidly down toward Miesso. Harry kept his eyes on the road, but he was nearly blind with the rage he'd unleashed.

"Julie told me," he said, "that the baby was yours."

Baria's right hand went up to the strap mounted on the door-frame by his shoulder. His right hand clung to the strap. His left still gripped the rubber hand mount on the dashboard. He stared straight ahead.

"You're driving too fast."

"Don't tell me how to drive. It's my life."

"And mine. Please, dear Harry. There was a time, you know, when you thought that birth was a Kulubi miracle. But I don't think birth is ever a miracle. Maybe an accident. Like death."

"I don't believe in accidents."

"Perhaps you should. Do you remember that fellow you met, Balcha Amara? The friend of the *azmari* the police beat up at Kulubi."

"I remember."

"He's a very famous writer, you know."

"I know."

"And one of his books, you can't read it, of course, is a fable about two infants still in the womb."

"I know the book."

"Yes. Then you know that those unborn infants saw how unjust and cruel the country was and how one didn't want to be born into such a place like our Ethiopia, and the other couldn't wait till he could get out of the womb and change it."

"I know."

"Yes. You know so much now, dear Harry."

"Yes."

"You see, I thought about Balcha's fable because he hit on something very deep. Perhaps deeper than he knew. Because, you see, there are two kinds of people in this world. People who let things happen to them. And people who make things happen."

"No one's that simple."

"Perhaps. Perhaps there's another son. Still not yet born. Because he's afraid to make things happen. There are men in this world who seduce women they want to go to sleep with. And men who let themselves be taken to bed by women who want them. There are men who kill, even men who kill themselves. And men who let themselves get killed."

"None of that matters. Jonathan is our son now. We don't want you in our life anymore."

He drove even faster. The green dome of a minaret's white

tower rose over the desolate town that sped toward them. Harry remembered it. Miesso. It was where he'd encountered the old man he'd mistaken for a beggar the year before. And where he'd argued with Julie a few days ago. About what? The baby's diapers. The length of her skirt. He hated the sight of this place. He wanted to race through it, to put it behind him with every other memory of Kulubi. The wind sang in his ears as they swept over a low bridge.

The car bounced crazily, hitting a rough spot in the road coming off the bridge. Harry gunned it through and up a slight rise. The road leveled off. The village was there.

"Harry, there's stones."

He swerved just in time. They missed the stones bunched in the middle of the road. But then his foot hit the brake. The car spun out of control. The village whirled around them. Then the village was gone and all he could see was blue sky.

The truck rounding the curve in front of the Mobil station had tried to stop. It couldn't. It caught the rear of the Volkswagen. The impact flung Harry's door open. He panicked and let go of the wheel. The car spun and his body pitched out.

Baria clung to the hand strap. His eyes were swollen with fright. He saw the red *O*, the flying red horse turn end over end. For a moment, the car seemed to stand on its blunt nose, then tipped over and smashed sideways into two of the benzine pumps. First one then the other exploded and burst into flames. The car's own tank went next. And, not more than a minute later, five revolver shots sounded from inside the car as the bullets in the gun in Baria's pocket exploded.

It was an hour before the charred remains of Baria's body could be dragged from the car. Flames and burning gas fumes had blackened his flesh.

"*Shankila,*" said one of the men from the service station. The others laughed.

"Shut up," said Tesfaye.

"But look how black he is. All over. Like a real *Shankila.*"

Julie sobbed. She hadn't understood the words. But she understood what she'd seen.

Tesfaye took her arm.

"There's no need for you to look at this."

"There is," she said. "I did it."

"Don't talk nonsense."

The baby, deserted where Julie had left it on the front seat of the station wagon, wailed its fierce complaint. Tesfaye ignored it and led Julie back to Harry.

A medical dresser of surprising competence had appeared from the village clinic. There were no doctors to be found outside the cities. Tesfaye knew they were lucky to find a man, though only trained to dress injuries and treat minor ailments, who was nevertheless skilled and knowledgeable. He wanted Harry moved as little as possible. There was evidence of concussion. His left arm was broken. The dresser suspected there might be broken ribs, and he was worried about spinal injuries.

He'd had a canvas lean-to set up on the shady side of the service station. Armed police held back a curious crowd that now shifted from the injured foreigner to the car and Baria's blackened body. Harry lay on a straw pallet under a single sheet, his head propped on a folded blanket. The dresser put his arm in a splint and bandaged his head and torso. Harry, still in shock, had drifted in and out of consciousness. His dozens of cuts and bruises had been washed and salved with antibiotic ointment.

Flies swarmed around him and Julie again begged the dresser to move him to the clinic. He shook his head and spoke to Tesfaye.

"Tell her there is nothing more I can do at the clinic. The less we bounce him or drop him off a stretcher the better it will be for him."

He was a small compact man of forty in a soiled white robe. He was attended by two solemn young boys. One carried bandages, scissors, and other medical equipment. The second boy had brought a pitcher of hot water, soap, and a towel.

Tesfaye nodded and translated for Julie. "Don't worry about the flies," he added. "They can't hurt him now, but moving him will."

"He has to be moved," said Julie.

"He'll be moved," said Tesfaye. "But safely. The police got through a call for me to Addis. A helicopter will come."

He didn't bother to explain to her that the nearest hospital or doctor was at the sugar plantation at Wonji, two hundred kilometers away over the roughest stretch of the highway. His phone call had reached Negash at the palace. A helicopter and medical team were being sent from the Air Force base at Bishoftu.

The baby's cries carried on the warm desert air.

"Can someone look after the baby?" said Julie. "I want to stay with Harry."

"Someone will," said Tesfaye.

Harry moaned. His legs twitched. The dresser crouched beside him. He made a quick check of the pulse. Harry's eyes opened.

"Can you hear me, sir?" asked the dresser in English. "Don't try to move the head. Can you see my hand?"

"Yes."

"Good." He moved his hand to the right, then slowly to the left. Harry's eyes followed it. "Very good. Don't try to move. You are going to be all right."

"Baria?"

Julie glanced at Tesfaye. He remained silent.

"Baria's dead," said Julie.

"That's what they told me," said Harry. "Someone. I must have been dreaming."

The dresser stood. He nodded to Tesfaye. "He'll be all right. Come. We can look to the child. And they can give us some tea just here."

He spoke to one of the policemen and led Tesfaye away. His two young attendants followed. As they crossed the road to the station wagon, Tesfaye looked up. He saw the sign in the distance. It was too far away to be read, but he remembered its legend.

Yih Kulubi Mengid Bizih No
This is The Road to Kulubi

Julie knelt beside Harry.

"I'm sorry," he said. "Was anyone else . . ."

"Just you. Just Baria."

"I was mad. I didn't see. What I was doing."

"Don't try to talk."

"He's dead. And us?"

"Don't try to talk now."

"We should never let it happen again."

"I know," said Julie.

"Not after this."

"I swear I'll try. I swear to God I'll try."

"To God."

"Yes. To God. I'm frightened."

"We have each other."

"Yes."

"It's what we keep coming back to."

"Yes."

"There's nothing else."

She looked down at him.

"Not God?"

He closed his eyes.

"Leave God," he said. "He's left us. It comes back to us. We have that. Nothing else."

"I'm frightened."

"Me too. I killed him, Julie. As much as if I'd put a gun to his head."

"Don't talk."

"You don't hate me?"

"No."

"You won't leave me?"

"Never."

"We have that?"

"Yes," she said. "We have that."

"Each other."

"Each other."

He trembled. She put a hand on his shoulder and knelt beside him. She knew she would never escape. Nor would he. He was the last man. He hadn't died. He never would. He would always be there. And so would she.

We get the miracles we deserve, she thought. Harry—his son that isn't his. And me—a burnt-out lover. She'd made the vow as a joke. Like Harry. She looked at Harry and saw in her mind the image of Baria's cindered corpse. Skin burned pure of its spots.

"I hate your Kulubi," she said.

"I know," said Harry.

"Not just what I told you before. Not lepers or the filth or the beggars. I hate your God."

She knew then that she did believe. God damn. Jesus Christ. For God's sake. All the curses Harry had told her were ways of acknowledging what her mind denied. Yes, she said to herself. I believe. And I hate God. God damn him.

"The baby?" said Harry.

"He's all right," said Julie. She started to weep.
"Don't cry, hon. A whole life. We still have a whole life."
"God help us," said Julie.
"He won't. There's just us."

EPILOGUE

The Burial

TESFAYE STOOD NEAR THE GATE OF THE CHURCHYARD APART FROM the dense crowd which squeezed close to the door of the modernistic brick building. He looked up at the hexagonal bell tower that soared over the adjacent spaces of Janhoy Meda. The monumental design gave an impression of great size, but the interior of the church was small. Big enough, Tesfaye knew, for the tiny German and Swedish communities that used it, but not for the hundreds who had flocked to Baria's funeral.

He had never known that missionaries had had a hook into Baria. Even now there were not many of them in Ethiopia. Until after the occupation they had been even rarer. Yet, you kept discovering people who had been educated, confused, sent abroad, and retrieved by some band that had established a clinic or a school among the *Shankilas* of some distant desert or jungle. For Baria it had been the Lutherans. Which is where the German pattern of his education must have begun, thought Tesfaye. And this is where it ends.

Baria Medhane Alem. Slave of the Saviour of the World. He had borne a slave name, but he was not a slave. He had carried what people took to be the marks of a leper, but he was not a leper.

Only through Harry had Tesfaye come to know Baria as more than someone whose work and legend were famous. We depend on foreigners for so much. But what a strange friendship. To bring us both here.

He had admired the beauty of Baria's poems. But from a

distance. The paintings had left him intrigued but confused. The man was something else again. He was the bull, the ox.

Despite the roseate patches that marred the brown flesh, women, even those who believed he was a leper, were drawn to him. There was that. There was his physical strength. There were the stories of his many children. One of his poems talked about all the seeds he had scattered on the wind. And the stories of his drinking and whoring. Tesfaye knew too well about that. And there were the foreign women. The Peace Corps chippies, the embassy wives, the neurotic women of inadequate scholars.

Tesfaye was drawn to the funeral, not just as a friend, but as one of the hundreds, the mob who came because one way or another they were drawn to the man. His legend. His death.

So many were here. So many for whom his paintings, his poems, the leper's skin he wore, his complex web of defense would have made him a stranger. All the fat aunts and fading uncles. The cousins and nephews seven times distant. His students, his friends, journalists who would write only a few lines. The thin intellectual cream of young Ethiopia. Hagos and Makonnen among them. He saw them standing by the door.

The service in the church may be German, thought Tesfaye, but the funeral is not. Among the hundreds in the compound and as far as his eye could penetrate into the interior of the church, Tesfaye could see no trace of pink or gray skin, not a wisp of blond hair.

In reserved front seats, tactfully scattered among the closest relatives, he knew there must be a stout delegation from the embassy, the cultural institute, the school, the mission, the old German families. He wondered if any would make the long trip to the cemetery.

Death moved quickly in Ethiopia. More quickly than birth. The life that was nine months in creation could end in nine seconds of violence. Baptism would wait forty days after the birth of a son. Burial would follow his last breath by no more than a day.

Death moved quickly. But funerals were slow. The services in the foreign church, Tesfaye guessed, would be efficient and swift. Germans at work. But what would follow would be agonizingly slow. Ethiopians at sorrow.

Now it was beginning. The people inside the church began slowly to move out. On some unseen cue, the ugly hearse with its carved border of chipped, painted flowers and pale angels backed into the churchyard.

Tesfaye stood at the edge of its path. But the crowd was caught between the pressure of the dead and the mourners leaving the church and the black, backward advance of the hearse. There was an attendant in khaki shirt and trousers and a messenger boy's peaked cap. Unidentifiable campaign ribbons decorated his shirt. "*Menged, Menged,*" he loudly yelled. The crowd ignored him.

The hearse, with its exhaust belching black fumes, made its own way. The coffin being carried from the church and the black truck backing toward it cut into the crowd. The driver raced the motor, jumped the clutch, slammed the brake. The hearse jumped, reared, stopped.

Like a wave that had struck a jetty, the crowd spumed, roared, fell back. Then the sea of white costumes again flooded quietly around the hearse.

The coffin's official pallbearers had already given way to the undertaker's menials, not the black-suited, white-gloved professionals of Europe and America, but ragged, shoeless porters. There were four. They bore the coffin on their shoulders.

When the varnished but unpainted white pine box became visible to the crowd, piercing ululations of pity and sorrow keened from the women. To Tesfaye the sound often seemed as mechanical as the calculated electronic cries of modern music, but now he couldn't repress the shiver that contracted his spine.

Perhaps a hundred women took up the wailing vibrations. Their cries seemed to lift the coffin out of its Lutheran confines of red ecclesiastical brick and into the sunshine that flooded the churchyard. No path was made, but, holding the coffin above their heads, the pallbearers were able to wade through, like men walking into a suddenly calmed river. The flood of people parted as the shabby pallbearers edged by, then eddied back around them as they passed.

The loud *telalackey* with the campaign ribbons was still shouting *menged, menged* as he flung open the doors. An old woman misunderstood him and started to climb into the hearse. The attendant pulled her down.

Tesfaye grinned as he listened to her loud protest. She thinks it's a bus to take people to the cemetery. As he said the words himself, he imagined saying them to Harry. Is that why I'm here?

he wondered. To act as usual as Harry's eyes and ears. And translate for him later.

Swathed in bandages, mummified in his hospital bed, eyes and ears and a slash of a mouth were all that was left of Harry. And even the mouth was useless. He was taped too tightly to talk. A tube carried liquid food to a vein in his arm. But he would live.

Baria, who was strong, had been killed. Harry, who was weak, survived. Is that why I'm here? wondered Tesfaye. Because the weak bury the strong. He knew he had been weak. But that last day at Kulubi he had vowed to be strong.

There had been no funeral for his father. Weakly, he had allowed that. Is that why I'm here? he wondered. He had vowed to do all that he could for the changes his father had wanted. Not to kill the mosquito. But to cure the malaria. He wondered how much he could do.

He edged his way to the churchyard gate. The falsetto *illils* of the women reached a new pitch of intensity. Without looking back, he knew the coffin was being placed in the hearse. He remembered the priests of Kulubi rhythmically raising the volume of the cries of the women by lifting higher the *tabot* they carried three times around the church.

He'd parked his green wreck of a car across the street. As he unlocked the door, he looked back at the swollen churchyard. Even if they'd wanted to, they would never have been able to carry Baria's pine box three times like a *tabot* around the stone German monument. The way was too small; the crowd, too thick. At Kulubi only a cordon of armed bodyguard troops kept the crowd from crushing Emperor, *tabot*, and priests against the sandstone walls of the church.

He climbed into his car. Someday, he feared the cordon would break. Or would turn and become part of the crowd. And then, when straw and steel, fear and tradition, respect and guns, would finally give way, the flood would sweep everything before it.

Now, the flood was sluggish. The funeral cortege moved through the heart of the westernized city. Perhaps a hundred automobiles, trucks, and buses crept among the thousand walking mourners. But Tesfaye, driving slowly among them, felt they were moving centuries deep in the countryside.

It had taken them thirty minutes to wind their sorrowful way from the German church through Sidist Kilo where the monument to the martyrs of the occupation cast its gray shadow over the white river of mourners. They climbed the ascending grade between the modern university campus still guarded by soldiers and the hospital that bore the Emperor's name where Harry now lay in white bandages.

They moved down through Afincha Barr where seven roads met at a bridge named for a *zabagna* with a funny nose. Then up a wooded hill where cattle grazed on untended slopes. They crossed the street named for a duke of Harar who, like Baria, had died in a flaming automobile. Then down a street where in alternating shops women and slabs of meat were on sale.

Opposite a church named for John the Baptist behind which *dabtaras* worked miraculous cures beside a muddy stream, the tide of mourners bent and began the long final leg of their journey to a cemetery named for Paul.

The river of mourning was fed by the weeping of hundreds of eyes. Old men and even some of the young wept, but it was mostly the women who bore the burden of tears. A low moaning sound almost like a song accompanied their crying. It came in waves, cresting when a church or landmark was passed, ebbing on the emptier stretches of road.

A hospital named for a *ras* whose name meant happiness, a school, another church on the right. On the left, dreary shops and then the police officers' club.

Dense growths of eucalyptus now blocked off the reminders of a city fading into its suburbs.

Modest homes and shops to the right and a drop to the stream on the left where cattle were being watered. Eucalyptus and olive trees, oaks and homes and more eucalyptus and, from someone's cookhouse, the sweet-acrid smell of eucalyptus burning.

Slower than time, they edged past the Pasteur Institute which now bore a new official name no one could remember. All traffic but the traffic of death was stopped. In low gear, Tesfaye's Volkswagen crawled, stopped, stalled. Mourners behind him pushed it to get the car started again.

In front of the facade of the hospital for the poor, he gave up and pulled off onto the shoulder. By now, all forward movement had become a trickle. The mourners had reached the gates of the cemetery. He rolled the car windows up, leaving a fraction open on either side to allow the expanding, sunbaked air in the locked oven to escape.

When he turned his back on the car, he again felt part of the steadily flowing yet somehow unchanging Ethiopian tide. In the midst of the crowd, not standing apart or insulated in his car, he no longer saw the massed mourners as waves of the sea or as a slowly flowing river. He felt he had become part of a lake, somnolent and still, riffled, eddied forward gently by the breeze.

A few of the mourners carried photographs of Baria. Many, particularly among the women, carried them shyly, pressed close to their breasts. Others held them high, brandishing them like banners. He wondered what his father's burial would have been like. How many portraits? What banners? How dense the crowd? If his father had been allowed a funeral.

Some of the photographs of Baria were simple snapshots. Many were large, framed reproductions of a highly retouched studio portrait. In living color. But with the vivid pink patches of Baria's vitiligo brushed over so that the face and hands were varying shades of the same sweet chocolate.

Where had the custom come from? From the Italians, Tesfaye assumed, like shaking hands a hundred times a day, sugared coffee, women in black for mourning instead of the traditional white, and young men having their shoes shined morning and afternoon. All the absurd customs the hollow city dweller considered part of his tradition and the hallowed countryside laughed at.

He flowed with the tide, his feet now on a macadam street; the smell of unwashed bodies and cotton and of burning eucalyptus in his nostrils; the taste of ash in his mouth and his eyes on the towering tips of countless slender, silver blue trees that brushed clouds of the purest white.

His eyes could tell him he was in the idyllic countryside. His feet reminded him he was in the city. His mind felt torn between. He knew many of the people he walked among were torn the same way, though few would have words for the thought. Torn, too, between the death they attended and the life they felt in their own limbs.

For some, fat and bothered by sweat and flies, that life was measured in annoyance and fatigue. For others the measure was their awareness of the slow passing of minutes that kept them from the thousand tasks and distractions the city promised when their interlude with mourning was done. But life couldn't turn them now from their attachment to death. Tesfaye knew he had often stood apart and mocked—"typically Ethiopian." But now, as he walked among them, he understood. Typically Ethiopian—like me.

Earlier that morning, from Baria's brother he had obtained a clear, black-and-white snapshot for use with the brief funeral story he would write for his paper. The crowd was moving even more slowly now, turning from the road to the wide cemetery gates. As he turned with them, Tesfaye took the snapshot from his wallet. Cupped in both hands, he carried it close to his chest.

In the cemetery he balanced himself on the exposed roots of a live oak tree, bracing himself against the dry, scaly bark. With the added elevation, he could see over the heads of the crowd thickly clustered around the grave. He was sure there were now well over a thousand people.

On the edges of the assembly, friends greeted each other softly, and a score of casual conversations were in progress. Tesfaye picked out a sprinkling of ministers and generals. The son of slaves had become a figure of importance since foreigners started buying his paintings.

A gray-bearded priest of the Ethiopian church went through the motions of reading from a prayer book. His mumbled words didn't carry over the crowd. Tesfaye was surprised to see several white faces like pale flowers in a field of grass scorched brown by the sun. There were perhaps a dozen. Most he recognized from the German embassy and cultural institute. There was a knot of Peace Corps types, scruffy boys and neat girls. He remembered Baria's cruel words about Julie—when you can't afford to go to the ladies . . . And then he saw her.

No face was whiter. Not simply drained of color but stark white like the pages of an unlined notebook. Sunlight, filtered through the leaves of ancient junipers and oaks, blanched out her features. Tesfaye wondered if she had powdered or painted herself to achieve that deathly white. It wasn't a face but a ghostly mask, stark white and enormous among the hostile brown faces of the women around her.

She stood defiantly close to the grave where only the family should have been. At least, he thought, she had had the grace not to bring the child. He recognized one of the women who stood near her as an aunt he'd once met on one of the rare occasions he'd been to Baria's house. That night, stuffed with *injera*, primed on *tej*, and led by Baria, she had been loud and bawdy. Now the sorrow that had subdued her was giving way to anger.

No one around the grave seemed to pay attention to the

priest. Tesfaye knew he was probably reciting from memory rather than actually reading the Ge'ez words which none of the mourners and possibly not the priest himself understood. He might have been ignored in any case, but Julie's presence at the edge of the open grave robbed the mourners even of their grief.

As though she were some graveside totem, most of the mourners not staring at the coffin had fixed their eyes on her. She must be crazy, thought Tesfaye. They might stone her to death. He noticed Wolde, the brother from whom he'd obtained Baria's photo, edging his way around the grave. He wasn't looking at Julie. But she was clearly his destination.

Finally, he edged up behind her, his eyes still on the grave above which the coffin was suspended on ropes tied to stakes. Wolde, taller than Baria but as stocky and hard, leaned close to Julie's ear and whispered what could not have been more than a single word. Julie spun around. Wolde, his face expressionless, his hands calmly folded, kept his eyes fixed on the coffin. His lips again formed a single word. Tesfaye was sure it was "Go."

Julie backed away from him. She bumped into the heavy-set aunt in black who pushed her brusquely aside. Julie didn't panic but began making her way as swiftly as she could back through the crowd which in a moment swallowed her up. Tesfaye could still trace her path. The indistinguishable mass of heads in the midst of the crowd parted in a curiously twisted pattern as she made her way. It was like tracing the movements of an unseen animal making its way on a still morning through dense savannah grass. She would have a long way to go. She'd been standing on the side of the grave farthest from the gate. Once she made her way back through the massed mourners, she would have to circle the crowd.

She had completed half an arc before Tesfaye began to catch glimpses of her, stumbling on high heels among the tombstones. When she was beyond the crowd, hurrying toward the gate, Tesfaye could see her more clearly. Color had returned to her face. He no longer saw a mask but a face of shame and sorrow. He watched her go. A brief, sudden breeze swayed the branches of the trees above them. The leaves stirred, then settled, like a sigh. She was gone.

Tesfaye shifted his position on the bared roots of the live oak. He wondered if she would go to Harry in his hospital or find some place alone to cry. Seeing her stumbling among the graveyard's rocks and weeds, he had been moved to pity for her. But even the pity had been an embarrassment. For a moment it had been her burial. Now it was again Baria's.

The black-clad, gray-bearded priest closed his book. He spoke now in Amharic, an apparent eulogy to Baria. His voice was louder, clearer, but still Tesfaye caught only occasional, formula phrases, "*B'Egziabehare Baria Medhane Alem* . . ."

Tesfaye admitted to himself a sense of relief that Harry wasn't there. He was spared the ordeal of translating words he wanted to ignore. He began to survey the crowd. Several of the women closest to the graveside were dressed entirely in black. Others wore a black scarf draped over head and shoulder to shroud the brilliant white of their national dress.

Women and girls in western suits and dresses had uniformly chosen black. But most of the hundreds of women and perhaps fifty of the men were entirely clad in the traditional white. Others among the men wore dark western suits, many with a black armband. Tesfaye had made do with a black tie. He fingered it self-consciously as he scanned the scene. It could be Baria's last painting. Title: *A Circle in Black and White*. With a pale rectangle against a background of earth colors at the center. Abruptly, his cool study of the crowd stopped. Eleni was there.

In flowing black, she stood near a stately juniper with a group of chattering girls. They were well back from the crowd, not far from the gate. She ignored the girls around her. Her attention seemed fixed on the rambling words of the priest. Her face wore a puzzled expression. As he watched her, she moved apart from the other girls, apparently to be able to hear the priest better.

Slowly, the puzzled expression narrowed into anger. Her gaze turned his attention back to the priest. To Tesfaye it seemed that the old priest was looking straight at him. By watching the wide, beard-shrouded mouth and straining to concentrate on his words, Tesfaye was able to pick out enough of the phrases to follow what the priest was saying.

"Yes," he heard, "it is known that Baria Medhane Alem followed foreign . . ." for a moment the words faded. "His back was turned to his people . . . alien doctrines . . . paintings not in our tradition . . . even his death at foreign hands . . ."

The voice was calm, betraying no anger. The tone hadn't changed from the monotonous drone of the first words when Tesfaye's attention had begun to wander. He wondered if the old man had been annoyed by the German church service. Or had some neglected relatives petitioned him to lace his graveside words with these poisonous barbs. He glanced at the aunt in black. Her eyes were cast humbly down. He couldn't see Wolde in the crowd.

"Woe unto him who would . . ." As the words droned on, Tesfaye stared at the old man's mouth. He felt that the priest's eyes, at which he could no longer bring himself to look, still were fixed on him. ". . . and deny his own church, his country, his people."

The words struck like shots fired over the coffin and aimed, not at Baria, but at himself.

"To forgive such betrayal we must look deep in our hearts . . ." Tesfaye's foot slipped from the roots on which he was balanced. He fell to one knee and skinned his hand on the trunk's dry bark. It was as he pulled himself back up that a voice on his right, a dull buzz in his ears that he'd been trying to ignore, began to penetrate.

He straightened himself, standing on solid ground among the roots. A young man, not more than twenty, stood on a low, square mausoleum that Tesfaye assumed must be the tomb of some wealthy landowner. He wore slacks, sweater, and a jacket that managed to look both slept in and clean.

Though he spoke both clearly and well in a voice that carried far more strongly than the priest's, at first his words were only an annoying blur in Tesfaye's mind. First Julie, then the old priest's continuing diatribe by the grave, and now this. Why couldn't they let Baria be buried in peace?

The young man on the mausoleum spoke with the fervor of the mad. His eyes glittered. Sunlight cutting through the leaves lit his handsome, unshaven face. He was saying he was a student. A student of what? Why didn't someone stop him? Several men stood around the base of the mausoleum. Some Tesfaye recognized as students from the School of Fine Arts where Baria had taught. They were grinning.

The old priest droned on. The young man on the tomb seemed to take strength from the droning. His speech soon eclipsed the scene at the open grave. The richness of his language, the purity of his grammar, began to sink in on Tesfaye before the meaning of his words. His Amharic was as beautiful as any Tesfaye had ever heard spoken. There was madness but also poetry, wit, and subtlety in his harangue.

A few moments before, as he listened to the priest, Tesfaye had again been happy that Harry wasn't with him . . . even his death at foreign hands. How would he have rendered that? But he wished Harry was with him now. The bizarre scene would be hard to fit into his TAT card sociology. But this was something Harry should see and hear. And tape. Automatically, he began translating for the friend he imagined at his side.

"They say that a man who takes his rest in a cemetery will be beaten into madness by devils. I ask them, 'What if the man is dead?' And they laugh. But for me, still alive despite them, this is my home. They shot at me yesterday when we tried to bury Tekle, our brother, but I live. Though I am not a leper, I live among the dead."

There was no way to translate the poetry, the beauty of the language. But poetry, Tesfaye realized, would always be lost on Harry's academic ears. He would always be the last to know.

"Do you know, brothers and sisters, do you know Baria Medhane Alem, the man with the face of a leper who was not a leper?"

More and more the attention of the crowd swung to the young man. He made no gestures, offered no shouts. But he lured them from the priest and held them in the strange spell of his words.

"Now, like me, he takes his rest among the dead. Do you know Medhane Alem? Who saved the world? In the cemetery of the church of Medhane Alem here in the heart of this city—does this city have a heart?—live lepers by the hundreds. Does the devil beat them into madness? Who has beaten them into the compound of the dead? In the heart of this city.

"And I, but yesterday or yesterday released from the madness of a madhouse, I fled to the graveyard, for I can testify, my lords, madness is a grave affair. How many yesterdays was it?

"Yes, they have put me down for mad because I spoke. Not prison, not exile. Not death. They put me down for mad so my words would be known as the words of a madman. Easy to dismiss. Easy to forget. They have done it to others. You know who they are."

Tesfaye looked around the churchyard, wondering if Balcha was in the crowd. The young man spoke as though reading a text from the great author.

"Because I spoke I was made mad."

Tesfaye turned back to the student. He hadn't seen Balcha, yet, he was sure he was hearing him.

"And now because I'm certified for mad, I can freely speak. In Amanuel, where they chained me, I spoke only to the mad. And whom do I speak to now, my worthies. Yes, I know you generals and ministers, my noble lords. When we demonstrated our ignorance, as your Ethiopian sources of rumor called it . . ."

Oh God, thought Tesfaye. The self-styled madman punned on the Amharic name for the government news agency and referred to an infamous editorial, "Demonstration of Ignorance," he had drafted on orders from Negash. He lowered his eyes. But the words kept filtering through.

"Your Ministry of Vomit said we were ignorant. Your doctors of mental disease said I was mad, and your priests say we are foreign."

"His mouth has ears," said a man standing near Tesfaye.

"Who is he?"

The man shrugged.

"And you say we aren't grateful. Hadn't Takel himself come riding to our schools, laden with apples of knowledge when we were young? And when we spoke out, the serpents said to us, 'Why aren't you grateful? Don't you remember the apples His Imperial Horse brought you? Didn't he bring you to the tree of knowledge and let you eat?

"Even paying from his own pocket for your schooling?"

Tesfaye's brain was spinning. If Harry were with him it wouldn't be possible to keep up with even the gist of the student's words and still try to explain a reference like that to "Takel," the Emperor's "horse" nickname. It had been the same at his father's when his father spoke words much like those he heard now. He looked at the student. Is he a ghost, risen from the tomb he stands on. A ghost for Balcha. Or the ghost of my father.

"Yes, generals and ministers, yes, brothers and sisters . . ."

Tesfaye had noticed that the student used the polite form for everyone—students, lepers, ministers, generals, the nobility, the poor, madmen, priests. The classic purity and heightened formality of his language mocked them all in the language of respect.

"You think I will be beaten into madness by devils today as other *azmaris* we know of have been beaten. But it isn't possible. Already I am mad. And already the slave who saved the world is dead, safe from all devils here. And yes, though I live here, though I stop here, I am not just resting by this burial. I am here by right. You think I don't know him, but I do. I know this slave. Listen . . ."

He began to recite a series of punning couplets and tercets. Some struck a religious theme but buried a secret story of love. Some spoke of sexual license and carried a hidden meaning of asceticism. All were based on traditional poetry. All were twisted to dance around Baria's life and death.

"*Esta balas belto addam kanfaresh*
Baria Medhane Alem tasakalalesh."

"Adam by your lip ate from that tree;
The saviour of the world was crucified for thee."

But the words also said "because of you, my heart was crucified for thee." He then rhymed on the father's debt passed on to the son and the man who now had a debt begun by his grandfather. But he turned the couplet to mean a debt of death owed to God because of a woman the debtor had seen.

"Who was the ghost by the grave?" cried the madman. Tesfaye cringed.

"The son of a slave, high rank to display,
Made love to the Christ's wife yesterday.
She fed him leaves and he withered away."

How much did this cunning distorter know? The ghost at the grave. Had he seen Julie? Tesfaye stared hard at the young man mounted on a stranger's mausoleum. Did even the mad know what Harry was the last to know? Or were all his words, his allusions, his twisted couplets made ambiguous enough to touch all who heard him in a different way. The crowd was held as Tesfaye was caught. He wondered if each of them might not say, yes, he knows, while each heard a different poem. He wondered if some weren't absorbed because they thought the madman was talking, not about Baria, but about themselves. The priest, ignored at the graveside, droned on. And the mad shepherd went on leading his flock.

"Yes, brothers and sisters, I knew him. I knew him though I was not his student. No. No one could teach me to be a painter of pictures—or even of houses." A poor joke, and yet it brought actual laughter from many of the mourners. Tesfaye wondered if he were going mad himself. "But this man we come with priests not to praise but to bury, this man taught many of us to see. To see poverty, cruelty, disease, bravery, and death. Yes, generals and ministers, he taught your sons to see."

Many eyes turned to General Gebre Kebede, commander of the police force. A month before his son, who had been a student of Baria's, had been sentenced to seven years' hard labor for printing and distributing antigovernment pamphlets. The general stared straight ahead. His sad eyes showed no anger. Tesfaye thought he detected a slight nod, as though of assent.

"They tell us students must live in their books and learn before we can speak. And it's true. But since I am certified mad, I live and learn among, not books, but tombstones. The dead have many secrets and great knowledge. You see me, like our teacher who had died, a night singer, a *lalibela,* singing by daylight to save me from the leprosy that infects us all. As Baria Medhane Alem sang in the night of his soul, in the soul of his poems and paintings, 'Hear the slave song we sing to save the world from the leprosy of these sad times.'

"The song of the slave with the face of the leper who wasn't a leper and who wasn't a slave. Listen. Listen to the mad who have learned the secrets of the dead. Listen, brothers and sisters, and listen ministers and generals, for the sake of the saviour of the world find it in your hearts to help a poor student . . ."

Incredibly, he was turning his mad but pointed monologue into a beggar's appeal for alms. He hadn't sung, but he performed in the tradition of the *azmari,* the jester, insulting them all and washing away the insults by belittling himself and appealing for alms. Tesfaye stared in amazemet.

Again he visualized Harry by his side. He would be trying to explain to the confused, questioning American what was happening, wondering aloud if this was what the student had been leading up to all along, the whole performance a prelude to an appeal for cash.

Maybe he's just another con man, he imagined Harry saying. A superior one, Tesfaye would have to answer.

There was movement at the gravesite. He turned to see that the old priest now was silent. The gravediggers had taken up the ropes on which the coffin was suspended. Slowly, they began to lower it into the shallow grave. Shrill ululations and loud, stylized sobs filled the graveyard, drowning out the student's repeated appeals for alms.

Tesfaye glanced at the mausoleum. The unshaven young man gave up. Several arms reached up to help him to the ground. One of the art school students shook his hand. Several people pounded his back.

At the grave, Baria's brother threw the first handful of dust onto the coffin. All the men near the grave followed suit, then the women and children. The gravediggers picked up their shovels and began filling the wound. A fresh waterfall of tears was let loose.

At last, the crowd began to move away from the grave. Tesfaye walked slowly with them toward the gates. Strait is the gate and narrow the way, he said to himself, but all will pass through. All but Baria.

Wolde, the brother who was evidently chief of the mourners, stood just inside the main gate. With a slight bow and a handshake, he returned the traditional "May God give you strength" with its ritual reply, "May the strength of God be given to him."

God is alive and well in Ethiopia, thought Tesfaye. Harry's words as they watched the spectacle of Kulubi. That foolish, half-dead man recovering on his hospital bed haunted him still. God is alive and well and may his strength be given to Baria. To see him through heaven or hell. But for the Baria we knew, thought Tesfaye, the strength of God comes too late. Let it be given to Harry.

The mad student who had raved from the top of the mausoleum now stood not far from Wolde. He chanted, *Sila Medhane Alem; sila Medhane Alem . . .*" For the sake of the Saviour of the World, give to a poor beggar. Tesfaye remembered the beggars of Kulubi . . . *sila Gabriel; sila Cristos.* The student was faring much better. He held a soiled cap in his hand. The cap quickly filled, and each time it did he dumped the contents on a small wool rug spread on the ground before him. The Amharic epigram "it is useless to trust in man" was woven into the flowery red, green, and yellow design of the rug.

Tesfaye saw dollar bills, a few fives, and a ten among the coins. As he passed, offering no alms, the student stared at him with bloodshot eyes. A smile curled the corners of his mouth. Tesfaye wondered if he recognized the reluctant author of "Demonstration of Ignorance."

The student bowed to him slightly.

"You spoke well," said Tesfaye.

"Thank you," said the student in English. He raised the cap he held in his cupped hands. Tesfaye offered no alms, but, continuing in English, asked, "When did Balcha brief you?"

"I spoke long," said the student, smiling. "My words weren't brief."

"You speak well," said Tesfaye.

He moved on, trying to slip into the knot of people bunched around Wolde. Finally, he stood before him. The brother who had banished Julie from the graveyard fixed coal-black eyes on Tesfaye. He didn't offer his hand. Tesfaye took an involuntary step back.

The hostility he read in Wolde's eyes puzzled him, for they barely knew each other. Then, as though the force of Wolde's thoughts made them his own, Tesfaye realized that the brother saw him as an accomplice. He had traveled with Harry, Julie, Baria, on the trip that had led to this graveyard. His own gentle brown eyes fixed on Wolde's. He nodded his understanding and said, "Forgive me, and may the strength of God be shared by us all who need it."

"May forgiveness be given to us all," said Wolde. He took Tesfaye's hand and clasped his elbow. "And may the strength of God be given to him."

Tesfaye had wanted to ask him if he knew who the student turned madman turned beggar was. Now he dared not. But the flow of thoughts between them seemed to continue. For Wolde, still holding Tesfaye's hand, nodded toward the student and said, "Never mind. He spoke the truth."

Outside the graveyard, Tesfaye was dazzled by the unshaded sunlight. An image danced before his eyes. The woman in black who had pushed the stumbling Julie away from her by the grave stood with the old priest. His death at foreign hands. Tesfaye blinked and visored his eyes with his hand. The priest and the old woman weren't there. He turned around. People streamed through the gate inside which Wolde and the suddenly prosperous madman were standing. There was no priest, no angry aunt. He felt dizzy. He had to escape the hammering of the sun. But his car was at least a hundred meters away. There was no shade here and the thick crowd was barely moving, as sluggish now as a river of mud.

He became aware of a voice.

"Don't say hello, Ato Tesfaye Tessema."

A woman in black stood before him. It was Eleni. She put her hand on his arm. The grace of her touch, her nearness, which might have dizzied him if he were calm, now served to steady him. A stray fluff of white cloud for a moment muted the sun.

"*Tenastelign,*" said Tesfaye. "Since you tell me not to say hello, *Tenastelign, Woizerit* Eleni."

"*Gash* Tesfaye, *l'irswo minim kilklil aydelum.*"

"*Muwt?* Nothing is forbidden?"

"Haile Selassie *muwt,*" answered Eleni.

"Kulubi Gabriel *muwt?*"

"*Ai,* Tesfaye." She took his hand but went on addressing him in the polite form. "*Y'irswo machina yet no?*"

"My car is a million miles away," he answered, "and I'll never get there alive."

"Why don't you come with me then?" said Eleni.

"Where?" He had planned to go from the cemetery to the hospital to visit Harry, to cheer him up, to tell him of the mad student's strange words, the couplets he had used and twisted. But now Harry, like the figures of the priest and Baria's fat aunt, had vanished. He had asked, "Where?" but he didn't care where. He wanted to go wherever she would take him.

"My car is just here," said Eleni. "I can drive you to where your car is parked."

"Oh." His throat tightened. "You have your own car now?"

"Of course. A Fiat 850. Red. Every modern young girl has to have her own car now. That way she can choose her own boyfriends."

"This younger generation," said Tesfaye. "In my day marriages were always arranged."

"And boyfriends?"

"Boyfriends can always be arranged."

He looked into her eyes as a few minutes before he had looked into the cynical bloodshot eyes of the student, the black hostile eyes of Baria's brother. Her eyes danced. He tried to hold them, but they danced away.

Someone pulled at his sleeve. It was Balcha. He nodded curtly at Eleni.

"Tesfaye," he said, "I've decided. Let it be banned."

"Your book?"

"My book. Let it be banned."

"I thought I just heard of part of it being published," said Tesfaye.

"I know nothing of that. Let it be banned."

Tesfaye nodded.

"Farewell, Balcha."

"Good-bye."

He turned and walked swiftly away, his arms swinging freely at his sides.

Tesfaye felt as though he'd been slapped.

"Coming?" said Eleni.

The white cloud slipped from the sun. The sudden light was blinding. He wanted to speak. To tell her what just had happened. To suggest driving her new Fiat away from town, to Gefersa, to Ambo, anywhere. But there was no boldness in him.

"*Inn hid*," he said, knowing they were going only to her car.

Light rain clouds were drifting toward them through the blue sky, spiraling down from the heights of Entotto. Tesfaye saw them. According to the guidebooks, it didn't rain in January. Thirteen myths of sunshine, he thought glumly. He knew he would welcome the rain.

Eleni warned him she couldn't talk while driving. "I'm too new at it." They crawled in low gear among the walking mourners. Their silence filled the car, seeped out the open windows, seemingly affecting those among whom the car moved, silencing those who still wept, creating a still pool within the mournful river.

"*Baka*," said Tesfaye.

"You don't mean 'enough,' " said Eleni. "You mean 'stop.' You know, I'm getting to prefer talking in English. Like being called Helen, instead of Eleni."

The crowd flowed past them as though the car were an island or rock in the river.

"*Min giziem, OAU*," said Tesfaye. Always the OAU, the Organization of African Unity. "Always your job. Making you an African. Taking you away."

What had he said to Negash? Men who become their jobs. Like Shaleka. The Emperor. Like Negash. Like me.

"I'm still here," said Eleni, still speaking in English.

"My father said Russian was his language. The Emperor talks to the Prime Minister's wife in French. I work and write in English, but I prefer . . ."

"You prefer Amharic."

"I'm an Ethiopian."

He looked again into the dancing eyes of this girl who would be African.

"Tesfaye," she said, looking away, "do you think you could make a good Ethiopian wife out of me?"

He studied the profile she showed him. He lowered his eyes and shook his head.

"No."

"No. I don't suppose anyone could. In fact, I don't think I'm cut out for this marriage thing at all. Not husbands."

Let me buy you a lemon, thought Tesfaye. *Lominat* for Timket. Timket is soon. He stared out the window at the passing mourners in white.

"You see," he said, "that's one of the beauties of this language of ours. You can say things. You've organized yourself into African unity. That's your life. And you don't want to marry." He turned to her. "And in our language the word for unity—*andinet* —can also be the word for single."

"I thought our word for single was *netela.*"

"That too," said Tesfaye.

"I hate our language. In Swahili the word for unity means one."

"*Mojo,*" said Tesfaye. "*Uhuru, mojo, harambe.* I'm not a Kenyan."

"Neither am I," said Eleni. "But the word now is *Harambe Africa.* There's even a song."

"I know the song," said Tesfaye. "But I'm not an African. Only an Ethiopian."

They were silent, then parted abruptly, each knowing a moment, a chance had been missed. Tesfaye stood in the roadway, single, alone, watching the Fiat make its way through the mourners, a small red craft parting the white waters. Even when he could no longer see the car, he could follow its progress, watching the mourners parting before it, flowing together behind it.

He looked up. The sun was gone. Gray clouds swirled before it. He went to his car and was no sooner inside it than a light rain began to fall, streaking the dust on the windshield. Rain in January. It shouldn't happen. Like Balcha's slap. His loss of Eleni. He turned on the ignition. The motor started. He tried the wipers. Magically, they worked. Just enough rain had fallen for the wipers to smear the dust that had gathered across the windshield. He prayed for more rain. He wanted to wash the dust of Harry and Julie, the dust of the dead Baria, the dust of Dire Dawa and Kulubi from his mind. He wanted to look through the windshield and see the smiling face of Eleni.

He had promised himself to do all that he could, but to go on being what he'd been. Now he knew he must be more. He had learned it from death. From his father. From Baria. And from the life that went on. From Balcha. From Eleni.

He could be only himself, but that self could never again stand apart. Be merely a witness, the observer, the recorder. Objective. The journalist he had been taught to be. He would be the witness, yes, but he knew he must be a conscience as well. A conscience first for himself. He must not become merely his job. An African, perhaps. For Eleni. For Balcha, a better Ethiopian. His paper would be only one weapon. Balcha's book would be published. He would seek Balcha out. Find his home. Beg if he had to. He vowed to find ways to make Ethiopia and the world know what Ethiopia was. Let Balcha's book describe to Ethiopia its prisons and let Ethiopia know that it is a prison. And perhaps one day the world would take note.

He vowed to see to that, too. Harry would be one of his tools. His ego shattered, his bones broken, Harry had said back in Miesso he was giving up the idea of writing his book on Ethiopia. The bones would heal, and Tesfaye planned to go to work on rebuilding that ego.

Harry would write his book. And Tesfaye, if he had to dictate the chapters, was determined the book would be more than a dry excursion into the theory of Ethiopian personality and culture. Harry's book would tell the world what Ethiopia is.

If Harry wanted history, Tesfaye would insist not just on the history of legend but the history of now, the death of his father, the murder of the student leader, all the plots, the intrigues, the suppression he knew.

If Harry wanted to explore the culture of Ethiopia, Tesfaye would point him to the culture that mattered, an *azmari* like Frehiwot, a writer like Balcha. Even the work of a painter like Baria. Who taught our sons to see. And who perhaps, at last, taught Harry to see.

Harry would write his book. A far better book than he had imagined. For Harry was going to be a weapon in a war Tesfaye declared. Like a dumb bullet, Harry might never know he'd been aimed and fired. And Harry would be only one weapon. Tesfaye was determined to build an arsenal in whatever way he could. An arsenal for a war, not of retribution, but of change. He did not want to avenge his father's death. He wanted to create a country in which his father's mad schemes and violent death would not be necessary. In Ethiopia all loyal opposition would be considered an enemy within. He knew he must be that enemy.

The rain quickened. Around him other drivers revved their motors, cursed the walking mourners, forgot the dead artist and the mad student, and drove slowly through the chaos of the crowded road. Tesfaye let them go and watched the falling rain and the filtering wipers slowly beginning to thin the streaked layers of dust. Not perfectly. The uneven rubber left arcs of mud. But he could see.

He shut off the ignition. The windshield wipers flopped like rag dolls. Rain clung to the window. People say that when it rains God is crying. He realized that he was weeping, weeping perhaps as long as God had been crying. He shrugged and let the tears fall. Not for Baria. Not for Harry or his dream of Eleni. Not for the mad oration of the student or his own sense of loss.

He sat until the crowd had cleared, then again started up the car. The rain was now a steady fall. The crowd had thinned like the dust. He backed onto the glistening highway and started for town. The windshield wipers now cleared the glass except for one blurry arc. A rainbow of gray, thought Tesfaye. He was still weeping. He didn't try to stop. He had decided to wage war. A war for change. He wondered how much he could change. Himself. Ethiopia. He wept, not for himself. He wept for Ethiopia.

GLOSSARY

Unless otherwise noted, all words and phrases are from Amharic. No effort has been made to indicate the Amharic alphabet, which has over two hundred characters. Amharic spelling has not been systematized, and the transliterations here are largely my own. They are designed for simplicity and quick readability. They will not please scholars. Deviations from the glossary spellings which appear in the text indicate that the character in question speaks Amharic poorly, as is the case with Harry, Colonel Wilson—and the author. Plurals generally have been formed in the text by adding *s* in the English manner rather than the common Amharic suffix for the plural, *och*. The listing includes the literal meanings of the names of major Ethiopian characters and a few important place names. Some figures of current or historic importance are also identified.

E.P.M.

Abate	my father; a term of respect for any elderly man
Abebe Bikila	Ethiopian who twice won the Olympic marathon
Abebetch (name)	she is a flower
Abuna (our father in Ge'ez)	head of the Ethiopian Orthodox Church
Addis Ababa	lit., New Flower; capital of Ethiopia; note: the commonly accepted English spelling is given here though Addis Abebe might be considered a more accurate rendering

Afa Negus	lit., mouth of the king; chief justice
Afincha Barr	lit., nose gate; a section of Addis Ababa
Agalgil	round pouch with shoulder strap; usually used for carrying food
Ahun	now
Ai	an expletive
Aichallim	impossible
Aimuwt	lit., may he not die; see *muwt*
Alegn	lit., I have; things are all right
Alem Bakagn	lit., for me the world is finished; name of a prison in Addis Ababa
Almetam	he hasn't come
Amharic; Amharigna	official language of Ethiopia and of the Amhara tribe
Amole	bars of salt still used as currency in some areas
Anbasa	lion; also name of bus company in Addis Ababa
Anchi	you (fem.)
Andinet	unity; single
Ante	you (masc., familiar form); can be used to indicate disrespect or affection; see *irsow*
Arat Kilo	a traffic circle in Addis Ababa; four (*arat*) streets meet here
Arbegna	freedom fighters; patriots
Asba Tafari (Ge'ez)	lit., Tafari wrought; a village in the Chercher Hills developed by Tafari Makonnen (Haile Selassie) when he was Regent; note: Asebe Tafari in Amharic would mean Tafari thought; many Ethiopians contend this is the correct form and meaning
Asira-and	lit., eleven; a derogatory term for Tigres who have parallel scars cut above the eye which resemble the number 11
Ato	equivalent to mister
Awo, awon	yes
Azmari	traditional minstrel
Baka	enough

Balabet	husband; landlord; local notable or someone of noble family
Baria Medhane Alem (name)	slave (of the) Saviour of the World (Christ); *baria* is similar in derivation and meaning to *shankila* (q.v.); both are used as racial slurs
Berberie	characteristic Ethiopian spice; similar to chili peppers
Bet	house; various usages as *tamari bet* (student house) to indicate school
Betam	very
Brundo	chunks of raw beef
Budda	evil eye or spirit
Buna	coffee
Buna bet	lit., coffeehouse; term for brothel
Bureau (French)	commonly used for office
Cas	slow
Cas bih Cas	lit., slow by slow; slowly
Chat* (Arabic origin)	a leafy plant chewed, particularly by Muslims, as a stimulant which has a strongly narcotic effect with prolonged and heavy use
Chereka	moon
Chibo	torch
Chika	mud
Dabo	bread
Dabtara	church scribe or singer; "witch doctor"
Das	temporary grass hut
Dejazmatch	lit., general who leads out of the king's gate; now a largely honorific title conferred by the Emperor
Demera	bonfire lit on the eve of Maskal (q.v.)
Dire Dawa (Galligna)	lit., empty plain; a city on the edge of the desert below Kulubi
Dulla	heavy wooden staff used both as walking stick and weapon
Egzier ystelign	thank you; implied meaning—may God give to you as he has given to me
Egziabehare	God

* "ch" words can also be rendered "tch" and there are two "tch" sounds in Amharic, one of which is an explosive.

Ewnet; Ewnetegna	true; one who tells the truth
Faranj, faranji	foreign; strange
Faranjoch	plural of *faranj*
Fird bet	lit., justice house; court
Gabbi	heavy white cloth of woven cotton used as cloak or blanket
Gabo	a bribe
Galligna	language of the Gallas, Ethiopia's largest tribe
Gari	horse-drawn taxi
Gashe, gashai	lit., shield, my shield; friend; often used with a name—Gashe Tesfaye; or, in the possessive, as a polite address to a stranger
Gedyelem	never mind
Ge'ez	ancient language of Ethiopia still used in the church; it bears a relationship to languages of Christian Ethiopian tribes roughly similar to that of Latin to the Romance languages
Genna	Christmas; a game like field hockey played only at Christmas season (January 7, European calendar)
Gesho	a plant, the leaves of which are used to ferment *tella* (q.v.)
Getie	lit., my lord; polite form of address to any person of importance
Getoch	plural of *getie* (q.v.), indicating even greater respect
Ginbot	Ethiopian month equivalent to May
Giraf	a whip
Gitem	lit., lock; a rhyme or poem
Gojo	a *tukul* (q.v.); mud house with thatched roof
Guad	corps, as in *Selam Guad* or Peace Corps; note: Ethiopians often use the term "Peace Cores" to indicate members of the Peace Corps
Gugs, Feras gugs	similar to medieval English joust
Gursha	a morsel of *injera* and *wat* (q.v.) placed by host or hostess in the mouth of a guest; any gratuity; a tip

Habesha	Ethiopian (Abyssinian); usually in a derogatory sense
Hager	country
Haile Selassie (name)	Power of the Trinity
Harambee Africa (Swahili)	roughly "Get Together Africa"—a song and slogan popular throughout the continent
Illlill	onomatopoetic term for characteristic cry of Ethiopian women at times of intense emotion; ululation
Indemin aderu	lit., how did you pass the night?, how are you this morning?
Indemin a lu	how are you?
Indemin nacho	how are you?, plural and polite form
Indet	how; an expression of surprise
Injera	pancakelike bread with which *wat* (q.v.) and other foods are eaten
Inn hid	let's go
Irsow	you; polite form
Ishi	okay
Ishi nega	lit., okay tomorrow; Ethiopian equivalent of Spanish *manana*, meaning—maybe sometime
Janhoy	a somewhat ambiguous but magnifying expression for Emperor
Janhoy Meda	lit., Emperor's Field; a large field in Addis Ababa used for holiday ceremonies and sports
Jib	hyena
Kabaro	a large church drum
Kabur	honorable; gentleman
Kabur Zabagna	imperial bodyguard
Katikala	a clear, very strong liquor
Kene	traditional church poetry, often rich in puns and ambiguity
Komata	leper
Koso	a red-flowering tree, the leaves of which are used to make a purge for tapeworm
Kulubi (Galligna)	lit., onion; village near Dire Dawa
Lalibela	twelfth century ruler; village where he had monolithic rock-hewn churches built; a night singer

Lalibeloch	plural for night singers who are usually believed to be lepers
Lomi; Lominat	lemon; brand name of a lemon-flavored soda
Magala (Somaligna)	market; the old areas of Harar and Dire Dawa
Makeda	Ethiopian name for legendary figure whom Westerners call the Queen of Sheba; see also *Saba* and *Sheba*
Mamitay	little sister; term used by foreigners for servant who takes care of children
Mariam	Mary; particularly in reference to the Blessed Virgin
Maskal	cross; feast of finding of the True Cross, Maskaram 17 (September 27)
Maskaram	Ethiopian month roughly equivalent to September
Matsenannat	comfort
Menelik	legendary son of Solomon and the "Queen of Sheba"; Ge'ez meaning—son of the king
Menelik II	ruler of Ethiopia, 1889–1913
Menged	road; as an imperative—make way
Messob	tall basket of brightly dyed straw used as food container and table for communal eating
Metcha Tuluma (Galligna)	underground Galla political organization; name derives from names of two brothers who were legendary founders of Galla tribe
Min gizie	lit., what time; always
Min giziem Philips	famous radio advertising slogan for electrical products of the Dutch firm, Philips
Minalbat	perhaps
Mota	lit., he died; village where Dejazmatch Tessema lives—and dies; there is a village of this name in Gojjam southeast of Lake Tana, but not in the Chercher Hills of Harar province

Muezzin (Arabic)	Islamic herald who calls the faithful to prayer
Muwt	lit., may he die; a way of saying I swear it's true
Nebr	leopard
Nefas Silk	a section of Addis Ababa famous for its brothels
Nega	tomorrow
Negash Mengistu (name)	Negash—one who should be crowned. Mengistu—the government or his kingdom
Negus	king
Netela	a long, shawllike wrap worn by women; single
No	he is; it is
Pagume	the five-day thirteenth month on the Ethiopian calendar (September 6–10)
Piazza (Italian)	major shopping area of Addis Ababa
Ras	lit., head; a title of the higher nobility
Saba	Ethiopian form of Sheba referring to Sabean (Red Sea) area; see *Makeda;* also name of commercial brand of *tej* (q.v.)
Selam (Arabic)	peace; same meaning in several Ethiopian languages; often used as a greeting
Selamta	greetings
Sera	work; conspirator
Seratagna sefer	lit., worker neighborhood; section of Addis Ababa below the Piazza (q.v.)
Shaleka	lit., leader of a thousand; major
Shamagile	old man; a term of both respect and contempt
Shamma	woven white cotton; a togalike costume; sometimes used as term for the national dress; see also *tibeb*
Shankila	a tribe originating near the Sudan border, formerly a source of slaves; hence, a slave or any person

	of darker color or Negroid features; see also *baria*
Sheba	lame; Western word used for Queen of Saba (q.v.); see also *Makeda*
Shermuta	prostitute
Shi Samanya (nickname)	lit., One Thousand Eighty
Shifta	bandit; often used of political rebels; can also be a term of endearment
Shinkwurt	onion; see *Kulubi*
Shum-shir	lit., appoint-demote; process of shuffling political offices
Shuro wat	a meatless stew made from chick-peas
Sidist Kilo	traffic circle in Addis Ababa; six (*sidist*) streets meet here
Siecento (Italian)	lit., six hundred; in Amharic indicates the 600 model Fiat or any small car used as a taxi
Sila	lit., concerning; with Christ or a saint's name—for the sake of; used by beggars as in *Sila Cristos*—give for the sake of Christ
Silet	vow or pledge; also the blade of a knife
Simu	his name
Somaligna	the language of the Somalis
Tabot	Ark of the Covenant; chest containing the stone or wood tablets on which the Ten Commandments are written
Tadess	lit., he or it became new or repaired; an all-purpose expletive and greeting most commonly used in a sense roughly equivalent to "what's happening?"
Tahsas	Ethiopian month roughly equivalent to December; feast of Gabriel is Tahsas 19 (December 28)
Takel	a "horse name" or nickname for Haile Selassie
Tamari; tamari bet	student; school
Tazkar	observance of the anniversary of a death

Teff	a grain grown only in Ethiopia; see *injera*
Tegegna	it is found
Tegna	he slept
Tej	honey wine
Telalackey	messenger
Tella	barley beer
Tenastelign	lit., may He (God) give you health; used for hello and good-bye
Tesfaye Tessema (name)	Tesfaye—my hope Tessema— he is heard
Tessema Bekele (name)	Tessema—he is heard Bekele—he blossomed
Tibeb	embroidered border on *shamma;* used as term for national costume
Tikimt	Ethiopian month roughly equivalent to October
Tiru	good; pure
Tiruwork (name)	pure gold
Tsehai	sun
Tukul	non-Amharic word used chiefly by foreigners for *gojo* (q.v.)
Tut	nipple; breast; also cotton
Tut abat	lit., breast father; foster father
Uhuru, Mojo, Harambee (Swahili)	Freedom, Unity, Cooperation; slogan of Kenya; see also *Harambee Africa*
Wada	to
Wadi (Arabic)	dry riverbed
Wandimu Getahun (name)	Wandimu—his brother Getahun—be a lord
Ware minch	lit., source of rumor; until recently used in Amharic name for Ethiopian News Agency
Washint	Ethiopian musical instrument similar to the flute
Wat	highly spiced stew
Wei good	an expletive indicating surprise or amazement
Woizero	Madam
Woizerit	Miss
Wushata	lit., he possesses lies; liar
Yellem	no
Yikirta	lit., forgiveness; excuse me

Yimuwt	polite form of *muwt* (q.v.)
Zabagna	guard; night watchman
Zare	today
Zim bal	keep quiet
Zorbal	harsh expletive meaning stop or go away
Zorbalu	plural of above